THE
ISLAND

BOOKS BY G.N. SMITH

FIONA MACLEISH CRIME THRILLER SERIES

The Flood

THE
ISLAND

G.N. SMITH

bookouture

Published by Bookouture in 2023

An imprint of Storyfire Ltd.
Carmelite House
50 Victoria Embankment
London EC4Y 0DZ

www.bookouture.com

ISBN: 978-1-80314-912-7
eBook ISBN: 978-1-80314-911-0

For my son, now a young man of whom I couldn't be more proud.

PROLOGUE

His body was half submerged, but there was no mistaking his fate. His throat and upper torso were covered in blood, but there were also rents to the clothing at his groin.

Normal circumstances would have dictated that Fiona try and preserve the crime scene. That she not contaminate any possible source of evidence. That was a non-starter. Even if the island wasn't temporarily cut off by the gale, it was far too dangerous to try and get a team here to extricate the corpse and sweep the crime scene. It was only a matter of minutes, maybe an hour at most, before the tide turned and the gale pushed heavy seas forward, to smash the *Each-Uisge*. Fiona's inspection was all the unfortunate victim would receive and she was fully aware of the fact as she bent to examine him. The man who lay before her deserved justice, every bit as much as the person who'd committed this heinous act deserved to be imprisoned.

ONE

When a kid goes missing there should be a full-scale search party. That's policing 101. Yet Fiona MacLeish was heading for the Luing ferry on her own. She was by no means the sum total of the response, but she was closest to the slate isle when the shout came in. As hard as she wanted to push the diesel Astra, the roads to Luing were so twisty they forbade high-speed driving. Narrow roads, tight corners and blind summits don't pull over when they hear a siren. A campervan dithered in front of her at one point; its driver, unsure of what to do in a place with hedges either side of the road, was preventing her from getting past for a torturous pair of miles. By the time she got to the ferry, she was sweaty, angry and more than a little keyed up.

Fiona ought to have had a fellow officer with her, but a dose of summer flu had swept through the station, decimating half the officers on and off shift. As it was, she was six hours into her seventh shift in eight days. She'd been given a basic outline of the Yorke family. Mum, Diane, Dad, Pete. No siblings for the missing Cait. No red flags against any member of the family from social services, the police's own databases, or any of the many other third sector agencies that fed information to the police. None of the family had a police record for anything more serious than a speeding ticket. Further information on the family would follow after more digging had been done.

So here Fiona was, standing on the tiny ferry that ran between Seil and Luing, eyes slitted against the spray kicked up by the wind whose intensity had been growing since dawn. As the first responder she would have a lot to do. She'd have to speak to the parents, organise whoever and whomever she could into search parties and co-ordinate everything with her sergeant on the mainland. More officers were on their way. That was a given, but with Luing's isolated location they'd be at least an hour behind.

A lot can happen in an hour. To an adventurous eight-year-old tourist, with a habit of wandering off and getting herself lost, a hell of a lot can happen. On a windswept island with rocky shores being pounded by crashing waves, the unthinkable can happen.

It had been forty-five minutes since Fiona got the shout. She knew from experience there would be at least a five-minute period between the police being informed of the missing child and her getting the order to head to Luing, post-haste. It would take a minimum of ten more minutes for her to get off the ferry and locate Cait Yorke's parents.

That put the count at two hours, plus however long the parents had spent searching for Cait themselves before dialling treble nine. Say another hour.

This meant Cait had been missing for three hours.

Fiona ran over what she knew as she googled Luing for extra information. Cait had been with some other children and they'd all gone off to explore ruins. The ruins were sited near Kilchattan Church, in pretty much the centre of the island, which was a good thing in terms of there being less chance Cait had fallen into the sea. It was also a bad thing, as from the centre of the island Cait could have travelled in any one of three hundred and sixty directions.

Google did its thing and offered up information about Luing. None of the information it gave filled Fiona with any great hope. Six-miles long and one-and-a-half wide, Luing comprised three-and-a-half-thousand acres. If a perfect rectangle, the island would possess fifteen miles of shoreline.

Luing was far from being a regular geometric shape, but the jagged shoreline with its inlets, coves and bays would more than make up for any shortfall. Worse still, there was a peninsular on the Atlantic side of the island, and several tiny isles that were sure to appeal to an inquisitive child with a bent for exploration.

From the centre of the island, the coast would be no more than three miles in any direction. For a child of Cait's age, three miles in three hours wasn't far.

Swallowing her sense of dread at what may have befallen Cait, and grabbing the safety rail to aid her balance, Fiona approached the crewman who stood at the bow, a rolled cigarette hanging squint from his mouth. Even though the ferry pitched in the waves his hands dangled relaxed at his sides, his body bracing one way then the other.

'Have you seen this girl on the ferry today?' Fiona held up her mobile and showed the picture Cait's mother had sent to Control.

In the picture Cait wore the uniform of the Manchester school she went to, and a gap-toothed smile. There was mischief in her eyes, a gap where her top front teeth had fallen out, and a ribbon in her hair.

'Not seen her.' The man's eyes narrowed as he puffed out smoke the wind instantly whipped away. 'She gone missing?'

There was no point denying it. In the four years she'd been stationed at Lochgilphead, this was the first time Fiona had travelled to Luing in an official capacity, and she'd never heard of anyone else having to come here. 'Yes. I think she's probably just wandered off, but I have to check in case, you know?'

Fiona wanted that to be the case. It would be a thousand times better for all concerned if Cait was still on the island. Luing was a much smaller area to search for the girl than Seil or the mainland. The police had to treat the girl's disappearance as serious, but in such cases everyone involved hoped the missing child had wandered off and got themselves lost. It was a far more preferable thought than any other.

The ferryman nodded. 'Afore you ask, I've never noticed owt odd the day, and I've no' heard any banging or crying.'

'Thanks.'

The ferryman was ahead of her, but that was fine, she had her answers. Fiona aimed a finger at the ferry's wheelhouse where a man controlled the craft. 'What about him. Is it likely he'll have seen anything?'

The snort from the ferryman as he shook his head said enough, but he couldn't resist sharing an opinion on his colleague. 'He hates dealing with passengers and avoids them at all times. He'd be far better suited to a cargo ship than a ferry like this.'

Fiona fished a card from her pocket. 'If anyone tries to bring a wee lass off the island before I return, can you halt the ferry and call me?'

'That'll no' happen the day. Once you're off, we're taking one load from Luing then heading up to Balvicar Bay to ride out the weather that's coming.'

The news the ferry was to stop running was a stiletto to Fiona's heart. She would have no backup, no help in scouring the island for the lost child. She alone would have to co-ordinate all the search efforts, and she had no idea how to do that. The one time Fiona had been involved in a search team, she'd been with the indomitable Sergeant Dave Lennox and ten other officers. A chief inspector had told Dave Lennox what he wanted done, and in turn, she'd followed the sergeant's instructions.

'When are you likely to start running again?'

'It'll be the morrow morning at the soonest.'

The timescale didn't surprise Fiona, and in some respects it played into her hands. If she hadn't found Cait by morning, there would be a clutch of other officers ready to travel across on the first ferry run of the day. They'd be able to assist her, and also search the vehicles of everyone leaving the island.

Fiona's eyes scanned the waves and took in the numerous white caps. None of them looked big enough to cause the ferry a real problem, but she knew the unspent remnants of Hurricane Chelsea had left Florida ten days ago, and was arrowing towards Scotland. It was due to arrive in the middle of the night, but its outer reaches were already buffeting the islands decorating the country's Atlantic coast.

The one positive Fiona could find about the ferry marooning her on the island was that if she couldn't leave, neither could anyone who may have snatched little Cait.

TWO

As the ferry neared the Luing terminal Fiona realised just how much calmer the seas were in the lee of a small peninsular jutting north from Luing. The ferryman would know both his craft and the waters between Luing and North Cuan on Seil well enough that he'd know when it was safe to run the ferry and when it wasn't. All the same, she'd be the only police presence and would therefore have to organise search parties, liaise with the parents and a dozen other tasks by herself.

From where she stood on the ferry, Fiona took in what was in front of her. The road from the small dock wound its way out of sight behind a couple of houses, and opposite the area where vehicles would disembark, a grey Portacabin sat with a forlorn slump. On the dock itself there were more cars than could fit on the small ferry, and while Fiona was resigned to spending the night on Luing, she could see anger on the faces of those at the back of the queue. That was so typical of the modern world. People had grown accustomed to getting what they wanted when they wanted it, that when they were denied, they went into meltdown. Had she not a missing child to locate, she'd have hung around ready to defuse any situation that may arise.

Rather than shoot off immediately in search of Cait, Fiona waited until the three other vehicles had disembarked the ferry, and parked her car where it prevented anyone boarding. The Astra was a bog-standard police car and in dire need of a service. The car's police comms radio had given up the ghost two days ago, meaning Fiona had to rely on her vest-mounted handset to speak to Control or fellow officers. To compound matters, there was a weird whine emanating from one of the front wheels. It was booked in for a service tomorrow, but now she was marooned on the island, she'd have to suffer the car's failings until a new slot opened up at the police workshop.

Of the cars waiting to board the ferry and leave Luing behind, the first Fiona looked into was a red hatchback. An elderly couple sat in the front and the back seats were bare. When she asked to see in the boot the old man behind the wheel told her it was open.

There was nothing in the boot bar a small picnic hamper, so Fiona closed the lid and tapped on the roof to signal to the driver he could now board the ferry.

After the hatchback was a pickup with a woman in her fifties at the wheel and no passengers save a collie whose head, complete with lolling tongue, poked from the open rear window. Its load bed was empty.

As Fiona walked to each car in line, she saw the same thing in the faces of drivers and passengers. Curiosity. She was looking for stress, nervous tics like a repeated tapping of a finger, and a forced jollity that may be employed to hide guilt.

Fiona saw none of these things. By the time she was at the fourth vehicle, the driver had exited and opened the boot ready for her to look in.

The fifth was different. It held a couple in their twenties, him a hipster, her wearing a leopard-print top and enough make-up to restock Clinique. The woman was out of her seat and aiming a sculpted talon at Fiona, her voice a belligerent screech. 'What do you think you're doing blocking the ferry? We've got to get across there. And if you think you're searching our car without a warrant, you've got another think coming. I know my rights.' When she'd finished speaking, the woman folded her arms and slammed them into her chest, as if the gesture proved her point.

'You're right, I can't search your car without your permission.' Fiona held her phone up so the woman could see the picture of Cait. 'This girl is holidaying on Luing with her family and she's now listed as missing. I'm asking to search your vehicle so I can let you leave the island. If you insist on a warrant, that ferry is going back without you. I'll also deem your refusal as suspicious behaviour and that will lead to me arresting you. It's your choice, you can co-operate, or you can make me suspect you. What's it going to be?'

The woman's top lip curled as she opened the car door. 'Pop the boot and let this cow take a look, Babes.'

Babes did as he was told. Something Fiona reckoned he'd be used to with the partner he'd chosen.

Fiona looked in the boot and found a collection of small cases. One looked like the camera bag her father had owned, and there was a tripod nestled against it.

None of the other three vehicles in the queue harboured a missing child. One had a baby and a boy around Cait's age, but even though Fiona wondered about a rapid makeover to sneak the child away, there was no quick and easy way they'd have been able to replace the front teeth Cait was missing.

With the vehicles searched, Fiona climbed back into her car. The Astra purred along the narrow road to Kilchattan Church, where Control said Cait's parents were searching for their missing daughter. Had Fiona not been scouring the rough fields for a tiny figure, she'd have taken time to appreciate the island's rugged beauty. As it was, she kept the car at little more than a trundle so she could properly scour the surrounding landscape and organise the list of tasks her mind was creating.

Half a dozen cars were parked in the gravel car park opposite Kilchattan Church, and as Fiona scanned the surrounding countryside, she saw knots of people wandering over towards them. Several of the people had children with them and this raised Fiona's hopes, as if these had been the children who'd been with Cait, they might be able to shed some light on where she'd gone.

A woman stood beside a car, her eyes red and restless as she rotated her gaze back and forth. When she saw Fiona's police car arrive she ran over, her strides long yet faltering as if covering the final yards of a marathon.

Her hands banged on the window of Fiona's door as the wind flapped pink hair sideways. 'Please, you have to find her. You have to find my little girl.'

Fiona exited the car leaving her cap on the passenger seat. The wind was already strong enough to make wearing it a choice between professionalism and the dangers of having to run after it. Mrs Yorke wouldn't care that she was bareheaded, all she wanted was her little girl back and that's what Fiona hoped she could deliver.

'That's what I aim to do.' There was no point in checking the woman's identity, her opening words and distraught nature were a plate-sized ID badge. 'But first, you have to answer a few questions so I can focus a search on the right areas. Shall we talk in the car where we won't have to shout?'

As soon as the car door slammed behind her, Diane Yorke was facing Fiona. 'What do you want to know?'

'From your call I know Cait was with other children who were also staying at Sunnybrae Caravan Park, and they went off exploring ruins. They fell out, as kids do, and when the other kids went back to their parents, Cait stayed behind. I have Cait down as wearing a yellow T-shirt and red leggings. Is that correct?'

'Yes. What else do you need to know?'

'The photo you sent to Control, how recent is it? Have her teeth grown in, has her hair grown or been cut off?'

'I took that picture three days ago. Is that recent enough?'

'It's perfect. Have the other children said anything about why they fell out with Caitlin? Have they mentioned her wanting to go somewhere they didn't?'

Thin lips pursed into a tight line as frantic eyes looked over Fiona's shoulder. 'They said they wanted to go and see if they could find an old settlement near Ardluing, but Cait didn't.' Apology drifted onto her face. 'Cait can be a handful if she doesn't get her own way.'

'Would I be right in saying the other kids went off leaving her behind?'

'Yes. She's stubborn like her dad and would have just sat down and watched them go. Short of the other kids picking her up, there was no other way for them to get her to go with them.'

This wasn't good. The kids leaving Cait behind and walking further away from their base at the top of the island meant that Cait had been missing longer than they'd first realised. This meant she could have travelled further and got herself into greater danger. There was also the unthinkable element; if someone had snatched her, then they'd had more time to spirit her off the island.

'Where do you think she'll have gone? What interested her? What was her state of mind?'

'I don't know where she'll have gone. Cait is interested in history and loves all animals. She was saying she was bored.' A tear rolled down Mrs Yorke's face. 'She threw a major strop this morning when we told her we planned to stay another night. If we hadn't changed our plans she'd have been in the car with us now.'

Fiona resisted the urge to offer succour. Mrs Yorke wouldn't believe her if she told her not to blame herself, and her former sergeant, Dave Lennox, had drummed it into her that she should never offer false hope, no matter how much she might be tempted.

'You said she loves animals, do you think that she maybe went to the shore to explore the rock pools?'

'God no, she hates the sea and is terrified of it. She refuses to learn how to swim and won't even play in a paddling pool. There's no way she'll have went near the shore.' Diane pointed over to the east of the island, where she'd been standing on the rise. 'My husband, Pete, is out that way looking for her.'

'I'll keep an eye out for him. Can you describe him?'

'He's six-two, got grey hair and a ponytail. He's a good man, a really good man.'

Fiona allowed her shoulders to droop at the news Cait was terrified of the sea. 'That has to be a good thing, though. If she's afraid of water and won't go near it, there's much less chance of her getting into trouble at the shore.

'Do you think she might have changed her mind and gone after the other children?'

'Nah. She's so stubborn she'd head off in the opposite direction rather than be seen to change her mind. Sorry, I know I sound a right bitch describing my daughter like this. I'm not making her sound like a good girl, am I? She is. She's a treasure most of the time, it's just, she's so strong-willed when she wants to be.'

'You make her sound like a normal kid. Moodiness is all part of childhood and you can't blame yourself for biology.'

The words were ash in Fiona's mouth. While Mrs Yorke couldn't take responsibility for biology, teaching a child how to behave in society was a parent's responsibility, and while she hadn't failed her daughter in this respect, there was room for improvement when it came to teaching Cait not to wander off by herself.

Fiona tried to think of what might interest Cait. She knew she liked animals and history, but disliked water. Cait would have been sullen and bored, but a part of her would have wanted to do something that would have given her joy, even if it was only to spite the children who'd left her. Spite was a powerful motivator, and in the hands of someone who was bloody-minded, it could turn malicious. Cait may well have decided to hide out somewhere so the other children got into trouble for leaving her. Fiona would take that version of events all day long, as every other alternative was far worse.

Luing was home to several former slate mines. While an open-cast slate mine would be of little direct interest to a young girl, there was a good chance that it would also possess a significant draw for a child who was interested in history. Maybe Cait planned to explore the mine, hoping to find dinosaur bones or cave drawings. A clincher for this theory was the former mines were in the north-west part of the island, almost a perfect one hundred and eighty degrees opposite to the direction the other children had travelled.

'Where are people currently searching?'

'Pete, my husband, has been to Toberonochy, just in case she went after the other kids, and everyone else is looking around here. Pete said it was best for me to stay in one place so that everyone knows where I'll be.'

'You're staying at Sunnybrae Caravan Park, aren't you? Do you have someone there in case she makes her own way back?'

'Yeah, my mother-in-law is there.'

'Right, I'm off to check the old slate mines, in case she went there. I'll be in touch as soon as I've checked them. Sooner, if I find her.'

* * *

Fiona set off for Cullipool, every part of her hoping Cait had followed this route and was safely playing in the old mines. A part of Fiona wanted to radio back and update Control of her movements, but Luing wasn't that big and if she found Cait in the next ten minutes, she'd feel silly about radioing back to basically say nothing. Better to leave all communications until facts were known and more time had passed.

As Fiona crested the low hill that ran the length of Luing, she reached for the switches that controlled the car's blue lights and siren. A wailing siren and flashing blue lights always drew glances. Humans were nosey creatures and as such were drawn to drama. Yet to a child who may be hiding away to spite other kids, they'd spell disaster. Little Cait would realise she'd be in trouble for hiding out and would be more likely to hunker down and stay hidden.

At the junction to the road that bisected the island on a north-south basis stood a shed labelled as a 'Fire Station', and another that appeared to be a garage or workshop. A man in grubby red overalls was bent over the bonnet of a car, but there was no sign of any other human life.

Fiona approached the man. A part of her was sure he'd have already been asked if he'd seen Cait, but she had to check anyway. 'Excuse me, have you seen a little girl?'

The man didn't answer. Didn't show any signs of having heard her. As she neared him, she saw the reason. Protruding from each of the man's ears were the tails of ear pods. It was the first sign of modernity Fiona had seen since arriving on the island.

Rather than startle the man, as his attention was on the engine he was bent over, Fiona took an extra step until she could wave a hand where he could see it.

The face that turned her way was covered with a Brillo pad

beard, and had brown Labrador eyes atop a nose that hadn't been reset after being broken.

Fiona used her mobile to show a picture of Cait. 'Have you seen this girl?'

'Nah.' A shake of the head. 'Some folks asked earlier, but I've been busy. Unless she was hiding in the air filter, I wouldn't have seen her.'

'Okay. If you do see her, get word to me right away.' Fiona jotted a couple of numbers onto her pad, tore out the page, and handed it to the mechanic. 'If you can't get me on my mobile, the second number is Lochgilphead station, they'll radio me to let me know.'

'She missing then?'

'Yeah.'

The man's eyes clouded. 'Time her folks called your lot and time it took you to get here. She must've been missing a while.'

'She has. Can you keep an eye out for her, please?'

'Of course. If I see her I'll make sure she's safe.'

With the conversation over, Fiona set off for the mines again. A quarter mile on from the mechanic's place her gaze became locked on something that was out of place. No matter how much Fiona wished she was looking at a young girl wearing a yellow T-shirt and red leggings, the wish was nowhere close to being fulfilled. Instead of little Cait, Fiona's gaze was fixed on the *Each-Uisge*, which appeared to be far closer to the shore than was wise in the current conditions.

The *Each-Uisge* was a pleasure cruiser that ran from Oban harbour and took trips around the various islands in the area. Its scarlet hull and white passenger cabin as familiar a sight around here as seagulls and clouds. Its name was Gaelic and translated as water horse. Whether its name was a tongue-in-cheek reference to its power, or a nod to the mythical water spirit whose usual form was that of a horse was unknown to Fiona, but it was the kind of detail she enjoyed speculating on. Gaelic speakers pronounced Each-Uisge as 'eck eesh-ga'. The name of the craft gave Fiona many opportunities to speculate, as she knew there were some who liked to use Gaelic names simply for the sport involved in hearing the names being butchered by tourists. She'd never liked that aspect of people's mentality, as she, along with many other Scots, had the same pronunciation issues with Gaelic as the tourists.

A couple of years ago, during one of Aunt Mary's visits, the two of them had taken a trip on the *Each-Uisge*. It had been a fine calm day and they'd both enjoyed the spectacular scenery of Scotland's west coast isles.

To Fiona it looked like the *Each-Uisge* was bereft of power, and if that was the case, it was only a matter of time before it foundered on the submerged rocks surrounding Luing. Fiona's instinct was to get herself as close to the shore as she could, so she could determine the pleasure cruiser's condition, but she couldn't abandon the search for Cait.

Torn between the two, Fiona maintained her journey to the slate mines, but she kept one eye on the *Each-Uisge* until she was convinced it was in trouble. As soon as Fiona was certain the *Each-Uisge* was going to run aground she reached for her radio.

It took less than thirty seconds for her to get through to the RNLI station at Oban. The news wasn't good. Their one lifeboat was already tied up with a rescue and would attend as soon as possible. They would, of course, contact their counterparts on Islay, the next closest station, but they could make no promises as all their vessels were already tied up and they knew the coastguard were also running at capacity. What was interesting about the brief conversation was the RNLI had received no other word about the plight of the *Each-Uisge*. The boat would surely have a radio, and if there was a loss of engine power, they'd have signalled for help. While Fiona didn't know or understand much about how such devices worked, she imagined the radio would have a battery backup for instances like this.

Fiona had a decision to make. Continue to search for Cait, who may well be deliberately hiding, or get into a position where she may be able to help save those on the *Each-Uisge* when it covered the last few hundred yards from its current position and ran aground. Which weighed heavier, the life of a missing child, or the dozen or two people aboard the *Each-Uisge*? How many lives could she save if the boat ran aground a hundred yards from shore? How could she abandon the search for a missing child? As Fiona deliberated with herself, a signal flare rose from the stern of the pleasure cruiser and climbed a scarlet arc. There was no doubt in Fiona's mind now, she had to try and help them.

But, there was still a little girl to find.

Fiona indicated at the sign for the ancient mine and pulled up to the gate. She had a small window before the *Each-Uisge* would be close enough to shore that she'd be able to help anyone on it. Therefore she had time to give the mine a quick check first.

THREE

There was a wooden gate blocking the trail into the abandoned mine. Four foot high and twelve wide, the gate was layered with lichen and algae, but its timbers were firm. A chained padlock secured it closed, but despite the warning sign saying the mine was dangerous and should not be entered, there was no real obstacle to prevent an inquisitive child gaining access.

Fiona climbed the gate at the hinge end, a trait she'd learned from spending the second half of her teens living in a farming valley in the Scottish Borders.

The wind was now strong enough that Fiona had to lean into it to progress forward. It plucked at the strands of hair that always seemed to escape her ponytail, billowing them back to tickle her ears.

With her eyes squinted against the wind, Fiona followed the overgrown gravel track as it wound its way towards the scar in the ground left by the former slate mine. Rutted and potholed, the track was solid underfoot, but it would be impassable to all but proper off-road vehicles with four-wheel drive.

A hundred yards or so from the road, the track cut left and started to descend. As Fiona rounded the corner she was able to see into the mine itself. It was an open mine where the slate had been mined by cutting into the side of a hill.

At the far side of the mine a cliff towered upwards; various weeds clung to its face, and a small tree that had somehow found a toehold and enough sustenance to sustain itself. The walls of the mine held little interest, as coming towards the track were two people. The first was a large man; the second a child, their left hand enveloped in the man's right. A springer spaniel was scampering around them, its tongue hanging out and its tail thrashing sideways with enough force to waggle its hindquarters.

Fiona scanned the child at once. They looked to be about the right age for Cait, but there was no way of telling if it was a boy or girl. Every part of the child was covered in dirt; from top to toe, there was a skin of brown mud. It was the kind of dirty only an adventurous child could get, but there was one key detail that gave her hope.

The man was waving his arm at Fiona, and the child was cowering against him as if worried about getting into trouble from the police.

As much as the wind allowed, Fiona increased her pace to get to them sooner. The child was now shrinking back, almost hiding behind the man.

Fiona tried to see through the mud adorning the child's clothes. A flash of yellow on the torso, or a hint of red at the legs would allow her to believe this child was Cait, but the mud was too evenly spread. At best guess it looked as if the child had fallen into the mud and had thoroughly coated themselves getting out.

The man's mouth opened and snatches of words were carried to Fiona on the wind, but they were dragged away before they could be heard properly. She opened her mouth to reply, then closed it. If she couldn't hear the man when the wind was carrying his words to her, there was no way she'd be able to shout loud enough for him to hear her.

The closer they got the more detail Fiona could see. As he talked to the child, Fiona could see a smile on his face as he offered reassurance. His body language was loose, which was a good thing. Better yet, the child trusted him which negated any suspicious thoughts about the man from her mind if the child turned out to be Cait.

The man shouted again. This time Fiona heard one word that set her heart racing.

'Cait!'

Without the rest of the words, Fiona couldn't guess if he was saying the child was or wasn't Cait.

She cupped a hand to her ear.

The man got it. He pointed at the child and gave a thumbs down as he again shouted the missing girl's name.

Fiona could feel the wind on her lips as her mouth tightened into a thin line. As they walked the last few steps towards Fiona, she dropped to a knee so she was eye level with the child.

'Are you Cait Yorke?'

The child peeked out from behind the man and gave a shake of her head.

'She's not Cait. She's my daughter, Ellie. We heard about Cait going missing and so we went looking for her.' As he was speaking the springer came bounding towards Fiona and jumped up at her. Its brown eyes wide and full of requests for pats and rubs. 'Millie, get down. Sorry, we were looking for Cait, and Millie ran off. Ellie went after her and fell into a puddle in the old mine.'

Everything the man said was plausible. It sounded like the truth and he had an easy way about him that made him sound genuine. Fiona would have believed him but for one thing. The child appeared to be frightened of her and was hiding behind the man. The fear seemed to be more than the usual stranger danger children had drummed into them. Had the girl already had a negative experience of the police? Or was it something else, something far more sinister?

In her head Fiona was picturing the man having abducted Cait and then, when she'd come along in her police uniform, he'd have made some vague threat that if the girl didn't play along with whatever story he told, the police would lock her away and she'd never see her mummy and daddy again.

FOUR

The child's fear of getting into trouble nipped at Fiona. If she was Cait, of course there would be a few words said about her going off by herself. That was natural and normal. There may even be a bit of a backlash from the worry of her disappearance, but there'd also be hugs and happy tears.

Fiona had seen parents reunited with lost children on three previous occasions. She knew the drill, it started with an enveloping hug that threatened to crush or suffocate the errant child. When finally released from the bearhug, the child would usually be held at arm's length and a minor admonishment like 'do you know how worried we were?' or 'don't you ever scare me like that again' was fired at the child before another hug was delivered. That was all fine, and just as it should be.

There had been a fourth occasion where Fiona had been involved in the search for a missing child. That hadn't ended well.

Like all those who'd been involved in the search, Fiona had felt a sense of failure for not finding young Thomas in time. She'd been fortunate to escape the horrors of helping to fish him from the river, or of having to break the terrible news to his parents.

Fiona bent to one knee, so she was on the girl's level, and beckoned her forward with a smile.

Cait had a distinguishing feature: an easy identifier. Above her left eye was a pair of marks left from picked chickenpox scabs. They sat side by side like an umlaut above her eyebrow.

The girl stepped forward, but she remained close to the man, her fingers gripping his hand. Her feet scuffed the ground as Fiona examined her face.

The mud covering the girl was on her face so Fiona looked up at the man. 'Can you clean above her left eye, please?'

As she made the request, Fiona was watching both the man and the girl. Him for any signs of aggression and her for how she reacted to his touch. For all he might have terrorised her into acting like his daughter for Fiona's benefit, there was no way she'd be a good enough actor to endure his touch without letting anything slip.

The man rubbed the mud away as the girl stood still. Millie capered forward and nuzzled at the girl's hand only to receive a practised stroke.

'Daaa... aaad. That hurts.'

Fiona didn't need to hear the pained tone, there was no umlaut of scars above the girl's eye. She was the man's daughter, Ellie.

'Sorry,' Fiona dropped the man a rueful smile. 'I had to make sure.'

A hand flapped away her apology. 'Of course you did. And considering the state Ellie's got herself in, she could have been anyone. Where do you think Cait will be?'

It was a good question. One Fiona only had bad answers to.

Now Fiona knew the girl she'd found wasn't Cait, she realised how much dread she was carrying in her heart. As the only police officer on the island, every horror that may have befallen Cait would have been hers to deal with. And yet Fiona knew she was being selfish. She was trained to deal with such things, and the one thing that mattered above all else – the only thing that mattered – was the safety of a child. A little girl yet to have her ninth birthday.

'And you are?'

'I'm John Prentice. I'm ashamed to say my son, Ellie's brother, was one of the kids who left Cait. I got it out of him where she wanted to go and when he said the quarry, I came to the nearest one. I hoped to find her playing in the quarry, but we've had no luck. I was about to look for other slate mines when you appeared.'

As charming and decent as Prentice appeared to be, there was something about him that was prodding Fiona's sixth sense in the chest. It could be a hangover from the experience she'd had while dating Herbert. In all possible ways Herbert had been a charmer of the first order. He held doors open for strangers, was unfailingly polite, and attentive to her every need. Herbert never missed a chance to flatter or compliment Fiona, and while it felt good to be treated like a princess, when she found out about the existence of a queen, she saw just how false Herbert's whole facade had been. She knew she shouldn't have been so easily taken in. Anyone who's called Herbert in Scotland has to be false, even if their falsity is nothing more than a defence mechanism against being lumbered with such an English name.

It was wrong to tar Prentice with Herbert's brush, but Fiona had learned a bitter lesson, and the whole going off to look for a missing girl could be interpreted in more than one way. Yes, he had his own daughter with him, but as her father, he'd easily be able to get her to keep a secret. Should Prentice be as false as Herbert, his motives for searching for Cait could be far darker than the parental responsibility for a child's error that he was presenting.

Had the child been Cait, Fiona would have been able to hand over the girl to her mother then rush off to see if she could in any way help those on the powerless *Each-Uisge*. A glance towards the sea confirmed Fiona's worst fear. The *Each-Uisge* was closer to the shore and still showing no indications of having any method of propulsion.

Fiona had an impossible choice to make. There was a missing child to find and a boat about to founder on the rocky shores of the island. Both parties needed her. The search for Cait could be over in minutes or might take days. The topography of Luing was uneven ground layered with reed outcrops more than large enough to hide a child. Smatterings of gorse bushes would provide the child with a ready-made den to play in. Another thought reverberating in Fiona's head was the change in children's behaviour from when she was young. As a child she'd played outside at every opportunity. She'd gone to the river with her friends, built makeshift dens and hiked miles. All the time she'd been doing so, she'd been able to learn safe ways to explore the outdoors from the older children, and on one occasion when Paul, a classmate who lived four doors down, had jumped into a river and broken his leg on the rocks, she'd learned what not to do. Even though Fiona knew she was being cynical, and thinking like her beloved Aunt Mary, she doubted Cait had the same meagre outdoors skills she'd possessed at Cait's age. Kids these days weren't allowed to play outside the way she had, nor did they seem to want to. Cait might be different, but she hailed from Manchester. A city. Yes, she may play in the city's parks, but there was no way she was used to an environment that could turn as inhospitable as an island like Luing.

The counter to this argument was there would probably be several people on the *Each-Uisge*. Common sense dictated the greatest good could be achieved by saving the greatest number, yet the idea of abandoning the search for a missing child went against every one of Fiona's principles, as did not rushing to offer any assistance she could to people whose lives were at risk.

Fiona knew she didn't have time to dither over the decision. Whatever she chose, she had to get on with it. Unable to make a firm decision, Fiona settled on a compromise. The *Each-Uisge* was coming ashore near Cullipool in Luing's northwest corner. There were sure to be some islanders and day-trippers or tourists there to help. It would take her only a few minutes to go there and assess the situation. If there was a way she might be able to offer help, she would. As galling as it was to pause the search for Cait, it was the logical thing to do. The number of people who may be on the *Each-Uisge* outweighed the missing child. It was a decision Fiona knew might haunt her, but in her mind she'd consulted her first sergeant. Dave Lennox had been a wise teacher and while he was as compassionate as anyone she'd ever met, when it came to choices like this, he could always put emotion to one side and look at cold hard facts.

'John, can you Ellie and Millie carry on searching this area, in case Cait got lost on her way to or from the quarry?' Fiona didn't like leaving the search for the missing girl with a man she wasn't sure she trusted, even if it was only her own neuroses fostering the mistrust.

With the request to John made, Fiona ran back to the car, ready to head to Cullipool to see if there was anything she could do for the people aboard the *Each-Uisge*.

FIVE

Fiona got into the Astra and was on the move before she'd even reached for her seatbelt. In her mind she was weighing up what she could do to aid those on the passenger cruiser, and what she might need to achieve it.

One by one Fiona checked off a mental list as she rocketed the Astra the half mile to where the *Each-Uisge* was likely to run aground.

There were far too many variables at play to make a solid plan until she had more information. How she might effect a rescue depended on where the *Each-Uisge* ran ashore, where and whether its lifeboats could be launched and a thousand other details.

The lack of detailed information chewed at Fiona. There was no way to know how close to the shore the *Each-Uisge* would run aground. Whether it would sink. How many passengers and crew it possessed.

Fiona considered radioing back and getting someone to find out how many people were on the *Each-Uisge*. Even as her hand connected with the radio she withdrew it. By the time she got an answer to how many passengers were aboard the boat, the information would be a moot point, as any rescue attempt she might be able to make would be underway.

No matter how she wracked her brain, Fiona couldn't see a way that she'd be able to help those aboard the vessel if it ran aground any distance from the shore. She had a rope in the car, and she was sure she could find some strong men at Cullipool to help her drag anyone ashore, if she could get the rope to them. Everything after that would have to be improvised depending on how things unfolded.

As she approached the village of Cullipool, Fiona was assessing all that lay before her. The *Each-Uisge* was approaching the collection of islands that lay to the village's south-west. A half dozen men stood on the grassy bank above the high-tide mark watching the stricken craft. One held a heavy shipping rope and two had mobiles to their ears, but there was no sign of any RNLI assistance. In the lee of the largest island a pair of sailing boats bobbed on the waves, their anchors holding them in place. Sailing boats would be more of a hazard than a help in the face of the relentless wind, and with the *Each-Uisge*'s proximity to the shore, their keels were sure to snag the rocks long before they could provide any help to those on the pleasure cruiser. Even if the water were deep enough for them to function, there was no way they'd be able to hold a position alongside the *Each-Uisge* that would allow the transfer of passengers.

As she was sure would happen, when Fiona climbed out of the police car, everyone turned to her with expectation. The way to meet those expectations was to have a clear plan. To issue specific requests to people so they each knew their role and what was required of them.

Fiona didn't have a plan. Couldn't have a plan until she saw what unfolded. All the same, she had to project confidence, even though her stomach was knotted and her mind unsure.

She clapped her hands together to get everyone's attention.

'Right. With luck the *Each-Uisge* won't run ashore at all, but we have to face facts, that's highly unlikely. Until we see where it does run aground, we don't know what we're dealing with, so for now, all we can do is get ourselves into the best position to help when it does run aground. Do any of you know these waters?'

An elderly man stepped forward. His face as weathered as the rocks the *Each-Uisge* was bobbing towards. 'Aye, I do.' A gnarled hand pointed at the island closest to the stricken craft. 'There's a riptide along the shore there that'll keep it out of danger for a while longer, but after another hunner yards, it curls in and heads for thon wee bay.'

Fiona followed his finger with her eyes and saw what his experience was describing. Right at the bay's mouth the waves seemed larger and more powerful. Instead of running largely parallel to the shore, the waves were turning into the bay and crashing into a variety of rock formations which lay between Luing and an islet the size of a football pitch.

'Is there a way to get across there?'

'Aye. The tide's oot just now so a young lass like you ought to be able to nip across the rocks between the waves. At my age I'm ower slow, but you should be fine.'

Again Fiona saw what he meant. The topography of the land formed a rocky causeway that would disappear as the tide came in. She and some of the younger helpers would have a few seconds between waves to cross from one high point to the next.

'Which way is the tide going?'

'Oot, but the water's no' dropped any for over an hour. Wind's holding it in.'

'When does it turn?'

'Half six.'

Fiona glanced at her watch and did the sums. She'd have ninety minutes to get to the islet, wait for the *Each-Uisge* to founder, rescue as many passengers as she could and get back across. If it took longer than that, she and whomever she rescued would have to spend the night on the islet. It had no shelter other than rocks, and there was every chance anyone they managed to rescue would need some form of medical assistance, if not actual treatment. An hour and a half was a long time to pause the search for Cait, but there was nothing to be done about that once she was committed to the rescue effort. All the same, she'd have to make damned sure she got herself back across to the Luing shoreline before she became marooned on the islet.

'Okay, folks, listen up. I'm looking for volunteers to help me. We leave in one minute so if you've any ropes, first aid kits, or snack food with you, grab it now and let's go do what we can to help those on the boat.'

As soon as she'd finished speaking, Fiona opened the boot of her Astra and got out everything she thought might be of use. When done she had a first aid kit, a rope and her cache of chocolate bars. Her next step was to remove her utility belt and stab vest: they were for the process of catching criminals, not rescuing civilians.

Four men volunteered. Fiona didn't worry about their names. In her head they were Baldy, Muscles, Big Nose and Glasses.

A glance out at the *Each-Uisge* being brought ashore by the incoming tide and the wind sent a shiver of dread and panic through Fiona as she watched it reach the end of the undertow and begin to rotate under the force of the waves. The craft now only had a couple of minutes before it foundered on the rocky shore of the islet or was holed below the waterline by a submerged rock.

SIX

Fiona dashed to the shoreline and paused until a wave ebbed enough that she could cross to the first rock that protruded from the swirling waters. She had no worries about getting wet, but the waves sweeping between the protruding rocks that formed the natural causeway were more than strong enough to knock her over. If that happened she'd at best get a dunking, at worst, she'd be sucked out to sea or smashed against the rocky shoreline. The crashing waves combined with the howling wind to spit salty spray at her, but she narrowed her eyes and kept her focus.

As soon as she judged it safe, Fiona set off for the next outcrop. The ebb and flow of the tide combined with a coating of seaweed left the rocks under her boots slick and greasy, but she powered forward as fast as she dared.

When Fiona got to the next rock she cast a glance over her shoulder. The first two of the four volunteers were on the first outcrop and two others were bent ready to dash and replace them on their perch. A look at the *Each-Uisge* gave her chills. She was now close enough to see the faces peering out of the windows. Each one pale and filled with dread as the craft neared the islet. Beyond the pleasure cruiser the seas were rougher than before and the wind stronger than ever.

Fiona didn't need to hear the voices of those on the pleasure cruiser to know they were willing her to find a way to get them to safety once the boat ran aground. The uniform she wore would place their hopes of survival on her shoulders. It would be Fiona they'd expect to have a rescue plan. She, they'd rely on. She couldn't fail them. *Mustn't* fail them.

The next outcrop was spaced further away than either of the ones Fiona had so far used to avoid the force of the waves. She'd have to sprint to reach it before the next surge flowed through the gap. Worse, it had been sheared by time and tide, so she'd have to climb up a three-foot-high step to evade the surging waters.

Fiona bent into a sprinter's stance and as soon as she judged the ebbing wave had lost the majority of its power, she set off, her boots splashing gouts of water up her legs with every thundering step.

Three steps into her wild dash her right foot skittered sideways, but she managed to maintain enough balance that she kept progressing forward. She wasn't fast enough.

A wave swelled between the two rocks, thumping into Fiona's legs as she clambered onto the safety of the next outcrop. She planted her hands onto the rock and flopped her upper body down, bending her legs so her heels bumped her backside. With only her knees and a few inches of leg to buffet, the wave that had almost done for her had too little purchase to dislodge her from the rock.

As the wave ebbed and she hauled herself onto the rock, the first two men joined her. A look back saw the others again setting themselves to cross from their perch.

'Shit.'

Fiona didn't need to follow Baldy's arm to know why he was cursing. The *Each-Uisge* was now tilted over on a forty-degree angle, and even over the crash of waves the sound of metal graunching on stone could be heard.

The wave ebbed and Fiona ran. Baldy and Muscles were at her shoulders and their presence reassured her. The two men were strong and powerful, and for whatever was to come, she was sure their physicality would be more of an asset than her sense of duty.

Fiona dashed up the shore of the islet, turning as soon as she was clear of the waters and setting a course towards where the *Each-Uisge* had foundered.

Even as she approached the nearest point to the stricken craft, Fiona was assessing what could be done to save those on board. The *Each-Uisge* was beached twenty yards from shore. Not a great distance, but there was a mass of swirling currents between dry land and the pleasure cruiser. In the seconds Fiona spent watching the waters ebb and flow, there was no sign of any rocks that could be used as stepping stones. Worse, the incoming waves slapped against the boulders of the shore with enough force to send gushing plumes into the air that the wind splattered onto the islet.

In the short time Fiona watched them she was soaked. Aboard the *Each-Uisge*, a crew member had exited the cabin and was balanced on the tilted deck, his feet resting in the V between deck and the cabin's windows. Every few seconds the craft would quiver and shake as it was buffeted by an incoming wave.

A basic plan came to Fiona, so she whipped the rope that was around her shoulders free and waved for Muscles to join her.

SEVEN

Fiona stepped back from the spray's reach and watched as Muscles prepared to throw the rope. He'd looped it and was rotating his shoulder, building up momentum so his throw would be as powerful as possible.

Up went Muscles' arm and then, as it came sweeping down beside his body, he let fly. The rope snaked forward, arrowing towards the *Each-Uisge* until the power of his throw was spent. When the rope landed it was at least six feet short of the pleasure cruiser.

Muscles wasted no time hauling the rope back to him. Even as he prepared for a second attempt, Baldy was nudging his arm and gesturing for the rope. Short and stocky, Baldy had biceps as thick as Fiona's thighs, but whether he could transfer that power into something as fickle as a rope was the question burned into Fiona's mind.

Baldy's throw went further than Muscles' had, but it still fell short of the *Each-Uisge* by at least three feet. It wasn't just that extra three feet that was needed. To reach the crew member who'd climbed out, the rope would have to travel a further six feet beyond the rail.

As Baldy wound up ready to throw again, Fiona turned away and started scouring the rocky shore. She knew what she needed, the difficult part was finding it.

After a minute's search, Fiona's eyes landed on her quarry. A flat rock that was more or less square. When Fiona lifted the rock and hefted it in her hand, she judged the rock to weigh about the same as a bag of sugar. Perfect.

With Muscles and Baldy still trying to launch their rope to the *Each-Uisge* by strength alone, she unwound her own rope and located an end. Fiona's hands worked with a quick nimbleness as she tied the rope around the square rock like ribbon on a Christmas present. Fiona had her Aunt Mary to thank for the knowledge of how to do this. Aunt Mary was a stickler for wrapping gifts with as much care as she put into selecting them, and after Fiona's parents had been murdered, it was Aunt Mary who took her in and repaired a broken teenager.

When Fiona was satisfied the rock couldn't slip free of the rope, she handed the rock to Muscles and stood back while he whirled it at his side. Muscles released the rope and the stone flew across the gap between the shore and the *Each-Uisge*. Instead of falling short like the previous attempts, the weight of the stone was enough to combat the wind and the rope sailed over the gap with ease, the rock landing beyond the stricken craft.

Now they had a lifeline reaching the *Each-Uisge*, there was the question of how to get the passengers off. Had the waters between the pleasure cruiser and the islet not been such a maelstrom, Fiona would have counted on the combined strength of Baldy and Muscles to drag people ashore, but with the waters as they were, there was every chance anyone who entered the waters would be smashed against the rocks. At the very least there would be broken bones, so she'd have to find another solution.

Instead of using the rope to drag people free, they'd have to

rig it as a skyline between the boat and the land so the passengers could use it to shimmy their way to shore. Fiona mimed
tying the rope off to the crewman, and while he secured his end,
she looked for somewhere to secure the landward end.

As her eyes scoured the rocky formations she saw no
obvious anchor point, but there was a huge boulder whose bulk
would provide more than enough of a counterweight.

Muscles was closest to Fiona so she handed him the end of
the rope. 'Can you wind this around a rock and brace against it?'

Fiona felt a hand pushing her aside as Glasses stepped
forward. 'Here, let me hitch it. The rope needs to be tense.'

There was wisdom in what the man was saying so Fiona left
him to it and waved to the guy on the *Each-Uisge*. When she
had his full attention she mimed looping her belt over the rope
and hauling hand over hand.

When it was tied off the rope created a skyline that hung at
least seven feet above the water. It was an imperfect solution,
but the best they had.

The guy gave her a thumbs up and then knocked on the
window, gesturing at others to come out.

Just as the first person attached themselves to the rope, a
huge wave crashed into the *Each-Uisge,* tilting it further over
and sending a torrent of water over everyone who'd clambered
out to join the first guy.

The man who'd lashed himself to the rope was now hanging
in mid-air. He had a hand on the rope and managed to pull
himself up enough that his other hand could also grasp the
hemp skyline. Due to the impact of the last wave and the man's
weight, the rope now sagged making it an uphill struggle for
the man.

Every new wave that came in was splashing up and
drenching the man, but he soldiered on until Baldy's powerful
arm could grab his hand and haul him onto the islet.

Glasses undid his knot and waved Muscles over. Together they hauled on the rope until it was as tight as they could get it. Rather than tie it off again, they kept their grip on the rope ready to add even more tension if necessary.

Fiona signalled the next person should make the trip.

EIGHT

Three passengers crossed without incident, but the fourth was a challenge. So far all those to cross had been slim people with youth on their side. The fourth was a heavyset woman whose pudgy face was whiter than the foam generated by the crashing waves.

The woman wore a loose sundress, ideal for a summer's day cruise, but wholly unsuited to crossing the skyline. Already the wind was threatening to expose the woman's modesty, and even though her dress flapped and whipped in the wind, she was clinging to the rail with both hands.

Worst of all, the woman had no belt to fasten her to the skyline. Her head was shaking, and while Fiona couldn't hear what was being said to her, it was clear she was refusing to travel across the skyline.

Instead of letting the others waiting go ahead of her, the woman refused to move from her position beside the rope.

Another crew member stepped up from below. In his hands were some short lengths of rope. The first guy used the short lengths of rope to fashion some slings. The first he put under the woman's arms and when it was tight, but not suffocating, he tied a loop in the other end that encircled the skyline. The second and third pieces of rope he used to fashion rudimentary slings that encircled her legs.

The woman's head was still sawing back and forth as she was guided to the point where she'd leave the pleasure cruiser.

Fiona could do nothing but watch. Her heart was racing as the woman gripped the rope with pudgy fingers and hauled herself towards land. It was a torturous process with the woman inching forward like a lame sloth. As she watched, Fiona could tell the woman's strength was going to fail her long before she reached shore. At the moment she was struggling to pull herself along the skyline, and as she wasn't yet halfway, the part of the skyline she was on was sloped downhill. When she got to the point when the skyline sloped upwards, the woman would have to exert every last piece of strength she possessed to drag herself up.

Not believing the woman could do it, Fiona grabbed the spare rope and thrust it into the hands of Baldy. 'Can you get this rope to her?'

The woman was at the point where Baldy's throws had always reached, but if they could get the rope into her hands, the people on the shore would be able to help.

The first throw fell short. Baldy's second reached the woman, but as her focus was on her hands, the rope bounced off her arms with the woman making no move to grab it.

Fiona fancied she heard a scream, but it could have been her imagination.

The next throw happened just as the wind dropped between gusts, and the rope sailed past the woman's hands and across the skyline. The woman's hands remained in place, her eyes wide when she turned her head to look at the shore.

Fiona looked at the rope forming the skyline and made a decision. The woman had to be moved. Not just for her own sake, but so those still on the *Each-Uisge* could be rescued.

'Here. Let me have the rope.' Fiona lashed one end of the rope around her ankle and tied off the other on her belt. 'When I've got to her, and tied the rope around her sling, haul me back.'

With her instructions given, Fiona unbuckled her belt, and refastened it around the skyline. One by one she looped her legs over the rope and then she grasped the rope with both hands and set off.

Hand over hand Fiona pulled herself towards the stranded woman. Spray from the crashing waves splashed up, cascading salty water into her. She didn't falter, didn't hesitate. By the time she was halfway to the woman, her muscles were burning with the effort, but not so much her pace faltered.

Fiona's brain was working every bit as hard as her body. She could hear the woman's screams and pleas for help. The first thing she'd have to do was calm the woman down enough to lash the end of the rope to the one supporting her. To do so, she'd have to clamber past her. Fiona was timing the gouts of spray gushing up at her, but the further she travelled towards the *Each-Uisge*, the less the spray became an issue as she was past the rocks the waves were colliding with.

The rope swayed above Fiona, and she thought for a horrible moment that her weight added to that of the heavyset woman would cause it to break, but her fears were assuaged when she risked a look at the woman and saw her thrashing about in a blind panic.

Not as bad as the rope breaking, but worse than she needed.

'Help. Somebody. Anybody, please. Help me.' The scream that followed was high-pitched enough to shatter glass. The woman's accent was so deeply Yorkshire it evoked thoughts of flat caps and whippets.

'It's okay. I'm coming.'

Fiona said no more. As good as her physical shape was, crawling out on the skyline was sapping her strength, and she'd had to hold her breath on several occasions when the spray was cascading over her.

When she felt her hands bump against the woman's, Fiona wasted a few precious breaths shouting an explanation of her plan.

'Please, you've got to help me. I've seen *Cliffhanger*.'

Fiona got the reference at once. In one of the movie's opening scenes, Sly Stallone had been unable to save a woman dangling on a skyline. His character had been haunted by the failure and, in true movie style, a similar scene had happened towards the end of the movie, allowing Stallone's character to find redemption. That was all Fiona needed; a negative image planted in both the woman's mind and her own. The fact the woman remembered the movie, even in a moment as stressful as this, spoke volumes about how terrified she was of falling to her death.

'This is real life. Not a film.' Fiona didn't care for the snarled way she yelled to the woman, but she had to transfer some of her dwindling confidence, as she'd never rescue the woman otherwise. 'Now, hold still while I tie my spare rope to your sling.'

The woman writhed as Fiona got close. The one good thing about the situation was there was no way the wild-eyed woman would release her grip on the skyline, so Fiona didn't have to worry about getting an elbow in the face.

It was a fight to get to where she needed to be, but despite the woman's struggles, Fiona got herself into a position where she could reach the rope sling supporting the woman's upper body.

Fiona knew this was going to be the hardest part of the rescue. Slung as she was by her belt, and her lower legs wrapped over the skyline, Fiona's torso was half supported by the hands she had clasped around the skyline. To undo the rope she'd hitched to her belt and tie it around the sling suspended beneath the woman, she'd have to release a hand from the skyline. This one hand would have to do all the work while the other kept her in place.

It took no more than ten seconds for Fiona to unpick the knot securing the rescue rope to her belt, but she knew tying the rope onto the woman's sling would be far more time-consuming. Before Fiona brought the rope free of her belt, she wound three coils around her wrist; if she dropped the rope the men on the shore would soon pull her back to land, but she'd have to start all over again, and the woman was already on the point of a full-blown panic attack, and a delay while Fiona started again would be catastrophic for her state of mind.

Fiona knew it was unkind to assume the woman's bulk had already placed a strain on her heart, but that didn't mean it wasn't true. She had to get this right first time.

Fiona's rope hand snaked between the woman's arms and located the loop the crew member had formed to encircle the skyline. With a series of careful movements and several muttered curses, Fiona managed to feed a couple of feet of the rescue rope through the loop and grab the end that sagged towards the woman's chest.

The arm Fiona kept grasping the skyline with burned with an intensity that increased exponentially as the seconds ticked past, but she gritted her teeth against the pain and the cramp of her clasped fingers. Even when her muscles began to quiver with the unfamiliar exertion, Fiona did nothing to ease her own pain. She had one shot at getting this done before the woman went into complete meltdown.

It wasn't just the woman she was saving: the lives of all those still on the *Each-Uisge* depended upon her clearing the skyline before the craft was further assaulted by the tumultuous waves created by the incoming gale.

Every attempt Fiona made to see what she was doing was thwarted by the woman's meaty arms and the flapping material of her dress, but Fiona wasn't giving up. She worked by feel alone until she was convinced she'd formed a secure enough knot for the woman to be hauled ashore.

Fiona gave the rescue rope a sharp tug as a test for the knot. It held, so she waved her hand to those on the shore and slung a second hand up to the skyline. A second later, the rope around her ankle was dragging her ashore.

Even before Fiona had undone her belt and collapsed onto the secure footing of the shoreline, she could hear the terrified screams of the woman over the crashing of the waves.

NINE

Fiona tracked the heavy woman's progress as she was hauled ashore. It was a stop-start affair as the woman would only release her grip to move her hands forward when Baldy paused to let her slide pudgy hands along the skyline.

Aboard the *Each-Uisge* the crew member had the other passengers lined up. A slight man was preparing to come next, and behind him were a boy and girl who looked to be in their mid-teens.

Fiona's jaw set in disgust. The kids should have been first off the pleasure cruiser. Certainly they should have been ahead of the men who were already ashore. Anybody with the tiniest shred of decency would have sent them before the woman. At the rear of the line were three young men, an elderly woman and a crew member whose burly physique gave Fiona hope that he'd help the old woman.

When they were untying the heavy woman from the makeshift slings that had carried her along the skyline, a huge wave crashed into the *Each-Uisge*, tilting it further over and causing the skyline to sag so it was mere feet above the frothing maelstrom between ship and shore.

'Tighten the rope.'

Fiona needn't have bothered speaking as Muscles and Glasses was already working to restore the tension on the skyline. It took a minute of grunting, but the hitch tied by the islander and their combined power did what was required.

While there was a delay as the rope was tightened, Fiona cast a rapid glance over to Luing. She was looking for Cait. If the child was anywhere near this coast, Fiona was certain the drama of this rescue would prove irresistible to a curious child.

No matter how Fiona strained her eyes she couldn't spot a small figure dressed in red and yellow.

A look back at the craft gave Fiona cause for concern. Where before the two ends of the skyline were around the same level, the fresh tilt caused by the recent wave had lowered the part of the pleasure cruiser where the skyline was attached. The slight man wasted no time in getting himself onto the skyline and making his way ashore. Despite it being an uphill slog most of the way, he got himself across in less than two minutes.

As soon as he'd released himself from the skyline, he was enveloped in a massive hug from the woman Fiona had rescued.

Next to cross were the two kids, the boy insisting the girl go first. The gesture was enough to restore some of Fiona's faith in human nature, although as a police officer, she'd seen plenty of scenes and actions that made her despair for humanity.

There were now six people left on the *Each-Uisge*. The original young crewman, three young men dressed in skinny jeans and hoodies, the elderly woman, and the burly crewman. Such was the tilt of the boat, they were standing on the craft's windows rather than the wooden deck.

Fiona had no chance of hearing what was being said by the three men, but it was clear the burly man wanted the others to cross first and then he'd bring the elderly woman with him as the last off.

The four younger men crossed in rapid succession. Aboard

the *Each-Uisge* the burly crewman was working with ropes to form a sling for the woman and a connecting rope so she'd be pulled along after him.

It was a good plan, and as exhausted and concerned for their safety as Fiona was, she was also beginning to feel a sense of jubilation as, if they could get everyone off the *Each-Uisge* without injury or loss of life, it would be the very best of a bad situation.

Fiona's eyes caught sight of impending disaster as the man was affixing his sling around the woman. Beyond the *Each-Uisge* a huge wave was barrelling straight at the craft.

A warning was shouted by all those on the shore, but the wind prevented the words reaching either of those still on the craft.

The wave hit the *Each-Uisge* with enough of a thumping force to rotate the craft until it was tilted on its side. The impact sudden enough to unbalance those on board. The elderly woman was gripping the rail with a hand so she only fell to her knees, but as the crewman had both hands on the sling he was wrapping around her, he went down hard, his reflexes shooting out an arm. The glass of the window the elderly woman was standing on starred under the sudden impact of the crewman's elbow. Then it sagged under her weight, but as she went to move off the now treacherous window it collapsed, dropping her into the passenger cabin.

The crewman looked down into the cabin, shook his head and turned for the skyline. Muscles had already restored tension on the skyline and the man crossed to the shore in record time. When his feet touched earth, his eyes were full of shame and his face was as white as the froth kicked up whenever a wave crashed into a rock, but Fiona could also see a lot more than a hint of guilt. His limbs were trembling and she could see he was in shock. It was understandable, he'd waited until last. Had volunteered to save the woman and he'd then failed. When the woman had fallen through the window, and had presumably received a serious injury or been killed by the fall, his nerve had failed him and he'd rushed ashore.

There could be no blame attached to the man for his actions, although a part of Fiona was thinking a professional sailor should have had the good sense to keep an eye on the seas.

She left him to be guided back to Luing by the others and turned for a final gaze at the *Each-Uisge*.

'Look.' Fiona's arm pointed at the craft despite it being obvious what she was referring to.

Out of the shattered window a frail hand was trying to find purchase. The elderly woman was still alive.

There was no doubt in Fiona's mind as to what she must do. She whirled to face the three men – Big Nose having taken on the task of escorting the rescued passengers back across to Luing – and pointed a finger at Glasses then Muscles. 'I need you two to keep that skyline tight. I'm going over to get her.' A nod to Baldy. 'Can you tie each end of the spare rope around me and keep a hold of the middle. You'll have to pull us both back.'

All three men set about their tasks with an acknowledging word and no further chatter. They got it. This was a time for action not talk.

It was gratifying the way they allowed her to take command, but Fiona wasn't fool enough to think they were following her leadership skills so much as obeying the uniform she wore.

As soon as Baldy had tied the two ends of the rope around her waist, Fiona looped her belt over the skyline and set off. Her feet touched down on the *Each-Uisge* two minutes later. The journey made easy by the downhill angle of the skyline.

The first thing Fiona did was grip the rail hard. The second, check the seas. They were still raging, but there was a regularity to both them and the waves that set quivers running through the *Each-Uisge*. Next, she tied off the two ends of the rescue rope and looked along the pleasure cruiser.

By now the elderly woman's head was poking out of the broken window and Fiona could see that apart from a cut to her forehead, the woman was unhurt. That was good news. A glance at the seas saw no abnormally huge waves coming their way. More good news.

The bad news was something else. Something Fiona hadn't expected.

As Fiona knelt down to help the woman clamber from the cabin, the woman's liver-spotted hand was pointed towards the front of the craft. 'He's dead. Murdered.'

TEN

A dozen questions hit Fiona's brain at the same time. As much as she wanted to ask them all and hear their answers, time wasn't on her side, so she ducked her head through the broken window and looked to where the woman was pointing.

The old woman's arm was aimed towards the front of the craft, where the fore part of the cabin became the wheelhouse. Fiona assumed it must be a crew member the woman was referring to. Perhaps the craft's de facto captain.

Whomever it was, Fiona knew her first responsibility was to ensure the safety of the woman before she investigated the claim of murder. Her own safety was Fiona's second responsibility, but the budding detective in her made her want to check out the woman's claim.

As she drew her head out of the hole, Fiona noticed the woman was standing on one leg. 'Are you hurt?'

'My ankle. I think it's broken.'

The woman's voice was tight, but Fiona applauded the way she was being economical with her words.

Fiona slung her legs into the opening ready to lower herself into the cabin. 'Let's get you out of there.'

As soon as she was in the cabin and had braced her feet on the row of seats, Fiona bent her knees, wound her arms around the woman's thighs and hoisted her upwards.

The woman had the good sense to aid Fiona as much as she could, and she slid her bottom onto the window frame as soon as she was high enough.

Now that Fiona was inside the cabin it would take no more than a minute or two to investigate the woman's claim of murder. She knew that she would have to get the woman to safety first, though. If something happened and the woman was hurt or killed, all the blame would lie on Fiona's shoulders. And so far as Fiona was concerned, that blame would be justified.

As soon as the woman was out of her way, Fiona climbed out and helped the woman make her way to the skyline. The makeshift sling the burly crewman had fashioned was still around the woman's waist, so Fiona looped it over the skyline, tied it off and untied one end of the rescue rope. She lashed this to the loop encasing the skyline and signalled to Glasses.

He had the old woman moving towards shore before the signal was finished.

Fiona looked over the exposed hull at the incoming waves. She knew that to go back into the cabin and check out the woman's claim was far above and beyond the call of duty, but she was a police officer and there was a potential murder to investigate.

Fiona wasn't a detective – she'd never been able to bring herself to sit the necessary exams due to the ongoing trauma of learning of her parent's murder upon exiting her History exam – but becoming a detective was her dream. With a detective's training, she'd have the skills and resources at her disposal to allow her to try and solve the one case that mattered to her above all others: the double murder of her parents.

Now, in Fiona's mind the reward outweighed the risk. If she could detect a clue before the sea claimed the *Each-Uisge* she may learn something that would help catch a killer. She'd endured almost twenty years of being denied the closure brought by answers and justice. Even if solving this case didn't advance her own cause further, she'd have the satisfaction of knowing she'd given something precious to another grieving relative.

The tilted cabin meant Fiona had to use the ends of the seats as stepping stones to navigate her way forward. Beneath her water sloshed back and forth.

Fiona wasted no time taking in her surroundings or pausing to maintain her balance. Time was as precious as oxygen and if the boat tilted further, she could be trapped until she ran out of both.

With the doorway to the cabin now being closer to horizontal than vertical, Fiona had to lower herself until she was thigh deep in the swirling waters so she could even look through it. What she saw was enough.

In the front cabin, a man was on his back. His body was half submerged, but there was no mistaking his fate. His throat and upper torso were covered in blood, but there were also rents to the clothing at his groin.

Normal circumstances would have dictated that Fiona try and preserve the crime scene. That she not contaminate any possible source of evidence. That was a non-starter. Even if the island wasn't temporarily cut off by the gale it was far too dangerous to try and get a team here to extricate the corpse and sweep the crime scene. It was only a matter of minutes, maybe an hour at most, before the tide turned and the gale pushed heavy seas forward, to smash the *Each-Uisge*. Fiona's inspection was all the unfortunate victim would receive and she was fully aware of the fact as she bent to examine him. The man who lay before her deserved justice every bit as much as the person who'd committed this heinous act deserved to be imprisoned.

Fiona began by exploring the clothing at the man's groin. As she'd noted in her visual examination, there were a number of rents in the material. To her grappling fingers they felt straight and un-tattered by age. Ripped jeans might well be fashionable, but the rips never risked exposing genitalia as these did.

As Fiona was cupping her hands in the water, the *Each-Uisge* gave a mighty shudder and tilted over a further few degrees.

Fiona's heart was in her mouth, but she didn't move her feet. Not yet.

With cupped hands, Fiona splashed water onto the corpse's throat until she'd washed enough blood away she could examine the fatal wound. Rather than the sideways slash she'd expected, there was a stab wound that went right through the Adam's apple. She got what it meant at once. His windpipe would have been punctured and, as he'd gasped for terrified breaths, his oesophagus would have filled with blood.

Fiona wished she'd had her mobile with her to take a couple of quick snaps, but she'd left her stab vest in the car and the mobile was secreted in one of its pockets.

As Fiona searched the man for a wallet, she observed everything she could about him. His facial features, hair, the sculpted beard, and any exposed skin she could see for distinguishing marks.

Another shudder ran through the *Each-Uisge* and Fiona's nerve broke. If she didn't get off the pleasure cruiser right away, she'd die in the company of a murder victim.

Fiona got back to the skyline without issue apart from the images of the corpse seared into her brain. She wrapped the spare end of the rescue rope around her shoulders in a bowline knot, and fastened her belt over the skyline.

Before she'd even signalled to Baldy, she felt him pulling her to shore. His urgency was welcome, if a little abrupt. It was only as she saw the wave about to crash into the *Each-Uisge* that she realised why he was in such a hurry.

The wave was larger than any other she'd seen that day, and as it slammed into the pleasure cruiser, she saw the craft rotate and felt the skyline slacken and lower her to the tumultuous maelstrom inches below her.

ELEVEN

Fiona had just enough time to grab a breath before she was plunged into the frothing waters. Something hard and unyielding slammed into her hip, but she managed not to gasp at the pain. She had a sense of movement, but no idea whether it was from Baldy pulling on the rope or the waters swirling around her.

Unlike the last time Fiona had been plunged into raging waters, the temperature wasn't icy, but it was still a lot cooler than the summer's day she'd been in before her ducking.

When Fiona felt the strong pull of the rope around her shoulders, she knew she'd have to do what she most feared and release the skyline so her fingers weren't nipped between the rope and her belt. Rather than fully release them, Fiona slid her hands along the damp nylon until she felt her head breach the surface.

As soon as she could Fiona gulped in a huge breath and swung her head around so she could see how far she was from shore.

Baldy stood on the edge of the rocky outcrop, ten feet away. Fiona could see the stress in his face as he hauled her land-

wards. Instinct was telling her to try and pull herself ashore to
aid him, but he was dragging her so quickly the practical part of
Fiona's brain told her to stay still lest her attempts to help
hampered him.

It only took Baldy a couple of seconds to reel her in, and as
soon as she could grasp the rock, Glasses and Big Nose grabbed
at her arms, dragging her bodily onto the rocky islet. No matter
how good it felt to feel terra firma beneath her soaking body, it
didn't escape Fiona's notice that one of the two men had
grabbed a handful of her backside as they were hauling her up
onto the rock. It could be entirely innocent with the offender
doing what was needed to save her, or it could be something
else. With a missing child and a murdered man to contend with,
a possible minor sexual assault was small beer, especially as
there was no proof it was deliberate. All the same, Fiona filed
the experience away for later consideration.

Fiona's legs were unsteady as she clambered to her feet, but
her mind was bang on track as the seawater dripped from her.
'Thanks, guys. You just saved my life.'

'You're either brave or stupid gan oot there like that.' Big
Nose's voice was layered with admiration as he looked at her.
'But you saved the auld wifie.'

'That's my job.' Fiona knew what she'd achieved, and while
one day she might look back at the moment with a sense of
pride, right now she had far too many other pressing concerns to
waste time thinking about what she'd already achieved.
'Where's everyone from the boat?'

Muscles pointed to the shore. 'We got them over to Luing.
The fat woman near got washed away but Deek made sure she
was all right.' The nod he gave towards Big Nose identified who
he meant by Deek. 'While you were in the boat, Grant carried
the auld woman back.' Again, Muscles' nod towards Baldy identified who he was referring to.

'Okay.'

Fiona set off across to Luing with the four men. After the ordeal of getting to and from the *Each-Uisge* it was an easy crossing, but Fiona's mind was elsewhere. Apart from the elderly woman who was being treated by an islander, all the others were specks in the distance as they were led to the houses of Cullipool.

It made perfect sense to Fiona the island community would rally round to help those who'd been shipwrecked. It was something that would have happened over many hundreds of years. Small communities always came through when the chips were down, and the island community was sure to be tighter than most due to their shared experiences of remote living.

The worst thing about the islanders' hospitality was the way the crew and passengers of the *Each-Uisge* were now scattered among the dozen or so houses that formed Cullipool. One of them was a killer and as such had to be identified and arrested.

It crossed Fiona's mind the killer might try to escape the island. If they were a crew member, they'd no doubt feel confident they could steal a boat and make their way to either Seil or the mainland. A desperate passenger may feel the same way when they found out Fiona had been on the *Each-Uisge*.

Somehow Fiona had to find a way to gather all the crew and passengers together and then question them to identify the killer. That wouldn't be too hard if that was all she had to do, but with little Cait missing, Fiona knew she'd have to divide her time between searching for the child and catching a killer. The task was a lot for her to undertake herself, but with no other officers able to get onto Luing, there was nothing she could do but her best, and she'd have to make sure her best was good enough.

When they were all on Luing, Fiona approached the elderly woman she'd rescued from the *Each-Uisge*. Her face was tight with pain as an islander strapped her ankle, but it was the words tumbling from her mouth that most concerned Fiona.

'He's dead. Murdered. I've never seen so much blood.'

The islander wore a kindly expression as she worked on the old woman's ankle, but Fiona could hear the quiet questions she was asking and the old woman's shrill answers. Fiona would bet the news would take less than an hour to ripple its way across Luing.

Fiona knelt beside the woman, the coarse material of her sodden trousers scraping her legs. 'Do you know who he is? If any of the other passengers or crew saw him? Did you see who killed him?'

'I think he must be the captain or whatever.' The woman paused to wince as the islander tied off a bandage around her ankle. 'I never saw him on the boat until after I fell through the window. All the time we were on it, the door to the wheelhouse was closed. I don't know if anyone else saw him.'

'Did you see who killed him?' This was the most important question. If the old woman could identify the killer, then it'd be a simple matter to arrest the culprit, and Fiona would be able to focus all her energies on searching for Cait.

'No.' The woman's hand covered her mouth for a moment. 'Dear Lord, I can't believe I was on a boat with a killer.'

Fiona felt a hand on her shoulder pulling her round. Grant stood in front of her, his face etched with concern as the sun reflected off his bald head. 'Is it true? Was someone killed on the *Each-Uisge*?'

'It's true.' There was no point denying it, and Fiona needed the help of these four men now as much as before. 'I think we need to contain the news, though. So far as the killer will be aware, we won't know of the murder. I need you, Deek and the other two guys to round up everyone who was on the *Each-Uisge* and get them to one place. If we can keep them together as a group, the killer can then be identified. Is there a village hall or somewhere like that you can use?'

'There's the Atlantic Islands Centre. It would do.' A nod

went towards Glasses. 'Fergus' wife runs it so we can easily get the keys.'

'Perfect. Where is it?'

'Just ower there.' Grant's arm extended towards Cullipool. 'What are you going to be getting on with?'

'There's a missing child to find as well.'

'Shit, I'd forgotten all about her.'

Fiona paused to look Grant straight in the eye. 'You look like you can handle yourself, but if any of the crew or passengers try making a run for it or threaten you in any way, don't engage with them. Just keep an eye on them and get word to me.'

With that said, Fiona set off for her car, her sodden clothes slopping water as she went. She had two calls to make; the first to Control to alert her mainland colleagues about the murder; the second to her closest friend, DC Heather Andrews, for advice on how best to find Cait and identify the killer.

TWELVE

The police radio on Fiona's vest had enough power to connect her to the duty sergeant at Lochgilphead, where she was stationed. He was a kind man who was a capable officer, but while he'd risen to sergeant, he was never going to progress further. His attitude was lackadaisical at best and he'd told Fiona he was actively counting down the months to retirement.

As Fiona had expected, he'd back-heeled her call up the ladder and she was waiting for an inspector to come on the line. While she waited she smoothed her hands downwards over as much of her body as she could reach. The seawater sluiced earthwards and by the time the inspector said her name, Fiona had removed her boots and was tipping the water from them.

The inspector was the one person Fiona hadn't wanted to take the call. Instead of her regular inspector, her call had been passed to DI Pauline Baird. DI Baird headed up the team Heather Andrews was a part of, and Fiona was more than familiar with her friend's opinion of the DI.

A ladder-climber of the highest order, DI Baird was rail thin with hair that resembled a squashed hedgehog. Her nature was all-business and she was wont to make sure those beneath her knew their station.

'No, ma'am, I haven't found the missing girl yet. As I reported to the sarge, the pleasure cruiser *Each-Uisge* ran aground, and I made the decision to pause the search while I tried to help save the lives of those on board. It was while effecting this rescue I found the murdered body of a man in the *Each-Uisge*'s cabin. Sorry, not the cabin, the wheelhouse.'

'I see. It seems like you may have made the right decision. I trust you secured the crime scene? Documented what you could without disturbing anything?'

'I'm afraid not. As I reported, the boat had run aground and was tilting over as the waves battered it. The *Each-Uisge* is now on its side filling with water. The islanders have told me the tide will be coming in soon. I only just made it back to dry land in one piece. If some of the locals hadn't pulled me back to shore I'd have drowned.'

'Shame.'

From Baird's tone it was impossible to detect if she meant it was a shame the crime scene had been lost, or that Fiona had survived the experience. As she'd had no run-ins with Baird, Fiona took the comment to mean the former, but she was getting to understand why Heather complained about Baird so often and with such venom.

'It certainly is, ma'am.'

'I think you misunderstand me, *Constable*. I think it's a shame you are the only person to have seen this victim. I've had my eye on you since that business down in the Borders before Christmas. You got a lot of press attention. It's no secret that you want to be a detective. And here you are, in yet another situation where you're the only officer around when there's been a murder. It is my considered—'

Fiona's knuckles went white as she gripped the radio. 'Excuse me, ma'am, just what are you suggesting? That I'm making up stories? That I'm imagining things? I know for certain one of the passengers saw the victim, and suspect others may have too.' Fiona wished she'd taken her mobile aboard the *Each-Uisge*, but at the time she'd been effecting a rescue, not preparing to visit a crime scene. Chances are the soakings she'd had getting to and from the boat would have seen her phone ruined anyway. All the same, it would have been nice to have had some evidence to destroy Baird's cynicism.

'Constable MacLeish, I would advise you to never, *never* interrupt me again. I am not making any accusations, merely pointing out coincidences that I have noticed. You are an officer of Police Scotland, and as a superior officer, albeit not one in your direct chain of command, it falls to me to assess all possibilities while accepting your version of events, unless proven otherwise. Now if you could find it within yourself to give me a professional report instead of letting your emotions get the better of you, I may be able to better advise you.'

Fiona's teeth itched with the response she wanted to give but daren't. Instead she sated her temper by using her free hand to give the radio the finger. 'I didn't have more than a minute at the crime scene, but I did what I could. The dead man was in his sixties with a close-cropped, balding head. He had a sculpted beard, stab wounds to his chest, a single stab to his throat and what looked like a dozen or more slashes to his groin.'

'Did you get an ID on your victim?'

'Not yet, but I haven't had chance to properly question any of the survivors. What I do know is that before he was murdered, he wasn't seen by the passenger I've spoken to. She thought he was the boat's captain.' Dropping the 'ma'am' from the conversation was a small act of defiance but it gave Fiona a lot of pleasure. 'Before you ask, there was no sign of a murder weapon anywhere, and there were splashes of blood on the dials in the wheelhouse, so I'd say it's fair to assume that's where the victim was killed.'

'I see.'

A silence came down the radio for so long that Fiona was tempted to drop an exploratory 'ma'am', to see if Baird was still there.

The radio crackled and fuzzed when Baird next spoke.

'I see from the report you gave you were the only person to board the boat. That suggests the killer is among the passengers and crew. I take it you have them all gathered together away from the islanders?'

'Not yet. As I was busy with the rescue, the islanders were taking in the various people I got off the boat. I wasn't aware of the murder until I boarded the boat to assist the last person off it. She is an elderly lady who has a suspected broken ankle. Ma'am, I know I'm changing the subject here, but when I asked Sergeant Ogilvie for some support, he told me no. Surely there's a way you can get some other officers to Luing to help me. A helicopter, or a boat.'

'I sincerely wish there was a way I could get some detectives out there to take over from you, but the gale force winds that are starting to reach land mean all helicopters are grounded. It's the same for all boats except the coastguard and the RNLI, and they're busy rescuing people who've got into difficulty. You're going to have to manage, so please don't bleat on about being by yourself. It's not the situation we want, but nor is it one we can change. Now, tell me about your search for the missing lassie?'

'There's nothing much to tell. There's various search parties made up from groups of islanders, and some of the other holidaymakers from the Sunnybrae Caravan Park at the top of the island.' Fiona stole a look at her watch. 'I haven't had an update for almost an hour, as I was busy with the boat rescue. With luck she'll have turned up safe and sound.'

'Yeah, that's what finds missing kids, luck.'

Fiona's mouth tightened as she sought an answer that wasn't as disrespectful as Baird's comment. She was loath to ask the woman's advice, but she knew her sensibilities ranked a long way behind Cait's welfare. 'If she hasn't turned up, what should I do? Where do my priorities lie? With the murder or the missing child?'

'I'm sorry, but until I have more information on both cases, you're going to have to make that call yourself. I expect regular updates from you, PC MacLeish.'

Fiona scowled at the radio in response to Baird's arse-covering, and reached into the front of the police car for her personal mobile. When she checked the signal bar she found it empty, meaning she couldn't pick Heather's brain.

There would be perhaps two hundred other people on the island, but with everything that was happening, and all eyes on her to find resolutions, Fiona had never felt so alone.

THIRTEEN

Fiona's uniform chafed at every part of her skin it touched as she climbed into the Astra. Compared to the self-recriminations she was throwing at herself, it was a mild irritant. All she could think about was that somehow she'd messed up. In her mind there were images of little Cait falling foul of disaster, either through her own adventurous spirit or at the hands of an evil human. Despite the knowledge she'd saved the elderly woman, and discovered a murder, Fiona couldn't shake the conviction she may have failed Cait.

As much as Fiona wanted to stamp down on the throttle to propel the Astra forward, the tumultuous roads on Luing forbade any kind of haste. The switch for the lights and siren called a mermaid's song to Fiona, but she knew there was nothing to be gained from it. Blues and twos worked when other drivers could see you coming. With all the blind summits and tight corners on Luing's meagre roads, they'd be less than useless. Fiona gritted her teeth and proceeded as fast as she dared, without ever topping thirty. There was also the knowledge that her blasting around the island with blues and twos on was as likely to alarm Cait as summon her.

When Fiona pulled into the lay-by opposite Kilchattan Church there were four cars and no humans. She scanned the horizons and saw a figure standing at the top of a hill a couple of hundred yards to the east. From what Fiona could see of the figure she deduced it was Diane Yorke, Cait's mother.

It made sense to Fiona that Diane hadn't waited by the road. In the woman's position she would have sought high ground too. The worst experience in Fiona's life had been the loss of her parents, but there had never been any doubt about their loss. Both had been murdered while she was sitting her History GSCE. As terrible as that day had become, Fiona had never had to face doubt; had never been given even a glimmer of hope things would turn out okay. Instead she'd been plunged into a nightmarish certainty that the two people she loved most in the world were gone forever.

Hope for Cait's safe return would eat at Diane and her husband. They would be distraught, sure to clutch at every straw, regardless of how flimsy. She'd seen it before and knew only too well how destructive hope could become when it was dashed.

To attract Diane's attention, Fiona reached for the switch that controlled the lights and siren. She was too late. Diane had spotted the police car and was running towards her.

Fiona squelched her way out of the car and started walking towards Diane. As a forbearer of the lack of news, Fiona inserted no urgency into her movements, as she wanted to portray calm competence instead of the out-of-her-depth feeling she was actually experiencing.

Diane's run faltered and Fiona could see the unsteadiness in her legs as she realised Fiona was standing alone. Diane went down in a tangle of limbs, reeds and hair. Fiona continued her measured walk towards her.

When Diane regained her feet Fiona was close enough to see the woman's mouth working, but the wind carried away every syllable. Rather than not give an answer, Fiona cupped a hand behind her ear.

Diane gave up speaking until she was within ten feet of Fiona. Her face was tear-stained and, thanks to the wind, her hair streamed out behind her head.

'Have you found her? Is she okay?'

'I'm sorry, but I haven't found her yet.' Fiona would have asked if Cait had appeared elsewhere, but there was no need. Diane's fraught state answered that question.

Diane's hands clamped Fiona's forearms. 'Please, you have to find her.' Her face changed. 'You're soaking.' A sniff. 'You smell of brine. No. No. Please. Please tell me she's not drowned. She wouldn't have gone near the ocean. Not her. She was terrified of it. Please. Please tell me she's okay.'

Fiona hesitated, to pick her words with care. It was a mistake.

Diane crumpled in front of Fiona, falling to her knees and sobbing as if she'd just had her worst fears for Cait confirmed.

'I'm not wet because of Cait. I haven't seen any sight of her. I'm soaked because I had to help rescue people from a pleasure cruiser that ran aground.'

'What?'

Diane was on her feet in a flash. Her nose an inch away from Fiona's as she gave voice to her anger and fears.

'You mean you stopped looking for my Cait? She's eight years old and missing. What kind of copper are you? How could you stop looking for her? Come on, tell me what you were thinking when you abandoned my daughter so you could play hero.'

Fiona said nothing. She'd already asked herself the same questions along with many others. There were rationalisations she could make, cold hard logic to back up her choices, and the certainty she'd saved at least one life, but none of them would ever salve her guilt if Cait wasn't returned to her mother's arms, safe and unharmed.

'Mrs Yorke.' In moments like this, familiarity was dangerous. 'Please, take a breath. It was one hour and I'm now focused on finding Cait.'

Except Fiona wasn't. She also had a killer to catch.

FOURTEEN

The lie chewed at Fiona like a dog worrying a bone. With luck she'd find little Cait soon and then she could give her full focus to the murder. DI Baird was right though, luck didn't find missing children.

Fiona radioed back to the desk and asked for the duty sergeant. He might not be the most hard-working cop, but he had grandkids around Cait's age and it was no secret he doted on them. He'd get her what she needed as quick as he could, even if he delegated the task to someone else.

'I need your help. I want a full topographical outline of Luing. I need to know about ancient mines, ruined buildings and so on. Basically anywhere a wee lass could hide.'

'Okay, I'll get someone on it. Be easy enough to get you the basic topographical maps, but ones that show ancient structures might take a wee while. Luing's no' exactly a world heritage site.'

The information Fiona had asked for was a double-edged sword. Cait could be happily playing in any such place, or she could be nowhere near any of them. As much as Luing was inhabited, the island only had three roads suitable for her car.

One from the top of the island down to the bottom with its two spurs; one going west to Cullipool, the other cutting east up a steep bank.

The best person or persons to ask about the island wasn't a copper back at the station, it was an islander. They'd know the places she was asking about and how to access them. The last thing Fiona needed was to waste time trying to find a structure that had long ago fallen down and overgrown.

Off to her right Fiona saw a group of people walking. There were four adults and five kids. Their clothes were flapping in the wind as was the hair of anyone who had it long enough to be affected by the increasing gale.

Fiona's eyes scanned the kids first. None of them wore red leggings, although one did have a yellow T-shirt. It was a boy, though, and he was dark haired, unlike the blonde Cait.

One of the adults, a woman, waved her over, so Fiona pulled up alongside them and climbed out.

'Have you found Cait yet?'

The woman's accent wasn't local. If Fiona had to guess she'd have placed it somewhere below Birmingham.

The question answered Fiona's query as to whether these people knew about Cait's disappearance or were their own search party.

'No. Have you seen any sign of her?'

'None.' The woman pointed behind them. 'We parked at Blackmill Bay and took a look along the coast, but we didn't see any sign of her.' A look to a man Fiona assumed must be her husband. 'She's only eight, you know? Honestly, to think my taxes pay your wages and you can't even find a missing child on a small island like this. No wonder the country's gone to the dogs, if all the coppers are as useless as you.'

The addition of Cait's age to the report did nothing to settle Fiona's inner fears. Instead it drove a skewer of dislike for the woman into her heart. She didn't need reminding of Cait's age.

Didn't need the woman's tone to hold accusation. Nor did she need the woman's ridiculous expectations adding to the burden of responsibility she already carried. She was on Luing to find the girl because she'd wandered off. For this woman to criticise her was too much after the roasting she'd just had from Cait's mother.

Diane Yorke could say what she liked, but this bitch better watch her mouth otherwise Fiona would put her right back into her box.

Fiona held the woman's eye longer than necessary before speaking. 'I'm well aware of her age, but unfortunately, I'm on the island alone and Cait has been missing long enough for her to have wandered anywhere. So, to help me co-ordinate a thorough search for her, can you please tell me exactly where you've searched so I don't waste time repeating your footsteps?' The last line was crucial to Fiona. The sooner she could learn the areas of the island that had already been searched, the sooner she could direct a search of the other parts.

The woman's husband stepped in front of her, earning a shove in the ribs. His voice was even, but there was no mistaking the undertow of apology. 'From where this road ends at Blackmill Bay, up the coast for about a half mile. There's bugger all to see except rocks, the sea and reed-covered grass. She's not in that area.'

'Thanks.'

Fiona paused and tried to think of the island's layout. From what she remembered and had seen, Luing was largely rectangular, but had a slight crook at its southern third. Where she was now, on the road that went left to Toberonochy and right to Blackmill Bay, was pretty much where the crook was. The roads to the south were little more than gravel farm tracks, and while they looked smooth to begin with, she didn't expect they'd stay that way for long.

The police Astra Fiona was driving was okay for scooting

about Lochgilphead and the surrounding towns and villages, but it was designed to only ever be used on paved roads. A rutted gravel track would either tear the underside of the car to shreds or see it stuck. Neither was an acceptable option. The car itself didn't matter, but the mobility it gave Fiona on the island was vital to her chances of finding Cait, and apprehending the killer. Plus there was that whine from the front wheel that she didn't trust. Fiona had to face facts, the Astra was lame, in every sense of the word.

The most galling thing for Fiona was the lack of knowledge she had about Luing. This was her first ever visit to the island, and while it wasn't like she could easily get lost, she didn't know it the way she knew the Munros she'd climbed around Lochgilphead. A proper detailed map of the island would have been a great help but she didn't have one. The shop halfway to Cullipool may have had one, or perhaps the Atlantic Islands Centre. She'd have to make a point of getting one the next time she was at that end of the island.

Maybe one of the people in front of her would have one. 'Do any of you have a map of the island?'

A woman at the back of the group, who was clutching a young girl to her side, nodded. 'I have an atlas in the car, if that's any use. It shows the island, but it's only about this big.' She held her thumb and forefinger an inch and a half apart.

'Thanks, but I need something more detailed.'

'Sorry, we've been before and don't have much need of a map. To be honest, we're here for watersports and fishing. If it wasn't for the gale, we'd be out on the water right now.'

'Your children. Were any of them with Cait when she went off?'

Four of the children shook their heads, but the fifth, a sullen boy, looked at his feet. Fiona stepped towards him, lowering herself as she went. 'Hey there.'

The boy didn't answer. Instead he looked at the man

standing by his side. The man was tall and thin with a hooked nose that gave him the appearance of a hawk.

'I'd prefer you not to question my son without my permission.' The man's tone was a Geordie burr, but it did little to soften the haughtiness of his words and demeanour.

This was all Fiona needed, an overzealous parent getting in her way. Yes, it was only right the boy was accompanied by an adult when questioned, but she was questioning him as a witness and the man was within three feet of his son.

'I appreciate that, sir, but so long as you are present I have a few questions for him. With your permission, of course. I'm sure that as a parent yourself, you can empathise with how Cait's parents must be feeling right now.'

The last sentence may have been an unnecessary barb, but Fiona wanted to pierce the man's self-importance before he became a full-on obstruction.

His face was tight when he gave a sharp nod. 'Very well, you may ask him some questions, but I'm a lawyer and Simon... ah... is very sensitive. If I feel he's in any distress I'll be shutting the interview down at once. Do you understand?'

'I understand.' Fiona did as well. Simon's father was looking out for his son. That was all well and good. However, provided the boy wasn't too sensitive, she'd be able to pick his brains. Fiona gestured at the ground a few feet away. 'Shall we move over here so we're away from the others?'

'That sounds like a good idea.' The man led his son across to the area Fiona had indicated.

When Fiona joined them she sat cross-legged on the grass, to further bring herself down to Simon's height. 'I'm Fiona and I need you to help me find Cait. You're not in any trouble, none at all. I just need to know from you a few things about how Cait was when she went off on her own. You know, angry, happy, excited or sad. Can you do that for me?'

Simon gave a nod but didn't speak. The fingers of his right

hand pulled at his earlobe three times in succession then paused before pulling three more times.

'You'll have to ask him your questions one by one. He'll answer them when he's had a think.' The father's voice was soft. 'Won't you, Simon.'

'Yes, Dad.'

Fiona read the underlying message the father was sending and the signals coming from Simon. The boy was on the spectrum. Asperger's or autism most likely, but whatever the official diagnosis might be, she'd have to be very careful with how she posed her questions lest she trigger the child in some way. With luck, Simon's father would recognise the signs she was on the wrong path and guide the interview long before she got to that stage. That was good for Simon, but it might not be for Cait.

Fiona gestured to Simon's father and then the ground beside Simon. 'Why don't you sit down beside Simon, help him through this?' She moved her focus to Simon and lowered her voice. 'Don't worry, I think you're far too big to need your dad's help, I'm just saying that to keep him happy.'

The corners of Simon's mouth twitched upwards as his father sat beside him. Now Fiona could see both of their faces without having to obviously switch her focus. The tiny nod of approval from Simon's father didn't go unnoticed.

'You and Cait were playing with some other children. Who were they?'

'Andy. His little brother Kevin. Kevin's nine and I'm eight, but I'm bigger than he is.'

'You are a big boy, aren't you? I bet you grow up to be as tall as your dad.'

When she saw the beam of pride on Simon's face at her comment, Fiona relaxed a little. She had no siblings and therefore no nieces or nephews. Most of her friends had children, but as her friends were all work-centric, she never saw their kids to interact with. Babies she could coo over, and teenagers who could hold an adult conversation she could handle with ease, it was the kids between two and fifteen that she struggled with and Simon was right in the middle of that group.

'Were there only four of you?'

'No. Leigh was there too. Leigh's a girl not a boy.'

'Thanks for clearing that up.' Fiona gave a side-nod back towards the other children. 'How come none of these kids were with you?'

'They're my cousins. They're staying in a house at Blackmill Bay. We're in a caravan up near where the ferry comes. Did you know the ferry is called *Belnahua*? Belnahua is an island over there.' Simon pointed a freckled arm. 'They used to live there and dig roof slates out of the ground.'

Fiona was desperate to get to the real questions, but she daren't put pressure on Simon in case he withdrew from her. 'That's fascinating. You're very clever to know that. So the five of you were exploring ruins near the church, and when you'd finished, there was a disagreement. Cait wanted to explore mines and everyone else wanted to go and look for an old settlement at Ardluing. That's right, isn't it?'

'Yes. The settlement was rubbish, though. Just a few stones sticking out of the ground. I wanted to see a proper castle, like Bamburgh or Alnwick. Do you know they filmed some of the Harry Potter films at Alnwick Castle?'

Simon's father gave an indulgent smile that told Fiona he was used to Simon's rambling speech. 'Simon, Fiona wants to know about what happened when Cait went off, not movie trivia.'

'You're very clever to know that, Simon, but your dad is right. I've come to Luing to help find Cait. The sooner you can tell me what you know, the sooner I can find her and take her back to her parents. They are very worried about her. When you decided to go to the settlement and Cait went off to look for slate mines, what direction did she go? Was it up towards the ferry? Over to Toberonochy or over to Blackmill Bay?'

Simon looked at his father, the smile now absent from his face. Fiona realised her mistake. Instead of sticking to one question she'd tagged on others as potential answers.

'It's okay.' Simon's father rubbed his son's arm. 'Take your time and tell Fiona what you told me.'

Simon's lip trembled as he turned back to Fiona. The boy's distress endeared him to her, but it also set her heart racing. They were about to get to the meat of the sandwich. Always the best part.

'She went that way.' His arm wobbled as he aimed it east, towards Blackmill Bay. 'Andy was annoyed with her for not coming with us and the rude things she called him when he tried to make her. He told her to watch out for the troll cave. To not go into it in case the trolls ate her. That was silly. Trolls aren't real.' Simon's eyes dipped to the ground. 'Cait's mum and dad asked us about this but we didn't want to say because Cait might get in trouble.'

Fiona had to fight to keep her expression pleasant and not scare Simon into silence. If he and the other kids had told their folks the truth from the off, Cait might have been found hours ago.

When it came to what he'd said, Simon was right. Trolls weren't real. But caves were. It was all Fiona could do not to slap the palm of her hand onto her forehead. On an island like Luing that had been savaged by the Atlantic tides for millennia and inhabited since the Bronze Age, there were sure to be some caves or at least cave-like hollows where softer rock had been scoured out. She'd theorised Cait might look for cave drawings in one of the mines, but never thought about caves along the island's coastline.

A cave was the perfect place for an adventurous child to hide out. Or, a captive one to be hidden.

'Simon, you're a superstar for what you've told me. Your mum and dad should be very proud of you.' Even as she was complimenting Simon, Fiona was rising to her feet. She had to get back to Cullipool at once. Not only were the passengers and crew from the *Each-Uisge* waiting for her, but the best chance she had of getting a detailed map or source of information on Luing was sure to lie at the Atlantic Islands Centre.

FIFTEEN

Fiona parked making sure the nose of the car was pointing into the wind. It was a struggle to get the door open and she had to lean into it, lest the increasing power of the approaching gale close the door on her. She fished her utility belt from the boot and set off.

The Atlantic Islands Centre at Cullipool was half full of people. As well as the passengers and crew of the *Each-Uisge*, there were the four men who'd aided in the rescue effort and two other men who Fiona hadn't seen before. Both of the other two men were old, their shoulders hunched from a lifetime of turning their backs to the elements.

Fiona guessed they'd be fathers to at least two of the men who'd helped her. They looked to be long retired and she expected they'd heard something from their sons and had come along to make sure they didn't miss any of the commotion that had arrived in their community.

Deek and Muscles stood in the doorway like a pair of bouncers, while Baldy and Fergus had stationed themselves behind the counter – no doubt to prevent anyone trying to escape via a back door. It all made sense to Fiona, and she dropped each of them a nod to thank them for their logical approach.

Where the faces of those rescued had shown jubilation and relief, now they showed discomfort that was turning to anger. Each of them would have got a soaking during the crossing, and Fiona's own sodden clothes were chafing as they dried.

'What the hell is going on? Why are we being kept here like prisoners?' It was the heavy woman who spoke, but she made no effort to rise from the chair supporting her.

'I'll explain everything in a moment, Mrs...' Fiona let the question dangle, but the heavy woman made no attempt to answer. In the end it was her husband who spoke.

'She's Irene Rogerson. I'm her husband, Richard.'

'Thanks.'

A young man rose to his feet. He was lithe, with wiry muscles and enough freckles to make him look perma-tanned. When he spoke his voice was a mixture of island drawl and anger. 'Aye. And where's Charlie? I didnae see him getting aff the boat.'

Fiona joined the dots in a flash. Charlie must be the captain, or whatever title the boat's driver held. She now had a name for her victim and someone who could tell her about him.

'I take it Charlie was the captain of the *Each-Uisge*?'

'Aye.' The young man's eyes bored into Fiona's as he waited for an answer to the unasked question.

'I'm afraid I have some bad news for you. Charlie's dead.'

It was against protocol to break bad news to non-family members before the family was informed, but the rule books never covered situations like this. The young man's eyes watered but no tears made it onto his cheeks.

As Fiona looked around the room she saw the large woman had a hand to her mouth and the teenagers were hugging. Other faces were shocked, but Fiona could also see relief in some faces as the passengers realised just how narrowly they'd cheated death.

'Are you sure? He coulda found an air pocket. He coulda got ashore anither way. It's no' like the *Each-Uisge* was the *Titanic* and he went doon wi' his ship.'

Fiona hesitated. This was the part she didn't want to get into. One of the people in this room was a killer and, for as long as she could, she wanted to let the killer think their crime had gone undetected. The hesitation was a mistake.

'There's stuff you're not telling us, isn't there?' Irene had risen from her chair and was walking towards Fiona with enough lumber to build a New York mansion. 'Did you see him die?' Once again, a hand went to her mouth. 'He was murdered, wasn't he? Oh my God, he was killed. I knew it must be something like that.'

She turned her gaze to her husband. 'I told you something was wrong. That there must be something up, otherwise we wouldn't have all been kept here. That boat should have had us back at Oban by now, and yet we're here instead. Kept prisoner by those four goons. I tell you now, we're all going to be murdered. That's what's going to happen.'

Distressed glances scoured the room as the passengers and crew all eyed each other with suspicion. Fiona had been here before and she could predict what was coming. It was only a matter of time before fingers were pointed and accusations made. Denials would be issued with vehemence and at some point, in the next hour or two, someone's temper would snap and there could be violence.

'Will you please sit down and be quiet?' Fiona could hear the anger in her own voice, and she hoped Irene could too. 'Those goons, as you call them, helped to save your life. Maybe you should be showing them gratitude instead of contempt.'

After the woman had retaken her seat with an audible whoomph, the lithe young man got close to Fiona, his eyes shining with unshed grief. 'Is that right? Was Charlie murdered?'

'I'm sorry to say it, but yes, he was murdered.'

As the young man's eyes closed in distress, Fiona wondered about his connection to Charlie. Maybe the captain had been a force for good in the man's life or perhaps he was a relative. It wasn't unknown for sons working alongside their father to use a Christian name when addressing them instead of Dad. It was a workplace thing, but if that was the case, she'd just informed a family member of a murder.

Fiona wanted to lay a hand on the man's shoulder, wrap a consoling arm around his shoulders, or just give him comfort in any way she could. She didn't do any of those things, as a primal instinct told her not to. The young man was fighting to maintain his composure, and it could be that an act of kindness broke the dam of his emotions rather than a callous word or business-like attitude. She'd been there. After the murder of her own parents, it was the little things that left her in a sobbing heap, not the world turning as it always did, and would.

'I have some questions for you. Is that okay?'

His head bobbed up and down, but his eyes were still clamped shut.

'What was Charlie's surname?'

'Tait.' The word only had one syllable, but somehow the young man managed to fill it with grief.

A man in his late forties appeared by the young man's shoulder. 'Have a seat, Davie. I'll answer her questions for you.' The man looked at Fiona and lifted an eyebrow. 'That okay?'

'Fine by me.'

It was as well. Davie was in no state to answer questions and, as much as Fiona wanted to identify Charlie's killer, she was conscious Cait was still missing and that it was only an hour, two at the most, before darkness fell. Without daylight the search parties would be unable to look for Cait, and if Cait was trying to make her way back, all manner of accidents could happen to her on the uneven terrain of Luing.

'You are?'

'Ian Caldwell.' Ian hooked a thumb towards where Davie was taking a seat. 'Me, Davie and Charlie were the crew on the *Each-Uisge*. It was Davie who caught the rope you threw. I was one of the last off.' Shame crept into his voice. 'I'm sorry I lost my bottle. The way you crossed and saved the old girl was the bravest thing I've ever seen.'

Now Fiona had Ian placed she could assess him as a suspect. As the last to emerge from the cabin he'd have been best placed to slip into the wheelhouse and knife Charlie. There was no sign of sorrow for the loss of a colleague about the man. That in itself was odd, but something, a sixth sense or fey feeling, told Fiona that while the burly Ian might look like her best suspect, there was more to Charlie's murder than met the eye.

'So there were three crew on the *Each-Uisge*. How many passengers did you have?'

Ian's eyes danced around the room at all the seated people, his lips moving as he counted. 'Eleven.'

The doubt in his voice along with the quick head count told Fiona he wasn't sure of the true answer.

'Have a look round this room, do you remember any faces from the boat that you don't see now?'

Ian's head shook. 'No, they're all here.'

'Is there any way that someone on the boat could have killed Charlie Tait and then got off before it ran aground?'

'Not at all. Yes, they could have jumped overboard and swum to the shore, but there's no way they'd have survived long in those seas. I told Charlie it was a risk going out in that weather, but he never listened to my opinion.'

Fiona scratched her chin as she thought. 'So you're

convinced Charlie's killer would be on the *Each-Uisge* when it ran aground?'

'Absolutely. Charlie kept away from the shore and the other boats until he lost power. Me and him had a look at the engine, first thing we did, but whatever was wrong with it was beyond what we could fix.'

'Did you try radioing for help?'

'We would have, but Charlie was too tight to replace the battery on the radio. He kept telling me the *Each-Uisge*'s engine would outlive us all and that I was worrying about nowt.'

Irene was on her feet again. 'For the love of God, will you stop asking stupid bloody questions and arrest the killer instead of hounding us. We were nearly killed, you know?'

'I know fine well you were nearly killed.' Fiona's nostrils flared as she rounded on Irene. 'If you remember, it was me who rescued you when you froze making your way off the boat.'

The woman flumped back down, her bulk pushing the chair back with enough force to pull a tortured squeak from its legs as they slid over the polished slate floor.

The elderly woman with the injured ankle twisted until she was facing the large woman. 'Listen you to me, that lass is a hero. She saved your life and when that young man abandoned me, it was her who came and rescued me. You, me and everyone else who was on that boat owes her their life. She's now trying to catch a killer, so you keep your fat arse in that chair, or so help me, I'll... I'll...'

The threat was drowned out by a new speaker before it could be made.

'Hey, I recognise her. She's that copper who got trapped in a flooded valley and caught a killer. She saved lives then too.'

Fiona looked up and saw it was a woman behind the counter, Fergus's wife, who was speaking.

Police Scotland had lauded her efforts back in December and had held her up as an example of the quality of Police Scotland officers. They'd made way more of a hoo-hah than Fiona was comfortable with. What they hadn't done was give her the opportunity to become a detective, a position she so desperately craved. Her parents' murders were still unsolved, and while Fiona had new information from her Aunt Mary to aid her private investigation, she knew she still lacked the skills she'd need to solve that most personal of cases.

'Good. She'll be able to catch the man who killed the captain.'

Fiona hated the notoriety that came with December's events. It was waning now, but she'd noticed a marked increase in expectation from the public when they recognised her. This had even bled through to her fellow officers, although DI Baird was the exception to prove the rule. She'd heard from her friend Heather that Baird had dismissed Fiona's success in apprehending a killer as 'beginner's luck'.

To shift the focus, Fiona tossed a side-nod at Ian and led him to an unoccupied corner.

'Davie seems really cut up about Charlie. Are they related?'

'Not as such. Back when he left school, Davie got into some trouble. Nowt serious, just a bit of shoplifting. He got done for drugs a couple of times. Possession, not supply.' Ian pulled a face. 'His mother's one of those bible-up-their-arse types whose idea of a good time is a whist drive for the kirk. His father buggered off years ago. No wonder. Anyway, Davie's mother kicked him out the second time he got done for possession. He'd worked summers on the *Each-Uisge*, which is how Charlie knew him. Charlie took Davie in and straightened him out. I'll be honest, Charlie and me rarely saw eye to eye. I do a couple of shifts a week on the *Each-Uisge* when I'm not on the fishing boats.' He gave a shrug. 'I've a daughter at uni, and another who'll be going next year. Their accommodation's not cheap, but I want the best possible future for them. That's why I'm working seven days a week.'

The tale of parental sacrifice plucked at Fiona's heart like it was a harp. Her own parents would have done the same for her had they been alive. Aunt Mary had moved heaven and earth to provide for her while she was training to be a police officer, but that burden should have fallen on her parents' shoulders.

Charlie's efforts in helping Davie painted him in a good light, but there was no escaping what the wounds to his groin suggested.

Fiona began a mental list of everything she had to do.

Identify all of the people who'd been in the *Each-Uisge*.

Question Davie about his relationship with Charlie.

Question everyone who'd been on the *Each-Uisge* about what they'd seen as the craft ran aground.

And above all of those things, find Cait.

Fiona wanted to rush out searching for Cait, and she wanted to stay put and get on with questioning those in the room. She opted for the latter first.

One by one Fiona went round the room jotting down the names and addresses of everyone present. When the list was compiled there were thirteen names on her list.

In addition to those she'd already got, Fiona collected the names of the teenagers, Harry and Melissa, the three young guys, David, Michael and Johnathan, plus the other three passengers; Isobel, Keira and Mark. Rather than try to remember all their full names Fiona concentrated on memorising their Christian names, although having a Davie and a David in the group was sure to confuse her.

After the list was complete, Fiona made a decision and prepared to tell a lie.

'Okay, everyone. I'm actually on the island to look for a missing child. I need you all to stay here. If you're all together in the one place, there will be safety in numbers.' Fiona aimed a finger at the woman behind the counter. 'Do you have any maps of the island? One that would show caves or ancient ruins.'

'There's some on the table behind you.'

'Thanks.' Fiona shifted her feet until she was facing Deek. 'Do you know the island well?'

'Lived here all my life.'

'Can you come along?'

'Aye.'

What Deek didn't know, what none of them knew, was that Fiona had no intentions of searching for Cait just yet. She planned to, within the next ten minutes, if not sooner, but first she wanted someone at the station to run all the names and addresses she'd collected through a police database. Where Tait's blood had splattered the wheelhouse, it was still viscous, which meant it hadn't had time to dry. Therefore it was likely he'd been murdered around the point the *Each-Uisge* had run aground. Now Fiona had time to think, she was mapping out the sequence of events. Tait and Ian had been aware of the engine failure and were trying to fix it.

As the boat neared the coast, Tait must have been in the wheelhouse either trying to steer the boat or get the radio working. If he'd been killed sooner, his body was sure to have been discovered. The wheelhouse was accessed through the passenger cabin, which made it easy to observe comings and goings.

When Fiona added the nature of Irene Rogerson into her thinking, she became more and more certain Tait had been killed at the last minute. Irene would have been on the backs of Ian and the captain from the moment the *Each-Uisge* lost power right up until the time it ran aground.

No matter which way Fiona looked at it, the murder of Charlie Tait screamed of a personal, targeted attack. She just hoped Cait's disappearance wasn't.

SIXTEEN

Fiona scanned the map she'd got from the Atlantic Islands Centre. It showed ruins in four places including the ancient settlement Simon had mentioned. Best of all it showed a cave a short distance south of Blackmill Bay. Cait had been headed in that direction when she'd split from the other children. Caves had been on her mind.

'Do you know the cave south of Blackmill Bay?' There was little point having Deek along if she wasn't going to pump him for his local knowledge.

'Aye. I haven't been there in years, though. Do you think that's where she is?' Deek's face pulled sideways. It wasn't an attractive look. 'It's a fair hike along the track. And unless she knew about the cave, why would she even head that way?'

'She was last seen down that way, so it's where I'm looking first.'

'Shit! I hope she's okay. Surely she'll head back when she's hungry.'

'Let's hope so.'

What Fiona didn't say was that Cait may have had an accident, or worse, fallen into the wrong hands. Something was amiss in the area. The captain of a pleasure cruiser wouldn't be murdered for no reason. Let alone have his genitals hacked at by his killer.

She'd always found islanders to be a different people. Many of them lived solitary existences battling the elements and the unforgiving landscape on a daily basis. Some spoke Gaelic as a first language and while they could be warm and welcoming, they could also be haughty and dismissive if you got on their wrong side. Tourists and mainlanders, even people from other islands, would get a friendly enough welcome, but there would always be an element of mistrust in the islanders' minds. Fiona knew from her move to Lochgilphead that while she was tolerated and liked by her neighbours, she'd never be classed as a local until she had at least three more decades of living in the town under her belt. It was the rural way.

As she drove off Fiona could feel the car being buffeted by the incoming gale. Other than the necessary muscle-memory Fiona employed, she gave no thought to the act of driving. Instead her mind was on the passengers and crew of the *Each-Uisge*. Ian and Davie knew Tait best, so there was a greater chance of them, either singly or working together, having a reason to kill him. While they'd had the opportunity, there was not yet a motive Fiona could detect. The best she could come up with was that they knew something about why the *Each-Uisge* had been without power. If Tait was lax in maintaining his boat and they'd known the engine wasn't in good condition, had they lashed out in fury after his failure to look after the craft had endangered them? It wasn't a strong theory, Fiona would be the first to admit as much. Sure, they might have got into a slanging match about it, but as she imagined the last few minutes aboard the boat before it struck the rocks, she pictured the crew working with frantic desperation to save the *Each-Uisge* rather than standing around arguing. If Tait had been rescued, she'd have fully expected the majority of the passengers to give him a piece of their mind. Yet, to draw a knife and inflict as many wounds as Tait had suffered was an extreme reaction when in fear for your life. All the same, it was as close to a motive she could think of until she had more information about everyone on board.

Fiona's next thoughts centred on the three young men. David, Michael and Johnathan had been their names. Unlike his namesake Davie, David had a stocky build. Michael was the tallest of the three and had a beard best described as scrawny. Both of them had tanned faces, but not the tan you get from a week in the sun, more of a slight weathered look, although both were too young to have spent a lot of years enduring the elements. Fiona pictured them as farmers or construction workers As for Johnathan, he was paler by comparison, but there was a studious look about him. His face revealed nothing, but his eyes held a level of intelligence neither of his companions showed. Fiona surmised that Johnathan didn't work alongside his friends, as his pudgy body wasn't synonymous with hard physical labour.

All three of the young men had been polite and respectful. They'd answered her questions without hesitation and, where they could, they'd helped others. No matter how she tried to picture one of them as Tait's killer, she couldn't begin to guess at what their motive might be.

Fiona couldn't think the same for the next three people she thought about. Mark, Isobel and Keira all hailed from Workington in Cumbria. Their surnames were all different, but Keira and Isobel looked alike enough for Fiona to guess they were sisters. Mark could have been dating either, but none of them had mentioned such a connection. Isobel was the heavier of the sisters, although she carried her weight well. Keira looked a year or two younger and while slimmer than her sister, she'd coated her face with make-up, a trait Fiona always considered a sign of insecurity. Mark, like the sisters, was in his thirties and to Fiona it seemed like he was fighting, and losing, a battle to contain an inner anger.

It made sense Mark, or any of the passengers, would be angry about the *Each-Uisge*'s power failure. That was natural, nobody would be happy about having their life risked, but what wasn't natural was the way Mark stared out of the window with a sullen expression etched onto his face. In another time and place, Fiona would have considered Mark to be good-looking. Not today, she didn't. Whether Mark's anger was from having fallen out with whichever sister he was dating, or a deeper issue that had travelled with him from Cumbria wasn't something Fiona yet knew, but it was something she intended to find out. The way Mark was acting withdrawn from the group rattled Fiona. Unlike the others he hadn't engaged in idle chatter about how lucky they'd been to survive.

That more than anything else made Fiona wonder about him. Was his anger a manifestation of frustration at not managing to kill Tait without the captain's murder being discovered? That made sense to Fiona, as did the theory that although Mark had killed Tait, he'd not got what he wanted from the kill. Maybe Tait had refused to give Mark the apology he demanded, or knowing he was about to die regardless of what he did or said, hadn't begged for his life. This line of thinking also tallied with the wounds on Tait. The slash to the throat was enough to end Tait's life, as were the stabs to his chest. Yet there had been far more wounds on Tait than were required to kill him. That spoke of a lot of anger, of a frenzied kill. Fiona knew she might have it wrong, but so far as she was concerned, Mark's behaviour was making him her top suspect.

Beside Fiona, Deek was shifting in his seat as he scanned both sides. It was a welcome piece of help, as Luing's narrow and tumultuous roads meant Fiona daren't take her eyes off where she was going for more than a fraction of a second at a time.

'I don't see any sign of her.' Deek pointed through the wind-screen in the direction of the front driver's side wheel. 'Sounds like you need a new wheel bearing.'

'I wondered what it was. Is it serious?'

'It will be if you don't get it fixed soon. If you leave it long enough, the wheel will either lock up or possibly even fall off.'

That was all that Fiona needed to hear. At low speeds the locking of a wheel wouldn't be too much of a problem, but if it happened when she was travelling at speed or cornering, then it could lead to disaster. Fiona vowed to herself that as soon as she returned to Lochgilphead, she'd refuse to drive the shit heap until it was fixed. Until then, she'd drive with the utmost care.

Upon reaching the tiny hamlet that was Blackmill Bay, Fiona looked to the left, in the direction of the cave. There was a gravel track running south past a dilapidated boathouse. Off to the south-east the mighty island of Scarba rose from the sea like a monolith.

When Fiona's gaze landed on the seas surrounding the island she could see a difference in them. Now the waves were roiling masses of angry water that slammed into shores and bashed into each other in an eternal fight for supremacy.

The gravel track was uneven and undulating, but there were no areas so rutted or potholed Fiona feared for the car's undercarriage.

Ahead of her she saw the track end beside a pair of cottages. A speedboat sat on a trailer, its canvas cover flapping a furious beat as the wind sought a way past it. Further ahead, the land curved round a bay, and it was here it rose high enough to have a cliff face that could house a cave. That was a quarter mile as the crow flew, and at least a half as the cop walked.

SEVENTEEN

With the car parked by the speedboat, they set off. Fiona's utility belt rasped the damp material of her trousers against her skin as she walked, and the hair she'd put into a tight ponytail that morning now whipped across her face every few seconds no matter how firmly she tried to wedge it behind her seaward ear.

At the shore, waves were crashing against the rocks with such force they created a noise akin to peels of thunder.

Fiona wanted time with her thoughts as she weighed her options, but at her side Deek was chattering away with a stream of questions. On the one hand it was good he was trying to help by educating himself, but on the other, his silence would have been more useful.

'How do you plan to find the girl and the killer by yourself? I'll help all I can, of course I will, but you're the only cop here and I can't see you getting any help before the morning. Not with the gale and everything.'

'I'm hoping to find wee Cait soon and then I can focus on finding out who killed Charlie Tait.'

'And if you don't find her soon? Which is your priority?'

'Good question.' It was as well, although with the weather making transport on and off the island impossible, it wasn't a tough decision. Not anymore. From what she'd seen on the *Each-Uisge*, the attack on Tait had looked personal. Plus everyone who was on the boat was now being watched over by the three islanders. So long as they were in the Atlantic Islands Centre, where there were at least a dozen witnesses to their actions, there was little danger of them trying anything. 'You're an islander born and bred. I'm sure you've spent plenty of time in a boat. If you don't mind me saying so, you're old enough to have seen a few storms like this over the years. Say the person or persons who killed Charlie Tait leave the Atlantic Islands Centre, could they safely take a boat out in weather like this? I'm thinking about a fast boat like that one we just saw on the trailer.'

Deek pulled a face. His oversize nose still dominating his features. 'You'd have to be desperate or mad to take a boat out in weather like this. A yacht would be useless as you'd be blown ashore, if your mast didn't snap. You need something like a trawler or a lifeboat with a proper hull to cut through the waves. That speedboat's hull is too flat to handle waves like these. It'd be pitched about all ways if you ran into or with the current. The second you tried to cut across the current the waves'd be constantly trying to capsize it. Even on the other side of the island where there's calmer waters, the island creates a whole mass of currents. If you knew these waters the way us islanders do, you might just stand a chance, but there's nobody on Luing foolish enough to try taking a boat out tonight. It'll be dark soon and it doesn't matter how modern your navigational instruments might be, you need to see where you're going in seas like those.' Once again, Deek's face contorted. 'Charlie Tait might have had a chance if he'd still been alive. But none of the others would.'

'What about his crew? Surely they'd know the waters? They sail them regularly enough, don't they?'

'They'd have more idea than most folks, but to really know waters, you've got to be the one at the wheel.'

The assessment tallied with Fiona's thinking, but her mind was already fast-tracking to a worst-case scenario. The killer would be expecting the group to be kept together until Fiona identified them. Desperate people did desperate things. To leave the Atlantic Islands Centre would be a huge sign of guilt, but once they left the building all they had to do was barge into a house and threaten a wife or child, and one of the islanders with a boat would have no choice but to ferry them ashore.

Fiona didn't know if there was a radar station that could track a boat travelling across from Luing to the mainland, but she doubted it. Warships and naval bases had those kinds of radars but whether they'd be able to track a small boat was questionable at best.

The nearest naval base Fiona could think of was HMNB Clyde at Faslane. That would be fifty miles away in a straight line, if a straight line could be drawn across all the mountains, hills and valleys between Luing and Faslane.

The next time Fiona had a signal and was talking to the mainland, she'd ask the question, but she doubted she'd like the answer.

'Who do you think the killer is?'

Fiona hesitated before answering. Deek might be providing useful help, but she didn't want to start pointing fingers in his presence until she had more evidence against the killer. The last thing she needed was him interfering in her investigation under the belief he was helping. 'I don't know, yet. It could be any of them, although I don't believe it's Delia.'

'She's the old girl who's got the bad ankle, right?' Deek scratched the side of his nose, his meaty finger dwarfed by the appendage. 'I reckon it's either one of the crew or that bloke with the two women. He looks like he's gone to the bookies with a dead cert and found it closed. His eyes are too close together. Always a bad sign.'

As much as Fiona agreed with Deek's choice of suspects, she didn't hold with the eyes-are-too-close theory. It was as outdated as witch trials. All the same, Fiona was tempted to keep the conversation going, as brainstorming could often produce good ideas. 'So you don't suspect any of the others? Irene and her husband? The three guys? Young Harry and Melissa?'

'Nah not really. Irene's a gobby cow, but she's all smoke and no fire. Them three lads seem all right, but I guess you never know. As for Love's Young Dream? Do me a favour, he's a teenage boy, the only thing that's on his mind is how quick he can get into her knickers. Trust me, the killer is either the angry bugger, or one of the two crewmen.'

If they'd been sitting across a table for this conversation, Fiona would have pulled a face at the crude way Deek dismissed Harry as the killer. He wasn't wrong, she'd thought much the same thing herself, albeit in a less vulgar fashion.

'How much further is this cave?'

Fiona was neither tired of walking nor under any physical duress from the exertion, but she was conscious of the time. In these conditions a half-mile walk took longer than the usual seven or eight minutes that was her normal pace. The going underfoot didn't help, as they had to pick their path among the tufts of reeds, rocky outcrops and patches of nice level grass. If the cave was a bust, it would be at least half an hour wasted. Probably a full hour if she factored in search time and the minutes it had taken to travel down from Cullipool.

'Not that far. Five minutes or so I reckon. If my memory's right, it's not that far once you get round those bluffs.'

Fiona said nothing, but she did lengthen her stride. The less she said the better. Not because she feared causing offence.

More because she could already feel her throat beginning to dry from all the shouting. Before long, it would feel raw and if she ended up hoarse, she'd have to shout even louder to make herself heard above the wind.

When they rounded the bluffs she saw the entrance to the cave. It was a dark spot some two hundred yards ahead. Instead of grassy and reedy ground, the terrain here was a gravel beach. The tide was a good five feet below the high-water line, but spray was crashing up, soaking the ground and the first few feet of the cliff base.

The stones beneath Fiona's feet crunched as she traipsed forward. The first gout of spray drenched her, but she didn't slow her pace. If anything she picked it up. The closer she got to the cave the more she got soaked, as the ground sloped down and she was nearer and nearer the point where the waves were crashing into the stones.

Each geyser of water thrown up by the waves was divided into a million parts by the gale and these were hurled landwards. Fiona had to close her right eye against the salty spray, but she never faltered. If Cait was in that cave she had to get to her before the tide did.

Fiona reached the cave and switched on the torch she'd retrieved from the car.

There was nothing much to see in the cave. It had weathered sides where millennia of tides had abraded soft rock from hard, a roof that sloped down until it was just two feet high at the back, and a shale floor.

Graffiti adorned the walls. Not the usual slogans about gangs or football, just names and dates scratched in by a stone or rock. One by one Fiona cast her torch over them until she found the one she didn't want to find.

Right at the back, in a hard to access place, in a childish script, were Cait's name and a date.

The date was today's.

EIGHTEEN

Fiona's first instinct was to get on her knees and crawl forward to examine Cait's name in greater detail, but she held back. Beside her Deek was muttering something but she wasn't listening to him.

Inch by careful inch Fiona tracked her torch over a section of the cave's floor that comprised a sandy patch. The sandy patch was damp, but it wasn't that which had caught Fiona's attention. Across the four-foot section of sand were footprints. Not one set, but two.

The smaller set ran from the back of the cave to the entrance. To Fiona's mind it was how Cait had made her way back from the rear of the cave where she'd added her name to all the others. The second set of footprints wasn't just larger, they were defined to the point where they were clear enough for Fiona to guess they were made by a pair of hiking boots.

There was no way of knowing how old the footprints were, but for Fiona it was far too much of a coincidence for them to be here and not be connected to Cait's disappearance. Most telling of all was the fact that a large footprint overlapped one of the small ones. That told Fiona the child had stepped on the sand before the adult. Whether it was minutes or hours later was impossible to know, but Fiona was sure that by the time high tide came and the gale reached full strength, all traces of the footprints would be obliterated.

Fiona pulled her mobile out and snapped the footprints from several angles then moved on to take a picture of Cait's name etched into the rock wall at the back of the cave.

'Deek, have you got a mobile on you?'

'I haven't got one. Don't have the need for one and the signal on the island is shite. Besides, they fry your brain.'

Fiona ignored the conspiracy theory about mobile phones and thought about what she could learn from the footprints. She bent to one knee and unlaced one of her boots. With great care she laid her boot next to one of the small footprints, making sure to keep the heels aligned. Next, she made a mental note of where the toes of the footprint ended on her own shoe. It wasn't the greatest method of measuring the size but it was the best she could do with what she had.

Fiona lifted her boot and placed it beside the larger footprint. It was short by almost an inch. She was a size six and reckoned the print must be an eight or nine.

'Deek, what shoe size are you?'

'Ten.'

Deek didn't need to be asked to offer his trainer. He pulled one off and handed it to Fiona. When placed on the other side of the footprint it was as long as Fiona's was short. That indicated the footprint was from a size eight hiking boot.

As she laced up her boot, Fiona's brain was moving faster than she could keep up with. A size eight shoe meant the wearer could be a male or female. There was also the fact that the larger footprint could have been left by someone searching for Cait a couple of hours after the child had left the cave. If that had been the case, then whomever left the larger footprint would have also seen Cait's name and date. That was the kind of information that would be shared with other searchers. It would be used to redirect the search for Cait to the locality of the cave.

Except nobody had reported it.

Fiona didn't want to believe the fears that were circulating in her brain. Her nature had always been to believe the best of people. It was something she'd been taught by her parents and, after their murders, Aunt Mary's inherent goodness had continued to foster the mindset. More than anything Fiona wanted to believe that by the time she left the cave and got a report radioed in, Cait would have turned up. The kid could be dirty and hungry, that'd be fine, just so long as she was unharmed and back with her mother and father.

When Fiona and Deek exited the cave there were two things she noticed before anything else. First, the tide had moved in and was now only a couple of feet from reaching the high-tide mark they'd walked along to access the cave; second, the sun was now settling below the horizon.

The two hundred yards' walk to the end of the bluffs was a purgatory experience. Not only were they walking face into the wind, but the higher water level meant the water had less time to be separated into droplets by the wind and now when they crashed into Fiona, they slammed into her as a solid mass rather than a collection of needles.

Halfway along the bluffs a monster wave crashed into the shoreline and up onto Deek, who was leading. His body shielded Fiona from the worst of the spray that cascaded towards them, but it hit him with enough force to push him backwards.

Deek stumbled into Fiona. Combined with the weight of the water buffeting her, Fiona lost her balance when he slammed into her. She went down, hard. Even though she twisted as she fell and stretched both arms out, something hard and unyielding thumped into her left shoulder.

Fiona yelped at the sudden explosion of pain. As she pushed herself back to her feet, her left arm felt numb and uncoordinated as fiery needles ran up and down its length. The shoulder itself was infused with agony. She wanted to swear and curse the pain away, but there was a member of the public present and as much as being professional was on her mind, the need to not appear weak was also strong. Deek knew she had two cases to solve, that she was alone as a police presence on Luing, and while he was good enough to help her, she knew that he'd also be on hand to document any mistakes she made during the cases. Those mistakes would include taking care of her own physical well-being.

As they trudged on, Fiona ran through a damage report on herself. She was again soaked head to toe. That didn't matter. Her left arm and shoulder now ached as though pummelled with a baseball bat, sadly a feeling she'd experienced for real during an arrest, but when she carefully wind-milled her arm in slow rotations it was possible, although it hurt enough for her teeth to clench against the pain. That was bad and it'd ache for days, but she still had the use of her arm so it wasn't as bad as it could have been.

By the time they'd passed the bluffs and were on easier walking ground away from the edge of the shoreline, Fiona had gathered her thoughts enough to feel ready to speak to DI Baird. She thumbed her radio and prepared to get routed through to the DI.

Nothing happened. She thumbed it again, bending her head to see its screen. The screen was cracked, but unlike her mobile which still worked despite the spiderweb of cracks on its face, below the cracks on the radio there was nothing but a blank grey-green screen.

Fiona let out a stream of unvoiced curses. She was marooned on a small island where there was a small child missing and an unidentified killer, and now her one reliable way of contacting the mainland for support was broken. To rub a generous dose of salt in the wound, Fiona had just had an idea that could help her find Cait. The problem was, it needed someone on the mainland to do the necessary research. With luck Deek would have a landline she could use. If not, she'd have to knock on doors until she found one, or travel around the island looking for somewhere her mobile would pick up a bar or two of signal.

NINETEEN

Deek's cottage in Cullipool was more modern than Fiona had expected it to be. In her mind she'd pictured a traditional fisherman's cottage, with aged furniture and wallpaper that had been hung decades ago.

It was a bachelor pad. That much was unmistakable. A plate lay on the kitchen worktop, its surface a mass of crumbs, grease and egg-yolk smears. The thought of food made Fiona's stomach growl. It had been hours since she'd last eaten and she didn't see any opportunity to eat coming her way anytime soon.

'There's a landline in there.' Deek pointed at an open door bedecked with chipped white paint as he moved towards a sink that was overflowing with unwashed dishes. 'I'll stay in here, give you some privacy. Do you want a coffee?'

'Thanks, and no thanks.' Fiona hadn't the time to sit around drinking coffee, and her old sergeant, Dave Lennox, had taught her the dangers of accepting a cuppa from the public. While often it was fine, there were numerous occasions when the cuppa was rank, or the hygiene of the provider was questionable. The sink full of dirty dishes put Deek in the latter category.

Fiona used her mobile to source the number she needed and called Heather Andrews direct. A DC in DI Baird's team, Heather was Fiona's closest friend and it was she who'd spent hour upon hour telling Fiona every detective technique she knew. As much as Heather's teachings helped Fiona in her day-to-day role as a police officer, she was learning all she could from her friend for personal as well as professional reasons, as the murder of her parents was the one case she wanted to solve above all others.

Heather answered on the third ring. 'DC Andrews.'

'It's me, Heather. I'm on Luing looking for a missing kid and I've discovered a murder.'

'I know, DI Baird has had me looking into stuff connected to your cases. You say what you need to say first, and then I'll fill you in on what I've got. DI Baird has just walked in so I'm going to put you on speaker.'

Fiona knew it was good of Heather to give her the heads-up Baird was there and listening in, but she'd have preferred to only talk with her friend. Now Baird was present she'd have to watch every word, as the DI would pounce on any wild thought she shared with the zeal of a lion attacking its prey.

'Thanks, Heather. Ma'am, I have updates on both cases, but unfortunately not ones you'll want to hear.'

'I didn't expect you to have them solved. Please explain why you're calling DC Andrews from a landline then go ahead with your report.'

Fiona spent a few minutes imparting everything she'd learned and answering their questions. Baird was sharp and insightful, but it was Heather's steady voice that purred reassurance into Fiona's ear.

'Ma'am, Heather, I've a couple of things I'd like checked out. First of all, and I know this may be a longshot, but as I've seen an adult footprint overlapped with one that could have been made by Cait in the cave, I think we now need to seriously consider that Cait may be with an adult on the island. I've a friendly local I can get to go round and knock on all the doors to ask, but I don't think that's going to help. If Cait's been snatched by someone they won't admit it. They probably won't even bother to answer the door.'

'I agree with that assessment, but I don't need to see your workings, so would you please get to your point? What are your ideas?'

Fiona's face burned at Baird's rebuke. 'Luing will only have a population of a couple hundred. Can we run their names through the PNC, the PND and every other database that you can think of?'

'I take it you're looking for someone with a record of violence against minors, sexual or otherwise?'

If Fiona hadn't felt so under pressure, she'd have blushed at the admiration that had crept into Baird's tone. As things stood, both with the cases and Baird's perfectionist nature, she had no time to live in the moment, it was all about what happened next.

'Yes, ma'am, but as private as some of the islanders' lives may be, they're a community that notices things. I'd also check for complaints against individuals. It could be that someone didn't follow a complaint up properly or something like that.'

'Are you suggesting Police Scotland may be in some way culpable if someone has snatched Cait Yorke?' The admiration that had been present in Baird's voice was replaced with her usual haughtiness.

'Ma'am, I think it's fair to consider that the offender may have charmed the officer who investigated. It may be that the complaint was made a decade or more ago and the offender has got better at covering their tracks. Or yes, someone made a poor judgement call. Police Scotland is staffed by human beings, and human beings make mistakes.'

'Not on my team they don't. I do not tolerate mistakes.' There was a pause and Fiona could picture Baird's face twisting in consternation as she contemplated the unpalatable. 'Regard-less, we will check out the islanders as your core idea is sound. What else have you been thinking?'

The faint praise was damning, but that was Baird's style.

'I want to know what you've learned about the passengers and crew. Do any of them have a criminal record? A known association with Charlie Tait? The crew will obviously, but have the passengers?'

'We're still looking into the passengers, and as for the crew, DC Andrews has already looked into them. I'll let her tell you what she's learned, but before I go, is there an answer machine at the number you're calling from?'

Fiona looked at the phone cradle to see if it had an inbuilt answerphone. 'No, ma'am.'

'Fair enough. DC Andrews will remain by this phone until we can get some support to you, or you have resolved the cases.'

The clack of heels echoed down the line as Baird left. It was petty of her to force Heather into the overtime the way she had. Fiona knew Heather was supposed to be meeting her new boyfriend for a late drink after her shift. Heather was falling for the boyfriend and would rue missing the chance to spend time with him. With the staff shortages they were facing Baird's hands were probably tied, but the way she'd committed Heather to the overtime unasked was typical of her management skills.

Fiona waited until she heard the click of Heather taking the phone off speaker before she said anything.

'How in the hell do you put up with her? Surely you don't have to pull an all-nighter. You've a date.'

'I cancelled the date as soon as I heard you were stuck on Luing, as I figured you'd probably need to speak to me at some point. He got all arsey about it so I dumped him. He's hot and all that, but if he can't handle broken dates, there's no way he's Mr Right.'

'Bless you, Heather. You didn't need to do that.'

'Of course I did. If the roles were reversed, what would you have done?'

Fiona didn't answer the question. They both knew that she'd have done for her friend exactly what Heather had done for her.

'Okay, what's the craic about the crew and the captain?'

The first part of Heather's report backed up what Ian had said about him and Davie, but it was when she started talking about Charlie Tait that things got interesting.

'I put a call in to the woman who runs the ticket place at Oban harbour.' Fiona nodded her approval, although she knew Heather couldn't see the gesture. Half ticket booth and half gift shop it was the go-to place for anyone who wanted someone else to take them out on the water. She also knew the woman in question, a right busy-body who was often a great source of information. 'What did she say about him?'

'Tait had told her that before he bought the *Each-Uisge* he used to be a crabber up at Ullapool. That makes sense, right? But when I ran his National Insurance Number, he's never worked within a hundred miles of Ullapool. Not for someone else, and not for himself. Now it could be that he was unregistered and selling on the black market, but things are tight enough up there that there's no way any reputable fish dealer would work with him.'

'So he lied. Therefore he's hiding something.'

'Well, duhhh.'

Fiona ignored the jibe. She was already wondering what Tait was hiding. 'Where had he worked?'

'Peterhead. Mostly on trawlers for twenty-three years until he appeared twelve years ago at Oban as the owner of the *Each-Uisge*.'

'Other than trawlers, where did he work?'

'He had a couple of jobs captaining supply boats for the oil rigs, but nothing on land. Seems the sea was in his blood.'

Fiona had seen Tait's blood in the sea. It was an image that would stay with her for life. She closed her eyes and focused on everything Heather had said, and some of what she hadn't.

Tait had the money to buy his own boat. Unless he lived the frugal existence of a monk, it was unlikely that he'd saved enough of his own money to buy the *Each-Uisge*. She had no idea how much such a boat would cost, but she was sure it would be tens of thousands of pounds at least. At Tait's age it was possible he'd saved for years, or that he'd received an inheritance or two, but it was still a possible line of enquiry.

'I take it you're looking at his finances, Heather?'

'Of course. I've also had a look at his record. It's clean. Very clean.' There was a pause that went on too long. Fiona knew her friend too well to let it lie. Heather could ramble on with the best of them and for her to end a sentence the way she had was unthinkable.

'What are you thinking, Heather? There's something you're not saying.'

'Tait has never had so much as a parking ticket or a caution. He's never been in a pub fight. No neighbours have complained about him. He's never called us about anything. My mother's got a longer police record and you know what a goody two-shoes she is.'

Heather's comments made sense. Fishermen tended to be hard, uncompromising characters. They had to be to endure the back-breaking work and terrible conditions. Such men got into pub fights, they fell out with neighbours and got themselves picked up for drunk and disorderly charges on a regular basis. There was rarely any real bad in them, they just drank more than they should and then solved problems with their fists. For Tait's record to be so clean after so many years working on the boats was unbelievable.

'Are you suggesting he's got a false ID?'

'I'm not suggesting anything, Fiona. Be careful you don't go down a rabbit hole with your thinking. It's too easy to do.'

'Hang on.' A new thought was pushing its way into Fiona's brain. 'We're missing the obvious, Tait was murdered. Mutilated first. That means someone wanted to harm him. Specifically him, as you'd have to be monumentally stupid to pick a place like the *Each-Uisge* to pick someone random as a murder victim.'

'Agreed.'

'No way a guy who's upset someone enough they'd kill him would have such a clean record. At some point he must have done something to piss someone off. The wounds to his groin suggest a sexual reason he was killed. Thing is, was he doing nothing more than sleeping with another man's wife or husband, or was he a sexual offender who'd managed to stay totally under the radar until today? Or are the wounds to his groin a red herring to through off any possible investigation? Done purely on the off chance his body was ever recovered.'

Heather's voice carried the same excitement it always did when they brainstormed ideas together. 'It could be any or all of them. As for his nature, you said before that he didn't get on with one crew member, but that he'd taken in a young lad and got him back on track before he ended up in real trouble. Sounds to me like he was a decent bloke at heart, but wasn't everyone's cup of tea. In other words, your average person.'

Fiona didn't answer. In her mind she was looking at Davie's face as she told him about Tait's death. Had Davie been acting? In her own stressed state had she misread relief as distress? She didn't think so, but she wouldn't bet more than a quid on it.

'You still there, Fiona?'

'Yeah, sorry. I was thinking. There are so many things to consider on both cases. Where should I look for her? How do I catch the killer?'

'You follow the evidence and you keep an open mind. It's

not much, but you're doing a great job and asking all the right questions, so keep on doing what you're doing. If I was in your shoes, I'd be doing and thinking what you're doing.'

'Thanks, Heather. I'll call back when I've something to report or time to check in for an update.'

Heather's last couple of sentences chewed at Fiona. She knew her friend was trying to give her a pat on the back, but the positive words felt like added pressure. In addition to identifying the killer, there was a missing child she had to find on an island that would soon be shrouded in darkness.

TWENTY

'Thanks, Deek. For the phone and your help. I'm afraid I'm going to have to ask more of you, though.'

'Ask away.' He gave a self-deprecating shrug. 'I'd call it civic duty, but the truth is this is the most exciting thing that's happened here in my lifetime. Besides, I get to watch a real-life investigation as it happens. It's like I'm in the middle of one of those cop dramas that are always on the telly. And just like the ones on the telly, the lead cop is a right looker.'

'Get on with you.' Fiona waved away the compliment, but its root registered another thought in her mind. It was an unwelcome thought and sat with her like the guest who invites themselves to a party. She hadn't seen many women among the islanders. There was the woman in the Atlantic Islands Centre, but other than her and tourists, she'd not seen a female.

Luing had a population of around two hundred. Of these, a half of the island's population would be split between Cullipool and Toberonochy, with the other half living in small farms, and the small cottages that decorated various parts of the island. Human beings were sexual creatures. They had needs they'd want satisfied. On a remote island where there were fewer women than men, there would be a number of men whose sexual appetites weren't even close to being met. It was a breeding ground for sexual frustration and that, in turn, was something that combined with other unknown factors could loosen moral codes and lower inhibitions. The imbalance between the genders was likely to be greater in some parts of the island than others. There was also the memory of the hand on her backside when Deek and Fergus had hauled her out of the water and up onto the rock.

It was abhorrent for Fiona to think of little Cait in the hands of a sexually frustrated islander, but she had to consider every option with an open mind no matter how disturbing it might be. What she must do was work out who might have taken Cait, and if she had been abducted, where she was being kept.

Deek's voice cut into her thoughts. When she looked his way she saw his eyes were locked on where her damp T-shirt was plastered to her chest. 'What do you want me to do?'

'That pickup outside, is it yours?'

'It is, yeah. Where do you want to go?'

'I want you to get someone else, a female neighbour would be best. Then go down all the tracks on the island. Start at Toberonochy and work south. Go over the fields if you can. Point your lights over the landscape as much as you can and get your neighbour to shine a torch over the bits your lights can't get to. You're looking for Cait. If you know of anyone else with a four-wheel drive vehicle, a quad bike, a whatever, get them out there looking too. Blare horns and loud music. Do anything you can to attract Cait's attention, but make sure there's a female with you or anyone else who's searching. A little girl will have been warned to never get in a vehicle with a man or men she doesn't know. I'll need you to keep going until you find her or someone tells you she's been found. Can you do that?'

'Of course. I'll get the farmer down there out looking too.

He and his wife are good people, they'll help us. Where will you be?'

'I'm going to speak to Cait's mother and then head back to the Atlantic Islands Centre.'

'I'll find you there.' Deek tossed her a set of keys. 'In case you want to use the phone again.'

The gesture was welcome, and at a different time and place, it may have made up for the way he was ogling. Not today it didn't. Not when there was a potentially sexually motivated murder to investigate. And Cait's lengthy disappearance to explain.

* * *

Fiona climbed into her car and fished her bottle of water from the door pocket. It was warm from the blazing sun that had streamed into the car all day, but it eased the scratchiness of her throat before she set off for the church in the centre of the island, to catch up with Cait's mother. Her heart grew heavier with every yard she travelled. The undulating landscape of Luing with its rocky outcrops and reed-strewn grasslands was a nightmare in terms of visibility, and if Cait feared she'd be in trouble for going missing there were a multitude of places where she could hide from search parties.

The one thing in Fiona's favour was the time of year. If this had been winter it would be pitch dark by now, plus there would be a far greater chance of Cait suffering from the elements than there was on a warm summer's night. For all there was a gale coming into the island, there was no great risk to Cait from the weather unless she sought shelter in a rickety building and, from what Fiona had seen, the only buildings that weren't solid stone were the few sheds at the centre of the island.

Diane Yorke was where Fiona had last seen her. Although

she was no longer alone. A tall, beefy man was with her, his arm draped over her shoulders as she cried into his chest. Her hair streamed out sideways, and she saw a greying ponytail flapping behind his head. He would be Diane's husband, Pete.

When Fiona walked over to them, they separated from their consoling embrace and faced her. Even in the dimming light, Fiona could see the gauntness of their faces and the dread in their eyes.

'I'm sorry. I have nothing positive to tell you, but neither do I have any bad news.' Fiona gestured round about her. 'I've roped in some of the locals with four-wheel drive vehicles to search the more inaccessible places, and I would suggest that you and anyone else you can enlist should keep moving about all the tarmac roads. Beep your horn, keep stopping to look and listen for her. Now it's getting dark Cait is bound to be scared and hungry. Our best hope is that she hears the horns or sees the lights and comes out of wherever she's been hiding.'

Diane went toe-to-toe with Fiona. Her nose an inch from Fiona's. 'That's it? That's your masterplan, is it? Beep our horns? My daughter's missing, she's been missing for hours and you want us to go for a drive, beeping our horns. Jesus fucking Christ, is that the best you can come up with? Where are the search helicopters? The dog teams? I know this island isn't exactly Ben Nevis, but what about mountain rescue? She's eight. Eight years old and all you're doing is getting people to drive around. You're useless, totally fucking useless.'

'That's enough, Diane.' The man pulled her shoulder and wrapped his spindly arms around her in what was half loving embrace and half restraining measure. 'The wind's far too high for helicopters and the seas are too rough for anyone to cross from the mainland. You know that. Just as you know our Cait is smart and resourceful. You know what she's like, she'll have found somewhere that interests her, and then when it started getting dark she'll have found somewhere to spend the night.'

Fiona nodded her thanks to Pete Yorke, and opened her mouth ready to speak. When she caught his expression she closed her mouth again. It was clear from his face he didn't necessarily believe what he'd told his wife, but he'd done what he could to calm her. As he looked over Diane's head, his face was a mask of despairing anger.

Fiona had debated whether or not to tell the Yorkes about the footprints and the etching of Cait's name in the cave. Now, in the face of their fury, she felt she had to throw them something of a crumb.

'I do have some news. It's not a lot, so don't get your hopes up, but there's a cave along the shoreline south of Blackmill Bay. Cait was in there.'

'How do you know that?'

The hope in Diane's eyes as she spat the question out made Fiona's heart ache for the woman's pain.

'Like so many other people who'd visited the cave she'd scratched her name and the date onto the cave wall. It was her name and it was dated today.'

'And you didn't see her? She wasn't anywhere in that area?'

'She was long gone and she won't have gone back. You told me earlier that she's afraid of large bodies of water. As I left, the tide was coming in and throwing spray up and into the cave. Even if she wasn't afraid of water, I don't think she'd have dared go back to the cave.' Fiona took a moment to let this news sink in before continuing. 'I've asked the islanders to start looking at the most southern part of Luing, as we know for certain she was in that area at some point today. I don't know for certain if there are any other caves down there, but the local I had with me didn't mention any. My thinking is that Cait went south hunting for more caves.'

Diane pushed herself away from her husband and wrapped her arms around Fiona. 'Thank you. Thank you. Thank you.'

There was no apology for the harsh words but Fiona didn't

care about that. As a police officer she'd been called a lot worse for a lot less. 'I'm going to leave you now and do what I can to co-ordinate the search. From what you said earlier, I know you have family with you. My advice would be to get a search party armed with torches to sweep down the other side of the island from Toberonochy. If Cait's gone south following the coast, it makes sense that she'd end up coming north on the opposite coast. Even for a child, it's not that far considering how long she's been... exploring.' Fiona chose her final word with care lest she trigger another round of panic in Diane.

Pete's eyes shone and Fiona could tell he was happy to have something practical to do. A task that would make him feel like he was making a contribution. 'I'll do just that. Diane, you wait here and when I get back you can use the car to do the horn and lights thing between Toberonochy and Blackmill Bay.'

Next on Fiona's mental list of tasks was a return to Cullipool and a conversation with everyone who'd been aboard the *Each-Uisge*.

As Fiona gunned her engine she was also crossing her fingers in the hope she was on the right track about something.

TWENTY-ONE

The Atlantic Islands Centre was ablaze with light, its floor-to-ceiling front windows spilling illumination out across the patch of grass that was its frontage.

Fiona's feet dragged as she entered the centre's café. At first glance it looked as if everyone was present, but when she looked in more detail, she saw there were two empty seats that had previously been occupied. The first belonged to Richard, the second to the teenage girl who was sitting with a boy she was cuddling into far too much for them to be siblings.

Grant had taken Deek's place at the door and it was to him she spoke. 'There's two of them missing. Where are they?'

'The bonny lass and the wee guy? She's in the bog, and he's gone out for a smoke. He's been out a few times. He's five, mebbe ten minutes a time.'

'He's not outside. Not at the front.'

'He goes round the back. It'll be the only bit he can light up in this wind.'

What Grant was saying made sense to Fiona, but all the same, when she trudged outside to find him, she was relieved to see him puffing away on a hand-rolled cigarette, rather than face down in the water that had filled the former mine behind the centre.

'Can you come back in, please?'

He showed her the half-smoked cigarette. 'I'll only be a couple of minutes.'

'Now, please.' Fiona put enough authority into her voice to make his refusal to do as she asked a bad idea.

The man grumbled as he ground out the cigarette and stuck the remaining half behind an ear, but he came.

Upon re-entering the café Fiona saw Melissa had returned. She had a decision to make. Here as a group, these people were safe. They might find the night uncomfortable sat in the wooden chairs or sleeping on the slate floor, but there were too many of them for the killer or killers to strike unseen.

'Have any of them tried to escape? Given you any hassle about being kept here?'

Before Grant could answer there was a huge splintering crash behind them. When Fiona whirled to see the cause of the commotion she saw that a piece of wooden debris had been slammed into the top of one of the huge windows fronting the café. The toughened and laminated glass had shattered into many pieces, but for now it hadn't sent any broken glass inside.

The pressure of the wind was already bowing the glass, bellying it inwards as it found a weak spot to exploit.

'Everyone, get back from the windows.'

Fiona didn't know who'd shouted, it may have been her, but right now all she could think was that the café was no longer a safe haven. She had to get all these people somewhere they'd be safe before she could continue with either investigation.

TWENTY-TWO

When Fiona's hand clasped the door handle she heard a shout. She looked round to see Fergus waving for her to join everyone else at the rear of the café.

'The back door will be safer.'

To Fiona what Fergus was saying made sense and lots of it. She cursed herself. She ought to have had that thought.

A great creaking and cracking sound made Fiona sprint the twenty feet across the café. When she reached the others she turned and saw the damaged window had been blown in by the gale, and now lay in a million pieces across the floor. Within seconds the wind was tearing into the café, overturning chairs and fluttering pamphlets and napkins around like they were confetti.

Just outside the window the piece of timber that had broken the glass lay on the paving slabs. Even from the brief glance Fiona gave it, she could see it was a hinged door. From its size Fiona assumed it had been torn from a boat by the increasing wind. The fact they were seventy or more yards from the nearest boat didn't bode well. If the wind was strong enough to rip a door off and throw it so far with enough force to smash a toughened window, what else would it throw their way?

As they filed through the café's kitchen and store room, Fiona was already wracking her brains as to where she could get everyone relocated to.

In most communities there would be a village hall, but from the notices Fiona had seen in the café, it seemed the one building had multiple uses.

Fiona gave her mind a quick trawl, flashing images of what she'd seen on the island. When she settled on a potential place for shelter, she grabbed Grant's arm and pulled until he turned to face her. 'Is there any way we can get into the church? Is it locked?'

'It's locked, but Auld Noreen has a key as she cleans it. Is that where you want everyone to go?'

'Yeah, it's a solid building and far enough away from the shore there'll be no chance of flying debris. Where does this Noreen live?'

'In one of the houses opposite the shop. We can get the key on the way. And it's Auld Noreen. She doesn't like being mixed up with the Noreen from Toberonochy.'

Were the situation not so serious, Fiona would have found amusement in Auld Noreen's petty ways, but she was intent on getting the whole group to the church without injury.

Once outside everyone sheltered behind the building. Richard putting the roll-up back to his lips and bending his back against the wind as he tried to re-light it.

The wind was now howling, its swirling tendrils rounding the building to pluck at everyone's clothing and hair.

'Listen up.' Fiona had to shout to be heard. 'We're going to go to the church.' She pointed at the nearest building. 'Those with cars, can you park them behind the cottage over there?'

As they trotted off, Fiona used the dim light spilling from the bulb above the back door to cast her eyes over the remaining group. Couples were cuddling each other as they looked with trepidation beyond the building. The elderly woman's face was stoic, but she'd placed a steadying hand against the wall.

Harry and Melissa were the only ones who didn't seem to grasp the severity of the situation. Their faces were rapt, and the girl had her mobile clamped in her hand. Fiona reckoned that while the girl might not have a decent signal, she'd leave the island with plenty of pictures and videos for her social media feeds.

Fiona realised she'd have to monitor the young couple: the last thing she wanted was for them to be recording her decisions and plastering her every move online.

Two cars pulled behind the nearby cottage followed by a large SUV. That made twelve empty seats, eleven if Melissa sat on Harry's knee. That was more than enough to transport everyone to the church and leave Fiona's car for Fiona alone.

Grant's muscled physique appeared round the corner and sought out Fiona. 'It's as wild as buggery out there.' He pointed to Delia. 'The old girl'll be knocked flat. I'll help her, you warn the others.'

As Grant wrapped a beefy arm around the elderly woman's waist, Fiona saw the young couple start to head for the cars. The wind caught them and blew them four paces sideways before they could lean far enough into the irresistible force to control their movements.

The older, wiser adults learned from the young couple's error and each of them was braced against the wind before they stepped into its full force.

Fiona made sure to bring up the rear, but as much as she prepared herself for the impact of the gale, she found it far worse than expected. There was grit in the wind that made her feel like she was being sandblasted. If that wasn't bad enough, the relentless pressure of the wind pushed every breath she tried to exhale back down her throat until she turned her head to the side.

By the time Fiona was in the shelter of the cottage, she was breathless and her eyes stung. Regardless of her own discomfort, she went to where Grant was helping the elderly woman into his car.

'Can you get everyone to the church and keep them there? I'll be along shortly.'

'Of course.'

Fiona wanted to check in with Deek before she joined the others in the church. When the group were assembled there, she could get Grant or one of the others to help out with the search. Whichever one of them drove the SUV would be the best candidate.

Before she even did that, she planned to enlist the help of another local. A man who'd so far been friendly to her.

To Fiona's left, the island's shop-cum-post office flashed past, and then she was at the garage again. Fiona drew into the yard and strode across to where the mechanic was working under the illumination of a lamp clipped to the car's bonnet. 'Hi, have you seen anything of her?'

The spanner in the mechanic's hand was laid on top of the engine. 'Not a sign. I'll gie you a hand looking for her if you want.'

'Thanks.' Fiona thought for a moment. In her mind she was mapping out the island and what she'd seen of it. As a way of not putting all of her eggs into the basket for the theory that Cait had remained in the south of the island, Fiona pointed over towards the northeast quadrant. 'There's a bay over there, and there's some kind of construction work taking place. Maybe she's gone to look at the boats in the bay or watch the buildings going up.'

'The pods? I doubt they'll be of any interest to a bairn.

Bloody things'll fall doon in a couple of years. Island like Luing, you need a proper stone building. I'll check, though.'

'Keep your eyes and ears open. If we find her elsewhere, I'll run along the road with my sirens and lights on.'

No sound came from the man, but his face held a harrumph as he leaned into the wind. Fiona got his point at once. With the wind howling as it was, there was little to no chance of anyone hearing the car's siren.

TWENTY-THREE

Fiona travelled south with a million thoughts for company. Not one of the thoughts gave her even the semblance of cheer. The longer Cait was missing, the greater the odds were of her either having had an accident or fallen into the wrong hands.

It was the same for the killer. The more time they spent in the group of rescued passengers, the more their desperation to escape would grow. Sooner or later they'd realise their only hope of evading prosecution was to disappear.

In Fiona's mind she imagined the killer biding their time. Not all of the people who'd been on the *Each-Uisge* could be arrested and found guilty, but when more officers came armed with all the information available from background checks, the list of thirteen names would soon be whittled down. Fiona had already dropped three names off her own suspect list. The elderly woman with the injured ankle, Delia, was the first. Her hands were gnarled with arthritis and Fiona couldn't see her having the strength of grip to wield a knife or the speed to attack Tait. Next were the teen couple, Harry and Melissa. Both were well-spoken and they were so wrapped up in each other they hadn't seemed to notice anything or anyone else. She believed

Deek's coarse assessment of Harry's focus was accurate, and the only real question in Fiona's mind was how hard Melissa would make Harry work for his prize.

Fiona could be wrong, she knew that, but in the absence of hard facts she was working on instinct. Fiona knew she could be wrong about the young couple's manners, too, as killers came from all walks of life. Some were erudite and wordy, whereas others had poor vocabulary punctuated with swear words. All the same, she couldn't see either Melissa or Harry tearing themselves away from the other long enough to murder Tait.

Irene wasn't the greatest suspect she'd ever known, although Fiona believed her hectoring nature could easily persuade someone like her beleaguered husband, Richard, into murdering someone she believed had crossed her. Having said that about Richard, he seemed more intent on killing himself with his rolled cigarettes than being someone who murdered at his wife's command.

Next there was the group of three young men. They'd been quiet the whole time. Not once had they given any problems. There had been no grumbles from them, no complaints, just polite thanks to her and the islanders for rescuing them. When asked they'd trotted out their names and addresses without hesitation.

After the group of three young men, Fiona was left with three passengers and the two crew members as the others on her list of suspects. Both of the crew were high on her list, and she still wasn't sure what to make of the other three passengers, although she harboured plenty of suspicions about Mark. The anger he'd shown earlier hadn't dissipated in the hours he'd spent at the Atlantic Islands Centre. There was also something off with the way neither of the women with him were showing any care about him. Perhaps they'd grown indifferent to his withdrawal, or their relationship with him was nearing a natural end.

Fiona turned towards Toberonochy and looked south for the lights of Deek's pickup. Every twenty seconds or so there was a flash of light appearing over the horizon, but so far as Fiona could judge, Deek wasn't returning north yet.

The road to Blackmill Bay seemed a lot narrower in Fiona's headlights than she remembered it being in daylight. All the way there she was casting her eyes south looking for any kind of sign that Deek had managed to get the farmer out looking too. A second set of lights was arcing back and forth, as if the person controlling the vehicle was casting wide sweeps as they progressed forward. Fiona approved of the technique, it would cover the greatest amount of ground in the shortest time.

The more Fiona considered little Cait's choice of destination, the more she began to wonder if Cait had started feeling hungry, or if she'd had the maturity to recognise darkness was on its way as she left the cave and had started hiking back north. If that was the case, there was every chance the mechanic might have found her at the eco-pods.

After watching the lights move around for a good five minutes, Fiona located a place to turn and set off north to check in with the mechanic. If he hadn't found Cait, she'd muster some more islanders and get as many of them as she could out with torches. And while they were searching for Cait, she'd go to the church to try and identify a killer.

TWENTY-FOUR

Fiona would have driven right past the church a second time had Grant not stood in the road flagging her down. The look on his face told her it wasn't good news.

Grant's hand was on her door handle before she'd pulled to a stop. Wasn't good news became really bad news in Fiona's mind. A ball of dread was forming in her stomach as Grant yanked the door open.

'They've only gone and buggered off.'

'Who has?'

'The two guys from the boat you kept talking to. And that bunch of young guys. You know the ones, they hardly spoke to anyone, including each other.'

Fiona pointed at the passenger seat. 'Climb in, take a breath and tell me what happened.'

As Grant rounded the car, Fiona tried to piece together what he'd said into a coherent thought. By the sounds of it, Ian and Davie had gone their own way and so had the three young men. If what Grant was telling her was right, and she saw no reason for him to lie, it meant her list of suspects now only had five names on it, as she couldn't see a killer remaining in a group when others had left it. How the killer planned to escape the island was a mystery, but both Ian and Davie were seamen and, if they'd been the ones to kill Tait, they'd be best placed to steal a boat and strike out for the mainland.

Grant thumped his door shut as he launched himself into the passenger seat. 'I'm sorry, that fat woman was being a right pain and insisting she was going nowhere with us, and then the next thing I know is that when I looked round they were all gone.'

'Let me get this straight, both the crewmen, Ian and Davie, didn't come with you. And neither did the group of three young men who were on the boat.'

'That's what I've been telling you. All five of the buggers just vanished when we were getting the others into the cars.' Grant's hand spread apart. 'I had a quick look for them, of course I did, but they were nowhere to be seen.'

Fiona nodded but the gesture was more to let Grant know she'd heard him than anything else. Her mind was already pushing across the possibilities of where the five men might have gone.

Another factor to consider was if they'd left as two separate groups or one. From what she recalled observing the five men, Fiona hadn't noticed any hint of kinship between them. That could have been an act designed to throw her off the scent, but it could also be due to the genuine fact they didn't know each other.

'Grant, did you see the five of them talking at any point?'

'No. The older guy was busy comforting the young one, who was upset about the captain, and the others didn't speak to anyone but each other unless spoken to.'

Grant's words tallied with Fiona's memory, but that still didn't mean the group hadn't planned to keep to their separate cliques should the need arise. All the same, Fiona couldn't see five people conspiring to a murder. Not when there was little chance the opportunity to kill Tait and get away with it would arise.

Fiona's fingers rattled off the dashboard as she worked over an idea. If Ian had been involved in killing Tait, he'd surely know how to incapacitate the boat's engine. Therefore, he'd created the opportunity. As a professional seaman he'd know all about tides and could have timed his tinkering with the engine so the *Each-Uisge* would run ashore on Luing or one of the surrounding islands. It was a risky thing to do, but if the boat was sabotaged with the right amount of care, he'd have been confident of his survival.

Except it hadn't gone as he might have planned it. Had Fiona and the islanders not been there to help, there was little chance those on board the *Each-Uisge* would have survived. That in turn meant that if the engine had been tampered with, the killer had risked the lives of a dozen innocent people as well as their own.

Fiona drew in a long breath as she considered this angle. If she was right, it meant she was hunting a killer who placed little or no value on the life of innocents.

'You know the island better than me, Grant. Where might they hide out?'

'There's the eco-pods that are being built. They'd be a good place to weather the storm. All the houses are occupied and, at this time of year, it's unlikely there'd be any vacancies at the bed and breakfasts.'

'What about the caravan park? Sunnybrae, isn't it?'

'It is. They'll like as not be full too.'

'Other than the eco-pods, is there anywhere else?'

'They might break into the cabin by the slipway at Cuan Sound.'

Fiona remembered the trip across.

There'd been a Portacabin on the right as she'd got off the ferry, but there had been a house on the left. As wild as the wind might be, it was a warm evening and there was no rain or snow to contend with. It might not be the most comfortable way to spend a night, but if they could find a stone wall to shelter them from the worst of the wind, the night wouldn't be unbearable. For someone trying to escape justice for murder, it would be more than acceptable.

TWENTY-FIVE

Fiona swung the nose of her car into the mechanic's yard, in case he'd returned when she was at the south portion of the island. He hadn't.

Once Fiona was past the fire station that doubled as the island's ambulance station, she switched on the car's blues and twos, in the hope it'd attract his attention.

A sign adorned with the name of a construction firm, pointing down a gravel track, made Fiona take the turn. She reasoned it would be the eco-pods, and as that's where she'd asked the mechanic to begin his search, it seemed like the best place for her to find him.

The gravel track was a new one that had yet to develop any ruts or potholes. It sprayed tiny stones upwards that clattered on the underside of the car as Fiona navigated her way down the slope. As she rounded a corner Fiona got a glimpse of the eco-pods.

Shaped like gypsy caravans the pods were coated with horizontal boards of a dark timber. They were arranged in a neat row, and Fiona could only imagine how beautiful their views would be in daylight. A stack of timber and other building materials were arranged in tidy piles, and there was a skip loaded with rubbish at the far end beside a Portaloo.

The sight of the Portaloo loosened something within Fiona and she released just how badly she needed a pee. The water she'd been sipping to ease her throat had brought effects of its own. A minute spent having a pee would affect no one, so she went towards the Portaloo with mixed expectations. She needed the release it'd offer, but as it was provided for the use of builders, she didn't expect it to be very hygienic.

The Portaloo was everything Fiona expected and less, but there was more than enough paper to wipe the seat into a semblance of clean, so she gritted her teeth and answered nature's call with a squatting hover.

As Fiona wandered past the eco-pods she saw the gravel track curled around to their fronts. On the track was a small white van that looked familiar. The answer came to Fiona as she strode towards the van. It had been parked by the garage, therefore it must either be the mechanic's, or one he'd borrowed as it was in his yard.

A closer inspection of the van found it empty, the keys still in the ignition. Their presence made a certain amount of sense to Fiona, as there was so little crime on the islands, the islanders tended to be more lax with security than mainlanders. Even if the mechanic wasn't the trusting type, with the ferry not running, nobody could steal his van and leave the island with it.

Rather than waste her breath shouting, Fiona scanned the terrain in front of the pods. Even in the darkness she could make out the different areas of sea and land. There were no moving lights suggesting the mechanic was searching by torch-light. Common sense told Fiona that he would have returned to his vehicle when night fell. Except he hadn't.

A fey feeling befell Fiona as she realised she'd asked the mechanic to search a place that Grant had suggested potential killers may choose to shelter. She hadn't known at the time, of course, but that did nothing to salve the guilt balling her intestines into a knot.

Fiona swung her torch towards the eco-pods. Their doors and windows were traditional wood, but they were yet to be glazed. One by one she cast her torch inside them. She didn't expect to find Cait, not that she'd complain if she did. It was the missing men from the *Each-Uisge* she was searching for. She'd had the sense to put her utility belt on, and in the hand she wasn't using for the torch she held a pepper spray ready for use.

The first two pods were empty shells with nothing but unclad walls inside. The third was better equipped. Its walls were clad and there was a toilet, sink and shower cubicle against a wall ready for fitting. That wasn't what Fiona's eyes focused on, though. She didn't care about bathroom fittings, not when there was a bloodstain in the middle of the floor.

Fiona cast her torch into every corner of the pod and then rotated through three hundred and sixty degrees to check she was alone.

She was, although the thudding of her heart sounded like the thumping footsteps of someone approaching at a run.

After a deep breath, Fiona opened the door and stepped into the pod. The blood on the floor could be from a builder who'd had an accident. That would be the best outcome by a mile. Perhaps not for the builder, but Fiona would take it over any of the other possibilities in her mind.

A dozen thoughts competed for supremacy as Fiona circled the bloodstain. She was intent on doing what she could to preserve the crime scene, yet she also had to check for any evidence she could find.

Even by torchlight, Fiona could see the stain was recent. Someone had tried wiping it with a cloth or rag, but there were none of the scuff marks that littered the rest of the floor through the stain. In total there would be a couple of square feet that was marked by blood. Not all of it would be where blood fell, as it had been wiped and no doubt that spread the stain, but it was still big enough to indicate a fair amount of blood had poured onto the floor.

Fiona swept her torch around the room in a slow arc. There were no tiny spatters of blood on the walls. Nor were there any others on the floor. Were she not afraid a killer might ambush her at any moment, Fiona would have closed her eyes in despair. If a builder had an accident severe enough to warrant such a large bloodstain, it'd have occurred with a power tool. The offending power tool would have spat blood across the room. That didn't happen, therefore what she was looking at must be a crime scene, as an injured worker would have bled their way out of the door. Which also didn't happen.

The knuckles of Fiona's hands were white as she gripped the torch and pepper spray. Now her theory of another murder was reinforced, she was expecting a killer to leap out at her from every direction.

Even as she stepped out of the pod and swung her torch into the darkness, Fiona was wondering who'd been killed. Had little Cait fallen into the wrong hands, or had she unwittingly sent the mechanic to his death?

No matter how she tried to work it out, Fiona couldn't decide which would be worse. Was the mechanic's life worth less because he'd lived longer? Or Cait's more because of what she might grow up to achieve? Neither would be good, and as much as Fiona didn't believe it was the case, she'd be quite happy to learn she was wrong and the blood had come from a construction worker who'd got careless with a power tool and had lopped off a finger or two.

The next thought she had was the potential location of the body. It would have made sense to use the mechanic's van to carry it away from the pods, but that didn't appear to have happened. When she'd cast her torch inside the van's rear it was empty, its plywood floor covered with toolboxes of varying shapes and sizes. None of those toolboxes had been tainted by a bloodstain.

Fiona reasoned that if the body wasn't transported in the van, it must be close. So she walked back along the track with a specific destination in mind.

The skip beside the Portaloo was three quarters full. In it were broken pieces of plasterboard, a dozen or so pieces of timber with nails protruding from them.

Before she began taking a proper look in the skip, Fiona walked around it, scanning her torch in every possible direction. She found no killers waiting for her. No predators lying in wait to add her to their list of victims.

Once she was confident she could put the pepper spray back in her belt, Fiona drew a pair of nitrile gloves from a pocket, swapped the torch to her left hand and started pulling detritus from the skip. Upon moving the third piece of plasterboard she saw a scrap of red cloth.

Cait's leggings were red.

So were the mechanic's overalls.

Fiona dug deeper and uncovered enough of the material to make an identification. Instead of tight leggings, the red material was the loose fabric of oil-stained overalls.

'I'm so, so sorry...' Fiona couldn't finish the sentence. She'd never learned the mechanic's name.

Tears streamed from Fiona as she moved enough debris to let her see the mechanic's face and put a trembling finger to his throat, to confirm he was dead. He was in this skip because she'd sent him here. This man whose name she didn't know had died after she'd sought his help. She ought to have concentrated on the fact there was a murderer on the island instead of looking for the lost child.

What had the mechanic seen or heard that had got him killed? Had he overheard a conversation about Charlie Tait's murder? Found little Cait being held captive by someone? Had that someone been an islander he could identify? Every possible reason for the mechanic's murder Fiona thought of had logic backing it up. And behind every one of those reasons was the mechanic's reason for visiting the pods: Fiona had asked him to come here.

As she stumbled her way back to the car, one thought was above all others in Fiona's mind. How many more people might die because of her mistakes?

Another, more chilling thought pushed its way into Fiona's mind. If she hadn't sent the mechanic to the pods, she herself would have visited them at some point soon. She could easily have ended up in that skip. As she sniffed herself back under a semblance of control, Fiona resolved to do whatever it took to bring the mechanic's killer to justice.

Fiona wanted to take some time out to compose herself, to get her thoughts in order and to let the redness from her eyes ebb away before she faced anyone. It was a nice idea, but she couldn't do it. She owed the mechanic far better than that. Cait too. With her jaw clamped firm, she set off to the Kilchattan Church. It was time to learn a whole lot more about the missing men.

First, though, she had to learn the mechanic's name.

TWENTY-SIX

Fiona had to battle every step of the way to get across the road from the car park opposite the church. It was only ten yards or so from where she'd parked, but by the time she'd travelled the short distance, Fiona was breathless and perspiring.

The inside of the church was quiet save the howling of the wind.

Irene, who else, was the first to come towards her, but Fiona stalked right past her until she was beside Grant. A side-nod had Grant following her to a secluded corner.

'Do you know the mechanic who has the garage by the junction?'

His eyes narrowed a little. 'He's my brother. What do you want to know?'

Fiona had to fight to keep her face from betraying her. It made sense the islanders would all know each other, but she'd been naïve to think they wouldn't be related.

'I'm sorry, Grant. So very sorry, but I have bad news about your brother.'

'What, he's not missing as well, is he?'

'I'm afraid it's worse news than that. I'm sorry to have to tell you this, Grant, but your brother has been killed.'

Grant's face went hard as he sawed his head side to side. 'No. You've got it wrong. He can't have been killed. He's a mechanic not a... a...'

'I'm sorry.'

Grant's fingers latched on to Fiona's shoulders and gripped hard. Fiona ground her teeth against the pain in her bruised left shoulder. Grant wasn't trying to hurt her. All he was doing was trying to make sense of the devastating news she'd just delivered.

'You said he was killed. How? What killed him?'

Fiona let silence answer the question.

'No. No way. Are you telling me he was murdered?'

'I'm so sorry.'

'Was he at his garage?'

'No, I asked him to help me search for the missing child. To check out the area where they're building the eco-pods. When I went to see if he'd found her, I found him instead. I'm so, so very sorry. It's too early to know for certain who killed him, but my guess would be whoever killed the *Each-Uisge*'s captain. I'm sorry, but once they'd killed him, they hid his body in a skip.' Fiona laid a hand on Grant's arm that he glared at. 'I'm so sorry.'

'Stop fucking apologising. Unless you killed him yourself you've got nothing to apologise for. Let me get this straight, he went looking for the missing kid, and he was murdered, right? Then the bastards dumped him in a skip like rubbish.'

'He was, yes.' Fiona tapped the useless radio still clipped to her stab vest, her stomach roiling at what she was about to say. 'I have to go call it in, to let my superiors know what's happened, and to declare the skip as a crime scene. But before I can do that, I'll need to know his name.'

Grant's eyes were as hard as any slate that had ever been mined on Luing. 'His name was William Peter Nichol. We all call him Will. Go on, go and make your call. We don't need you here.'

The bland tone Grant spoke with was at odds with the pain in his eyes. Fiona would have preferred him to rage at her rather than dismiss her in such an offhand fashion. The guilt Fiona felt at Will's death would never leave her, she knew that. If Grant or his family could find even temporary solace in berating her, blaming her for the loss of their loved one, she'd take anything they threw at her. Every word, every accusation they wanted to voice, she'd listen to them all and offer no defence. They deserved their voice and she deserved their scorn.

As Fiona reached the church door she became aware of a presence behind her.

It was Grant, his face twisted and hard.

'You better find whoever killed Will before I do, because if I find him first, you'll need a body bag not handcuffs.'

The realisation of a fatal mistake she'd made hit Fiona with enough force to double the already oppressive guilt she felt about Will's death. After rescuing everyone from the *Each-Uisge* she'd overlooked the most obvious thing: she'd not searched for the murder weapon.

Fiona had assumed the killer would have ditched their weapon into the sea rather than keep it on them. Yet even by what she'd seen from the light of her torch, it was clear Will had been killed with some kind of bladed weapon, perhaps a knife just like Charlie Tait. Fiona gripped the steering wheel until her hands ached. If she'd patted down everyone who came off the *Each-Uisge*, she'd have found the knife and the murder suspect. Even the act of patting down the passengers and the crew in turn would have been enough to put such fear of discovery into the killer they'd have had to react before she got to them. Fiona knew that had she searched people for the murder weapon, Will would still be alive.

'He has a knife, Grant. It's what he used to kill both your

brother and the captain of the *Each-Uisge*. If you try and attack him, there's every chance you'll end up as his next victim. Plus, we don't know whether or not the killer is working alone or whether he has help.'

'I don't care.' Grant's face now resembled a vengeful gargoyle. 'Knife or not, I'll beat the bastard to death for what he did to Will.'

From the shaking timbre of Grant's tone, Fiona didn't think the man before her was making an idle threat fuelled by grief. One way or another, she had to identify and catch Will's killer before Grant did, or the island of Luing would be stained with even more blood.

TWENTY-SEVEN

She didn't rub the grit from her eyes when she made it into Deek's cottage; instead, Fiona bent forward and blinked until tears had washed the worst of it away. She'd returned to Cullipool to report the second murder and seek both advice and information. The lack of mobile communications was a complication Fiona could have well done without. Not only did it waste her time travelling back to the cottage, it meant she had to wait for updates that might change her strategy.

'DC Andrews.'

Heather's purring voice sent strength and reassurance directly into Fiona's subconscious. Fiona had feared she would break down upon hearing her friend, but the opposite had happened.

'It's me.'

'How are things there? Have you found the bairn yet? The killer?'

'Bad. No. And No.'

'Shit, Fiona, tell me everything and don't worry, Baird's not here, and nor is anyone else.'

Fiona brought her friend up to speed in the most profes-sional way she could, but when it came to telling her about Will's murder, she heard the cracks in her own voice.

As she always did, Heather read between the lines of Fiona's emotional story. 'You're not to blame for his death, Fiona, you do know that, don't you?'

'I asked him to help. I didn't even find out his name until I spoke to his brother. How am I not to blame?'

'You could only be more wrong if you put pineapple on a pizza. You expect way too much of yourself. You're a copper, not a detective. Think about what would happen if there was a missing kid on the mainland in decent weather. There'd be police, mountain rescue and as many civilians as volunteered. There'd be sniffer dogs and a whole chain of command following the best recognised practices for finding a missing child. And don't get me started on the amount of manpower that would get involved in a murder case. In either of those situ-ations, your role would involve nothing more than standing around somewhere or tramping over a hill as part of a search party. God's sake, Fiona, you've got two huge cases at once and you're on your own in the middle of one of the worst gales to hit Scotland in fifty or more years. Listen to me, you have to give yourself a break and recognise you can't be everywhere doing everything.'

'That's just it, Heather. I do have to be everywhere doing everything. Wee Cait needs me to find her. I have to be smarter. I have to think of consequences and potential dangers all the time. I need the help of the islanders, but I'm now afraid to ask them in case they end up dead.'

'Then don't ask them, and if they volunteer, make sure they know the risks.'

'What about Grant? He's hell-bent on finding the killer and beating him to death. Either he'll succeed or he'll be killed for trying.'

'That's on him. You've other fish to fry. You've been a cop long enough to know that people say things in the heat of the moment that they don't really mean. And what's the odds of this Grant actually finding the killer before you do? You're the cop. You're the one who has all the training, and while you might not be a detective, you've a great head on your shoulders and you've discussed so many cases with me you're as good as a detective anyway. Go with your gut. Anyway, that's all the pep talk you're getting. I have some information for you.'

'Good. What have you got?'

'We ran all the names and addresses you sent for those on the pleasure cruiser. They all checked out except three. Those three turned out to be false. We checked the databases, they returned nothing. The names didn't match the addresses and in one case the address turned out to be a pub not a house.'

'People live in pubs. They can rent a room.'

'I know, but the pub in question is a proper dive bar with no accommodation. Not even the owner lives there.'

The fingers of Fiona's left hand drummed on her thigh as she thought about what Heather was telling her. 'Nobody pays for anything with cash these days. If you can identify all the card transactions from the people who bought a ticket for the *Each-Uisge* you can cro—'

'Way ahead of you there, Fiona. We've already thought of that. Oban station sent a body round to speak to the woman from the ticket place. She took a look at the payment methods for the *Each-Uisge*. Want to guess what she found?'

'All of the payments were on a card except for three?'

'Correct. There's no CCTV in the ticket office, but we paired up the transaction times with the CCTV footage we were able to get, and we're as sure as we can be that the three cash payments correspond to the people who'd given false names and addresses.' A pause came down the line and then a sigh. 'I'm guessing you're already aware it's the group of three young men who gave false names and addresses?'

'Yeah. I didn't clock it at the time, but there was something off about them. They were too calm, too quiet. It never occurred to me that any of them would give a false address.' Fiona's fingers were drumming ever harder on her thigh. 'However, can we be sure they are the killers? There's every chance they had records, or even warrants out for them for something else. If that was the case then they'd still give me false names, and then do a runner at the first opportunity they got. If they were known to us for something else, the last thing they'd want is for us to involve them in a murder investigation.'

'I hear you, but it sounds very coincidental, and as if you've already got someone in mind as the suspect.'

'I do and I don't. Open mind and all that. However, if the loss of power to the *Each-Uisge* was sabotage, who better to do it than one of the crew?'

'Hang on. You said three cash payments. Are you saying the young men arrived individually?'

'That's right. There were ten minutes between the first two and then another five before the third arrived. All of them had their hoods up and their faces down. We've someone at the CCTV control room going through footage, to see if we can pick them up elsewhere in Oban before they walked along the front to the ticket office, but as things stand, we've not got a clear image of any of their faces.'

'Everything you're saying speaks of planning. This wasn't a spur-of-the-moment thing, it's been planned in detail before they got anywhere near that boat. If the wounds to Tait's groin aren't enough of an indicator he was specifically targeted, what you've told me is.'

'I agree.' There was a slurp as Heather took a drink of something. 'We've requisitioned the cash from the till, and someone's testing it for prints, but you know how flimsy that evidence is. Best-case scenario is that it'll get us their real names and will add to the burden of proof when we finally get to interview them.'

'Mind you...' Fiona wasn't ready to release the idea Tait had been killed by a crew member. 'You know what guys in their twenties are like, they all walk about dressed like that thinking they're cool, even as the sweat's running down their backs. For all we know they'd arranged to meet on the boat.'

'I get what you're saying, but we're still working to find out what their real names are.'

'That's good. When we know more about them, we'll be able to work out if the killer is one of them or one of the crew. What about Tait himself, have you learned any more about him?'

'Not a lot. We've been to his place, it's rented so there's no mortgage in his name. We found plenty of documents such as driving licences and they're all in the name Charlie Tait.'

'Was there anything that might have been of sentimental value? Something too precious for him to leave behind when he started over under a new name? That might give us a clue to his real identity.'

'There was no mention of anything like that. The guys who searched were instructed to look for such things. I've requested someone from Ullapool ask around to see if he's known up there. I found a photo of him online they can use.'

Fiona scratched her ear as she thought. 'You said earlier his back story didn't check out against his employment record. Either he's totally crooked and has a false ID, or, and I don't say this lightly, he's a protected witness who has been given a new identity. What are your thoughts on him?'

'I'm leaning towards a false ID. Someone in witness protection wouldn't buy a boat and then run pleasure cruises off it.

While the odds of them being seen by someone they're hiding from are slim, the amount of pics that end up on social media are bound to have them afraid of their whereabouts being made public.'

Fiona agreed with Heather's assessment. 'What else have you got for me? Did you get a hit on anyone who could be classed as a sexual predator?'

'We've got through about three quarters of the residents. There are no known sexual offenders living on Luing. A couple of complaints were made nine years ago against a man who lives in Toberonochy, but they were looked into and dismissed.'

'What's his name? His address? Does he still live there? What were the nature of the complaints?'

'Whoa. One question at a time. He's Edwin Hamilton. He's been on the island for twenty-six years. He's fifty-seven. Nine years ago a Betty Jamieson made three complaints against him in the space of a month. She didn't think it was right he was chatting to teenage girls. The investigating officer reckoned she was jumping at shadows. His report says Hamilton came across as having learning difficulties.'

'Doesn't sound like much, does it?' Fiona wasn't at all in favour of mob justice, but in a small community like that on Luing anyone who showed any signs of being a sexual predator would soon be run off the island. None of the islanders whom she'd involved in the search for Cait had mentioned Edwin Hamilton, which made her doubt the claims against him. All the same, she got his address from Heather. Better to waste a half hour checking Hamilton out than to dismiss him out of hand and be proven wrong.

'What else do you have?'

'That's it for now. We should have the rest of the islanders checked within an hour or so if you're able to call back.'

'I'll do my best, but no promises.'

As Fiona strode out of the cottage towards her car, she was

making a mental list of everything she must do in order of priority. Right at the top of that list was going to Edwin Hamilton's Toberonochy home and making sure he didn't have Cait. As low as the possibility might be that he was guilty, the sooner she eliminated him as a suspect, the sooner the demons creating images in her mind would lay down their tools.

TWENTY-EIGHT

Fiona saw the lights were on in the church as she passed it. She knew she ought to stop and try asking if anyone had seen what direction the five missing men had taken when they left the group, but the urge to find Cait was stronger than her fears for the rescued passengers.

Like the majority of Cullipool, the houses at Toberonochy comprised rows of aged cottages. The big difference between the two being the sheltered harbour at Toberonochy.

Edwin Hamilton's cottage wasn't hard to find, not when there were only a dozen to choose from. From the size of the garden, Fiona guessed it would have one bedroom. Unlike the neighbouring homes, the cottage's garden was neat grass, with no shrubbery or flowers to add colour.

The door to the cottage was bright blue, and from the light it reflected from a street lamp, Fiona judged it to have been freshly painted. Likewise, the rest of the cottage appeared to be in good order. It meant nothing. Fiona had attended the homes of victims that were little better than a tip and immaculate homes whose inhabitants had committed heinous acts.

No lights shone out of the house. That wasn't a great

surprise considering the hour. Fiona thumped the heel of her hand against the door four times and waited.

There was no answer. None of the windows showed a light being switched on as Hamilton made his way to the door. Fiona banged again. Harder.

A door opened. Not Hamilton's, but the neighbours'. In the doorway stood an elderly woman. She had a flannel dressing gown that hung to her ankles, large glasses and a pinched expression. 'He's no' in. He's out looking for thon wee lassie that's gone missing.' The woman's nose crinkled. 'As you should be.'

And with that, the woman slammed the door behind her.

Fiona could have said a million things in response to the woman's criticism, but in her heart, she could find little argument. All the same, she tried the handle of Hamilton's door.

It opened just as she hoped it would. Those who lived in isolated communities were often blasé about their home security. The general thinking was that they knew their neighbours well enough to trust them. A prime example of this was the way Will had left his keys in the van's ignition while checking out the eco-pods.

It was a nice theory and in instances like this, it played right into Fiona's hands. Without a warrant, nothing she found could be used in court, but at this point Fiona didn't care too much about evidence. She was checking the house for a missing child, or a clue as to whether or not Hamilton was a danger to Cait if he was the one who found her.

Fiona switched the light on as she stepped into the cottage. She was in a short hallway that had four doors leading from it. They'd all lead to the four essential rooms in a home. Kitchen, living room, bedroom and bathroom.

A rack by the door held two pairs of trainers, dirty work boots and a pair of wellies. Fiona lifted a welly and looked at its sole. It was a size eight. The same as she reckoned had made the footprint that overlapped Cait's in the cave.

The first door Fiona opened led to the living room. There was all the usual furnishing. TV, sofa, coffee table and a battered recliner.

It was the stack of magazines on the coffee table that both interested and repulsed Fiona. She lifted the pile and counted eleven magazines that were aimed at teenagers. Specifically teenage girls. Fiona saw some of them had corners of their pages folded as bookmarks. When she followed the bookmarks, the pages they held depicted images of teen girls modelling skirts and dresses. On the mantelpiece, right in the centre where a clock usually sat, there was a picture of a girl in a dress. It was an old picture, Fiona could tell that from the style of the girl's hair and the clothes she wore. To have such a pride of place the picture must be precious to Hamilton. Fiona's best guess was that it was taken in the eighties, and the girl was someone Hamilton had been sweet on.

Bile rose in Fiona's throat as she contemplated Hamilton's fascination with teen girls. Cait wasn't yet close to being a pre-teen, but that didn't make her any less vulnerable to a predator fixated on young girls.

Fiona wasted no time in checking the rest of the cottage. Cait wasn't anywhere to be found, but a laptop plugged in beside the bed told a tale of its own.

When Fiona opened the laptop it became obvious Hamilton's laxity with home security extended to his electronic devices, as she was taken straight to a home screen.

Hamilton's search history was Fiona's first destination. It was there she found links to two kinds of websites. The porn videos, although commonplace, were disturbing enough when she saw a couple featured the female stars dressed as schoolgirls, but when coupled with hundreds of links to images of teen, and pre-teen, girls modelling dresses and skirts, they set off a deafening siren in Fiona's mind. For the first time since Cait had gone missing Fiona's worries for the child crossed from fear to outright terror. If someone with Hamilton's appetites had Cait, Lord alone knew what he'd do to her.

A quick search through the house left Fiona wanting to punch something, or someone. Hamilton would do, many times over.

It was a landline she was looking for. A way to share what she'd found with Heather and those on the mainland. Not that Heather or anyone else could do much to help her, but she had to pass on what she'd learned about Hamilton. If nothing else, it would make damn sure help came at the earliest possible moment.

Protocol forbade using a suspect's personal equipment to communicate with other officers, but Fiona had a work around; she pulled her mobile from a pocket and hunted until she found Hamilton's router. With the code from the router logged into her phone, she accessed her email account and fired off a brief report to Heather.

Fiona took a look out of the kitchen window. There was a shed in the garden so she padded out the back door and along the weed-free path. She'd snapped her collapsible baton out and held it ready to strike.

The shed was full of gardening tools, and empty of kidnapped girls.

Fiona went back through the cottage, switching off every light she'd put on. There was no knowing when Hamilton would be back, and the fewer signs of her entry she left, the better.

With her mind working overtime, Fiona's priorities had again changed and with what she'd learned about Hamilton, she put finding him on the same level of urgency as finding Cait.

As she didn't know what Hamilton looked like, the neighbour's cottage had to be her first stop.

The neighbour opened the door in seconds, but before Fiona could speak, an accusing finger was pointed in her face. 'I saw you. Saw the lights you put on in Edwin's house. You went through it, didn't you? I've seen *Line of Duty*. That's an illegal search, that is. Don't you think you'll be doing the same in my house. Now be off with you. You'll not find that wee lassie here.'

'It's not just her I'm looking for. I need to find Edwin Hamilton as well.' No way could Fiona tell the old woman why she needed to find Hamilton. 'It's very important, but I don't know what he looks like. That's why I've had to bother you so late at night.'

The lines around the woman's mouth flattened out as she spoke. 'Why do you need to find Edwin? He's no' the brightest bulb on the Christmas tree, but he's a good man. He's been doing my garden for years and he'll no' take a penny for it.'

'I really can't say. Please, what does he look like?'

'He's got long white hair, right down to his shoulders. I've offered to cut it, but he'll no' let me.'

'How tall is he? What's his build like?' Fiona could do without the side details. Right now, every second counted.

'Near on six foot, and built like a sailor's kit bag, he is.'

Fiona had heard the unflattering term before. Hamilton's body shape was that of a uniform cylinder.

'Do you know which way he went to search for her?'

'Aye. He went down the coast in case she'd gone to look in the rock pools.'

'Thanks for your help.'

Fiona was halfway back to her car by the time the door slammed.

A man who was displaying a keen sexual interest in young girls had travelled south on a path which would have brought him into contact with Cait, if she'd carried on south from the cave and followed the coastline round and back north. That was, if he hadn't already snatched her in the cave.

TWENTY-NINE

Fiona drove out of Toberonochy, her mind a whirlwind of competing thoughts. At the junction to Blackmill Bay she parked the car, and sat with the engine idling as the gale rocked the car. The movement did nothing to calm the maelstrom of her mind and she knew that's what she needed most.

It would be easy to rush south searching for Hamilton. Easier still to charge about like a headless chicken hunting for Cait.

Cold hard logic told Fiona that all she had against Hamilton was circumstantial suspicions garnered from evidence uncovered during an illegal search. So far as Fiona was concerned, logic could go hang. Everything she'd seen in that cottage screamed of Hamilton's fascination with young girls. While Hamilton may have never been known to assault a minor, Cait's disappearance gave him a gilt-edged chance if he was the one to find her. The thought of Cait in his hands was all that Fiona needed to throw everything she had into finding the child.

Rather than rush into another mistake, Fiona sucked deep breaths into her lungs and forced herself to think with as much clarity as she could muster. Deek and a farmer were searching down this coast. As Fiona scanned the southern part of the island, she could see lights flashing back and forth. Sometimes they were the bright glare of halogen headlights and at others they were the pinprick of torches. Back and forth the lights traversed as Deek and the farmer stuck to their task.

If he'd possessed one, and there had been a mobile signal worth a mention on the island, Fiona could have called Deek's mobile and asked him to also look out for Hamilton. If she could get a fix on his whereabouts, she'd be able to arrest the man then cross-examine him in the hope of finding out if he'd taken Cait, and if so, where he'd hidden her. Even if Hamilton said nothing, the place where he was found would give a focal point to the search for Cait.

Fiona wanted to trust the islanders to do the right thing. To search for Cait with decency in their hearts, but a new idea was kicking down the door of her fears, and it was one she was loath to allow into her mind.

Coupled with what she'd found in Hamilton's cottage and the way Deek had stared at her chest earlier, plus the grab of her backside, Fiona couldn't help but wonder how much sexual frustration and deviancy may exist on Luing. The island was small enough to have limited opportunity for its inhabitants to meet potential conquests, and she'd seen enough of the islanders to recognise a tight-knit community.

If Fiona had received Deek's scrutiny when she was glammed up for a night out, she'd have thought a lot less of it. But soaking wet, with bedraggled hair, no make-up, and what was sure to be stress all over her face, Fiona knew she was a long way from her best. And Fiona was a realist, even at her best she wasn't especially pretty, nor did she have the kind of figure that attracted attention. When she went out with Heather, it was her friend who guys hit on first.

Fiona's fingers drummed on the steering wheel as she worked through darkening thoughts. Maybe the woman who'd reported Hamilton had it right and a portion of the other islanders were covering for him. Maybe Hamilton wasn't the only one on the island whose tastes lay in that direction. Was the woman who'd complained about Hamilton the one sane voice? Ought she speak to that woman to get the truth about what the residents of Luing were really like?

As unpalatable as these ideas were, Fiona recognised sitting isolated in the dark as she was, it was easy to jump at shadows of the mind. Despite all the depravity and unthinkable acts Fiona had encountered as a cop, she retained her faith in humanity, still believed the vast majority of human beings knew right from wrong and would invariably make the correct moral decision.

It was this belief that allowed Fiona to process the bad days and rejoice in the times when humanity shone bright. The belief shepherded Fiona's mind away from the darkest mental images and allowed her clarity of thought.

The islanders and tourists had been searching for Cait for almost seven hours now. Other than what she herself and Deek had found in the cave, there had been no sign or sighting of Cait. That meant one of four scenarios was at play. The first was the best option, it saw Cait, lost and hungry, wandering about the island trying to find a grown-up who'd return her to her parents. The second was that Cait had hurt herself, a twisted ankle or perhaps even a broken leg and was unable to respond to the lights and horns of the searchers. She'd have an uncomfortable night, but the temperature was high enough for exposure not to be a credible threat to her. The third option was that Cait had found somewhere to hole up for the night and had fallen asleep. With the gale blowing as hard as it was the horns of searching vehicles would only be heard downwind, and even then, the howling of the wind was likely to drown them out. The fourth option was the one Fiona least wanted to be true, it saw Cait in the hands of someone intent on doing her harm.

Someone like Hamilton. The first three scenarios were all by far more palatable.

Fiona worked through potential ideas for Cait's whereabouts in her mind and settled on a new theory. If Cait had continued south from the cave, rounded the southern point of the island and started coming back north, it was possible she'd passed Toberonochy before Hamilton had set out looking for her. The neighbour had said Hamilton had been in and out all day and that she'd last seen him going out as darkness was falling. That was a couple of hours ago; more than enough time for Cait to have passed Toberonochy provided she hadn't found something that attracted her interest and delayed her journey. Cait and her family were staying at Sunnybrae Caravan Park, at the north of the island. While a larger island may be big enough for a lost child to wander in circles, Luing was narrow enough that Cait would never have to travel far without encountering a shoreline to help her navigate her way north.

The theory of Cait following the shoreline back to Sunnybrae was one that gave Fiona a hint of hope. If Cait was trekking up the east side of Luing there were few places where she'd encounter houses. According to the map Fiona had got from the Atlantic Islands Centre, there was a hamlet accessed by a gravel track running north-south from a road that began near the place where Will the mechanic had his garage and ended near the Kilchattan kirkyard halfway down the island. The memory of the helpful mechanic compressed Fiona's chest until all she could get were short sharp breaths.

Fiona forced herself to take shallow breaths until her breathing was back under control. As she set off north to find the road, she was trying to put herself into the mind of a headstrong eight-year-old.

To the best of Fiona's thinking, Cait would follow the shore. Not right at the edge because of her fear of open water, and because she'd soon learn it was easier to walk along the grass above the high-water mark than on the fissured rocks and gravel banks closer to the sea. By the same token, Fiona didn't think Cait would stray too far from the shoreline. It was her guide, her one constant reference point, and while Cait might not be old enough to understand the psychology behind her decisions, the desire to keep the sea in view would still affect her decision-making processes.

Where Fiona couldn't second-guess Cait was what the girl would do if she saw the lights of houses shining out from the hamlet. Would she seek the help of adults, or would she continue with her journey alone, more afraid of stranger danger than being on her own in an unfamiliar place at night?

Cait's mother had described her as headstrong and determined. Admirable qualities though they may be, a frightened shrew of a child would never have gone missing the way Cait had. Not that Cait could be blamed for her disappearance. That was merely the product of kids being kids. Although, if Cait had been taken by someone, she wouldn't have had a choice in the matter.

Once again, Fiona felt a pull to head to the church and check on the well-being of those rescued from the *Each-Uisge* before continuing with the search, but she pushed the urge down and steered her car onto the southern end of the track, not only was there a potential paedophile out looking for Cait, but if her thinking about Cait's route was right, Cait was on a course that would take her close to the eco-pods: the very area where Will had presumably been killed by one of the five men who were her suspects for the murder of Charlie Tait.

THIRTY

Gravel rattled against the underside of Fiona's car as she drove along the track. To back up what she'd suggested Deek ought to do, she'd turned on the car's lights and siren. Cait may or may not respond to the blues and twos, but Fiona hadn't switched them on with the sole purpose of attracting Cait's attention. While they may draw Cait's moth to her flame, they'd also warn the killer she was in the area.

Fiona's thinking was that a police presence may just be enough to deter the killer from striking again. Since she'd aided in their rescue from the *Each-Uisge*, they'd know there was a police presence on the island, but what they wouldn't know was how great a one there was. Had the force not had its numbers decimated by illness, there would have been another officer with Fiona. Two was the norm and it was something the public were used to seeing.

Therefore the killers would expect that Fiona had support, and the other officer had been tied up with whatever reason had brought the two of them to Luing. Even the most paranoid killer wouldn't expect a police response before they'd committed their crime. Now, though, they'd killed twice and would be sure to think the blue light was coming for them. In Fiona's mind they'd go to ground. While this may make them harder to find in the longer term, the island was isolated by the gale and when that eased enough for access to and from the island to resume, the police and coastguard could ensure nobody got on or off the island.

The one flaw in this thinking was the killer might choose to take a hostage, and what better hostage than an eight-year-old girl?

Fiona's car skidded on the gravel at a slight bend. As much as Fiona wanted to conduct a slow journey that allowed Cait to see her lights and come forth, she was more concerned with making sure the killer was aware of her presence. Her plan was to blast north until the track ended and then take a much slower return journey south so she could look for Cait, three men walking in a group, and an older and younger man together, or a lone figure with shoulder-length white hair. There was also the possibility of the killer having struck out on their own, so Fiona was alert for any combination of human beings or people travelling on their own.

A part of Fiona wondered if she should raise the alarm so all the islanders locked their doors and kept themselves safe. It was a drastic action and one that could have far-reaching consequences. Cait's family would up their fear levels to catatonic in an instant and in Fiona's mind there was little point adding that level of terror to their already existing worry. The killer or killers had targeted Tait, and so far as Fiona could assume with any degree of certainty had killed Will because he'd found them hiding out at the eco-pods after they'd took off while leaving the Atlantic Islands Centre. A wee girl wouldn't offer them anything close to the threat Will had, and that's what Fiona was banking on.

Should Fiona decide to raise the alarm, she'd have to knock on doors to spread the word. There were at least eighty properties on Luing and they were spread out across the northern two thirds of the island. To visit that many people and deliver her message would take hours, hours that would be far better spent trying to locate both Cait and the men who'd absconded.

Another possibility of alerting the islanders was the chance of a vigilante group getting together. Island communities were tight-knit. They stuck together and looked out for one another. The residents of Luing might well decide that their best form of defence was attack. If that happened, more people would be at risk, including Pete Yorke, a stranger to the islanders who was out looking for his daughter. A few of the houses may be second homes, but for the most part the homes on islands such as Luing were passed down from generation to generation.

For the time being she reasoned that it was best not to go down the route of warning the islanders as to the killer in their midst.

The same logic Fiona had used to plot Cait's supposed route worked the opposite way for the killer. The nearest point of the mainland was across Cuan Sound to the north of the island, but even when Fiona had crossed hours earlier, the current had been strong and the waters choppy. Now the gale had picked up, those fast-moving waters would be even more treacherous. It made sense the killer would be desperate to escape the island. That they'd make their way down the more sheltered east coast of Luing to look for a boat they could steal. It would be a foolhardy thing to do, but by killing Will, the killer had proven their desperation, and people desperate to avoid detection did foolish things.

Another train to Fiona's thinking was that by illuminating her way along the track in such a conspicuous fashion, she'd be highlighting its existence to Cait, as she was sure the girl would be tired. If not from the late hour or the exertion of a day spent tramping over the island, then a combination of both. Tired people seek out the easiest option and while the track wasn't exactly smooth like a motorway, it would be a lot easier than going across fields or broken shoreline. A further bonus of drawing Cait towards the track was the killer was much more likely to stay away from any kind of roadway, and therefore not encounter the missing girl.

A collection of buildings appeared out of the dark, but it was little more than a farm and a couple of farmworkers' cottages. Fiona kept going, pushing her car as hard as she dared on the uneven gravel track. Other tracks fed from the main one, but Fiona paid them no heed for the moment. They could be investigated more fully on the return journey. Going north was about making her presence known, coming south was when the real searching would be done.

As much as Fiona willed her headlights to pick out a small figure in red leggings and a yellow T-shirt, they didn't. Nor did they uncover anyone else.

On two occasions Fiona saw the flash of torchlight to her right. Each time she slowed and turned the blues lights off for a few seconds, but so far as she could tell, those holding the torches didn't try to signal her back.

When the track met a road near the north part of the island, Fiona turned the car around, wound both front windows down and set off at a crawl. As the car pulled itself along the track, Fiona swept the torch out of one window and then the next. She gave priority to the passenger side as that was where the coast now lay. The car's blue lights helped illuminate the land either side of the track, but no matter how much Fiona strained her eyes, she saw no human shapes.

On and on she trekked, her car doing no more than hauling itself along in a low gear. Back and forth her torch scanned the landscape without success. The car's siren was searing a white-hot pain across the front of Fiona's head, but she didn't turn it off.

A track leading off to the left appeared in Fiona's headlights. She'd counted three on her journey north. Now she was paying greater attention to her surroundings, Fiona realised the curves in the road had skirted around a pond.

Fiona guessed the pond was the site of a former slate mine like the one behind the Atlantic Islands Centre in Cullipool, the arrow-straight track towards the sea being the route the slates had been transported off the island.

This track was rougher than the other, although Fiona wasn't going nearly fast enough for it to be a problem. At the end of the track, there was nothing but beach. Even on the lee side of the island, there were breakers crashing into the shore from a tumultuous sea.

Fiona backed up until she could turn in a gateway and made her way back to the main track and set off south again. The slow crawl of the search was counter-intuitive to her. As much as she knew the search had to be conducted with care and not rushed, so desperate was her need to find Cait so she could get on with the business of catching a killer, all she wanted to do was bury her foot on the throttle so she could fast forward to the part of the day when she either returned Cait to her parents, or found Hamilton and got him talking.

The further she travelled without finding anyone, the more Fiona was unsure whether it was a good or bad thing.

THIRTY-ONE

Another track went left. This time the pond was on the other side of the road, but that wasn't a huge detail. So far as Fiona was concerned, the former mine could be on the moon, so long as she found Cait before Hamilton did.

Instead of petering out to nothing at the shore like the other track, this one aimed straight at a collection of vertical posts that marched out into the waves crashing into the shore. Fiona didn't need to be a detective or archaeologist to work out this was a former jetty.

Off to the right the blue lights atop Fiona's car were being reflected back at her by the once white walls of a crumbling cottage.

Fiona's heart skipped two beats. One, for the hope Cait had chosen the ruin as a place to hole up until morning, and two, in case the killer had chosen it for the same reasons. As Fiona exited the car, she made sure she wore her stab vest and utility belt. Even though she braced herself against it, the wind almost knocked her flat.

A police torch was in Fiona's left hand as she stepped towards the cottage. Her right hand clasped her pepper spray.

When it came to taking on a suspect, the collapsible baton on her belt was the usual go-to tool, but as Fiona feared encountering more than one person, she'd gone with the pepper spray, as a quick blast from it would incapacitate multiple suspects far quicker than a weapon that could only affect one person at a time.

'Cait? Are you in there, Cait? My name is Fiona, and I'm a police officer. I've come to help you get back to your mummy and daddy.'

Even though Fiona spoke the reassuring words in a loud but friendly voice, they felt hollow to her.

No answer came. No slight figure crept into a doorway where she could be seen.

It wasn't a surprise to Fiona. Not only would her words be whipped away towards the mainland by the wind, if they were heard, they may not be trusted. Cait's state of mind wasn't something Fiona could begin to accurately guess at, having never met the girl, but it stood to reason that she'd be scared. Either of strangers, or the reaction of her parents when she was returned to them.

After a scan of the area to make sure the killers weren't sneaking up on her, Fiona cast her torch at the cottage's crumbling walls. The roof had long ago rotted away and the walls were no longer at their original height, but there was enough wall left for Fiona to see where the door and windows had once been. Rather than step into the dark space without first checking it out as much as she could, Fiona approached the gap of a former window and used it as a way to scan the insides of the cottage. There were two rooms. Both with grassy floors, exposed stone walls – and no human beings.

Fiona exhaled and turned her attention to the surrounding area. When she'd done her quick sweep, the far reaches of her torch had picked out other ruined structures. One to the south of the line between the track and the jetty, and three to the north.

The cottage to the south was so ruined Fiona's torch had scanned its every corner before she got within twenty yards of it. When she turned north Fiona saw the three structures in greater detail. The closest two were thoroughly dilapidated, their walls less than two feet high.

It was the closest one that held Fiona's attention. Of the five cottages, it was in the best repair by a long way. A roof still rested on its walls, although Fiona could see it was nothing more than bare wood, its slates having long ago been removed by human hands or winter storms.

The rotting remains of windows and a door cluttered the holes in the cottage's walls. As a place to shelter, or hide out, it was perfect. Fiona stalked forward, heart racing and every nerve in her body jangling with anticipation of what she might find.

As before, she approached the window after a scan of her surroundings. Off to the side the police car's blue lights flickered, at times reassuring, at others blinding.

Fiona's torch illuminated the inside of the cottage. It was dank and unwelcoming, with patches of the old lath and plaster hanging from the walls like a bad case of psoriasis. This cottage was larger than the others and, from where she was, Fiona could only scan one room.

The door resisted Fiona's efforts to open it. Whether a human had shot an old bolt across or a shift in the building had jammed it, there was no way Fiona was getting through the door without tools.

With a swallow, Fiona stepped back to the window, did another scan of her surroundings. She leaned her upper body through the opening and repeated the entreaty she'd sent Cait a few minutes ago.

Again there was no answer.

No wonder, the exposed sarking gave the wind something to rail against. A solid item to whistle through.

Fiona gave up with reassuring tones and took in a deep breath before raising her voice to a yell. 'Cait. I'm a police officer. Come out if you're in there.'

Nothing happened, so Fiona made a decision.

The windowsill was too high to step into the cottage, so Fiona opted for a less glamorous method and leaned through the gap until she could drop her torch and collapsible baton the remaining foot to the floor and then slid her way in until she could walk her hands forward. In the open, pepper spray was the best way to incapacitate opponents, but if she discharged any from the canister in a confined space, the pepper spray would affect her as much as her targets.

As much as it pained her injured shoulder, Fiona executed the move in record time. At the back of her mind was the thought the killers could be lying in wait for her, so she made sure the first thing she picked up was the baton.

Fiona's torch swept back and forth, but landed on no humans. In her mind she could hear Dave Lennox mimicking the swooshing whoosh of a lightsabre every time he used a torch. His love of *Star Wars* was legendary at the station, and many were the times someone would deliberately mix up a *Star Wars* reference with a *Star Trek* one to distract him from whatever his latest grumble was.

As much as she'd never understood the attraction of the franchise, Fiona would have been quite happy to have a lightsabre in front of her as she stepped to the part of the cottage that her torch hadn't yet illuminated.

At a corner, she kept her back against the far wall, just as Sergeant Lennox had taught her. His teachings had been both wise and well-explained. Lennox had instilled in Fiona the principle that in any situation where she may be ambushed, the further she was from where the ambush might come, the better her chances of avoiding the ambush, or mounting a defence against it. Another teaching was that when moving through a potential ambush zone, the quicker she moved, the harder target to hit she'd be.

Fiona stepped into the next room with two rapid strides, her torch flashing at the dark recesses it hadn't yet searched.

A relieved breath gushed from Fiona's mouth as she found no attackers lying in wait for her. It was sucked back in when her torch picked out a child's footprints in the dust on the floor.

THIRTY-TWO

The torch in Fiona's hands cast an unsteady light as she bent to examine the small footprints. At first look they seemed to be the same size as the ones she'd found in the cave, but she needed better proof than just her own recollection.

Fiona retrieved her mobile and compared the footprints in front of her to the pictures of the ones in the cave.

They were different. The ones found in the cave had clear tread marks, whereas the ones in the cottage were much less defined. To Fiona's mind the trainers that had left the footprints in the cottage were much older, their soles worn through use. It crossed her mind that Cait's trek across the island could have added weeks' worth of wear to her trainers, but it didn't seem likely, not when she saw the two prints side by side.

Fiona returned to the window convinced it must have been one of the other kids who'd explored the cottage. Simon had said they were coming this way, and while it looked like there was only one set of footprints in the cottage, she could picture a gang of kids with only one having the nerve to enter the cottage.

Before she climbed back through the window, Fiona cast her torch around. Not for a moment had she forgotten there were five murder suspects on the island, and she was damned if she was going to make it easy for them to attack her.

Two minutes later Fiona was back in her car and setting a course south again. She'd only gone three hundred yards when she encountered a man walking on the road. As her lights picked him out, she saw he was tall and solidly built. A stream of white hair whipped sideways from the man's head, and the sight of him was enough to make Fiona's heart race. Edwin Hamilton was one of the people Fiona was seeking, and while she'd never met him, the figure standing by the track matched the description Hamilton's neighbour had given.

The man stepped off the track as she approached, the torch in his hand pointing at the ground. Fiona appreciated he had the sense not to dazzle her, but the fact his other arm was flagging her down set further alarm bells ringing. The car's lights were encasing the man in flashes of blue, and he'd turned his head to the side.

Fiona reached for the switch that controlled the blue lights. When they were off she wrapped her fingers around the collapsible baton on her belt. One way or another, Hamilton was going to tell her where he'd stashed Cait.

Except it wasn't Hamilton standing by the track. Fiona recognised the man as Pete Yorke, Cait's father.

It was only as she stepped out of the car that Fiona realised just how keyed up she'd been at the prospect of coming face-to-face with Hamilton. Deep in her gut she believed he'd found Cait and had hidden the girl somewhere he could live out his fantasies with her.

'Have you found her?' The question tumbled from both Fiona and Pete's mouths at the same time.

Because of the gale and the noise it was making, they had to stand toe-to-toe to make themselves heard.

Pete's arm extended in the direction of the ruined cottages. His voice cracking as he spoke. 'When I saw your car stop down there for a few minutes I... I feared the worst. I thought you'd found her, and she was... she was dead.'

Fiona had to bite the inside of her mouth before answering. Pete was a mess. She could see he was trying to be stoic, but the effort was taking more out of him than he had to offer. The worst thoughts she was having about the fate that may have befallen Cait were bad enough for her, but if he was having the same ideas, they'd be a million times worse.

'I was checking out some cottages beside an old jetty. Sorry for any scare it gave you. I left the blue light on in the hope she saw it and came forward.'

Pete nodded, his mouth clamped in a tight line. 'Where can she be? We've been searching for hours and other than the foot-prints you found in that cave, there's been no sign of her. And why are you looking up here when she was halfway down the other side of the island?'

It was an unfair question, as he was in this area too, but Fiona explained her theory about Cait following the shoreline back to Sunnybrae at the north of the island.

'That makes sense.' Pete gestured towards the centre of the island. 'Me and my dad have been criss-crossing these areas in case she is trying to get back to the caravan. Where can she be?'

It was a good question and not one Fiona had an answer for. No way could she tell Pete about Hamilton. That would only make matters worse for him. Besides, if he ran into Hamilton on his search, there was every likelihood Pete would attempt to beat Cait's whereabouts out of him.

Fiona had never condoned vigilante action – every scenario she'd envisioned where she'd caught her parents' killers had ended with them in prison – and while it might be a quick route to finding Cait, there was always the slim chance she was wrong and Hamilton wasn't involved in Cait's disappearance. Which-ever of these scenarios unfolded, she'd have no choice but to arrest Pete. Not something she wanted to do.

'Where is she? Where can she be?'

The desperate plea in Pete's tone wrapped a noose around Fiona's heart. She wanted to offer him some form of comfort, but she didn't dare put a false hope forward. Pete was already struggling to hang together, and whatever unfolded, his wife would need him.

As a way to dodge the question, she brought up one of her own. 'Your wife said Cait is headstrong. How headstrong is she? Would she ignore everything you've taught her about not speaking to strangers? Or would she have possibly sought out an adult to help her get back to you?'

'She knows her own mind.' Pete scrubbed a hand over the lower part of his face. 'But I'd like to think she's smart enough to not do that. I get why you're asking, but if she'd done that, wouldn't the adult have brought her back to us by now?'

'Yes.' Fiona tried to keep her face neutral. She'd made a mistake by asking the question and now she had to tread a fine line between conjuring dark thoughts and offering false hope. 'But there's every chance Cait is terrified of the trouble she'll be in for going missing. It could be that whomever she's gone to for help is having to calm her down, maybe they're giving her something to eat.'

'You don't know our Cait. She's only eight, but she's afraid of nothing. Diane can barely handle her now. I spend half my life acting as peacemaker between them, or the bad guy who has to discipline her.' His head sawed. 'Cait is so strong. She's kind, considerate and all that. She's a wonderful kid in every way that you can imagine, but when she thinks she's right, or she's made her mind up about something, she'll argue until she's blue in the face. We've grounded her, taken away her tablet and other such things like TV time. She never bats an eyelid. She just deals with the punishment and then does her own merry thing as soon as she can. God knows what she'll be like when she's a teenager.' Pete's face crumpled. 'Please, please find her. Right now, I'd give anything to deal with all the teenage angst she can throw my way.'

Fiona laid a hand on Pete's shoulder as she looked into his tear-filled eyes. 'I'm doing everything I possibly can. If it's at all within my power to find Cait and bring her back to you, that's exactly what I'll do.'

Pete nodded and turned away, his torch sweeping across the fields towards the sea.

Fiona took the cue and climbed back into her car. As much as she wanted to keep searching for Cait until she found her, she also knew there was a responsibility on her to protect the islanders and tourists from the killer. Plus, she wanted to speak to someone other than Hamilton's neighbour to find out what the locals thought of him.

She'd also had an idea about how to identify the tourists on the island, but there was research she needed to do before she could get that information.

THIRTY-THREE

Multicoloured light emanated from the church's one stained-glass window as Fiona drew to a halt with the car's bonnet facing west, into the wind. When she went to open the car door, the pressure exerted on it by the gale was such that she had to use all her strength to swing it wide enough to allow her to exit the car.

The gale wasn't content with making car doors hard to open. It slammed into every part of Fiona, forcing her to brace herself and actively lean into it so she could walk the twenty paces to the church.

Fiona's breath was ragged from the effort of walking into the wind by the time she opened the church door. The sight she was greeted with didn't help put air in her lungs.

All of those she'd helped rescue were on their feet and waiting for her to enter. Muscles stood by the door, his face grim, but no grimmer than any of the assembled group's faces.

'About bloody time. You can't do this. You do know that, don't you?' Irene's arm swept over the assembled group. 'What you're doing to us all is either false imprisonment, or kidnapping, you and that ape you've got guarding over us. You're going to pay for this, you mark my words. There's a kitchen here but nothing to eat, and tell me, how in the hell are we supposed to get any sleep on these pews when they're nothing but solid wood? You have a duty of care to us; don't you realise that? You should have arranged a hotel for us all. Instead you've been off God knows where. We're lucky to be alive and you treat us like this. I'll be writing to your inspector about this. And the press.'

Fiona's nostrils flared as she stepped forward until she was invading the woman's personal space. 'It's neither false imprisonment, nor is it kidnapping. Any one of you can leave at any time you choose. However, until proven otherwise, you're all suspects in the murder of the *Each-Uisge*'s captain, and your leaving *will* cast suspicion on you. You're right, I do have a duty of care for you. That's why you're here. Because the Atlantic Islands Centre was no longer safe. As for beds and food, I'm sorry but I can't magic them up from nowhere. Your safety is far more important to me than your comfort. Do you honestly think there's a hotel on this island? A hotel with enough vacancies to accommodate you all?' Fiona shot a look at Muscles. 'How many hotels are there on Luing?'

'None.' His face was implacable but Fiona could hear an undertone of mirth in his voice. She guessed it was because she was busy putting Irene in her place and that the woman had been a thorn in his side. 'There's a couple bed and breakfasts, and Sunnybrae Caravan Park. This time of year, I 'spect they'll all be full.'

'Thanks.' Fiona faced the woman again. 'You heard him. What do you expect me to do, magic up a hotel?' Fiona couldn't resist pointing at the altar. 'If you want miracles maybe you should be at the other end of the room talking to someone with a far higher power than I have.'

'How dare you speak to me like that? I'm a taxpayer. I pay your wages. Just you wait until I speak to your inspector.'

'You've complained about me not being here. That's

because I'm on the island to look for a missing child. An eight-year-old girl who's yet to be found. If you want to complain about me, feel free, there's a form on the Police Scotland website for just such things. If you want to go to the press, be my guest, there's islanders who'll testify that I risked my life to save yours. I dare say some of the people in here will do the same. Can you imagine how that'll play out in the press? On social media? My own opinion, that you're an ungrateful cow, will be the least of your problems once the online trolls start commenting.'

'Are you threatening me?' She turned to her husband for support. 'Did you hear that? Her threatening me?'

'Sit down. And, shut up.' Fiona put authority into her words. 'That wasn't a threat, that was a realistic version of what will happen if you go to the press. You heard what Delia said earlier, you even made a comment. You said, and I quote, "Good. She'll be able to catch the man who killed the captain." You can go to the papers all you want, but right now, whether I like it or not, I'm a press darling. Do you really want to see whose side they'll take when they learn I saved your life? When it becomes known you wanted me to put your comfort above the welfare of a missing child?' Fiona aimed a finger at the nearest pew. 'Now, sit, before I arrest you for obstructing a police investigation. That is an actual threat. I'm sure you'll recognise the difference.'

Nobody met Irene's eye as she eased herself down, not even her husband.

It hadn't escaped Fiona's attention that of the islanders she'd asked to help watch over the passengers, only Muscles was present. She'd speak to Muscles in a minute, but first she had to speak to the passengers.

The altar would be a perfect place to speak to the assembled group and observe their reactions, but the last thing Fiona wanted to do was assume the role of preacher. Instead she cleared her throat and waited until she had their attention.

'I'm sorry about the lack of facilities here, folks. I really am. But there isn't a lot I can do about it. Once morning comes and the gale passes, there'll be other officers joining me. As soon as we can we'll get you somewhere more comfortable, get you something to eat.'

Delia, who'd been the final passenger to leave the *Each-Uisge* looked around her, and then leaned forward to place her liver-spotted hands on Fiona's arms.

'You saved all of us. A few hours of discomfort isn't a problem. Go, find that little girl. And find the killer. That's your job. You're a police officer, not a nursemaid. And don't worry, that fat woman might have the loudest voice, but she's not speaking for me.'

'Thank you.' The words almost caught in Fiona's throat as she spoke.

After so many hours of stressing about Cait, and the killer running loose, it had been all she could do not to tear into the large woman. And as so often happened, it was an act of kindness and understanding that came closest to piercing her emotions.

Fiona led Muscles right to the door before she spoke to him.

'I need to speak to someone called Edwin Hamilton. He's not at home. Do you know where I might find him?'

Muscles glanced at the ceiling for a second. 'Nah. I've no idea where he'll be.'

'What's he like? Is he a decent guy?'

'He's all right, but he's dolly dimple.'

Muscles' derogatory rhyme for simple was one Fiona had heard before, although she'd never liked such cruel slang. However, if her fears about Hamilton's intentions were on the money, his lack of intelligence could lead him to not have the same understanding of right and wrong. It wasn't a thought that sat well with Fiona and she knew she had to find Hamilton as soon as she could.

'Okay, what about Grant and the other guy? Fergus, isn't it? Why aren't they here with you?'

'Aye he's Fergus. He's away with Grant, they're cousins.'

Fiona began to feel a ball of dread growing in her stomach. 'Where have they gone?'

The answer Fiona wanted to hear was that Grant and Fergus had gone to get food or bedding for the passengers, or that they'd decided to join the search for Cait. Either of those options would be fine, but it was another option that she feared hearing.

'They've gone to find Will.' Every part of Muscles' face tightened. 'And then they're going to look for whoever killed him.'

Fiona ran out of the church and let the wind propel her sprint to the police car. She had to stop Grant and Fergus from disturbing a crime scene, or committing murder, and then she had to get back to searching for Cait, Hamilton and the missing five men from the *Each-Uisge*.

THIRTY-FOUR

The one beauty of the darkness was that Fiona could tell from the lack of headlights coming her way there was no other traffic on the road. It meant she could increase her speed and get to the skip by the eco-pods a lot faster than she could have if it were daylight. Or it would have if she'd not feared rounding a tight corner or cresting a blind summit to encounter a little girl walking in the middle of the road.

As unlikely as Fiona thought it was that Cait would now be walking along the road, she didn't dare take the chance in case she was wrong. The lights and siren were back on, but now for their designated purpose rather than as a beacon to attract Cait.

Grant had earlier said she'd need a body bag for Will's killer if he found him before she did. While Fiona had at first believed Grant, she'd later dismissed his words as an emotive threat, spoken with far more venom than actual intention. That was another mistake she'd made. She ought to have stuck with her initial impression that Grant planned to be true to his word.

Neither Grant nor Fergus were the largest of men, but they both had a certain power to them and if Grant was half as angry as Fiona thought he was, he'd take a lot of stopping. The killer had at least one weapon and they were prepared to use it with deadly force. The fates of Charlie Tait and Will proved that. The killer could either be alone or in a group of two or three. If it was the group of three and they each carried a weapon, it was likely Grant and Fergus would be killed, or severely injured. Should the two men overpower any of the three and get a hold of a knife, Grant's desire to exact a biblical toll may well happen.

Whichever of these scenarios came to pass, Fiona had to prevent Grant and his cousin finding the killer. The one good thing she had working in her favour was how the gale and the darkness made searching the island far harder than better weather would have.

As Fiona steered the car onto the track leading down to the eco-pods, she had a clear plan in mind. Find Grant and Fergus, stop them from taking revenge and then carry on with her searches for the killer and Cait. It sounded simple, but before she could do that she had to find Grant and Fergus. The last thing she needed was another two people to scour Luing for.

Fiona rounded the corner at the bottom of the slope and swore when she saw what her headlights had revealed. She drove forward until she was in front of the debris beside the skip. The last time she was here, the debris was in the skip, not beside it.

As much as the gale raged around her, it was the thumping of her own heart Fiona could hear loudest as she approached the skip. It took no more than a brief glance for her torch to confirm her suspicions. Will's body was no longer in the skip.

For a brief second Fiona thought she'd got her diagnosis wrong, that Will had been wounded and dumped in the skip to die rather than after he'd died. When Fiona remembered checking Will for a pulse and not finding one, she recognised her desire to believe she'd mistaken the severity of Will's stabbing was fuelled by wishful thinking.

The removal of Will's body from the skip was understandable if done by one of two groups of people. Grant and Fergus wouldn't want to see Will lying among rubble and rubbish from a building site. Nobody wanted that for a loved one.

On the other hand, and this theory sent a prickle running up and down Fiona's spine, it could be the killer had hidden themselves earlier and watched her discover Will's body. If that was the case, they could have decided to hide the corpse to limit their culpability.

Whomever had moved Will, they would have disturbed a lot of forensic evidence. Worse, they'd have contaminated the scene just by being there. Fiona had worn gloves when she'd pulled the debris covering Will aside, but her hair had whipped in the wind, and knowing what she did about forensic protocol, she knew she was bound to have left some trace of herself behind.

Once again, Fiona drew the pepper spray from her utility belt. She had one thing left to check before she left the eco-pods and began another search of the island.

Fiona stepped forward until she was looking at the narrow road in front of the eco-pods. She found what she expected to find. Will's van was no longer where it had been parked.

As she'd worked out earlier, the van would be the perfect vehicle to move Will's body. Either Grant had claimed it to take Will home, or the killer had used it to dispose of his body.

Grant and Fergus had both been in Cullipool when she'd first gone there, so logic dictated that's where they'd live. It's where she planned to look for the missing van first.

In Fiona's mind, the best place for the killer to dispose of Will's body would be the sea. The way the tides and currents were with the gale behind them, the corpse may never be seen for days, or maybe ever. The problem with this for the killer was the van would collect evidence from them as they used it. The simple way to deal with this was to burn the van out, but a better way would be to run the van into the sea with Will's body behind the wheel, as a burning van would draw attention as soon as it was seen.

All of the current harbours and docks on the island had a house, cottage or hamlet beside them. But the two tracks she'd followed down to the sea were ideal places where the killers could jam Will's foot onto the throttle so he'd drive the van into the sea. So long as he remained undiscovered, they'd have a chance to leave the island and disappear.

Apart from one thing. If they *had* witnessed Fiona discovering Will's corpse, they'd know their crime was recorded. Fiona's phone had flashed when she'd taken pictures of Will in the skip. If it was the killer who'd moved Will's body, Fiona could see only one way for them to be sure to keep his murder quiet until they left the island. Kill her.

THIRTY-FIVE

As she made her way into Cullipool, Fiona's headlights swung out across the seas. What she saw was a maelstrom of waves curling and crashing. Spray was being blown sideways until it battered up onto the shore. In some areas the road was damp from the spray's furthest reaches, and at one point a mass of roiling froth slammed into the side of her car with enough force to rock it sideways.

Fiona gritted her teeth and kept going. The road hooked right in a ninety-degree bend and when Fiona saw a white van parked outside the one cottage that had lights on she let out a relieved sigh. The van was Will's, therefore the cottage would either also belong to Will, or it would be Grant's home. Either way, the fact it was Grant and Fergus who'd moved Will's corpse was a blessing. It meant there was less of a direct threat to her than had Will's killer moved it.

To try and find shelter from the effects of the gale, before parking Fiona drove past the cottage until the road turned again.

The cottage Fiona parked beside offered little shelter

against the wind, or so Fiona thought until she stepped onto the short street where Will's van was parked.

Funnelled as it was between the two rows of sturdy cottages, the wind was even stronger here, and the only way Fiona could walk into it was to lean so far forward she was in danger of falling on her face if the wind eased.

The wind didn't ease, instead it made every step a slog and at one point as Fiona was in mid-stride, a stern gust pushed her back two paces before she could do anything about it. Had she not been about to pass a window that was spilling light onto the road, Fiona would have taken the easy option and dropped to her hands and knees to travel the last few yards.

As she passed the van, Fiona glanced through the window and saw that a space had been cleared in the back. Will's body wasn't there and she guessed it would now be lying on a bed in the cottage.

Fiona's knock was answered within five seconds.

Fergus stood in the open door, his face showing no sign of apology. 'You'd best come in.'

The cottage was bedecked with framed pictures of Scottish scenery. Fiona recognised the Falls of Dochart at Killin, Eilean Donan Castle and McCaig's Tower at Oban, among others.

Fergus herded Fiona into a small kitchen where Grant stood with his back to the worktop. At the table sat a couple who were both looking into the tumblers of whisky in front of them. Neither looked up. Their hair was white and from the styling of their clothes, it required no great feat of deduction to work out they were Will and Grant's parents.

The woman was sniffing into a paper handkerchief, while the man kept wrapping his fingers around the tumbler of whisky and then releasing it.

Fiona recognised their pain. She'd felt the same debilitating numbness after learning of her parents' murders. The five stages of grief were a real thing and she'd gone through them all. The denial, where no matter how she tried, she couldn't accept the tragic news. That had sat with her a long time. When anger had arrived, it had been more intense than anything she'd felt before or since. Fiona had raged against the world for a time, and had it not been for Aunt Mary's loving care, she would have never been able to let go of the cold fury that enveloped her every waking thought.

Will's parents had a long road ahead of them. They'd try bargaining with whichever deity they believed in, wallow in depression, and finally find a form of acceptance.

Fiona had travelled that road, it was a journey made all the more arduous because of the way her grief had been instigated. Yet she'd never had the closure that came with the knowledge her parent's killers had faced justice. As she looked down on Will's mother and father, she made a silent vow to herself to do everything in her power to make what amends she could to the devastated family for her part in their loss. Whatever it took, whatever she had to do to atone, she'd bring Will's killer to justice.

All Fiona wanted to do was embrace the couple and draw their pain from them like a salving balm. It was beyond her; beyond any mortal human. Fiona knew that better than anyone and she'd had the very best in Aunt Mary.

'Mr and Mrs Nichol, I'd like to offer you my sincere condolences for the loss of your son.' Even to Fiona's ears the words sounded trite and formal. She wanted to do better, to try again and allow them to know how much she too was hurting at Will's murder. Fiona didn't say anything else, though. This wasn't about her and how she felt. It was about the deceased, their family.

The woman didn't look her way, but the old man lifted his head and stared into her eyes before giving her the tiniest of nods.

Grant looked at Fiona, his face a pained mask. 'D'you find him?'

Fiona didn't have to ask who he meant. 'No. I'm sorry. I looked, but I was also looking for the girl who's gone missing.' Even to her it sounded like she was making excuses.

'I told you before. I'll kill him if I find him. I promise you I will.'

The promise from Grant brought a howl from his mother that cut through Fiona.

Grant's father lifted his tumbler of whisky an inch then slammed it down, the action sloshing a healthy slug of Scotland's finest onto the table. 'You'll do no such thing. I'll not hear of it. We've lost one son tonight, I'm buggered if I'm losing you to the jail. Do you hear me, Grant?'

'I hear you, but... the bastard who stabbed Will deserves to get a taste of his own medicine. I don't care if I end up in the jail. I'll happily do the time.'

'Aye, an' what about your mother and me? You go to jail for murder, you'll be in there long after we're deid. It's bad enough we've had one son die without another throwing his life away.'

Grant turned his back on the room and faced the worktop with his head bowed and his shoulders bobbing at the sobs he was trying to suppress.

'You, lass.' Grant's father aimed a gnarled finger at Fiona. 'I ken you're on Luing to look for a missing lassie. Grant telt us you asked Will to help you find that wee lassie, and that you think he must have been killed by whoever killed the captain of the *Each-Uisge*. You no doubt blame yourself for Will's murder. I don't want my son to have died for nothing; if you can find that wee lassie, and make sure my son's killer ends up behind bars, neither I, nor any member of my family will blame you.'

'Thank you. I swear I'll make sure Will didn't die in vain.'

'I don't want your promises, they're no use to me. My son was a good man, but he'd lived at least half of his life. He was married until cancer took his wife two years ago. That lassie's got all her life to live yet.' The old man's voice caught as tears formed rivers on his jowls. 'If Will's life has to have any meaning, you can't let that wee lassie's folks hear news like we've heard tonight.'

Fiona's lip trembled as she nodded. There was no way she could trust herself to speak again, not when confronted by the stark grief in the room. The news about Will's wife passing from cancer just added to the sorrow. Will had carried on wearing his wedding ring. She got the reasons why he did that. The watch on her wrist was her father's, and the necklace around her throat her mother's. The wearing of their jewellery kept them close to her, with her at all times. What possession of Will's would his family cling to for succour?

Will's mother rose from her seat, laid a hand on Grant's shoulder. 'You're more use helping find the lass than being here.' When she turned to Fergus, Fiona saw the redness surrounding her eyes. 'You go too. Make sure you bring Grant back. I'll not have my last boy end up in the jail.'

With a grim nod at both of the grieving parents Fiona made her way to the door. How she was going to deliver what she needed to was beyond her, but after the grief she'd just witnessed, she'd die before she gave up.

THIRTY-SIX

As she had a new theory in mind, Fiona drove the short distance from Cullipool to Sunnybrae Caravan Park, at the north of Luing. A place where tourists stayed would provide the best hideout for a stranger in a small community. There was always a chance there would be an unoccupied caravan they'd be able to hole up in, unseen for a few hours, until the storm abated and they could make an attempt to leave the island. As much as she felt compelled to charge around the island looking for Cait and the killer, she had enough sense about her to do whatever she could to conduct a more intelligent search. As well as looking over the caravans for a sign they'd been broken into, she also had another idea at play. So far her investigation into the islanders had turned up one potential suspect if Cait had been abducted. By noting down all the registration numbers of the cars at the caravan site, she could get Heather to check the tourists in case one of them had a red flag against their name.

Grant was in the passenger seat, and Fergus was in the back. Neither had spoken and as much as Fiona understood they'd need time to deal with their thoughts, time wasn't something she had a lot of.

'Are either of you okay to answer a few questions?'

Grant turned his head until he was looking out the passenger window.

'What do you want to know?' To Fiona, the low tone of Fergus's voice held pain, but he was at least speaking to her.

'There's a guy from Toberonochy who's a person of interest with regards to Cait's disappearance. He's not at home and is apparently out looking for Cait. I just wondered if you knew of anywhere he might take her apart from his home.'

'If you told us his name we'd have a chance of helping.'

'It's Edwin Hamilton.'

A snort erupted from the passenger seat, but Grant kept his head away from Fiona.

'What do you know about him, Fergus?'

'He's known as Soft Eddy. He works part time at the farm and part of the time helping the fishermen. But if you think he's got the lassie, you're mistaken, Soft Eddy is like a child who's never grown up beyond his teenage years.'

'What's he like as a person? Is he good, kind? Does he creep anyone out? Does he have a wife or girlfriend? Has he ever had one?'

'He's a simpleton.' Grant's voice was gruff, whether it was residual anger or an attempt to mask his pain, Fiona couldn't guess, but at least he was speaking again. 'He'll help anyone he can. I've never heard tell of him creeping anyone out. If he's ever had a girlfriend it'll be news to me. So far as I know, he's still got the wrapper on. Even the Lynx has always left him alone.'

'The Lynx? Who's that? And why are they called the Lynx?'

It was Fergus who gave Fiona the answers, his tone matter-of-fact. 'The Lynx is how Alison Vivers is known. Every time she sees a younger man, especially ones in their teens and twenties, she's all over them, despite being well into her sixties. Hence the nickname. She's a man-eater.'

Fiona didn't just hear what Fergus was saying, she also heard what he didn't say. Alison Vivers' carnal appetites would be a source of amusement or opprobrium for some, and a rite of passage for others.

There was nothing to be gained by thinking about Alison Vivers as a one-time lover of Edwin Hamilton. Either it had happened, or it hadn't, but she didn't think it would have, after all, both appeared to be attracted to people much younger than themselves.

Instead Fiona's interest in Alison Vivers lay in her attraction to younger men. Four of the five suspects were in their teens or twenties, had she invited them into her home? Or was the woman's reputation more legend than reality? So many times she'd had character assassinations presented to her as gossip or known truths, and then when she'd dug into the facts she'd found isolated incidents had been exaggerated out of all proportion to reality.

'Would you class Hamilton as harmless or dangerous?' Fiona couldn't bring herself to use the nickname Soft Eddy. Nor did she want to say what she'd found in his home and on his laptop.

'He's harmless. Gullible as can be, but harmless. He hasn't a bad bone in his body. How you've got him down as a person of interest is beyond me.' Grant turned to face Fiona. 'But then again, you're hardly Miss Marple, are you?'

Fiona let the barb slide. Regardless of what his father might have said, Grant blamed her for his brother's death. That was fair enough, she too blamed herself.

'Fergus, where does this Alison Vivers live?'

'There's a cottage by Sunnybrae Caravan Park. She lives there and she cleans the caravans between uses.'

This was a piece of good fortune. Fiona wanted to speak to

someone regarding the site and now she could also check Vivers hadn't taken in the missing men.

With Fergus pointing it out, Fiona found the entrance to the caravan park without any trouble. A pair of cottages sat on the right against the bank, with a central road snaking between two rows of static caravans.

Fiona drove between the first two caravans and pulled to a halt. A minute later, she had the registration numbers of the cars parked by the caravans noted down. In less than ten minutes, she had the registration numbers of every car in the site listed. It was potentially a waste of time, but if there was someone with a history of sexual offences against minors staying in the caravan park, she needed to know.

'Which is Alison Vivers' cottage?'

'The one on the right, but why do you want to speak to her?'

'I have my reasons.' Fiona didn't dare explain there was a chance one of the missing men from the boat might be in the house, not considering how angry Grant was. As much as Fiona wanted to believe he'd listen to his parents, she'd seen more than her fair share of people ignoring sound advice when gripped by grief and rage.

THIRTY-SEVEN

The woman who opened the cottage door wasn't anything like Fiona had expected. From the way Fergus had spoken of Vivers, it wouldn't have surprised Fiona if Alison Vivers had answered the door in a leopard-print negligee and pink fluffy slippers.

Alison Vivers was decked out in a blue pair of slacks and a crisp white blouse. Her intelligent face had high cheekbones and wine-dulled eyes.

'Mrs Vivers?'

'That's me, how can I help you?' A shadow crossed Vivers' face. 'It's not my sister, is it? You're not here to give me bad news, are you?' There was a hint of a slur in her voice, but not enough to suggest she was too drunk to be worth questioning.

'No, it's nothing like that. I'm here to ask you a few questions, that's all.'

'You'd best come in then.'

The cottage was tastefully decorated and clean enough to double as an operating theatre. Whatever the local men said about her sexual exploits, Vivers took pride in her home.

As Fiona trailed after Vivers to the living room, her eyes were casting into every visible nook and cranny while also sweeping the room for signs Vivers wasn't alone. There was one wine glass on the coffee table. One mug on the draining board and one ashtray resting on a chair arm. The ashtray held only white-tipped cigarettes, each bearing a smudge of the soft pink lipstick Vivers wore.

'First of all, are you here alone, or is there someone else here?'

'Sadly, I'm here by myself. I'd like to say there's a man waiting for me in the bedroom, but there isn't.' A wry grin twisted Vivers' mouth. 'I don't suppose you've a young recruit with you? One you could leave behind for a few hours. I'll be gentle with him, I promise.'

As amused as Fiona might have been about the forward request on another occasion, she had no patience for such nonsense tonight. 'Mrs Vivers, I'm here to discuss a missing child and warn you there is a killer somewhere on the island, not pimp out my fellow officers.'

'I'd heard about the missing child. Has the poor wee soul not been found yet? And what's that about a killer? This is Luing, we don't have killers here. You must have got that wrong.'

'I'm afraid that yes, there is a killer on the island. I would advise you to keep your doors and windows locked after I leave and not to open them to anyone you don't know *extremely* well.' It was all Fiona could do to keep the snarl off her face, but she didn't have enough in her to keep it out of her voice.

Vivers' face was now contrite. 'Okay, I'll take you at your word. Why are you here to see me?'

'I learned you work as a cleaner on the Sunnybrae site. Do you have a list of who's staying in each of the caravans?'

'No. I get an email every Sunday telling me which caravans I need to clean on which days.'

'How do the guests get keys to the caravans? Do you hand them out, or does someone else?'

'The caravans all have combination locks. The guests get the combinations as part of their welcome email.'

'Fair enough. Do you know if all the caravans are currently occupied?'

'Aye. At this time of year they're always full.'

'I see. Do you have much to do with the guests of the site?'

Vivers shook her head, tumbling silver hair across her shoulders. 'No. I try to keep my distance from them, otherwise I end up getting pestered to death. Directions to places, ferry times. Someone once knocked me up in the middle of the night to ask what time the shop opened.'

Fiona could sympathise with that aspect of the woman's life. As a cop she'd been asked all manner of inane questions by a public who treated her like an information booth.

'What do you know of the current residents? What have you noticed about them? Are there any of them who've maybe creeped you out in any way?'

'From what I've seen, there's two or three families. A few older couples and a bunch of guys in their fifties. I think they're in number five.'

Fiona recalled seeing caravan five. As well as a car, there had been a trailer with four kayaks strapped to it. The bunch of guys may well be a collective suspect in Cait's disappearance, but Fiona didn't think it likely. As a rule, paedophiles tended to commit their heinous attacks alone, so for there to be a group of them operating together in such a remote place seemed improbable. On the other hand, paedophile rings existed and it was more than possible that a group of them had decided an isolated place like Luing would make a perfect hunting ground. Whatever the case may be, Fiona was experienced enough to recognise the dangers of tunnel vision when concocting theories.

'That's good. You're doing well.' It never hurt to compliment witnesses. 'You never mentioned how they made you feel.

Did any of them make you feel uneasy? You know, gave you the shivers or something like that.'

Again, Vivers shook her head. 'Not at all, but one of the guys with his family seemed withdrawn. Normally you see the dads playing football or something with the kids, but this guy never seemed to interact with his family at all. He just carried the stuff in. I've seen him a few times, standing outside his caravan. Not smoking or fiddling with his mobile, just standing there looking around.'

'Do you remember which caravan he was in? Can you describe him?' Fiona gabbled the questions as her mind was racing with possibilities. It could be this man was just slow to unwind from his daily life. There could be marital problems and he was struggling to put on a jolly face. Another thought Fiona had was that he might be a mother's new boyfriend and the kids hadn't warmed to him. Maybe a holiday on Luing was his idea of hell, and he didn't have the good graces to pretend otherwise. All of these could be possible reasons for him being withdrawn, but it could also be that he was planning something more sinister. More than any other factor, Fiona's senses were jangled by the man's habit of standing outside the caravan looking around.

As scenic as Luing, the surrounding islands and mainland might be, the caravan site wasn't in a place where the views were the most spectacular ones Luing had to offer. It was, though, in one of the island's more sheltered parts. From what she worked out of where Vivers would have been able to see the man, he would have been standing at the front of his caravan by the road between the rows to be in her eye line. Fifteen paces along the side of the caravan would afford a far more picturesque view. Yet he hadn't made that short trip. He'd just stood there. Fair enough the man might not smoke, and the mobile signal was sketchy enough that he'd be unlikely to access much on his phone, Fiona blamed the weather conditions for her mobile signal being so bad as she knew a lot of islands such as Luing generally had decent coverage, but the man Vivers was telling her about had forgone taking a few paces towards a breathtaking view and stood not doing anything bar looking around.

He might, of course, have been thinking. With no distractions, the man might have stepped outside the caravan for no other reason than to clear his head. That was a reasonable assumption, but with a missing child who by rights ought to have turned up by now, Fiona was rapidly approaching the point where she was ready to think the worst of everyone. What if the man wasn't clearing his head? What if he was scheming? What if he was standing outside the caravan so he'd become a familiar face? Kids tended to trust adults they knew, or who were at least familiar. Had the man been standing outside his caravan so that when he got a chance to snatch Cait, or another child who found themselves alone, they'd come within his reach?

'It was number seven. He's a big beggar. Tall too, with a ponytail.' Vivers' mouth twisted. 'Sorry, when I saw he was in his thirties, I didn't pay him much attention.'

'Do you have a contact number for the person who owns and operates the site?'

Vivers got a pen and paper and jotted down a number from memory. 'That's the main office, but it'll not be open until nine tomorrow morning.'

'Thanks, you've been very helpful.'

Fiona knew coincidence often made a mockery of statistics and trends, but she didn't think the odds of there being another man who matched Pete Yorke's description staying at the same small caravan site as the Yorke family were high enough to factor into her thinking.

The more Fiona considered her earlier thoughts about the man's reasons for standing outside the caravan against the description of the man who sounded very much like Pete Yorke the more she was kicking herself. A seasoned detective would have known to learn about the family dynamic. To look for things other than a child's stubborn nature that might be behind Cait's disappearance.

Pete Yorke's behaviour in standing outside the caravan now took on a dozen more sinister forms in Fiona's mind. She had to get more information. One way of getting that was to speak to Cait's mother, another was to get Heather to do some digging.

Fiona voted for the easy option. Diane Yorke was antagonistic towards her. That it was down to terror at Cait's disappearance was understandable, but Fiona wouldn't win any favours by cross-examining the woman about her husband. Besides, Fiona told herself, she also needed to check in with Heather anyway. The number plates needed matched to their owners, and she wanted to check if there was anything Heather had for her. With luck, her friend would have unearthed something that would help her find at least one of the parties she was looking for.

THIRTY-EIGHT

Deek's cottage was in darkness when Fiona approached it, and his pickup was nowhere to be seen. This was a bad sign; if he hadn't returned, he hadn't found Cait. That would be the best news she could hear.

With the layout of Deek's cottage in her mind, Fiona made sure to park outside the living room window.

'I need to call the mainland, can I trust you two to wait here while I make the call?'

'We'll be here.' Fergus' voice was a low rumble like a distant peal of thunder.

Grant snorted his agreement, his gaze straight ahead.

Fiona wasted no time getting into the cottage and putting a call in to Heather. From the window she could see Grant sitting in the police car. She knew she didn't have a lot of time. Grant and Fergus wouldn't wait long. Either they'd head round the corner to check in with Grant's folks, or they'd head out on their own search. Whether the wishes of Grant's parents would hold enough sway they'd look for Cait rather than the killer was anyone's guess.

Heather answered on the second ring. 'DC Andrews.'

'It's me. I have a list of things for you to check out.' Fiona recited all the number plates she'd listed at the caravan site. 'Don't just check out the owners, check the immediate family, anyone who may be travelling with them. Also, I need you to take a deep dive into the family of Cait Yorke.'

'Will do, and why do you want the family checked out even further? What's jangled your antenna?'

Fiona explained her suspicions about Pete Yorke in as concise a fashion as she could. Heather's only comment was a low whistle.

'Okay, Heather, that's it from me, what have you got?'

'We've already took a close look at the family as it's standard procedure. Pete Yorke is Cait's biological father according to her birth certificate. He married Cait's mum nine months after Cait was born. There's been no concerns about him raised by any of the welfare agencies, and none by the school. If what you're thinking is right, it's either something new, or extremely well covered up.'

'Try digging deeper if you can. What else have you for me?'

'Edwin Hamilton, I showed your email to DI Baird, and she told me to tell you that finding him is as urgent a priority as finding Cait. Just so you know, she did quite a bit of grumbling about the illegal search, but don't worry about that. I'd have done exactly the same in your position. We've also heard from Ullapool. Nobody called Charlie Tait is known to the local crabbers, and the way the investigating officer told it, the people he spoke to have been crabbers for years and all know each other.'

'Did they ask about a former crabber who'd left the area?'

'Of course, nobody of Tait's age was known to have left the industry. There'd been a few younger men who'd work a winter or two then moved on, but that's all.'

'Okay. I take it you've got people doing everything they can to trace his past.'

'Well, duhhh. We've got a team from Glasgow doing that right now. They're doing all they can to find out who he was before he appeared in Oban as Charlie Tait.'

'The mechanic who was murdered.' Fiona drew a breath before continuing; even though Heather was her friend, she was still admitting to something lots of fellow officers, not least DI Baird, would count as a mistake. 'His family went looking for him and moved his body. It's now at the family home in Cullipool. What with the gale and everything, there's little chance we'll ever get any forensic evidence.'

'That's unfortunate.' Now it was Heather's turn to pause. As she waited for her friend to continue, Fiona was preparing herself for the criticism she expected to be aimed her way. No matter that Heather wouldn't say anything as bad as what she'd already thought herself, what she did say was going to hurt. 'But unavoidable. I'm telling you now, Fiona, don't beat yourself up about it. You're there by yourself. What were you supposed to do, abandon the search for the missing girl and the killer so you could guard the crime scene?'

Fiona had gone through the same reasoning, and while it stood up to scrutiny, she had still found a way to find fault with her actions.

'No, but I could have stressed to the family that moving his body might jeopardise our investigation. That we needed to sweep the dump site for evidence before removing his body.'

'Do you think they'd have listened? He was dumped in a skip and covered with building site rubbish. Would you want that for anyone you loved? They wouldn't care about that, and even if they did care for our investigation, they'd probably think the gale would have blown the evidence away anyway.'

'Stop it, Heather. Stop trying to put sauce on shit and tell me it's a sausage. I messed up. Big time.'

'No, you stop it. I'm saying this as a fellow officer as well as a friend. You're in an impossible position, but every second you spend beating yourself up is time wasted. You need to be at the top of your game, there's no doubt about that. So focus on what you can achieve and stop running yourself down.'

Fiona saw the wisdom in Heather's words, but she didn't believe anyone could ever say anything that would take away the guilt she felt for her mistakes.

'I need to crack on, Heather, but there's one last thing I need you to do for me. The woman who made the complaint against Edwin Hamilton. Find out if she's still alive and still on the island. Maybe if I speak to her, she'll be able to tell me where he might be. I'll check back when I can.'

Fiona considered asking the islanders who were helping her about who the woman was and where she might be found, but in the end she decided against it. Communities such as Luing's might know everyone's business, but there was also a lot of family connections and loyalties among them. The last thing she wanted was for anyone to get word to Hamilton she was looking for him. If he had Cait and knew she was searching for him, there was no telling what he might do.

THIRTY-NINE

Fiona put the phone back in its cradle and looked out of the window. Grant was still in the front seat which was something to be thankful for. Her mind was bouncing ideas around like they were tickets in a raffle drum. Every idea was colliding with a dozen others and, as Heather had said, she needed to be at the top of her game. To have an acute focus so her time was spent in the wisest fashion possible.

The searches she'd conducted so far had led to no discoveries. That meant one of two things. Either she'd been searching in the wrong areas, or the people she'd been searching for were actively hiding from her. That made sense with regards to the killer, and if her fears about Edwin Hamilton's intentions were right, he'd be hiding too. While Hamilton might have learning difficulties, he was capable of living by himself, therefore he'd know right from wrong. As for little Cait, Fiona didn't believe she'd be hiding now, not this long after she'd gone missing. Cait would be hungry and scared. As much as she might fear a telling off from her parents, she'd also want to be back in the safe embrace of her family.

Except that embrace might not be so safe.

Pete Yorke was Cait's biological father according to the birth certificate. That counted for a lot, and yet it also counted for nothing to some people. And that was the sugar-coated version of what may happen behind closed doors. If Fiona's worst suspicions about Pete Yorke were right, there was every chance Cait was in hiding too.

As much as Fiona disliked the dark thoughts she was having, she knew she had to conduct her searches on the basis that Cait wasn't hiding from her. She'd scoured the east side of the island down to Toberonochy. Plenty of people were looking in the centre, and Deek was checking the southern end of the island. That left the west coast up from Blackmill Bay, past Cullipool and round the top of the island to the ferry dock at South Cuan.

The west coast of the island was accessed by a gravel track. She was prepared to chance the police car on the track if necessary, but while what she'd seen of the track suggested the car would be okay, there was no telling what it was like further from the tarmacked roads.

Fiona climbed back into the police car and gunned the engine.

'Where to now, Miss Marple?'

The barb from Grant was expected, so it didn't sink deep. 'We're going to look down the west coast of the island. I saw a track near the shop.'

'You'll need a four by four. This car won't get half a mile.'

'Then we'll go as far as the car will take us and walk the rest.' No way was Fiona going to allow Grant's objections to stop her doing what she believed was best for Cait.

'Good luck with that. The way the wind is, you can hardly stand straight. Take me to Will's garage. There's an old Land Rover there. He was doing it up as a pet project. It won't be comfortable, but it'll get us where we need to go.'

'Thank you.' Fiona didn't miss the way Grant's voice went

from scornful to pained as he spoke about the use of his brother's Land Rover.

When Fiona pulled into the garage's yard, the headlights of
her car picked out the Land Rover. It was an ancient model that
had a cab and an open load bed at the back. There may have
once been a canvas awning covering the load bed, but there
wasn't now.

Grant let himself into the garage building and emerged with
a set of keys in his hands. Instead of handing the keys to Fiona,
he strode to the Land Rover, where Fergus was already feeding
himself into the passenger seat.

'When you get on the track keep blaring the horn, and don't
go too fast. We need to do as thorough a search as we can.'

The look from Grant told Fiona she'd best say nothing
more. She clambered into the back of the Land Rover, sat on a
wheel arch and clamped her left hand around a hitching hook.

The Land Rover started with a tremendous rumble and
were it not for the cleansing effect of the wind, Fiona was sure
the vehicle would have been shrouded in a cloud of black
smoke.

Grant set off and the Land Rover rumbled forward, its
motion a series of jerks and crunches as Grant fought with the
aged gearbox.

When they left the track, Fiona cast her torch towards the
shore in a series of arcing sweeps as Fergus did the same. Every
minute or so a pothole would jolt the Land Rover, bouncing
Fiona on the unforgiving wheel arch. She knew the two men
had deliberately worked it so she was in the back and would
have an uncomfortable ride. They couldn't know the left arm
she was using to brace herself was on fire due to the fall by the
cave, or that the way she was looking into the wind dried her
eyes out to the point she had to keep blinking moisture into
them.

The discomforts were something Fiona vowed never to

complain about. They were a penance for her enlisting Will in a task that led to his death.

As the Land Rover travelled further from the road, the track became rougher. The jolts that had been infrequent now came with the regularity of a clock ticking. At one point when the Land Rover's nose was pointing up a crest, Grant let the vehicle slow to a halt and then crunched something in the gearbox. Fiona guessed he'd engaged the four-wheel drive, as the aged Land Rover hauled itself up the slope without any drama.

It was when they crested the slope that Fiona noticed a difference. Instead of staggered blasts of the horn, Grant was letting out a long blare.

He was trying to get someone's attention and he certainly got Fiona's. She turned her head so she was looking forwards, the wind whipping tendrils of hair across her face. A couple of hundred yards ahead was a light.

Not the piercing glow of headlights, but the pinprick of a torch. The torch was held in a steady hand and it was aimed at the Land Rover.

Fiona recognised the thumping in her chest as hope. The fervent desire that whoever held the torch aimed their way was signalling that they'd found Cait. She wanted Grant to gun the throttle, to race the Land Rover to the person with the torch. However much the sprint might beat her up, it would be worth it to find Cait.

Grant just kept the vehicle plodding forward. He was right to do so. Deep within her Fiona knew that as she turned back to her task of scanning towards the shore. If Cait wasn't with the torch carrier, there was a chance they'd miss her if they stopped their search as they connected with whoever held the torch.

Where before Fiona had been grateful for the slow pace of the Land Rover, she now cursed it as her torch failed to find anything but grass, reeds and rocks.

Fiona kept shooting glances over the cab to check the proximity of the torch. Whomever held it had no qualms about dazzling those in the Land Rover. All Fiona could see was the light arcing their way. It cloaked the identity of its user and when Grant finally stopped the Land Rover and left the engine idling, she had to shield her eyes against the torch's glare.

The person wielding the torch switched it off and stepped into the beams of the Land Rover's headlights. At first Fiona thought it was Pete Yorke again, but when the man turned to show his face she realised it wasn't him she was looking at. It was Edwin Hamilton. The simple-minded man with what appeared to be a fetish for schoolgirls.

FORTY

Grant and Fergus were out of the Land Rover and walking towards Hamilton before Fiona could leap down from the load bed. As pleased as she was to have located the man, finding him presented her with a series of problems.

Due to the illegality of her search of Hamilton's cottage, she couldn't arrest the man without having to admit entering his house. Plus if she did arrest him, he'd have the right to a lawyer, and would have to be released after twenty-four hours unless he'd been charged. Most of those twenty-four hours could be lost by the time other officers were able to access the island and then transport Hamilton to Oban station for a formal interview.

It made sense, then, to not arrest Hamilton, to try questioning him without the interference of a lawyer who'd obfuscate things. However, by not arresting Hamilton, she couldn't detain him, couldn't put the fear of God into the man so he answered her questions.

There was also the presence of Grant and Fergus to consider. They knew Hamilton and, while he might not be their best mate, if they felt he was innocent, there was a chance they'd take pity on the man and do what they could to advise him not to talk to her. To Fiona their lack of faith in her professional abilities was obvious and therefore any questioning she did of Hamilton must be conducted away from them.

Hamilton was dressed in camouflage cargo pants, his torso covered in a dark blue checked work shirt over a black tee. On his feet were a pair of hiking boots. The clothes weren't conspicuous in any way. There were no flashes of colour about them, nothing that would catch the eye from a distance. In short, they were a good choice for someone who didn't want to be seen.

As Fiona approached Hamilton she caught the way he was looking at her. There was nothing but idle curiosity on his face. Not one part of his features displayed any signs of fear. Fiona didn't like that. She wanted Hamilton to be worried about police involvement. The more nervous he was, the more likely he was to tell her what she wanted to know. Either through fear of prison, or from a mistake she could use to lever apart any fiction he created.

The wind was so strong it hissed in Fiona's ears with such volume the only way she could communicate with anyone was by putting her mouth to their ear and shouting.

She made a decision and pulled Grant a couple of paces from Hamilton.

'Has he found her?'

'Do you see her?' Grant raised a hand in Hamilton's direction. 'He might be numb from the neck up, but he's all right.'

After making mistakes with previous choices, Fiona was reticent to pick a course of action without first learning more.

'How far are we from the end of this track?'

'About a half mile. It comes out halfway between Toberonochy and Blackmill Bay. Why?'

'I need to talk to Hamilton. Somewhere quiet. I need you to get him into the back with me, carry on to the end of the track, and then take us back to Deek's. Can you do that?'

'Of course.'

Grant put his mouth to Hamilton's ear and pointed at the Land Rover. Hamilton's mouth pulled wide and showed crooked teeth as he strode towards the vehicle.

The rest of the trip until the track met tarmac roads was uneventful. Hamilton kept his back to Fiona. Like her, he was scanning his torch left and right across the land between the track and the coast.

When the tyres swapped gravel for tarmac, Grant wasted no time in gunning the engine. As much as Fiona appreciated the haste, the uneven and winding roads of Luing weren't suited to such rapid travel and Fiona had to cling on with both hands.

The Land Rover whooshed past the church and where Diane Yorke's car was parked without the slightest indication Grant was going to stop. As much as Fiona would have liked a minute at each point she was also desperate to get Hamilton into Deek's cottage so she could start questioning him.

It was only minutes, but by the time Grant halted the Land Rover outside Deek's cottage Fiona's muscles were cramped and bruised from the helter-skelter journey.

She climbed out and waved for Hamilton to follow her. Like an obedient puppy he ambled after her, his greasy white hair streaming from one side of his head.

Grant and Fergus stayed where they were, so Fiona opened the passenger door and pushed her head into the cab of the Land Rover. 'Are you going to wait here?'

The question was two-fold. If they were outside the window, they weren't scouring the island so Grant could exact his own version of justice on his brother's killer. But Hamilton was a large man, and while she had her baton to protect her, she didn't fancy having to subdue him in the tight confines of Deek's cottage if he got violent. With Grant and Fergus to help restrain him, there was a lot less chance she'd get hurt. Fiona knew she was being ultra-cautious, but the business with Will had embedded itself into her psyche, and she couldn't bring herself to believe that Hamilton night not turn on her if she started cross-examining him.

Fiona's fears weren't just for her own safety. If anything happened to her, there would be nobody to co-ordinate a daylight search for Cait, nobody to track down and arrest the killer.

'No.' Grant pointed north. 'People have searched every part of Luing for that wee lassie, except up there, so that's where we're going.'

Grant's logic made sense, but Fiona knew he didn't just want to find Cait. 'And what if you come across the missing men from the boat?'

'We won't. There's nowt up there except hills, gorse bushes, and wee lochs where the old slate mines were. Those bastards will want to be somewhere they can steal a boat. They're bound to know they're trapped on the island and will be caught if they stay here. They've killed two people, and will be desperate to get off the island before some competent coppers arrive and start looking for them. If they've been there, they'll have moved on.'

Fiona wasn't convinced by Grant's explanation, and while a lot of what he said rang true, there were other thoughts triggered by what he'd said about there being former slate mines in the area. The barb about the arrival of competent officers was one she accepted as her due.

'What about the mine works? I'm guessing they'd have a jetty at the nearest point they could. Is there anywhere up there those men could hide out?'

Fergus's face twisted at the question. 'There's gorse bushes and small woods all over the island, cuts everywhere someone thought it'd be easy to get at the slate. If those guys knew how to camouflage themselves, they could hide out on Luing for a lot longer than you'd keep searching.'

'I meant a building, a cave, or somewhere like that.' Fiona's cheeks burned at Fergus's implied insult to her ability and dedication.

'There's some caves there. That's why we're going.' Grant's face was dark as he reached for the gearstick. 'We're looking for the lassie. If we find the men who murdered my brother, we'll make a citizen's arrest. If they decide to resist arrest, that's their problem. I promised my folks I wouldn't kill them, and I'll keep that promise, but if they say the wrong thing, I'll make sure they regret it.'

The Land Rover surged forward along the road leaving Fiona helpless to prevent Grant and Fergus from leaving.

Fiona drew the keys for Deek's cottage from her pocket and led Hamilton inside. She chose the kitchen as a venue for the conversation over the living room. She didn't want Hamilton to get too comfortable and the kitchen table would hopefully make him associate their discussion with a formal police interview.

FORTY-ONE

Hamilton seemed amiable and friendly, but considering the size difference between him and her, Fiona was cautious about how she dealt with him. The pepper spray on her utility belt couldn't be used in a room as small as the kitchen, as it would affect her almost as much as him.

Fiona gestured to one of the wooden chairs tucked under the kitchen table. 'Why don't we sit down, make ourselves more comfortable?'

After the bruising ride in the Land Rover, the last thing Fiona wanted was to sit on a hard wooden seat, but she was desperate to do what she could to both put Hamilton at ease, and make him feel he was being formally interviewed.

'Can I get a wee-wee first?'

The request was innocuous, but Fiona was still wary of it. Some suspects did all they could to delay an interview. Others would try to use the privacy of a bathroom to climb out of the window. Hamilton's vocabulary and appearance suggested he didn't have the necessary cunning to use the bathroom as an escape route, but she didn't know if he was playing her. In the end, she nodded permission. Unless she arrested Hamilton, he was free to do whatever he pleased. And the second he was arrested, he'd have the right to legal representation. Something he couldn't get until morning, therefore any chance she had of getting Cait's whereabouts from him would be delayed. Not knowing what harm Cait had already suffered, there was no way Fiona wanted anything to delay her finding the child.

Hamilton lumbered back into the kitchen, his face open. From the time he'd flushed the toilet to his emergence from the bathroom, Fiona could tell he hadn't washed his hands.

'Mr Hamilton. I have a few questions for you. Don't worry, they won't take long.'

'What about the girl? Shouldn't we find her first?'

'Are you saying you didn't find her when you were looking?'

'Of course not.'

This was the kind of vague statement Fiona was hoping Hamilton would make. She pounced, her choice of words designed to confuse. 'Are you saying that of course you didn't find her, or that you're not saying you didn't find her? If it's the second one, then it's a double negative, which is a positive. So if you did find Cait, where is she now?'

Hamilton licked his lips as his eyes skittered around the room. He looked everywhere except at Fiona. 'I don't understand what you're saying. I didn't find Cait. I was looking for her. She's a little girl. A schoolgirl. She should have someone to look after her.'

There was a lot to unpack in Hamilton's words. The use of the term 'schoolgirl' was a huge red flag for Fiona. And his insistence she ought to be looked after could be taken several ways. Fiona had to choose her words with care. Clever insinuations flew past Hamilton without causing any damage beyond confusion. She'd watched his face as she tried to tie him in verbal knots and had seen nothing except bewilderment. There had been no flashes of anger or deception, no hint of a thought process that would untangle her words for him. He'd just floundered his way past the questions and issued a denial.

'You're right, she is a schoolgirl. She's eight years old. If she's out there alone, she'll be terrified.'

'I know.' Hamilton's tone matched the earnest expression on his face. 'That's why I was looking for her. She needs to be with someone who'll look after her.' He tapped his chest with a forefinger. 'If I found her, I'd look after her.'

'How would you look after her?' Fiona dreaded the answer to this question. After what she'd found in Hamilton's cottage, his idea of caring for Cait might be a nightmare for the child.

Hamilton rose until he was standing. His hands delving into the side pockets of his cargo pants. Although Hamilton's face was calm, Fiona reached for her collapsible baton in case he was reaching for a weapon.

When Hamilton's hands emerged from his pockets they were holding a can of Coke and a selection of chocolate biscuits. At the sight of a KitKat, her favourite biscuit after chocolate Hobnobs, Fiona's stomach let out a low growl. She was long overdue a meal, and while eating was at the bottom of her priorities, the sight of those biscuits had her salivating even as her cheeks reddened.

'If you're hungry, you can have one.' Hamilton used one of his chunky fingers to push the pile of biscuits across the table.

'No thanks.' Under no circumstances was Fiona going to have a biscuit, however well-meaning Hamilton's offer may be. The whole sweets-from-strangers thing was alive, well and sitting in front of her. Yes, it might be that in Hamilton's uneducated mind some biscuits and a can of Coke would be something Cait would want, but a grown man giving chocolate to a child was the way a lot of horrible stories began. She had to get back to questioning Hamilton, to probing him in the hope he knew more than he was letting on.

'You brought those for Cait, which would give her something to eat and drink. How else were you going to look after her?'

Hamilton's eyes tightened as he considered the question. It was the first sign Fiona had seen that he was giving actual thought to what he said instead of blurting out his answers. This was a key point in the interview. Whatever he said next would be key to his real intention behind his search for Cait.

FORTY-TWO

Hamilton's fingers drummed off the table as he stared into Fiona's eyes. 'I was going to take her back to her mum and dad. If she was hurt, I would have carried her. She's a little girl, she should be with her mum and dad.'

'Is that what you'd really do, take her back to her parents?' After what she'd seen in his cottage, Hamilton's words were hard for Fiona to believe.

'Of course. She's a little schoolgirl. She should be with her mummy and daddy.'

The words came in an instant and sounded genuine, but Fiona couldn't let it sit without challenging further.

'You're right, she should. But, there's a reason I had to talk to you. Do you know what it is?'

Fiona watched as Hamilton crumpled in front of her. One second he was a hulking brute with a childish eagerness to help, and the next he was wrapping his arms over his head as he gently butted the table with his forehead. Fiona let him have a few seconds of this and then laid a hand on his elbow. 'Edwin, this isn't helping me or you. Nor is it helping Cait. Can you stop that, please, and talk to me?'

When Hamilton eased himself back up she saw the damp-ness of his cheeks and the pain in his eyes.

'Do you want to tell me about it?'

'I was just talking to her. She was staying with Betty, Betty Jamieson. All I did was talk to her. Betty went mad. She called the police on me. For talking to a girl. We were only talking. Nothing else. I told that to the policeman back then. I told him the truth. I was just talking to her.'

'That's what I heard. But when there's a girl missing on the island, I'm sure you can understand why I had to talk to you.'

'No. No.' Hamilton pushed himself away from the table and rose, his feet propelling him backwards until he bumped into the worktop, tears streamed down a face that was aghast with the realisation of the crime of which he was being accused. 'You can't think that. I haven't done nothing. Not to the girl I talked to, and not to the girl that's missing. Please, you have to believe me.'

'I want to, Edwin.' The use of his Christian name was delib-erate. Now the accusation was out there, Fiona wanted him to think of her as a friend. 'But despite the fact people have been searching the island for hours, nobody has seen any sign of her. That makes me think someone has already found Cait, but hasn't taken her back to her mum and dad. After what happened with you and the girl all those years ago, my inspector has told me that you have to be classed as a suspect.' Although it was Fiona's own work that had put Hamilton on the suspect list, she was happy to give Baird the credit for the idea if it would get the truth from Hamilton.

'I was looking for the girl because I wanted to help her.' Hamilton's jaw set hard. 'What happened years ago was a misunderstanding. Betty never liked me. She's been mean to me ever since.'

Hamilton's disintegration in front of her would have been

tragic to witness had Fiona not harboured the grave suspicions she did.

'Tell me, Edwin, and I'm only asking this because I want to believe you, if a team of police officers got a warrant and entered your home right now, would they find anything that would make it look like you should be a suspect? Is there anything in your house that would make the police think you are obsessed with young girls? And you also need to think about what websites you've looked at. All of that would be noted by the search team.' Fiona raised a hand. 'Please, think very hard before you answer.'

The question was a workaround. If Hamilton admitted what was in his house, her illegal search would never have to come to light. If he didn't, she would have to arrest him to prevent him from returning and burning the magazines she'd seen. The web history could be deleted by Hamilton, but the forensic techies would get it all back provided Hamilton didn't destroy the laptop or toss it into the sea.

Hamilton took some deep breaths, looked around the room, and drummed his fingers on the table some more.

'Are you going to arrest me if I tell you the truth?'

'I can't answer that until I know what the truth is.'

There were two slow nods from Hamilton. 'I'll tell you the truth, but only because it will mean you stop wasting time talking to me. My little sister died when I was sixteen. I loved her so, so much. Aisling was so clever, way cleverer than I am. She loved clothes. Skirts and dresses. I have lots of magazines that she would like. She used to always get magazines and turn the corners down on the pages of stuff she liked. I used to give her some of my wages every week so she could go to Oban and get the clothes she wanted.' Hamilton's voice caught. 'I miss her every day. Aisling never let anyone call me Soft Eddy. I use the magazines and the internet to look at dresses and skirts she would have liked. It makes it seem like she's still alive. She's not, though. That girl Betty went mad at me for talking to. She looked a bit like Aisling. Reminded me of her. It was nice talking to her until Betty came and started shouting at me. Calling me all sorts of rude names.' Hamilton's head dipped and his shoulders bounced as his voice trailed off.

Despite the tears dropping onto the table, Edwin drew a battered wallet from a pocket, opened it and showed a picture to Fiona. It was a smaller version of the picture on his mantelpiece.

'That's Aisling. Isn't she beautiful?'

'She is. How did she die?'

Fiona saw Edwin's eyes move to a spot above her head. 'Her and Mummy were in a car crash. Aisling was killed in the crash. Mummy wasn't, but she blamed herself for Aisling dying. I think Daddy blamed her too. Both Mummy and Daddy drank too much whisky. Even when the doctor told them to stop they didn't.' Edwin shook his head in violent swipes. 'Mummy and Daddy drank themselves to death within three years of Aisling dying. I wanted to find Cait so that another mum and dad don't feel like mine did. If Cait has a brother or sister, I don't want them to be alone like me.'

Rather than speak, Fiona got up, rooted in the cupboards until she found glasses and poured them both a drink of water from the tap. If Edwin's story was true – and she didn't believe he could have layered so much emotion into his voice if it was a lie – then his life was tragic.

Against a throat scratched from all the shouting Fiona had done to make herself heard since arriving on Luing, the cool liquid felt like a honeyed balm.

Like her, Edwin had lost his parents at a young age. Fiona hadn't a sibling to lose, but after what she'd gone through, she knew the drawn-out loss of Edwin's family would have been heartbreaking for him. Had it not been for her Aunt Mary, she would have never got over her parents' murders. All Fiona could do was hope Edwin had had a relative who'd looked after him the way Aunt Mary had her.

As Edwin sipped from the glass, Fiona stayed on her feet. 'I'm sorry, Edwin, what you have just told me is awful, but you do know I'm going to have to check it's true?'

'It's true. Please. Believe me. I couldn't make up lies like that. I'm not a liar and I wouldn't never tell lies about Aisling. Or Mummy and Daddy.'

'I don't think you're a liar, Edwin, but I still have to check.'

Fiona walked through to the living room. She needed to get an update from Heather, relay Edwin's story to her friend so it could be checked out, and most of all, she had to park the memories of her parents that were flooding her thoughts. She could go back to the memories another time, it was something she often did, but after hearing Edwin's story, her parents were at the forefront of her thoughts, and as much as she missed them both, she didn't have time to entertain thoughts of the past.

FORTY-THREE

'Fiona?'

The stark way Heather answered the phone pumped adrenaline through Fiona's veins. Heather's tone was filled with excited anticipation and that signalled to Fiona her friend had something worth sharing.

'Yeah, it's me. Before you head into what you're about to say, I need you to check something out for me. You should be able to do it while we're speaking. And before you ask, I haven't found Cait Yorke yet.'

'Speaker. DI Baird present. Tell me.' The curt sentences didn't worry Fiona in the slightest as she detailed Edwin's story to Heather. Her friend was being brief and that suited Fiona just fine.

Even before she'd finished relating Edwin's tale, Fiona could hear the rattle of keys as Heather started the requested task. 'There's something else, Heather. Can you get me the details of the person who made the complaint against Edwin? Was there any malice in it? Or was it just someone getting their knickers in a knot?'

'Baird here. You have Edwin Hamilton in custody?'

'No, ma'am. He's with me and he's helping me with my enquiries, but I didn't want to slow my *pace*.' Fiona hoped Baird would pick up the emphasis she'd put on the last word. The Police and Crime Evidence Act would see Edwin released after twenty-four hours if he wasn't charged.

'I see. You've met him and as such as I have to bow to your greater experience of the individual, but I'm not sure it's the path I'd take myself. Nor do I recommend it, but as I said, you're the officer on the scene.'

How typical of Baird to make sure her own backside was covered. 'I understand, ma'am, but surely my immediate course of action will be dictated by what DC Andrews learns?'

'Perhaps. Now stop arguing semantics with me and listen. DC Andrews ran the registration plates you gave her. All except one car belonged to individuals over the age of thirty-five.' Fiona couldn't see why the age of the owners was relevant, but she knew better than to interrupt Baird with a question whose answer was imminent. 'This car belongs to a Frankie Shand. He's twenty-eight and when DC Andrews dug him up online, she found a whole lot of twos that added up to a whole lot of fours so to speak. Most of his pictures feature him and his two mates. The mates are tagged in the pictures. Sometimes the things you find online gladden your heart.' Fiona assumed Baird was talking about someone else's heart, as it was widely considered she was missing the vital organ. 'This is most definitely one of those times. The mates are Philip Kerr and Luke Williamson. And all three of them fit the descriptions you've given us for the men who absconded after the *Each-Uisge* ran aground.'

The David, Michael and Johnathan she'd met would really be Shand, Kerr and Williamson. 'That's great news, ma'am.' Fiona ignored the airbrushing of her rescue of the boat's passengers. 'I'll get a few locals to help me round them up.'

'I've already told you once not to interrupt me, Constable. Now will you please shush, as I have more information to pass to you? In the case of Shand, Kerr and Williamson, Facebook has been the gift that has kept on giving. There's all the usual pictures you'd expect of three young men. They're in pubs, beer gardens, football matches and so on. There's always the three of them in the pictures, and sometimes there are other people. Now before you get excited and ask if Charlie Tait is in any of the pictures, he's not. But after trawling through each of their profiles, DC Andrews reckons that around thirty-three per cent of the pictures all feature either boats, or pictures that appear to have been taken from boats. The boats in question are yachts, trawlers, dinghies and so on. Those boys are used to being on the water. If one of them, as seems more than likely, turns out to be Tait's killer, they've hunted him down for something he's done in the past. Either to the killer directly, or a family member of theirs.

'We've dug into the lives of the three of them. Shand and Williamson have pretty much worked on various boats out of Wick since leaving the school at sixteen. Kerr works in a dock-yard doing repairs and maintenance. There's a drunk and disor-derly against Kerr's name, but the report on it says he was singing 'Flower of Scotland' at the top of his voice while walking home from the pub. Neither of the others has a record. We have officers en route to their home addresses, but consid-ering how intertwined their lives are, I'd say it's fair to assume all three are on Luing and are the men who gave you false names and addresses. That's all I have on them. You're on the ground there and are solely focusing on this case, what are your thoughts?'

The switch between absorbing the torrent of information from Baird and being expected to have digested and examined it caught Fiona unprepared. 'First of all, ma'am, you've got a lot in a short time. What we've learned about them getting aboard the *Each-Uisge* suggests they were covering their tracks right from the moment they boarded the pleasure cruiser because they were on there for the sole purpose of killing Tait. Now we know who they are and where they're from, we can start looking at their lives a lot more closely. We can also assume that Tait was either from Wick, or somewhere relatively close, otherwise their paths would never have crossed; and the injuries to Tait's groin suggested a very personal reason for his slaying. You've disproven Tait's backstory about being a crabber from Ullapool, but it makes sense he was originally a crabber or fisherman from Wick, as the more little truths you seed into a big lie, the more convincing you make it.'

'Agreed. Carry on.'

'Tait was known to have arrived in Oban twelve years ago. His identity is suspect against his backstory, both the one he's told people and the one that's official. My guess is that he got a new identity, either a black market one, or one that was given to him as a protected witness. His chosen career is far too public a one for the idea of him as a protected witness to stand up, therefore he's got an illegal ID. That tells me he's running from something in his past. He was killed after his groin was mutilated. That hints at his past crimes, but may be a red herring. It could be he dated a mother of one of the three men and gave the boy a hard time. He might have bullied them mercilessly in their first jobs. I'm not an expert on the fishing industry, but I've seen enough of it to know that it's a hard and unforgiving environment, where political correctness doesn't exist. This might be a bit of a wild theory, ma'am, but what if the engine failure that caused the *Each-Uisge* to run aground wasn't an accident? One of them, Kerr I think you said, works in a boatyard doing repairs and maintenance. What if he sabotaged the engine so the *Each-Uisge* would be without power when it was in a position that would see it washed ashore at Luing? Then it would be a case of killing the captain and getting off the boat alive. Having said that, ma'am, the same scenario of someone scuppering the boat can also apply to the two crewmen, Ian Caldwell and Davie something or other.'

'Your theory does seem wild. Why would they take the risk of drowning themselves and all the other passengers? If they were on a suicide mission they'd have sunk the boat at sea.'

Fiona had already thought through that possibility. 'Those guys all know the sea. If it was the lads from Wick there was a lot of planning shown elsewhere, so perhaps they picked their spot with great care. I'm also thinking Kerr did just enough to the engine that it wouldn't run aground. Had it not been set to run aground at a place they could be rescued, he'd have probably undone his sabotage. My guess is that Tait was killed only moments before the *Each-Uisge* foundered. If it was one of the crew, there is every chance they'd know the tides and currents as well as Tait himself.'

'That makes more sense. I'm not saying you're right, but at least we have a workable theory about what happened on that boat. We still need a motive, though. Plus one for the killing of the mechanic. There was no need for them to kill him. Even if he'd found them in those eco-pods, he presented no threat to them.'

Fiona heard papers rustling.

'Right, here's the details of the woman who made the complaints against Hamilton. She's called Betty Jamieson and still lives at number six Slate Row in Toberonochy. She's seventy-three and has a long history of fostering children until she gave it up five years ago. According to what we know of her fostering, she specialised in taking in kids who'd been sexually abused. That's all we have on her.'

'It's enough, ma'am. What you've said about her has me thinking she'd overreacted when she saw Edwin talking to the girl. That's understandable, of course, she was bound to be over-protective to her charges considering their experiences.'

Fiona ran over what she'd just said in her mind. It fit.

Although it painted Betty Jamieson as an overzealous carer, protecting her charges like a lioness, Fiona found nothing wrong with that. For children suffering the traumas associated with sexual abuse, someone being overzealous was far preferable to them being indifferent.

'You believe Hamilton, don't you?'

'I do, ma'am. He's still grieving his sister all these years later. With what happened to my parents, I know what that's like. You can't fake the amount of emotion he had when telling me his story.'

'I'm not sure, but DC Andrews is waving at me like she's won the lottery, so I guess she wants to speak to you now.'

Heather's voice came over the line. 'His story checks out, Fiona. His sister died in a car crash and his parents died a few years after. The mother after two-and-a-half years, the father a week short of three.'

'Ma'am.' Fiona shifted her position so she could see into the kitchen where Edwin was stacking the biscuits into a Jenga pile. 'What course of action do you recommend regarding Edwin Hamilton?'

Hamilton's eyes widened at the question, but he made no move to leave the kitchen.

'Keep an eye on him, and don't let him go back home. If Cait isn't found by morning, I want a team with a warrant in his cottage at the first possible opportunity, and he can't have the chance to destroy any evidence.'

'Anything else, ma'am?'

'We're still doing the deep dig into the Yorke family. Why these things can't happen during regular office hours when we can easily speak to other agencies, I'll never know. Now find Cait, and get that killer into custody.'

If only it was that easy.

FORTY-FOUR

Fiona looked at Edwin as she laid down the phone. She understood and agreed with Baird's point about not giving him the chance to destroy any of the evidence in his home, but that didn't explain what to do with him until Cait was found or backup could get onto the island.

'Edwin, I'm not going to arrest you. But there are some men I need to find. I think they're at Sunnybrae Caravan Park. I want you to come with me when I go look for them. Can you do that?'

'I want to look for Cait. She needs to be back with her mummy and daddy.'

'She does, but the men I'm looking for are bad men, and I think it will be safer for Cait if we find them first.'

Edwin's eyes opened wide as he rose from the chair. 'If they are bad men, you can't let them find Cait. We have to stop them.'

'We will. But first we have to find them. I've heard they might be staying at the caravan park.' Fiona strode across the room and put a hand on Edwin's arm, pulling him back. 'If they

are there, you need to stay out of the way. The men are dangerous, Edwin.'

'Don't worry about me.' Edwin balled a fist and stepped
aside so Fiona could leave Deek's cottage first.

It was only when Fiona stepped out of the door that she
realised she was without transport, her car having been left at
Will's garage. A mile away.

Fiona set her jaw and started walking. Every step was a
purgatory hell where the wind battered her with gusts and sent
grit to scour her skin and fill her eyes.

The one positive thing about the hike to the garage was that
once they'd reached the halfway point the road turned inland,
which placed the gale at their backs, propelling them forward.

As they passed the Portacabin that housed the island's only
shop, Fiona saw the conservatory of one of the island's few
houses was lit up. The tops of heads poking above the reclining
chairs told Fiona there were four people in the conservatory.
The dresser at the house wall being laden with beer cans told
Fiona how the four people were amusing themselves as the gale
raged. She considered stopping to talk to them, in case they'd
seen any of the people she was looking for, but discounted the
idea. First, the number of beer cans on the dresser made it
unlikely she'd get any sense out of the party animals, and
second, the lead on Frankie Shand and his mates was too good,
and she wanted to get to them before they decided to vanish
into the night.

FORTY-FIVE

As she drove the short distance from Will's garage to the caravan park at the north of the island, Fiona's mind was racing hard. She was worried about Edwin. For all he was a bruiser of a man, he was slow-witted, and had no idea of the dangers Shand and his mates presented. The last thing she wanted was for him to get hurt. She was a police officer, she wore a Kevlar vest and had the collapsible baton plus the pepper spray to use for both defence and attack. Edwin had nothing more than his size.

If Edwin had been a police officer, kitted out the same as Fiona, she would still have had reservations about tackling three murder suspects. The odds were against them and she needed to at least even those odds if not swing them in her favour.

Had it not been for the murder of his brother, Grant and his cousin Fergus would have made ideal companions. Both were capable men who had an island toughness about them that Edwin would never achieve. However, Grant had spoken of revenge against the killer, and even if she could prevent the islander from beating them to a pulp, the fact she'd let a victim's family member accompany her on an arrest could signal the end of her police career if Grant followed up on his threat.

As Fiona made the drive, she kept casting her eyes across the north-west section of the island. It was where Grant had intimated they were going and she wanted to catch a glimpse of him, to reassure herself she didn't have to worry about him confronting the killer. No matter how she strained her eyes, she couldn't see a sign of them.

Time and again a gust of wind buffeted the car, forcing Fiona to correct the steering as the gale fought with the mechanical object defying its irresistible force.

Part of Fiona wanted to flick the switch on the car's blue lights, but she gave up that idea in favour of stealth. Outnumbered as she was, she wanted to get to the caravan park unseen. Alison Vivers had mentioned there was a group of four guys in their fifties staying at the site. She'd seen the kayaks outside their caravan and it was these men she planned to enlist.

Five against three were better odds. If she could persuade Edwin to stand at the back and not get involved, she'd lead a team of six. With an overwhelming force like that, there was a good chance Shand and his mates wouldn't try to fight their way to freedom. That was far and away the best she could hope for.

When Fiona drove into the caravan site for the second time that night, she wasn't greeted with the same atmosphere.

Solar lights stuck into the ground at regular intervals illuminated an unfolding disaster.

Where earlier there had been an eerie quality to the caravans gently rocking in the wind, there was now a great element of chaos in front of her. A dozen or so people were sitting with their backs against the various cars that had been driven from their allocated spaces beside the caravans. Some small children were huddled into their parent's arms and an older lady was fighting to preserve her dignity as the wind tore at her dressing gown.

Across the grass, all the caravans were moving under the force of the gale. One had slewed round as if on an invisible axis, but the others were feeling the full power of the wind on their flanks. This pressure was threatening to roll the caravans onto their sides.

Fiona's first thought was the safety of the public. Her second, the whereabouts of Shand and his mates. There were two caravans under threat that still had a car next to them, and the closer of the two cars was registered to Frankie Shand. The car's presence suggested a whole lot of things to Fiona, and none of them were good.

FORTY-SIX

Fiona whipped her head round to face Edwin. 'You stay here, all right? I'm going to find out if there's anyone still in those caravans.'

Rather than wait for an answer, Fiona opened her door wide. It was a mistake, as with the commotion of the tilting caravans distracting her, she hadn't been mindful to park nose into the wind. The door yanked her arm straight and the sudden jolt caused her fingers to lose their grip on the door handle.

The gale showed the car no mercy as it whipped the door past the end of its normal arc, buckling both door and bodywork. Fiona guessed the hinges would also be twisted, but she didn't have to guess as to whether or not she'd get a bollocking for the damage to the vehicle.

As well as the injury to the car, Fiona also felt the burn of humiliation on her cheeks. The people who'd escaped their caravans had seen what happened and one or two of the faces watching her now held wry smiles.

The wind was so strong in Fiona's face that she now gave up any pretence of staying upright and dropped to her hands and knees to cover the ten yards to the nearest person. Before she went anywhere near Shand's caravan, she had to learn if there was anyone in the other caravan which still had a car at its side.

A short man in his forties, with a pre-teen girl swaddled in his arms, was the closest of the caravan's occupants, so Fiona made her way to him. 'Is there anyone in any of the other caravans?'

'I don't know.' His face took an apologetic turn as he pointed at the two caravans with cars beside them. 'I banged on a few of the front windows when I left our van, but I didn't hang around. Folks came out of every caravan bar those two. I don't know who's in the first one, but the second has an old couple in it. I should have gone back to bang again, shouldn't I?'

'No. You did the right thing staying safe.'

Fiona left the man to work through his guilt and moved on to the next person. It was one of the four men in their fifties. Even with the wind as powerful as it was, Fiona could smell the alcohol emanating from him. His eyes were glassy and there was a lethargy about him that suggested were it not for having to evacuate the caravan, he'd be snoring by now. 'The caravan on the other side of yours, is there anyone in it? Have you seen its lights on tonight?'

The man shrugged as he shook his head. Like his three companions, he was massaging various areas of his body. Fiona reckoned that when the seas got too rough for kayaking, the men had hit the drink hard and only woken up when shaken from their beds. Her plan to use them as backup was in tatters, but the bucking of the caravans in the wind negated that plan anyway.

Fiona rose to her feet. By leaning back into the wind she could make faster progress than crawling, and time was now of the essence. If Shand and his mates were in their caravan, they could stay there and take their chances. The furthest caravan, with the old couple in it, had to be her priority.

As Fiona progressed forward in the fashion of someone

losing at tug-of-war, her mind was working every bit as hard as her body. The presence of Frankie Shand's car told her that he and his mates were long gone from this part of the island. If they'd been in their caravan, they'd have evacuated it, the same as all the holidaymakers had. They'd have moved the car. After what they'd done today, there was no chance of them finding sleep, not when they'd be afraid of every knock on the door.

It wasn't just the presence of the car that made Fiona so sure they weren't here. She was by no means an expert on such things, but she knew static caravans like the ones at Sunnybrae would be moored to the ground, to protect them from being moved or tumbled over by high winds. Every caravan had barely been moving when she'd been here earlier, and yet now they were all bucking like a rodeo bull. That didn't ring true: it was both possible and plausible the caravans the wind hit first would be under sufficient pressure their mooring straps gave way. What she didn't believe credible was the idea the mooring straps on every caravan would succumb at the same time. A domino effect would be more likely, the first caravan or two being swept along into the next and acting as a buffer was Fiona's best guess at what would actually happen should the mooring straps give out.

Except all the caravans were facing the same issue. That spoke of foul play. When she cast a glance under the seaward side of the nearest caravan, she could see its nylon mooring strap was flapping in the wind. Even though it was moving she could see the end wasn't frayed, it was too neat a break. The strap had been cut. There was no doubt in Fiona's mind as to who had done this: the killer had already twice used his knife today. The key question was why had it been done?

Fiona knew the answer. She saw it in the mirror every morning when she brushed her teeth. There was no toothpaste yet created that could cleanse the bitterness from Fiona's mouth. When she'd visited the caravan park earlier, she'd only knocked off her siren and blue lights when she'd seen the gateway.

Shand and his mates must have either fled the caravan at once, or hunkered down out of sight, confident there was no way the police could know they'd rented a caravan. It didn't matter which, what mattered was the desperate measure they'd taken afterwards. With no roads offering them an escape route, they'd left the car to its fate and severed the tie-down straps on all the caravans. Whether they intended to cause injury to others to create a massive distraction for Fiona, or had only done it so they could retreat to another part of the island was something that could be puzzled over later.

As a priority, Fiona had to check on the old couple who'd never left their caravan. Now she was halfway along the small road between the two rows of caravans, Fiona felt more threatened than she had at any time since arriving on Luing.

Even with the steady roar of the wind filling her ears, Fiona's head turned when she heard the grating screech as a caravan topped onto its side. The caravan's windows popped from their frames and a torrent of lightweight debris streamed from every new orifice.

A sheet wrapped itself around Fiona, and as she wrestled to free herself of it, she lost her balance and tumbled to the ground. It took several undignified writhes for Fiona to untangle herself from the sheet, but she succeeded.

Fiona learned the hard way standing up was a different matter. If she faced the wind, she could stand, but whenever she turned to carry on towards the old couple's caravan, the power of the gale knocked her flat before she could lean back into it. Every attempt to put her back to the wind saw her driven forward until she was flattened onto the abrasive tarmac a few feet from where she'd started.

In the end Fiona gave up trying to stand and completed the journey as fast as she could crawl. When she got to the old couple's caravan, she could see it was rocking from its normal position to one that saw it tilted thirty-degrees over.

The door to the caravan was on the right-hand side as she faced it. The same side the car was parked at. Not just the same side, but the same distance along. Anyone entering or exiting the caravan through that door would have to risk being crushed between caravan and door.

Fiona's jaw was tight as she sidled up against the car and used it as a windbreak so she could again stand. She had no idea whether or not the old couple were in the caravan, but there was no way she wasn't going to check. The killer had harmed more than enough people today, and she was damned if she wasn't going to do everything in her power to make sure no one else died because of their callousness.

FORTY-SEVEN

Fiona judged the rear of the car to be closer to the caravan door than the front, so she made her way along until her shoulder was against the car's rear bumper. Time and again the caravan rocked towards her. So far as she could judge, there was no noticeable increase in the height of each rock, but she knew it was only a matter of time before one of the stronger gusts caught hold of the caravan.

The big question in Fiona's mind was whether or not the door was locked. Had the old couple settled in for the night to wait out the storm? Or had they been up and awake when the mooring straps were cut?

As there was only one way to find out, Fiona ducked out from behind the car and let the wind propel her to the caravan door, her fingers grasping desperately for the handle.

The door opened, but only until a gust of wind caught it and blew it closed again.

Fiona worked the handle again, and thrust her spare arm between door and frame. At an oblique angle, the pressure wasn't an issue, but as she squirmed her full arm and then body into the gap, the rocking of the caravan scraped not just the door's inner handle, but the entire lock mechanism against the soft flesh of her upper torso. It was yet another injury on her already bruised left shoulder. As things stood, every movement of her arm set off a new lance of pain.

There were two steps leading into the caravan and Fiona climbed them backwards, her shoulder against the door so her body had a little room to move. A violent buck tilted the caravan as she drew her feet inside, causing her to fall backwards.

The only protection Fiona could give herself as she fell was to tuck her head forward until her chin was tight against her sternum, and to extend her left arm downwards in the hope of it breaking her fall.

Fiona let out a pained yelp when something hard and unyielding thumped into her shoulder blade. It was the same shoulder she'd injured on the way back from the cave, and while she'd hurt the front earlier, this extra assault from the other side jangled every nerve ending in the area.

As she tried to rise, Fiona found that while her left arm still worked, every movement she made set off a dozen distress flares in her shoulder. Somehow she made it up onto her knees and took a deep breath so she'd be heard over the racket of the caravan being pummelled by the gale. 'Hello, is there anyone there.'

'We're here.' The male voice was old and infused with phlegm, but there was a strength underpinning it.

'Are you hurt?'

'I'm not, but June is. We think she's broke her leg.'

Fiona fought to keep her face neutral as she moved towards the bedroom, where the man's voice had come from. Upon entering the bedroom she found June on the floor and her husband kneeling beside her. When Fiona saw the oxygen tank at the man's side, and the thin hose looped under his nose, she had to redouble her efforts not to show her dismay. Instead of getting the old couple out on hands and knees, as she'd planned, she'd have to find another way.

The first thing Fiona did before she bent down to examine June was to grab the sheet from the bed and tear four strips from it. June would have to be moved out of the caravan – how she'd achieve that was yet to be determined, but she couldn't stay where she was. If the caravan was blown over, June's broken leg would be the least of her troubles. There was another risk, one Fiona dared hardly consider. Every caravan had a gas bottle attached. At some point, if it hadn't already happened, the hoses connecting the gas bottle to the caravan would be pulled apart and the flammable gas would be released.

All the metal that was being tortured by the gale was a potential source of sparks, and there was no telling if the caravan would collapse on itself if the wind managed to over-turn it, so Fiona worked with as much speed as she could to tie June's legs together. As a splint it was rudimentary at best, but it was Fiona's only option.

'I'm sorry. I'm not trying to hurt you, but we need to get you out of here.'

June never made a sound as Fiona tied her knots, but the winces on her lined face told of her agony. The woman was thin to the point of frailty, but she was made of tough stuff.

Fiona would have liked time to check for shock and other injuries, but she didn't have it.

Fiona was finishing up and trying to devise a way to get June and her husband from the caravan that didn't involve her carrying them, when the whole caravan began a series of wild bucking movements.

Back and forth it rocked until the car side gave a lurch and dropped a few inches. Fiona had barely time to work out it must have dropped off the support blocks that kept it level before the wind caught a firm grip of the already tilted structure.

Instead of rocking as it previously had, the caravan began to rotate. It happened in slow motion at first, but speeded up the more the wind could press on the underside.

Fiona braced herself against a wall that was about to become a floor and did her best to make sure June didn't suffer a further injury as the caravan toppled. She wanted to do the same for June's husband, but couldn't protect him without abandoning June.

Just as the caravan reached the point of no return, a huge cracking and splintering sound rent through the air as it landed on the car.

The caravan halted its rotation at a more than forty-five degree angle. Now the greatest worry in Fiona's mind was that if the wind dipped a little, the heavy chassis would pull the caravan back to an upright position. If that happened, the wind would surely flip it again and the whole process would continue until the caravan disintegrated.

Fiona edged herself towards the bedroom. 'I'm going to find a way out. I'll be back in a second.'

No matter how much caution Fiona exercised, she was in constant fear of the caravan completing its rotation or crashing back to the ground. As she exited the bedroom, she saw a huge bulge in the side of the caravan where it had landed on the car. With its passenger-protecting design, the car had acted as a sturdy boulder the flimsier caravan had moulded itself around.

With the car now bulging the door inwards, the only exit route from the caravan Fiona could see was the large front window. First though, she would have to complete the job the impact had started and kick the window out to form a doorway of sorts. Before Fiona began, she reached forward and rapped her knuckles on the window pane.

She got the sound she was hoping for. Instead of the hollow thunk glass made when rapped, she got the softer sound of Perspex being assaulted.

Fiona got herself into position, and prepared to slam the heel of her foot into a corner of the window. Just as she was winding up the kick, a face appeared at the window. Her first thought as she reeled back was the killer had come to make sure her investigation was halted right here, right now.

FORTY-EIGHT

There was a shift in the light and the face at the window became clearer. Fiona exhaled as she realised it was Edwin rather than the killer.

Fiona waved Edwin back and took a savage kick at the window. It flexed in its frame but didn't otherwise move. She tried again, harder. The window remained resolute, half attached, half free, and totally in the way.

Edwin stepped forward, gripped the bottom corner that hung free and exerted his muscles; not in a direct outwards pull, but a sideways one which twisted the window out from the opening. It was a smart move and not one Fiona would have ever thought of. Edwin may never win *Mastermind*, but he had a certain wisdom about him.

Fiona leaned forward so she could shout in Edwin's ear. 'There's an elderly couple in here. At least one of them needs to be carried out.'

'Okay.' Edwin's face was impassive.

The caravan was still rocking as Edwin clambered up its towbar and fed himself through the gap. Instead of watching him, Fiona made her way back to the bedroom and quickly told the couple what was about to happen.

Edwin lumbered through the doorway, his face grave as he took in the scene. With four people it was cramped in the bedroom, so Fiona climbed onto the bed and gestured for the old man to do the same.

June's eyes pressed shut and Fiona saw her mouth tighten, but she never uttered a single moan or word of complaint as Edwin lifted her with as much tenderness as was possible in the cramped space. His face showed no strain as he lifted her and cradled her in his arms.

The narrowness of the bedroom door and passageway to the living area would have made Edwin's task hard at the best of times, but tilted over as the caravan was, Edwin had to rest his backside on the wall and shuffle his way forward.

Fiona touched the old man on the elbow. 'Do you think you can make it to the front by yourself?'

The man's eyes never left his wife as he nodded, his hand reaching for the oxygen bottle.

'I'll take that. You lead.'

Fiona hefted the oxygen bottle in one hand and used the other to brace herself off the wall as she trailed after the man. Their progress was slow and Fiona could see beads of sweat developing all over his head as he made his way along the now sloping passageway.

When Edwin reached the window Fiona saw him halt and glance over his shoulder. His face showed relief when he saw how close she was to him.

Fiona understood Edwin's concern. It was one thing to carry June, but there was no way he'd be able to climb out of the window with her in his arms.

June turned her head Fiona's way. 'Vic, are you there?'

'Of course.' Vic reached out a trembling hand and smoothed June's grey hair. 'How's your leg?'

'Sore, but it's not as bad as having kids.'

As Fiona climbed out of the window, the roar of an engine made her turn her head. A large SUV was reversing towards them at speed. Again her first instinct was that the killer was approaching, but when she saw the brake lights come on and the vehicle draw to a halt she felt her heart slow.

All four doors of the SUV opened and disgorged the four kayakers. Two of them set about lowering the back seats while the others came across to help Fiona transfer June through the window.

When the two men had a firm grip of June, Fiona stuck her head back through the window. 'Edwin, pass me some of the loose seat cushions.'

Edwin looked puzzled, but did as he was asked and handed Fiona two cushions. Rather than clasp them to her chest and increase the surface the wind could exert its inexorable pressure on, Fiona gripped the cushions by a corner and let them flap about behind her as she leaned into the wind and trudged the six steps to the SUV. She got there at the same time as the men carrying June, and managed to lay the cushions down before the kayakers placed June upon them.

'Get my Vic out safe. Please I beg you. Make sure he's safe.'

'We'll have him out in a jiffy.'

Fiona nodded her thanks to the man who'd made the promise.

As the men settled June, Fiona made her way back to the window, took the oxygen bottle now in Edwin's hand and waited for him to pass Vic through the window.

Whether it was a freak lull or the gale gathering its resources for a more determined assault on the caravan was unknown, but there was a dip in the wind that saw the caravan ease back towards its usual position.

Inside the caravan, Edwin was gripping Vic under the armpits as the old man's feet were scrabbling over the windowsill. It all made sense to Fiona until the wind picked up again and pitched the caravan back over.

This time it went further than before, its side moulding further around the car that was the only thing preventing it from toppling all the way over.

Edwin and Vic disappeared from Fiona's sight as she reared back from the window. The caravan's towbar glanced off her shoulder, but it was already numb from the earlier injuries, so she paid the latest hit no heed.

The caravan remained in place long enough for Edwin to regain his feet. Now when he lifted Vic, Fiona could see the old man was hurt. Blood ran from a cut above his ear and he appeared to be docile and barely able to move. The oxygen line was missing, but Fiona retrieved the gas bottle and drew the line to her as Edwin readied a second attempt at passing Vic through the window.

Strong hands gripped Fiona's shoulders and she felt herself being guided away from the caravan as the kayakers stepped up to the window.

With their combined strength, the kayakers had Vic out of the window in no time, and even as they carried him to the SUV, Fiona was at their side reattaching the oxygen line around Vic's head.

As soon as the oxygen line was in place, Fiona was turning back to look for Edwin. He was leaning out of the window, a seat cushion in each hand. She ran to grab them from him. 'Come on, get out of there before it collapses on you.'

Fiona backed away with the cushions, but her eyes never left Edwin as he turned and fed first one leg, then the other out the window.

As Edwin was leaning on the sill ready to lower himself to the ground, the caravan gave a series of wild bucking movements as it surrendered to the wind. Fiona released the cushions and ran forward.

Edwin fell out of the window, his legs hitting the ground and jolting him backwards away from the structure as it began to fold in on itself. By the time Fiona reached him he was lying flat on his back, panting. Both of his great arms were wrapped across his chest and there was agony on his face. It made sense his ribs hurt, they'd been balanced on the windowsill as it bucked beneath him. Not only would his weight have slammed him down onto the sill, but it would have bucked up to strike him there.

Fiona didn't think twice about her actions as she gripped Edwin's collar with both hands – the caravan's towbar was now close to vertical, and if the chassis of the caravan rotated much further, it would come down on him.

As soon as she'd dragged Edwin clear of the towbar, Fiona stopped moving and went round to his side. 'Let me see the damage.'

Fiona had to peel Edwin's arms from his chest, but there was no blood visible which was a good sign. Nor was there any on his lips. An even better sign, as a broken rib puncturing a lung was second on Fiona's list of fears for Edwin, after being stabbed by a nail from the windowsill.

Edwin's face was tight as he breathed and Fiona could sense the man was close to tears. If not from his own agony, from his childlike outlook on life.

Fiona felt Edwin's injuries as if they were her own. He was hurt because he'd come to help her. Vic and June had been placed in peril because she'd not managed to round up everyone from the *Each-Uisge*, or first check them for a knife after the rescue. Cait was still missing, and Grant and Fergus seemed hell-bent on finding the killer first so they could take a biblical revenge on them.

The last time Fiona had felt this helpless was the day her parents had been murdered.

FORTY-NINE

Fiona gathered the group of caravanners together and went round them in turn. Rather than speak to every person, she did what she could to identify family groups and spoke to one person so they could relay her words. She was telling them about the church. Where it was, how it'd provide safe haven for them all. By the time she'd relayed the same message several times her voice was little more than a pained croak.

As everyone fed themselves into cars, they shot glances at the destruction of the caravan site. By now most caravans had either toppled or slammed into their neighbours. It would be a nightmare to sort out, and if as she suspected the killer had severed the mooring straps, the whole area would be classed as a crime scene. That was an issue for another person on another day.

Edwin hovered by Fiona's car, an arm across his chest and a poor attempt at stoicism on his face. He was hurting, and despite his best efforts to hide it, he wasn't fooling anyone. Fiona planned to drop him at the church. He was better there where he could be looked after, and now he was injured, Fiona didn't want to risk him being anywhere near Shand and his mates in case he got hurt further.

Fiona wanted to catch up with Grant. He may have news of either Cait or the killer. The fact there were caves in the part of the island he was searching made her think he stood a good chance of success. While the last thing she wanted was vigilante action, she wouldn't be too concerned if Grant and Fergus delivered a dollop of retribution. Vic and June could have been killed if they'd stayed in their caravan. As it was they were lucky to have only relatively minor injuries. Edwin was the same.

The evacuation of the caravan site was now complete and the holidaymakers would be safe in the church, but the way Irene had complained about being hungry and thirsty stuck with Fiona. Right now, she'd kill for a cup of coffee and a bite to eat.

Alison Vivers stood in her doorway, watching, and Fiona took a step towards the woman before drawing to a halt. It would be easy to ask for the cleaner's help. If Alison Vivers' cupboards didn't contain snacks, she was an islander and would either be able to get stuff from other homes, or know where the shopkeeper lived.

As much as finding a way to provide food and drink would be a win for Fiona, she didn't do it. With a killer running amok on the island, the last thing she wanted was for anyone to leave the security of their home and potentially put themselves in harm's way. The church had a kitchen so anyone holed up there could at least get a drink of water. A few hours of being hungry would only be an issue if there was a diabetic in the group.

A look at her watch didn't help Fiona's peace of mind. It was almost one in the morning. Daylight would come around five. That was four more hours before the searches for Cait and the killer had a chance of bearing fruit. Four more hours for the killer to find a way to escape the island. Even were the gale to blow itself out, it would be at least four more hours before any attempt would be made to deliver support to the island. June, Vic and Edwin all needed urgent medical help.

Fiona climbed into her car and gestured for Edwin to do the same. Unlike June, he ahh-ed and oww-ed with every movement. Fiona let him make his noises without commenting on them. Without Edwin, there was no way she would have got the elderly couple out of the caravan.

Instead of turning left towards the church, Fiona turned right towards the ferry dock. There were no ferries running, she was sure of that, but it might give her a glimpse of Grant's and Fergus's progress.

With the car parked on the slipway, Fiona told Edwin to stay put and clambered up a banking to give herself a better chance of seeing signs of human life. On top of the exposed banking the gale was so strong Fiona made no effort to stand against it and sank to hands and knees.

Across Cuan Sound she could see lights in the houses on Seil. Over in the distance in the direction of Mull, there were a cluster of pinpricks of illumination. On Luing, there was nothing. No headlights from the ancient Land Rover. No torches wobbling a path across the landscape. Nothing.

No matter how she tried to endure staring directly into the wind, Fiona had to give up after a minute. Not only were her eyes dried out by the relentless gale, but there was grit and dust being blown into them as well.

By the time Fiona climbed back into her car she'd blinked what felt like a million times.

Edwin unwrapped an arm from his chest and put a hand on her forearm. 'It's okay. I feel like crying too.'

Fiona said nothing as she twisted the key. The tears falling from her eyes were a biological reaction to the grit that had been blown into them, they'd stop soon. If she allowed tears of grief and worry to flow, there would be no stopping them.

It took less than half a mile for Fiona to catch up to the

convoy that was heading to the church. Whichever one of the kayakers was driving the SUV had obviously chosen to let the vehicle pull itself along in a low gear so as not to jolt June more than necessary.

The slow pace grated on Fiona, but there was nothing she could do about it. Instead she took the time to think, and whenever the contours of the land allowed, she scanned for signs of Grant and Fergus, the five missing men and Cait.

It was the thinking time Fiona needed most. She'd noticed the way Vic had been holding June's hand when she'd found them, and though she'd thought nothing of it at the time, now she had time to think it cast back memories of her parents' murders.

Fiona's mother and father had taken a week off work to decorate the lounge together, the same way they always tackled projects around the house. When they were found by a neighbour, they were dead. Aunt Mary had told her they were lying in pools of their blood; and the police had said that before they died, they'd each moved towards the other and they were found to be holding each other's hand. Whether it was true or not, Fiona chose to believe they'd both had enough strength left to say 'I love you' to each other one last time. To think of them having that chance to say goodbye gave her comfort as well as a burning sense of determination to catch their killer.

The knowledge her parents' love story was so strong they'd drawn comfort from each other in their dying moments had helped Fiona manage her own grief, while also enraging her their story had been cut off mid-chapter. She would have given anything to have seen them live to their seventies like Vic and June. Not just for her own self, but for them to have lived a long life at the side of their beloved.

Fiona gave a sigh of relief when Kilchattan Church was picked out by the SUV's headlights. As much as she never wanted to disrespect the memory of her parents, she needed to have her focus elsewhere. Even as she'd been driving to Sunny-brae Caravan Park to apprehend Shand and his mates, an idea had been forming in her mind about where Cait might be and she'd been desperate to check it out.

The SUV parked with its rear bumper at the stone gateposts in the metal fence fronting Kilchattan Church. When Fiona pulled onto the verge she saw two things that made her chest constrict.

FIFTY

The gravity on the faces of the two men who'd been in the SUV told of tragedy, but Fiona didn't get the chance to go and speak to them as Diane Yorke was striding her way.

Diane's face was a twisted mask of hate as she jabbed a finger in Fiona's chest. Despite the wind doing its best to carry the woman's words away before Fiona could hear them, Diane was shouting more than loud enough for Fiona to hear.

'You're useless, you know that? My little girl... my baby, is out there all alone and what have you done to find her? Nothing, that's what. For all the use you've been, I might as well have lit a fucking bat signal.'

Fiona took the abuse and kept her face neutral, as making it stony would further infuriate Diane. To show empathy and understanding may have worked to calm Diane, but Fiona didn't dare travel that route. Not with fresh memories of her parents in her mind and the looming bad news she expected from the SUV.

'I'm sorry, I haven't found her yet, but I'm still looking. I've got islanders out looking too.'

'Oh, you're sorry, are you?' The sneer on Diane's face was

twice as vicious as the one in her voice. 'Do you think that makes everything okay? Do you think your apology will bring my daughter back to me? Don't just stand there being useless, go and find my daughter. And I've heard there's a killer on the island. Is that true? Should I be worried about a killer as well as everything else that could have happened to her while you've been swanning about like you're trying to look busy?'

Fiona ignored the insults and focused on what she knew was heightening Diane's fears the most. 'Sadly, yes, I am involved in another case as well. That much I can tell you.'

'Another case? Is that how you describe murder? Is that all any of this is to you, just another case? My little girl isn't just another case. She's the most precious thing in the world. Fuck you and your other case. You need to find my daughter before anything happens to her, you useless bitch.'

The rest of Diane's vitriol was lost to the winds as Pete appeared and enveloped his wife in a hug that pulled her face into his chest.

When Fiona forced her way to the SUV she found the kayakers working together to carry June into the church. June was mumbling something, but her words didn't carry to Fiona.

Rather than disturb their task Fiona ducked her head and shoulders into the open tailgate of the SUV.

The car's internal light showed Vic's face to have a waxy, ashen look to it that hadn't been there before. She clambered in and reached for Vic's wrist. No matter how many times Fiona shifted the position of her fingertips, she couldn't detect a pulse.

Fiona sat with her head bowed for a moment as she considered things. It could have been the brief spell without oxygen, the blow to his head, or the exertion of the escape from the caravan triggering a heart attack that had killed Vic, but one thing Fiona was sure of, his blood was on the hands of whomever had cut the mooring straps on the caravans. Had the straps remained intact, Vic would be asleep in bed beside his wife. Fiona also saw Vic's blood on her own hands. If she'd better contained the passengers from the *Each-Uisge*, the killers wouldn't have been able to run amok on the island.

The four kayakers returned, and one of them pointed at Vic. 'Shall we take him inside or leave him here? The old girl asked for him to be brought in, but there's kids in there too.'

While not a believer herself, Fiona was of the opinion the church would be a much more respectful place for Vic's body. The man had a point about the children, though, so she scanned her memory of the church. Although it was a long, single-storey building with a porch built at the doorway, there must be a room at the back where the minister changed or whatever.

As she thought, she looked along the church and saw a second door at the far end indicating such a room existed.

'Put Vic in the vestry, or whatever it's called. If June wants to be with him, take her in there too, although I think one of you ought to stay with her.'

'Don't worry, we'll look after her. Two of us are doctors.'

'You're doctors?' Fiona pointed at her car. 'The guy who helped us get them out of the caravan has banged up his chest. I think he may have a cracked rib or two. Make sure you take a look at him when I send him in.'

With the men lifting Vic's body from the SUV, and everyone else inside the church, Fiona made her way back to the car. Edwin was where she'd left him. Both his arms cradled his chest but his eyes were locked on her.

The 'come over here' waves she gave Edwin were ignored, and when she opened the passenger door he made no move to leave the vehicle.

'Edwin, the men who helped us back there are doctors. I think you should let them take a look at you. You've clearly hurt your chest.'

'I'm fine. That little girl is still lost. I have to help you find her.'

'No, Edwin, you have to leave that to me. You have been hurt once because you helped me. What you did back there saved their lives. That's more than I can ask of you.'

Edwin turned his head to face Fiona. 'We saved her. He's dead, isn't he?'

'I'm afraid he is. He died on the way here.'

'He probably died because I dropped him. He banged his head. I couldn't stop him from falling. You saw all the blood. It's my fault. I have to save Cait. Have to.'

Fiona understood the power of atonement. Every one of the emotions Edwin didn't know how to express were assaulting her psyche. Finding Cait wouldn't bring Will or Vic back to life. It wouldn't erase the guilt she felt for their deaths, nothing could do that. But, finding Cait before something awful happened to her would mean there would be no additional culpability to add to an already overbearing burden.

'You need to take care of yourself too, Edwin. You may have broken your ribs.'

'I'm fine. You can't make me go into the church.' Edwin's face took on a petulant look. 'If you do make me get out of your car, I won't go in the church. I'll go looking for her. You needed my help at Sunnybrae, and you may need it again. We're a team now.'

Fiona abandoned the argument and walked round the car. The only way to make sure Edwin did as he was told was to put him under arrest, and after his efforts at the caravan site, he deserved better.

She consoled herself with the theory that if he was with her, she'd at least know his whereabouts and would be able to prevent him from returning home, as per DI Baird's instruction.

Betty Jamieson had been a foster carer who specialised in caring for children who'd suffered sexual abuse. According to what Heather had unearthed she'd been filling the vital role for many years.

Fiona's theory was that Betty had perhaps gone looking for Cait too. After years of caring for young girls, she'd be unable to switch off the maternal urges that had made her such a long-time carer. It made sense that Betty would have wanted to help out. It was a natural reaction and one that had been echoed by many of the islanders and tourists on Luing.

The only flaw Fiona could find with her theory about Betty Jamieson having joined the search was that if the foster carer had found Cait, she would have surely returned the girl to her parents, or at the very least contacted the police or social services to inform them Cait was with her. As neither of these things had happened, Fiona began to doubt her idea, but not enough she planned to not follow it through.

Five minutes after leaving Kilchattan Church, Fiona stopped the car and turned off the engine. There was a light on in the house she planned to visit, and she didn't know if it was a good sign or not.

FIFTY-ONE

Betty Jamieson's house was set back behind others and accessed by a gravel track. Unlike so many of the homes at Toberonochy, this one had two storeys, although the upstairs windows were dormers that extended out from the roof like a pair of bug eyes.

'Why have you stopped here?'

When Fiona turned to look at Edwin she saw discomfort on his face. It wasn't that he was suffering from his wounds, more that he was uneasy, as if he didn't want to be here.

'I need to go and speak with the lady who lives in that house.'

'Why? She's nothing but a mean old cow.' Edwin's eyes widened. 'No. Please don't say you think I've got the missing girl. I haven't. You can check my cottage if you want. She's not there, I swear it.'

'I don't think you have her, Edwin. But I need you to wait here.' Fiona put a sternness into both her voice and body language that felt too brutal for the nature of the man she was speaking to, but she needed him to do as she requested. 'If you get out of the car before I tell you to, I'll arrest you. Do you understand me?'

'Yes. I'll stay here. Please don't arrest me.'

Fiona left the car and walked up the track, leaning hard into the wind as she went. When she got within thirty feet of the house, the gravel gave way to paving blocks, each one outlined by moss. She was pleased at the development, as the theory she was following meant sneaking up to the house may be necessary. She knew it was overkill on her behalf, as the gale was sure to overpower any noise she made, but if she was right in her thinking, she didn't want to take any chances.

There were two large windows either side of a red door. The one to the left of the door was the one that had light spilling from it. Light also gushed from a glass panel above the wooden door.

Rather than knock on the door, Fiona decided to check out the illuminated window first. There were curtains drawn, but as she approached the window she noticed there was a chink in the curtains a half-inch wide.

Fiona eased herself forward so she could look through the gap and gaze through. She saw an old fireplace with a log burner where a grate would have once sat, above it the mantelpiece and chimney hearth were festooned with framed photographs of people. At this distance Fiona couldn't tell who the pictures were of, or even if they were male or female, but she guessed they'd be the children Betty Jamieson had fostered over the years.

With a series of slow advancements, Fiona moved her head sideways, the gap in the curtain acting like a periscope showing her one part of the room after another. In front of the fireplace there was a coffee table with an empty plate and glass. At the far side of the fireplace there was a bookshelf and as the scan continued there was the arm of a chair bedecked in a riot of colour Fiona guessed would be a floral pattern.

The next advancement brought a leg into view. It was the trousered leg of an adult, and from the shoes, a woman. Fiona's heart pounded as she realised Betty Jamieson might see enough of a distortion in the light emanating from the gap to realise there was someone outside. Another reason Fiona's heart beat so hard were the shoes she'd caught sight of. They seemed to be a large size for a woman. Larger than Fiona's size six for sure.

There was only one thing Fiona could do, so she did it. She kept up her scan of the room.

When she saw more of the figure in the chair, Fiona's shoulders dropped to their normal height. Betty Jamieson was in the chair, but from the way her head rested on her chest, she'd fallen asleep there.

The sight of the sleeping woman gave Fiona the confidence to lean forward and complete her scan of the room.

It was a scan she'd never complete.

A child was asleep on a couch every bit as colourful as the armchair. A blanket hung from the child towards the floor where it had been pushed off in their sleep. The child wore a yellow T-shirt, red leggings and had long blonde hair.

Fiona turned away from the window and rested both shoulders against the wall. There was no doubt in her mind the girl asleep on the couch was Cait Yorke. Where there was doubt was in the circumstances that had led her to this house.

Had Betty Jamieson taken in a lost and hungry child who'd fallen asleep after a bite to eat? As a former foster carer, she'd provide a safe refuge, but she'd also have more than enough about her to make sure the girl was returned to the safety of her parents. Or would she? If something was amiss with the family, who better to tease truth from a troubled child? Maybe the girl had opened up to a kind stranger about the special secret her father made her keep. In that case, it made sense Betty Jamieson kept Cait until the morning, when she could report everything she'd been told to the appropriate agencies.

If the pictures on the wall were of Betty's former charges, their presence spoke well for the woman's caring nature.

However, if everything at home was as it should be, there was no logical reason for the woman to keep Cait. There was a car parked beside the house, and Cait was old enough to tell Betty where she was staying. Even if Cait didn't know the name of the caravan site, there was only one on Luing so it would have been easy for Betty to return Cait to her parents. But, she hadn't.

With no support from fellow officers, Fiona knew there was only one course of action open to her. She walked to the front door and swung the heavy knocker three times.

The door opened a crack and the creased face of Betty Jamieson appeared behind the security chain. 'Hello. What are you doing waking me up at this hour?'

'I'm here for Cait Yorke.'

'She's no' here.'

'Then who's the girl asleep on your couch?'

'That's wee Gemma. She came back to see me. She stayed here fifteen years ago. She never did like sleeping in a bed. Every morning I'd find her on the couch fast asleep.'

Fiona could see Betty believed every word she was saying. The real Gemma would now be in her twenties, but in Betty's mind, Cait was the girl Betty had fostered years before. She had to get in and speak to Cait. Convince Betty of her mistake. Poor Betty must be suffering a form of Alzheimer's to believe the eight-year-old Cait was the same girl she'd fostered fifteen years ago.

'Please, can I come in and speak to Gemma? It's important.'

'Bugger off. I'm not letting you wake the bairn. Come back in the morning.'

'I need to see her.' Fiona put authority into her tone. 'Please let me in, or I'll do you for obstructing a police officer.'

As the door eased to, Fiona saw a mottled hand reaching up to the level of the chain. When the door didn't reopen after a few seconds, Fiona tried the handle. Locked. She swung the knocker five times but the door remained closed.

Fiona took two steps back and decided on a course of action. By rights she ought to have a warrant to search Betty's house, but she could get round that by classing Cait as a kidnap victim. It was stretching the truth, but there was no saying what Betty would do considering her state of mind.

The door was made of timber, but it had paint flaking from its surface, so Fiona readied herself and then slammed the sole of her foot beside the handle. All she achieved for her troubles was a vibrating throb that ran right up to her hip. The pain didn't prevent Fiona from taking a second or third kick, but the door was too stout for her to breach it.

FIFTY-TWO

Edwin had the window open and was looking at Fiona as she approached his side of the car. It was a risk involving him, but she didn't see another option. Had this been the mainland she'd have been able to call for support and a team of officers would have arrived with a Big Red Key to bash the door in. The only way she could breach the door of Betty's house was to kick it down, and she had neither the weight nor power to do that. Edwin, on the other hand, was taller and heavier and stronger than she was.

'I need your help.'

The car door opened before she could say more.

'I know, I saw you trying to kick the door in.' Edwin looked down at Fiona. 'Do you promise I won't get into trouble for helping you? Mrs Jamieson is mean. It was her that reported me for talking to that girl. I know it was. She's never liked me.'

'I promise you won't get into trouble for helping me get into her house.'

Together Fiona and Edwin trotted back to the house as fast as they could with the wind trying to blow them off their feet.

Edwin didn't waste any time sizing up the door or lining up

to strike with maximum impact, he just ducked a shoulder and charged. The howl of agony he gave as he crashed into the door was audible over the din of the gale, and his face contorted in agony as he recoiled away from the solid wooden obstacle.

Rather than shout in Edwin's ear, Fiona showed him how she'd been using the sole of her foot to slam against the part of the door where the lock was located.

There was a nod from Edwin and he adjusted his position to use his foot instead of his shoulder. Edwin had an arm clasped across his chest as he lurched forward and gave the door a mighty kick.

Fiona could see the door frame had splintered under Edwin's assault. She raised her voice to a yell. 'Again. Go on Edwin, you can do it.'

A second hefty kick thudded into the door and it snapped open, only to be halted two inches into its arc by the security chain. Edwin didn't hesitate, or try to recover his balance, he just launched his weight at the door, taking the full impact on his shoulder.

The door swung wide, so Fiona pushed past Edwin, her baton in hand in case Betty Jamieson tried attacking her.

The house smelled of roast chicken, which made Fiona's stomach growl as she made her way to the living room.

'Betty, Cait. I'm a police officer. My name is Fiona, where are you?'

Although she used a loud voice, Fiona stopped short of a full-blooded shout. There was no telling what Betty had said to Cait about the noise of them kicking the door in, and the last thing she wanted to do was frighten the child.

There was no answer and when Fiona pushed the living room door open she found no sign of Cait or Betty. As she spun from the room, Fiona's mind was racing with possibilities for their whereabouts. If there was a back door to the house, then Betty could whisk Cait from it and disappear into the night.

The idea of being so close to rescuing the child and having to scour the island for her again burned at Fiona as she dashed through the house looking for the kitchen. She found the kitchen and from it, a small utility room with the back door.

The door was closed and there was a key in its lock. Fiona tried the handle, but the door didn't open so she removed the key, tossed it into a cupboard and made her way back to the central hall.

Edwin was leaning against a wall, a sheen of sweat running over his face and a grimace twisting his mouth enough to worry Fiona into a halt.

'You okay, Edwin?'

'Yeah. Go find her.'

Instead of returning to the living room Fiona tried the other door in the hall and found a dining room. A salt cellar and pepper pot were centred on the polished wooden table, but like the living room, there was no sign of life.

Fiona took the stairs two at a time, her feet thudding on the treads as she went. At the top there were four doors. Two to the left, one dead ahead and one to the right.

The door in front of Fiona was ajar enough she could see a peach sink on its equally hideous pedestal. Logic suggested the door on the right would be the master bedroom, with two others crammed into a similar space on the other side of the house. The question was, had Betty gone to her own room with Cait, or had she taken her to the one where Gemma used to sleep all those years ago?

Fiona went right. The thinking behind her decision was that everyone feels safe in their bed and, confused as she was, Betty might be taking refuge in the place she felt safest.

The bedroom had all the usual furniture, but no humans. All the same, Fiona swung the wardrobe doors open and checked in case Betty was trying to hide.

She wasn't.

'Owww. Stoppit, you're hurting me.'

As soon as she heard the child's voice, Fiona was moving. She grabbed the handle of the nearest bedroom door and barged into the room.

Cait was on her knees by another wardrobe, and Betty was trying to push her in but the child was resisting.

Betty never looked Fiona's way.

'Gemma, you have to get in. The bad people are coming for you. You don't want that, do you?'

'I'm not Gemma, I'm Cait. I don't want to stay with you until morning like you said I could. I want my mummy and daddy.'

Fiona stepped forward, the baton back in its holder on her belt, and her hands reaching for Betty's arms. 'Betty, let go of her. You've got it wrong. She's not Gemma.'

'Liar.' Betty whirled, her eyes wild and both hands clawing at Fiona's face. 'She's Gemma. You're going to take her away from me. She's only just come back to see me, and you're here to steal her away. After all I've done for that lassie. How can you do that to us? How do you sleep at nights?'

Fiona might not have been powerful enough to break down the door, but she had more than enough strength to restrain the elderly woman in front of her. 'Betty Jamieson, I'm arresting you for kidnap, and assaulting a police officer.'

Of all the arrests Fiona had made, this was the one of which she was least proud. Betty Jamieson was confused. Other than the attempt to hide Cait in the wardrobe, it looked very much like she'd been kind to the child. All the same, her actions couldn't be allowed to go unpunished. As soon as Fiona had Betty in handcuffs and was satisfied the old woman couldn't harm anyone, including herself, Fiona cast her eyes down at Betty's feet.

'What size shoe do you take?'

'What? I'm size eight, why?'

'Just curious.' There was no point in explaining the question, Fiona had the information she needed. The footprint she'd found overlaying Cait's in the cave was judged to be a size eight.

Fiona shifted her gaze to Cait.

'It's okay, Cait. I'm going to take you back to your mummy now. She's missed you. Have you missed her?'

Cait nodded, her eyes on Betty who was now mumbling curses. 'I've missed my daddy more. He's funny, but Mum's always telling me to behave.'

Fiona could feel a smile widening her mouth. Not only did Cait's words quell the latent suspicions she'd had about Pete Yorke, but also the girl's assessment of her parents chimed with Fiona's memories of her own father and mother.

The smile faded when Fiona revisited the thought she'd had earlier relating to her parents' murder. Had they been slain because of a sexual crime they'd blown the whistle on? At first thought it seemed unlikely, as if they'd gone on record against someone, the police would have had a solid lead to follow in the hours, days and weeks after their bodies were discovered. However, the more Fiona considered the idea they'd made an anonymous tip, the more she believed they'd been identified as the tipster by the person they'd told on.

FIFTY-THREE

Fiona drove them all back to the church with her blue lights flashing. More than anything she wanted to attract the attention of Diane Yorke. The woman's barbs were forgotten in her mind, and she was anticipating one of those rare moments in policing: the indescribable pleasure of reuniting a lost child with their parents.

Beside her in the front of the car, Cait was sitting in silence. Edwin and Betty were in the back, and while Edwin was also quiet, Betty was havering away about how Fiona was wrong and that she ought to never have been arrested as she was fostering Gemma.

The collapse of Betty's mind was tragic to behold and it was the one thing that was tarnishing Cait's rescue. It was wonderful that Cait had come to no harm, that above everything else was what everyone wanted, but Fiona could feel nothing but pity for the elderly woman. For all Betty may have kidnapped Cait, she'd done so out of mistaken identity as her mind crumbled due to Alzheimer's or dementia. When it came to giving her report, Fiona planned to tell nothing but the truth, but she was already crafting sentences that would explain

Betty's actions in a sympathetic light, and Cait was unharmed, although she was now fearful of the older lady.

When Fiona's headlights picked out the standing figures of Diane and Pete Yorke, she knocked off the blue lights, beeped her horn and flashed the car's headlights. Both of them were running her way as she drew to a halt and switched on the internal light so Cait was illuminated.

As soon as both parents saw Cait in the front of the car, they reacted in different ways. Diane was at the passenger side, yanking the door open, squeals of delight filling the car as she hugged Cait. Pete's run faltered as his knees wobbled, the huge beaming smile on his face collapsing as relief pulsed tears from his eyes.

Fiona reached to open the door, turning her head to Edwin as she did. 'Can you keep an eye on Betty for a minute, please?'

Edwin nodded. His eyes shining as he witnessed the reunion. Fiona got exactly how he felt: she had the same emotions in her chest.

By the time Fiona had climbed out of the car, all three of the Yorkes were hugging each other. It was an embrace as precious as any she'd ever witnessed, and while the sight would never assuage the guilt she felt at what had happened to Will and Vic, Fiona counted it as a win.

She stood to one side until they peeled themselves apart enough to notice the rest of the universe. Cait was in Pete's arms with Diane snuggling into her.

Diane untangled herself and stepped towards Fiona. 'Thank you, thank you, thank you. I'm so sorry I was so horrible before.'

'Don't worry about it.' Fiona had already forgiven the harsh words, as she knew they'd been spoken under immeasurable distress. 'All that matters is that Cait is back safe and sound.'

'That's very good of you. Where was she?'

Fiona didn't want to give too much away, as her mind was

already moving forward onto what she must do next in the hunt for Shand and his mates, plus the crewmen, but she didn't see how she could hide the truth. Cait would relay everything that had happened to her parents anyway.

'A local woman took her in. From what I can tell the woman's suffering from Alzheimer's or a similar condition, and she mistook Cait for someone she used to foster. While Cait may be a little traumatised, the woman hasn't harmed her in any way.'

Diane's mouth twisted as she peered in the car. 'That her?'

'Yes. I've arrested her and she'll be charged. I'm not sure she'll ever stand trial, though.'

Both of Diane's shoulders drooped as she exhaled a long breath. 'I don't know if I want to kill her, or thank her for looking after Cait. God knows what could have happened if she'd been out on the island all night.'

'You should be thankful. Maybe not to her, but to the fact Cait is okay. She'll be dealt with, but will probably end up in a form of social care.' As relieved as Fiona might be that Diane wasn't screaming vengeful threats at Betty, the hard part of the conversation was still to come. 'I don't know if you've heard yet, but the caravan site where you were staying is wrecked. All the caravans are overturning in the wind and everyone from there is in the church.'

A nod. 'I've heard. We'll go there too now we've got Cait back.'

'That's good, but I have other work to do and need somewhere to keep this lady, as there's no way she can come with me. The church makes sense as there'll be other people there to watch over her. Can I trust you and Pete to leave her alone?'

Diane's eyes clouded as she considered the question. 'Don't worry, Pete's mother has Alzheimer's. We know how it twists the mind. I still don't know whether or not I hate her, but I won't bother her.'

* * *

Fiona walked Betty into the church and sat her down as far away from all the others as she could. Muscles came over, puzzlement on his face, so Fiona gave him a rapid explanation and asked him to make sure she was both safe from anyone who might wish to harm her, and prevented from causing trouble.

'What are you going to do?'

'I need to speak to one of the passengers then I'll try and find Grant or Deek, and then I'm going to continue looking for the five men who disappeared during the transfer from the Atlantic Islands Centre. Can you get one of the doctors to take a look at Betty and Edwin?'

'I'm going with you, Fiona. We're a team.'

Fiona turned to find Edwin at her shoulder.

'I'm sorry, Edwin, Cait's been found, you're hurt. You've done more than enough. You need to rest now.'

'But—'

'No buts, Edwin. You're staying here.'

Fiona walked down the aisle clapping her hands together as she went. 'Listen up, everyone who was on the boat.' Fiona paused while they stopped chatting among themselves and turned her way. 'The five guys who were on the boat with you, but aren't here. I know all about the two crewmen, as I spoke to them earlier, but I need you all to help me with the other three. I'm going to go round you all and I want you to tell me what you can about them. Yes, I did get their names earlier, but I didn't have a lot of time, so I want you to refresh my memory by telling me anything you can about their ages, height, body shape, any tattoos they may have had and every other detail like that. If you heard them speak what did they say? Where were their accents from?' Fiona gestured at the nearest table where Delia sat. 'Can you start, please?

'They would be late teens, twenties.' Her lips pursed in

disappointment. 'I'm sorry, but I didn't pay them any attention. I was looking out of the window the whole time.'

Round the room, the conversation went back and forth until Fiona had expanded on her memory of the three men. All were in their twenties. All wore ripped jeans and hoodies. One had a wispy goatee. Nobody had heard them speak. Not even to each other. No one had seen any tattoos, or recalled an eye colour.

Fiona took a walk over to the table where the teenage couple sat.

'Hi.' She gestured to the girl as she looked at the boy. 'Can I speak with her alone? You can stand by the door so you can see us if you like.'

The boy nodded and rose. Written all over his face was his obvious fear the girl was in trouble. The girl's face was calm, but Fiona had questioned enough people to spot the little nervous tic high on her left cheek.

'What's up? Why do you need to speak to me alone like this?'

Fiona tried to give a reassuring smile but it felt like she was grimacing. 'Don't worry. Everyone else on the boat is waaay old. They wouldn't notice what three young guys looked like. Wouldn't care. By the same token, the young guys wouldn't pay them any attention. You're young and pretty. Yes, you appear to be with someone and all that, but I just figured you'd have checked them out. You know, from habit.' Fiona tried another smile and leaned in. 'I check guys out all the time. And I bet those guys checked you out.'

'I didn't. I wouldn't.' The hint of a smile touched the corners of the girl's mouth as her cheek both flushed and twitched. 'At least, not when I'm with Harry, and even then, it's never more than looking. I love Harry. I'll be with him forever.'

Fiona thought better of commenting on the girl's assertion her and Harry's love would be forever. The most pertinent thing was getting the girl talking. Bursting her bubble would have the opposite effect. 'Come on. You must have had a wee look. There's nothing wrong with that. Don't worry about me telling Harry. I've nothing to gain from that. What I'm doing is trying to catch a killer. That's all I care about.'

'I caught one of them checking me out. He smiled at me. Creep. He had a missing tooth. Right here.' She pointed at her upper left incisor. 'I flipped him off and he never bothered me again.'

'Did he speak at all? How did he react to being flipped off?'

'He didn't speak, and he just turned away.'

'Okay. Your accent sounds local, where are you from?'

'Oban.'

'Cool. Did anything about those guys look familiar? Have you seen them in a pub or anything like that?'

'I've never seen them before. And if one of them killed the boat's captain, I never want to see them again.' The girl's shudder at the thought was violent enough to bring Harry running.

'Thanks.' Fiona rose from her chair and left the couple alone.

Fiona left the church and climbed back into her car. Against her instinct she found that she missed having Edwin with her. He might never be permitted to join Mensa, but his presence at her side gave her a sense of comfort. Now she felt alone and exposed. All the same, Edwin had been hurt at the caravan site and had aggravated that injury with the assault on Betty's door. There was no way she could risk further injury to him.

FIFTY-FOUR

Fiona went south from the church intending to head towards Blackmill Bay. That was the direction Deek had last been seen heading and she wanted to catch up with him. Not only to share the good news that Cait had been found, but to see if he'd found any sign of Shand and his mates.

Before she got to the junction towards Blackmill Bay, however, Fiona saw lights flash through the sky. She recalled from her visits to Toberonochy that a track ran south through a farmyard on the way there.

As the lights came from that direction, Fiona reasoned Deek must be using the track and made her way towards it, and rather than wait for Deek to arrive, she set off in case he took a turn off somewhere and moved away from her.

The rough track pitched the car around and on more than one occasion Fiona heard the underside scrape on something. She kept going, there was a new thought in her mind and as much as she didn't want to believe it would happen, she was afraid it would.

Deek's light kept coming her way and when they met he pulled his Jeep off the track until their doors were only a few inches apart. Even with both windows down and them yelling, it was a struggle to be heard. She could get what he was saying, but the wind was blowing her words away long before he could hear them.

'You what?'

Fiona cupped her arms as if rocking a baby then gave a thumbs up. The relief on Deek's face told her he understood. She pointed at him, made the sign of the cross and then put her hands together as if praying.

Deek's meaty hand curled into a fist with his thumb pointing at the sky as he dropped a nod her way and set off.

With Deek on his way to help Muscles take care of everyone at the church, Fiona found a piece of land flat enough where she could turn her car around, and then she set off for Toberonochy. The more she tried putting herself in the killer's position to try and anticipate the next move they would make, the more she was convincing herself they would be desperate to get off the island.

Fiona had spent every second since delivering Cait back to her parents trying to work out whether the killer was acting alone, or whether he was in cahoots with one mate or several. Ian and Davie were crewmates and it seemed they had a decent relationship. Shand and his two buddies wouldn't have travelled all the way from Wick together if they weren't close. According to Heather, there were a lot of pictures online of the three of them enjoying each other's company. It could be the killer was working alone, that they'd spotted an opportunity and taken it. The idea of the killer working with the knowledge and help of his friends made things more complicated. No matter how strong a friendship might be, very few people would stand between their mate and a police investigation. However, if they were involved, it could mean Fiona might have to try and arrest up to three people at once.

What Fiona didn't, and couldn't, know was whether there

was a connection between the two groups. If the five of them were working together, she wouldn't stand a chance against that many people. All she could do was try to find them – identifying the killer among them could wait for reinforcements to arrive.

Of Fiona's five suspects, four of them worked on boats and the fifth was a nautical mechanic, so it stood to reason they'd be confident at piloting a boat. Whether they'd risk the crossing to the mainland in this weather, at night, was unknown, but they'd be increasingly desperate, and desperate people did desperate things.

The killer would know that she was aware of the murders and would have reported that back to the mainland. It was to be expected that coppers would be stationed at the ferry port on the north side of the Cuan Sound, either to catch anyone coming across or to access Luing themselves, so it made logical sense the killer would head for the mainland instead of Seil. While all the recognised ports and jetties may be under police surveillance, there were many miles of shoreline where they'd be able to run a boat aground if they could steal one.

To Fiona's knowledge there were three small harbours or working jetties on Luing. The one at Cuan Sound was devoid of boats and likely to deliver the killer straight into police hands, so that was out. So was the harbour at Cullipool, as it faced the Atlantic Ocean and while it might be a place a boat could be stolen from, it was on the side of the island where the seas were at their roughest. That left the harbour at Toberonochy, on the east side of the island. Not only was it facing the mainland, but it was the most sheltered harbour. If the killer stole a boat from there, they would have the best chance possible of surviving the trip across to the mainland, although there was the island of Shuna to get around before they could strike out.

This reasoning was why Fiona was on her way to Toberonochy.

As Fiona thought it through she realised the way she'd advertised her presence with the blue lights atop her car while looking for Cait would have been taken another way by the five fugitives. They'd have figured she was after them and that in turn would have made them even more desperate to find a way off the island. Their attack on Tait appeared to have been thought out in advance, and Fiona now wondered if the killer or a possible accomplice had made a contingency plan should they be stuck on Luing. If so, they might have enacted it hours ago.

The idea of three young men from Wick choosing Luing as a holiday destination didn't add up in Fiona's mind. Mainland Spain, one of its many party islands, or somewhere like Ayia Napa made a lot more sense. Those places were geared towards the hedonism enjoyed by young people. Luing was geared to water-based entertainment and solitude. There wasn't even a pub on the island. As much as the three men spent their professional lives on or around the sea, the idea of them taking a seafaring holiday didn't sit well with Fiona. And she couldn't think of a credible motive for any of them to murder Tait. Fiona was aware the information she had wasn't enough to formulate theories. When Heather had dug deeper into the men's lives a reason for them targeting Tait might emerge, but until that digging had unearthed something, all she could do was guess.

She could be wrong, of course. Ian hadn't tried to hide the fact he didn't get on with Tait. That could have been a double bluff, a deliberate statement made at a time when he still believed he might get away with the murder he'd committed.

As for young Davie. Tait had taken him in, helped him turn his life around. That wasn't a motive for murder, but who knew what had happened between the two of them? To live and work with someone takes a lot of patience and understanding from both parties. Had Davie's patience with Tait run out? Had he played along and bided his time?

When Fiona pulled into Toberonochy, she made straight for

the small harbour. She hadn't counted the number of boats present when she'd arrived earlier, but she didn't recognise a gap where one had previously been.

Fiona's headlights dipped into the shale bank of the harbour and illuminated two men wrestling with a boat at the water's edge. So intent were they with their task, neither man turned when her headlights landed on them.

As much as Fiona's heart raced at the sight, it only took a second for her to realise the men were trying to haul the small boat from the water rather than launch it. Not only that, but one of the men had long grey hair that streamed from his head. These weren't the men she was seeking, they must be islanders.

Fiona climbed out of the car, after pointing its nose into the wind, and trudged down the shale bank towards the men. It would have been polite to wait until their task was complete, but Fiona didn't dare waste the time. She approached the man whose grey hair the gale was streaming out from his head.

'Are there any boats missing?'

The man tossed her a glare. 'No, now let us get on with saving this one afore it gets swept away.'

Fiona was about to step away from the man and head back to the car when a thought struck her. If two men could drag the boat up the bank, three could easily haul it back to the water's edge. She pitched in to help the men until they were satisfied they had the boat as high up the bank as they needed it to be.

At the stern of the boat a small outboard motor was bolted to a flat plank. Fiona pointed at the outboard. 'Can that be removed?'

'Of course. Why?'

'There are people on the island that I'm after, and I don't want them stealing a boat and heading off to the mainland.'

'They'd have to be bloody mad to try sailing a wee boat like this to the mainland in this weather.'

Fiona tapped the front of her stab vest by her heart. 'Trust me, they're desperate enough. Please remove the motor.'

'Got a better idea.' The man lifted the hood of the motor and reached inside. When his hand came free it held a short piece of wiring that had connecting plugs at each end. 'It'll no' start without this.'

'Nice one.'

Back in her car, Fiona set a course for the north of the island. Her suspicion the killer would try and leave the island by boat either alone or with company still stood, but she was also wondering about Grant and Fergus. They ought to have returned by now. If she was wrong about the killer leaving the island, there was a chance the two islanders had found one or more of the missing men, and she didn't dare think of how that might have gone down. Therefore she was on her way to find them before there was another murder to investigate.

Fiona grabbed the plastic water bottle from its home in the door pocket and dribbled the last of the water into her mouth and allowed it to trickle down her throat. As warm as it was, it tasted worse than cold sprouts, but it did soothe the roughness of her throat.

The journey to the north of the island was short, as she was getting to know the roads on Luing and could go faster now she was confident there would be nobody walking the road in search of Cait.

Fiona wanted to check Cullipool first in case she could see a glimpse of light from the Land Rover Grant drove, but as she passed the house with the conservatory, Fiona saw something that made her stamp on the brakes, reverse back and climb out.

FIFTY-FIVE

The door was white and plastic. That wasn't a material Fiona had expected to find on Luing where so many of the traditional building methods still held sway. There was a doorbell on the left. Fiona stabbed it hard and kept her finger on the button. Drunk people have less awareness of what's going on around them. Dave Lennox and experience had both taught her that.

A woman opened the door. She was mid-fifties and had short hair that might have held a style some hours ago.

'Help you?'

Fiona didn't have time to answer before the woman hiccoughed. The one saving grace about the wind was that Fiona didn't have to smell whatever was on the woman's breath.

'Yes, I'm here to see Ian Caldwell and his mate Davie.'

The woman opened the door wide, her knuckles white as she clung to it for support with one hand and made an exaggerated 'come in' gesture with the other.

Fiona didn't ask the woman's name and it wasn't offered.

The woman with no name lurched her way to the conservatory. Ian Caldwell was no longer on his feet as he had been when Fiona had spied him while driving past. He was now slouched in a seat whose back faced the road. A glass of whisky was in his hand and from the glazed expression he wore, it was a long way from his first.

Fiona stood in the doorway where she could keep an eye on everyone in the room. A man she didn't recognise lay asleep on her left, his soft snores barely audible above the wind noise, and Davie was next to Ian.

'Ey up. The copssh are here.' The glass was deposited on a table that neighboured his chair and his now free hand rose in an untidy salute. 'What's up?'

Fiona was too experienced to take Ian's drunkenness at face value. There was plenty of time since his leaving the Atlantic Island Centre for him to have travelled to the eco-pods, kill Will, make his way to Sunnybrae and slash the mooring straps and then travel back here to nail enough whisky in a short time to get him as drunk as he appeared to be.

'How long have you been here?'

It was Davie who answered, his voice clear and unaffected by alcohol. 'Since we left that café slash museum place.' A nod towards the sleeping man. 'That's Ian's half cousin. Ian reckoned we'd be better off coming here than sitting in a church all night. You should have heard the stories about what they got up to as kids in Tobermory.'

Something in Fiona clicked. She thought about everything she knew about the five men who'd not gone to the church with the others. If Ian Caldwell was the killer, then he was either cocky as hell or as dumb as a rock to sit and get pissed in full view of the road where she might find him just as she had.

More than that, she thought of Shand and his mates, the way they'd all paid cash for the trip on the *Each-Uisge*, had arrived on the boat together and not engaged with any of the other passengers. There was no motive Fiona could determine, but there was too much other evidence pointing towards the men from Wick for Ian and Davie to be considered suspects for much longer.

'Davie, I understand that you both lived and worked with Charlie. I need you to think long and hard before answering me. The three men who were on the boat, but like you didn't go to the church, were around your age. They're the most likely suspects for Charlie's murder. Have you seen any of them before today? Near your home, perhaps, or in the pub where you and Charlie drank?'

'Charlie didn't drink. He said he used to, but got bored of it. I don't bother with it meself. Since I moved in with Charlie, I don't take nothing that'll tempt me to do owt stupid.'

Was Charlie bored of drinking, or had he got to the point where he'd had to dry out? That was the question Fiona asked herself. In her experience, few Scots didn't drink at all, and fewer fishermen.

Fiona kept her tone gentle. 'That wasn't what I asked.'

'Sorry.' Davie's apology was as much on his face as in his words. 'No, I've no idea who they are. Never seen them before. I'll be honest, though. I don't pay too much attention to the passengers unless I have to.'

A leer crept onto Ian's face. 'He notices the young women.'

Ian got a furious look as a protest tumbled from Davie's mouth. Fiona paid neither comment any heed. Single men and women have always sought out a mate and would continue to do so until all human life was extinct. She'd have been more surprised if Davie hadn't been the way he was.

'Never mind that, Davie. Would you say you knew Charlie well? Did he trust you? Tell you things about his past? Was he married?'

'Yeah, I knew him well enough. He used to be a crabber up at Ullapool. Christ, the stories he told about it. He'd go on and on if you let him. Mind, some of them stories were pure gold. Would make a brilliant film, they would.'

'I bet.' Agreeing with the subject being interviewed was always a good way to keep them onside. 'What about his love life? Did he ever mention a wife, kids?'

'Not to me. Said he liked the single life and didnae want any damned woman filling his hoose with cushions and flowers.'

'Okay. What about other family. Brothers, sisters, parents?'

'He never mentioned any. Never went to visit anyone like that.'

'Did he get cards from them? You know, at Christmas or on his birthday?'

'Nope. Poor bugger only had me.' Davie's expression collapsed in grief. 'And he was killed when I was within fifty feet of him. I failed him. I should have been there to protect him.'

Fiona rested a palm on Davie's shoulder. 'There's nothing you could have done. Charlie was stabbed. If you'd tried to protect him, you'd have been killed too.'

There wasn't a lot else to say, and with everything else she had to contend with, Fiona patted Davie's shoulder and made to leave. On a technical level it was still possible Davie or Ian may be the killer she was hunting, but Ian wasn't fit to walk, let alone try to escape the island, and if Davie was acting innocent, he deserved every award Hollywood had to offer.

'Davie, did you see which way the three others went when you left the passengers after leaving the café place?'

'Alls I saw was them going up towards the top of the island. Me and Ian ducked behind a row of cottages and hid in a bush for a few minutes in case the locals came looking for us.'

It made sense the trio from Wick had gone that way. Once away from the well-lit areas, they'd be able to set a course for Sunnybrae. They'd gone off course though and ended up at the eco-pods at some point. It might even have been their original plan to lie low there for a few hours until the ferry ran again and they could get back to Seil. That plan had been changed when she sent Will there looking for Cait.

Along with the pang of guilt, came the realisation of yet another mistake she'd made. Davie had been the first on deck. Therefore, if he'd been the one to kill Tait he would have had to push his way through the passengers all the way from the wheelhouse at the front, to get to the entrance and exit point at the rear. He'd stayed on station until he'd crossed the rope. Unless Tait had been killed long before they crashed, there was no way Davie could have been the killer.

Fiona had long ago reasoned the odds of Tait being killed before the *Each-Uisge* foundered were almost non-existent. Anyone intent on murder wouldn't kill someone in a room next to a bunch of witnesses. Nor would they risk one of the passengers looking for the captain. Not with someone like Irene on board, and with her nature being what it was, there was little doubt Irene would have been a pain in the arse long before Tait was killed.

The more Fiona pressed her memory of the rescue, the more she could picture the faces as they'd emerged. The three young men from Wick had been among the last to exit the cabin. The pudgy one who'd called himself Johnathan had helped Delia maintain her balance.

Ian had joined Davie at the rope, helping the passengers until his nerve failed him and he abandoned Delia. Like Davie, he'd never left that position until taking the skyline to solid ground.

The killer was one of the three men from Wick. He had to be, all the other suspects on her list hadn't had the same opportunity they'd had. Now Fiona had to find the men from Wick. Grant and Fergus were looking to avenge Will, and if the two parties met there was every chance there would be at least one more murder.

FIFTY-SIX

The need to relay Cait's rescue to those on the mainland was high on Fiona's agenda, and there were some lines of enquiry she wanted Heather to check out, so she drove the short distance to Deek's cottage to contact her. As she'd approached Cullipool she'd watched for the headlights of the Land Rover but hadn't seen a sign of them.

'Heather, it's me. I've found the missing girl and have reunited her with her parents.'

'Brilliant, Fiona. Well done you.' Heather's voice changed. 'Ma'am. It's Fiona. She's returned Cait to her parents.'

'Before you ask, Cait seems unharmed. Now listen up, please. I know you've probably been digging into the background of those three guys from Wick and the two crew men, but I've had an idea I need you to check out for me. Before you do anything, though, I've eliminated the crewmen from my enquiries.'

'Please explain your reasoning, PC MacLeish.'

Fiona spent a solid five minutes explaining to DI Baird about the cut straps at the caravan park, and how she'd found Ian and Davie sitting in a conservatory that was in full view of the road. When she detailed the rescue of the elderly couple and Vic's death she heard breaths being sharply taken.

'It would appear your logic is sound. I agree that the crewmen should no longer be viewed as suspects. That brings us back to the three men from Wick. What do you want DC Andrews to look into for you?' The way Baird always used ranks and surnames was something Fiona had grown familiar with, but she'd never get used to such unnecessary formality in what was supposed to be a tight unit.

'I've been thinking about why Tait was killed. The wounds to his groin suggest something to do with sex is the reason he was killed, but they might be a red herring. We know the killer or killers are from Wick, while he's been in Oban for over a decade, so we need to find the connection between them. I've been wondering if it's something like the Scouts, Boy's Brigade, the Sea Cadets or any other youth group that's run by adults. You said the three lads are either twenty-six or twenty-seven. Twelve years ago when Tait turned up in Oban they'd have been fourteen or fifteen, that puts them the right age range for members of an organisation like the Scouts or Sea Cadets. My guess, with Wick being such a port town is that Sea Cadets is more likely. I don't know their ranking structure, but had he been their captain or whatever? Had he lived and worked up there on the boats and knocked up one of their mothers or sisters? Is he the dad of one of them? A dad who abused his son and his son's friends, either physically, emotionally or sexually? If you haven't already got people knocking on their mothers' doors with a picture of Charlie Tait in their hands, you need to make it happen as soon as you can. If it's not related to sex, we still need to find a connection between them and Tait. Person-ally, I believe it has to do with sex, as they never expected Tait's body to be discovered. Therefore, he was stabbed in the groin as that's the part of him that had caused the killer the most offence.'

When the reply came it was DI Baird's voice. 'Do you think we don't know how to do our jobs, Constable MacLeish? Do you think that because you found Cait Yorke you're the only one who can use joined-up thinking?'

'Of course not, ma'am. But my queries still stand; are those things being done as we speak?'

The silence was more informative than the entire contents of the British Library.

'Ma'am? Heather?'

'It's me, Fiona. DI Baird has just left the room. I can't believe you spoke to her like that. Anyway, to answer your question, there are officers enroute to speak to the families of the three guys. I don't know if they've pictures of Tait or not, but I'll make sure some are sent to them right away.'

'Thanks. I'll check in again soon.'

Fiona left the cottage and made her way to the ferry point at South Cuan, her eyes constantly checking the landscape for signs of Grant. By the time Fiona parked on the ferry ramp, she hadn't seen a single hint they were still in that part of the island.

As a last resort, Fiona again clambered up the bank and looked into the wind. A hundred yards ahead was a hill and she picked her way up it until she could see further. Except she could see little except faint pinpricks of light that may be Grant and Fergus holding a torch or maybe lights from Mull, several miles beyond.

Fiona swept her torch back and forth across the landscape as far as its beam would illuminate. Upon finding no sign of them she covered the torch with a hand and let out a series of ten flashes. If Grant and Fergus were out there, they'd hopefully see the flashes and come to investigate.

Five long slow minutes ticked by and with nothing gained beyond a sense of exhaustion at fighting her way into the wind, Fiona turned and made her way back to the police car.

The police car sat where she'd left it. Nose into the wind at the top of the slipway. As Fiona approached the car's front a sense of unease grew within her. Something wasn't right and she couldn't put her finger on it until she looked along its flank. Both driver's side tyres were flat. She tried to think of anything she'd hit like a pothole that could have flattened both tyres at once, but came up short.

Fiona aimed her torch at each tyre in turn and found the same thing, a four-inch slash at the top.

There were only three people on the island Fiona could think of who had cause to do such a thing. Frankie Shand and his two mates, Williamson and Kerr.

Fiona's free hand fumbled the collapsible baton from her utility belt and snapped it to its full extension. All Fiona could think of as she swept a circle with her torch was the hunter was now becoming the hunted.

FIFTY-SEVEN

Fiona stopped whirling round and tried to gather her thoughts. If she climbed back into the police car and locked the doors she'd be safe from any attack Shand and his mates may launch at her. Slashed tyres or not, the car could still be driven if they tried to force their way in. Alison Vivers lived two hundred yards away. Her house offered a source of refuge, a safe haven to wait for morning, when she'd be able to better watch for any attacks that may come her way.

It wasn't in Fiona's nature to hide away. Nor was she confident the killer or killers wouldn't try storming wherever she holed up. If that happened it was better for her not to be seeking refuge in the home of an innocent.

If they were coming for her, there was no way she was going to put anyone else in danger. Men like Fergus and Grant might deter with their size and obvious toughness, but two women would be seen as an easy target.

As much as waiting in the car seemed like the wise thing to do, Fiona didn't see it as a viable course of action. In the car she might be safe from the killer or killers, but they'd also be safe from her. Fiona's investigation into their whereabouts would end if she cowered in the vehicle, and that wasn't something she could live with. Not after two men had died because of her mistakes.

Another way of looking at the attack on the car was to see it as a non-lethal way to slow Fiona down. The killer had targeted Tait, that was a given, but it was only chance that caused them to run into Will and there was always the possibility he'd been killed as a desperate way to keep their whereabouts secret. The cutting of the mooring ropes on the caravans was more a distraction tactic than a direct assault. There was nothing to be gained from harming anyone at the site, therefore Shand and his mates must have reasoned the occupants would all evacuate before anyone was hurt.

It was a nice idea, but it did little to quell the thumping of Fiona's heart as she decided there was only one course of action left to her: she'd have to walk back to the church and enlist Deek and Muscles to help her. They had vehicles, they were large and powerful men whom the killer would fear tackling. It was about two-and-a-half miles back to the church. Less than an hour's walk, or a twenty-minute run on a sunny day. At night, in the wind, and with killers who may choose to ambush her at any moment, it was a different matter.

Fiona never once allowed herself to break into a jog as she trudged along the road, although doing so would massively reduce the time it took her to get to the church. The way she was constantly turning to keep a watch behind and on both sides of her would be impossible at a run, and there was the fact that whichever way she faced, the wind was always trying to push her eastwards. Any stumble when she was running would likely see the gale flatten her long before she'd recovered her balance. Another factor to keep Fiona from breaking into a run was her exhaustion. She'd been tired when she drove onto Luing, almost twelve hours ago. Now she was running on thinning fumes and stubborn determination. Most of all, though, she wasn't running because if she encountered the killers, she wanted to be at her best, not puffing and gasping before any confrontation began.

A huge part of Fiona knew that she was offering herself up as bait by walking along this road alone in the dark. It wasn't an idea she relished, but with the collapsible baton in her hand she had a chance. The heavy police torch in her other hand could also be used as a weapon. As plans went, it was a poor one, but to Fiona it was a better plan than hiding from them. She also had the stab vest she wore to protect her from knives. Three on one was never good odds, but she'd witnessed enough uneven fights to know that if she could take one of the three out of the equation before the others could attack her, the other two would lose confidence. Then it would be a case of taking one of the remaining two down and talking the third into surrendering. She'd seen Dave Lennox take down four attackers in this way as she handcuffed a fifth.

Headlights beamed around a corner some hundred yards in front of Fiona. She doubted the killers had a vehicle at their disposal, but rather than stand exposed on the road, Fiona clambered up the bank where she couldn't be run down.

Once she'd got herself upright and braced against the wind, Fiona shone her torch down into the roadway. If it wasn't the killers driving, she could get a lift from whomever was.

Even before the vehicle lumbered out of the dark Fiona knew who it was. The earthy rumble of the Land Rover's ancient engine was unmistakable.

FIFTY-EIGHT

Fiona climbed from the back of the Land Rover and followed Grant into his brother's workshop. They'd tried conversing by the side of the road, but short of yelling into each other's ears there was no way either of them could make themselves heard before the wind carried their voice away. Fergus stood just behind Grant, his glasses reflecting the strip lights illuminating the garage.

'So you had your tyres slashed, eh?'

'That's not all.' Fiona spent a minute giving Grant a quick update on everything that had happened since he and Fergus took off to search the island's northwest section. To Grant's credit he looked shameful when he heard about what happened at the caravan site, although he gave a fist pump when she told him she'd found Cait.

'So what's next? It looks like they're targeting you. Don't worry, Fergus and I will stick with you until they're caught.'

'Thanks. But my thinking is that they're going to be desperate to escape from Luing before morning. As soon as it's light, any attempt they make to get to the mainland will be clearly visible. Once the wind dies down enough for the ferry to run again, this island will be swarming with police.'

Grant rasped a hand over his stubbly chin. 'That makes sense, but do you really think they'll risk crossing in this weather, in the dark?'

'I don't know. But they're sure to know they're going to end up in prison if they stay on the island. Maybe not all of them. One will have been the leader, the person to stab your brother and the captain of the *Each-Uisge*. Maybe one or both of the others will point the finger at the leader and end up cutting some kind of deal. But if they're all mixed up in it, they'll be desperate to get to the mainland; it's their only chance of getting away with the murders they've committed.'

'There's no way the bastard who killed my brother is getting away with it. So help me, I'll kill him myself if I have to.'

'It won't come to that if we can figure out what they're planning.'

'How the hell are we meant to do that?'

'I've got some ideas, but first I have questions.'

'Then ask them. What do you need to know?'

'You're used to sailing or boating or whatever, aren't you? When's the next low or high tide?'

Grant looked at his watch. 'Aye, I've been on the water since I was five. It's high tide again in a couple of hours, but the gale will be holding the tide in as well, so it'll be a proper high tide.'

'I thought as much. What time is sunrise?'

Grant turned to Fergus with a raised eyebrow. 'You're the early bird.'

'It was ten past five this morning.'

Fiona checked the watch on her wrist. The watch had belonged to her father. It had a brown leather strap she'd replaced five times since inheriting the time piece, and a clock face with Roman numerals. By wearing the watch, and one of her mother's necklaces, every day, Fiona felt she was carrying a piece of her parents with her at all times. The necklaces changed depending on the occasion, but the watch never did. Like her father it was solid, reliable and best of all for Fiona, comforting.

It was now 2.55 a.m. High tide was in a couple of hours and so was sunrise. From living in Lochgilphead for the last seven years, Fiona had learned about slack tides. At either side of high or low tide there was a window when the tide was slowing down its movement in one direction and preparing to set off in another. These windows could last an hour either side of high or low tide, or be as short as five minutes depending on such things as weather, the topography of the sea bed, and whether or not there were any channels or headlands for the tides to follow or break upon.

Fiona spied a map pinned to a wall and as she walked towards it she waved for Grant to follow her. 'In normal weather conditions, how long would it take you to sail to the mainland?'

'The ferry only takes five minutes.'

'No, not the ferry to Seil, the mainland.'

Grant gave a shrug. 'From my berth in Cullipool, I could be there in an hour. It all depends on the boat you have and which way the tide is running.'

'The tide is currently coming in so I'd guess it's less than that. However, the sea is rough as all hell. Would I be right in saying the killers would have to travel at an appropriate speed rather than their best speed?'

'Aye, but it would be dangerous as buggery. The currents go in all directions as they go round the islands, split off up Loch Melfort, or travel back up towards the Clachan Bridge. We know the currents, but at night and in this weather, anyone who tries to sail to the mainland without knowing the currents is likely to end up running aground.'

Fiona had been afraid of this answer. If Shand and co were lost at sea it might not be the greatest loss to society, but unless their bodies were recovered, the families of their victims would never receive full closure. She also believed the chances of them running aground would be heightened because they'd travel without any running lights.

As much as she had to find and arrest the killers, Fiona also knew she had to capture them before they set sail, so she could prevent them from undertaking such a risky attempt to escape justice.

Fiona pointed at the map. 'Okay. Hypothetically speaking, if you were in their shoes and could steal a boat, where would you sail from and where would you try and land?'

Grant's meaty shoulders gave a shrug. 'It'd depend where I was setting off from. Cullipool is a non-starter as you'd need an ocean-worthy vessel to even attempt it in these seas. I would sooner go to jail than sail out of Cullipool tonight. There's Toberonochy, but if you went from there, the currents are a mess between Luing and Shuna, and then you'd still have to travel past Shuna to get to the mainland.' Grant paused to scratch his chin, then aimed a finger at the map, his nail at the top-right quadrant of Luing. 'If it was me, I'd pinch one of the RIBs or inflatable dinghies from Ardinamir Bay and head to Torsa, carry the boat overland and then head across towards the mainland from the other side of the island.'

From the way Grant traced his finger across the map to a small island just off the northeast coast of Luing then to the mainland, Fiona saw the wisdom of his plan. All the same, she had more questions.

'What's a RIB, and how heavy are they?'

'A Rigid Inflatable Boat. Even with an outboard attached they'd only weigh just over a hundredweight.'

The old-fashioned measure of weight brought a hint of nostalgia to Fiona. Aunt Mary had lived in a farming valley and

Fiona had often heard the measure used by the farmer and his workers. In reality, a hundredweight was around fifty kilos.

Those fifty kilos would take lugging across an island during a full-blown gale, but for three desperate young men it was doable. Doubly so as the gale would be at their back.

'What about navigation? How would they know where they are?'

'There are lots of apps for mobiles that will do the job, most of them work off satellites and won't be affected by the gale, but I don't think they'll care where they end up, so long as they get to the mainland.'

Grant's thinking made sense to Fiona. 'Does anyone live on Torsa?'

'There's a holiday let. I'd say it'll have someone in it. There usually is at this time of year.'

The fact more innocents may run into Shand and his mates sparked a flare of concern in Fiona's gut, until she realised the trio were trying to sneak away from Luing, so were unlikely to make a contact with anyone on the island lest their escape route be detected.

Fiona wanted to charge off to Ardinamir Bay at once, but she knew she had to slow herself for a moment's thought.

It made sense the killers would try escaping either round or over Torsa. From the havoc they'd wreaked on Luing, it was clear to Fiona they'd stayed in the north part of the island. Torsa was off the northeast coast and while the killers might all be experienced sailors, they'd also be familiar enough with the caprices of tide and current to know the folly of trying to sail across to the mainland. It made sense they'd do what Grant had suggested.

What Fiona didn't want to do now was commit to a course of action that may be wrong. If there was evidence of a missing boat in Ardinamir Bay, she'd have two choices, follow the killers across to Torsa, or stay on the island and run the risk of them escaping. She couldn't possibly get to Torsa without enlisting Grant's help. The crossing to Torsa was sure to put both of them in grave danger, but if by some miracle Shand and his mates got across to the mainland and survived landing their boat, they'd likely be in an uninhabited part of Scotland. A part that was rugged and mountainous. There were forests, crags and glens for them to hide in until police resources were redirected. Come night, it wouldn't be hard for them to slip across the A816 that ran down from Oban to Lochgilphead and escape the search net. Once they'd done that, they'd be able to steal a car from somewhere and then disappear into the ether. Maybe they'd be picked up one day, and maybe they wouldn't.

One way or another, Fiona had to stop Shand and his mates from getting to the mainland, but even as she was thinking this, she couldn't help but wonder if she was making another mistake. If she was wrong, she'd waste at least a couple of hours and, during that time, there would be nobody to protect the innocents on Luing.

FIFTY-NINE

Fiona wandered around the interior of the garage workshop. The motion helped her think, and as much as she was weighing up her options, she was also aware she had little choice. On her third circuit of the space, she noticed something fixed to a wall.

'Grant, may I use the phone?'

'Aye.'

Heather answered on the second ring.

'It's me again. Have you got anything?'

Fiona's heart both plummeted and soared as she listened to her friend pass on her findings. The news was everything she'd feared and more.

'Thanks. Is DI Baird there?'

'No, she's in her office. Do you want me to go and get her?'

'Don't bother. My latest theory is that Shand and co will try and cross to the mainland from Torsa. It's both high tide and sunrise at five. I reckon they're going to try crossing just before that. If I'm right, they'll make land somewhere on the west side of the peninsula that juts down at the north end of the entrance to Loch Melfort. If there are any spare bodies, it might be an idea to get them out that way just in case I can't stop them.'

'What are you planning, Fiona?' There was no mistaking the concern in Heather's tone.

Fiona hesitated. If she told Heather her full plan and Heather didn't advise her otherwise, it could well lead to trouble for her friend should she be wrong. 'To stop them. I'll be in touch when I've got more news.'

The phone was replaced and Fiona was striding away from it before Heather could press her for more details. By the time Fiona reached the garage door, the phone was ringing a loud jangle. Fiona stepped outside. What Heather didn't know, couldn't hurt her.

* * *

The journey to Ardinamir Bay was short. On the smooth roads, the rear of the Land Rover made no fresh assaults on Fiona, although the wind seemed determined to flick the ends of Fiona's hair into her eyes. To combat this, Fiona closed her eyes and tried not to think too much about the consequences of being wrong again.

The track from the road down to Ardinamir Bay was gravel, something Fiona worked out from the rattles emanating from the underside of the vehicle.

When looking at the map, Fiona had recalled seeing the island of Torsa when visiting the eco-pods. At first she'd thought it was part of Luing until she'd noticed the narrow channel between the two islands. The mainland had been visible and had she not known Torsa was an island, she'd have thought the two were connected.

At the ratcheting of the handbrake, Fiona opened her eyes and climbed from the rear of the Land Rover. Grant had parked by a small farmstead. Beyond the farm a narrow track ran down-hill to the water's edge some forty yards away.

Grant set off down the track with Fergus at his side. Fiona

had to stretch her legs to keep pace with them, and even though she was feeling like she couldn't walk another step, she pushed herself onwards.

As a counter to the exhaustion that was slowing her, Fiona also felt a weird excitement. Her best guess was that she was experiencing the thrill of the chase.

Under Fiona's torchlight, they found a collection of small rowboats that were all tied to iron rings that had been set in concrete.

The presence of the boats was a kick in the teeth for Fiona's idea. If there had been none, she'd have felt confident her idea had been good, but now, Fiona could feel her cheeks redden at being proven to have made yet another mistake.

As a last check Fiona cast her torch further along the beach. She discovered another boat. This must be one of the inflatable RIBs Grant had mentioned to her. Unlike the first collection of boats, this one had an outboard motor attached to its stern instead of a pair of oars nestling in its body.

Another difference was the way the RIB was secured to an iron ring. Where the rowboats had been tethered with ropes, the RIB was tied with a padlocked chain. Fiona's heart beat faster as she stepped towards the RIB, her torch following a second chain from the iron ring to a point behind the RIB.

When Fiona got close enough to spy the end of the second chain she let out a hissed 'yesssss'. A padlock lay hooked through the last link, its surface covered with a collection of fresh dents and scrapes.

The discovery was a big one. It indicated someone had recently bashed the padlock loose with a rock or some other blunt instrument, and in her mind there were collectively one and individually three suspects: Shand and his two mates.

Now it was time for the big question: should she follow them to Torsa, or stay where she was?

To follow them was to risk her own life, and to endanger a

civilian whose expertise she'd need to get her to Torsa. To stay and await morning and support made sense, but it ran the risk of killers escaping justice.

After almost twenty years of knowing her parents' murderers had never been identified, much less punished for their crimes, Fiona knew she had to follow the killers to Torsa, regardless of the risks to herself.

Fiona turned and almost bumped into Grant. Such had been her focus on the chain and its implications, she hadn't noticed the islander arriving at her side. She leaned into him so she could speak into his ear. 'It looks like we're right and they've stolen a boat. Are you prepared to help me get to Torsa?'

Grant didn't give an answer. At least, not a verbal one. Instead he reached for the outboard, fiddled with a couple of small levers and then pulled on the ignition cord.

At the fourth pull, the engine splattered into life. Grant switched it off and reached for a rock. Fiona aimed her torch at the padlock securing the boat and watched as Grant popped the lock mechanism with a well-aimed blow.

With help from Fergus they dragged the RIB to the edge of the water. The waves in the bay were much less ferocious than the ones on the Atlantic side of the island, but they were still violent enough to change the water level by four feet at a time.

'Wait a minute.' Fiona pointed at Grant and Fergus in turn and then gestured for them to lift up the stern of the RIB. As soon as it was more or less sitting level, Fiona stepped to the stern, released the lever holding the outboard up so it wouldn't drag on the beach and unscrewed the fuel cap.

Fiona dipped a finger into the fuel tank and hoped against hope. Their luck was in, her finger touched oily liquid before her first knuckle had entered the tank.

Together the three of them carried the boat until they were waist deep in the swells. Fiona gestured for Fergus to get in first and he obliged. As soon as he was in he started the motor while Fiona clambered aboard.

Grant made to join them but Fiona leaned forward to put her mouth next to his ear. 'Can you stay and help the guys at the church? If we don't return by the time other police get to Luing, let them know where we are.'

'I can, but you need me in that boat. Fergus doesn't know the water like I do. If I'm not piloting that boat, he won't go.' Grant folded his meaty arms. 'And neither should you.'

Grant's words left Fiona torn. She needed Grant to get her to Torsa, yet the trip across was fraught with danger. If the boat got swamped they'd all be sure to drown. And she had to consider whatever might happen should they catch up with Shand and the other two. She wore her stab vest and had police equipment to help her, if necessary. Grant had his bare hands and a lot of anger.

Fiona didn't like the idea of only Grant being with her when she tracked down Shand and his buddies. Fergus's presence might be the difference between him recalling the promise he'd made his parents, and the red mist taking over. To have both would be good, but she needed to leave someone on Luing to relay their story.

As Fiona shouted into Fergus's ear she could hear the rasp of her faltering throat from all the shouting she'd had to do to make herself heard.

There was disappointment in Fergus's tone when he answered.

'Aye, I'll do that.'

SIXTY

As Grant backed away from the shore and turned the boat towards Torsa, Fiona felt oceanic waves rock the boat as waves of self-doubt assaulted her every action. Had she just set off on a trip that would see her drown? What if Shand and his buddies had stolen the RIB, but instead of actually using it, had set it adrift to act as another distraction? What if Shand was now in a house on Luing with his mates and a knife against the throat of the homeowner? As much as Shand might believe a hostage situation might buy him and his mates safe passage from the island, it never worked out like that.

With the RIB turned and heading towards Torsa, it was now hitting waves head on. Every few seconds the bow of the RIB would rise to the skies before dipping down as they crested a wave and slid into the ensuing trough.

At the rear of the RIB, Grant sat erect, his face forward and his right arm on the handle controlling the outboard. Time and again the little boat would change course. At first Fiona thought it was the impact of the waves that was directing the boat's course, and Grant was correcting it with the skill of a rally driver sliding out of a corner sideways and driving a straight line from there onwards.

The further they travelled the more Fiona realised it was Grant adjusting the boat's course at all times. Like a savant he seemed to divine from nowhere the correct path as he guided and steered the boat on a course only he knew existed.

Fiona's night vision had returned after she'd holstered her torch, and although the RIB kicked up spray that stung her eyes, she kept her gaze on Torsa. It was as they passed an anchored sailboat Fiona experienced the first lunge of her stomach that wasn't in tune with the RIB's rhythm.

Every other time Fiona had been on a boat, the boat in question had been large enough to ride out whatever waves it encountered. A gentle cruise on Lake Windermere with her parents was a fond memory, and not just for the ice cream and waffles that had followed it. At times she'd take a ferry ride out to one of the islands, or join Heather and their circle of friends for a boozy sail up and down Loch Fyne on a chartered boat. All of those craft were at least ten times the size of the RIB. All of them had lifejackets if required, life rings and, in the case of the ferries, lifeboats.

Not once had Fiona been on water anything like this rough, and her stomach was making her fully aware of its displeasure at all the pitching and yawing. Her injured shoulder was protesting every jolt that travelled through it as she clung to the RIB's safety line.

With her in the RIB was a man who blamed her for his brother's death and not so much as a safety rail. Fiona wrapped her hand around a rope running along the side of the RIB to her left. If Grant had visions of creating a trip so rough Fiona fell overboard, she wasn't going to make it easy for him.

The skin of her fingers grew raw from the friction of clinging to the rope, but she never let her grip slacken. No matter how many times Fiona glanced back at Grant to make sure he wasn't moving towards her, she couldn't reassure herself he didn't have a dastardly plan in mind for her.

Time and again the seas tossed the little RIB around like a dog worrying at a rat. Fiona's stomach lurched with every pitch and she twice had to swallow down bile. The one saving grace she could find was that they were making progress.

As they neared Torsa, Fiona could pick out the shoreline with ease. Even in the dark she could see the white froth created by the seas crashing into the island's rocky shore.

Fiona would have worried about where they'd land had Grant not seemed so confident when boarding the boat. She trusted he knew of a small dock on Torsa. The island had a holiday cottage, therefore there must be somewhere for tourists to park their boat, as there was no other way to access the island.

A hundred yards from shore, Grant altered course. Instead of heading straight for the island he was now approaching it at an oblique angle. Waves crashed onto the shore in front of them, and the boat corkscrewed in wild gyrations as it was no longer running with the waves, but Grant held the course steady.

No matter how Fiona peered ahead she couldn't see where they'd reach shore. For a terrifying moment she wondered if Grant's plan was simply to run the RIB straight into the coast rather than find a dock.

When they were thirty yards from shore, the waters beneath the RIB changed. Instead of being a pulsating mass with a common destination, they roiled and cascaded in all directions.

Grant held his course and then all of a sudden, they were in the lee of a large rock and Fiona could pick out a small stone jetty with a little boat tied up. Her first thought was that it was the boat the killers had stolen, but if Grant's suggestion was correct that they'd carry the RIB over land to shorten the distance they'd be on the sea, their RIB would be with them. Grant and Fergus had said the island had a house on it that was a holiday let. The boat must belong to the house's residents.

When Grant nudged the RIB's bow against the jetty Fiona leapt out and lashed the bow line to a short post.

A minute later the rear of the RIB was tied up and Grant was standing beside her.

'How the hell did you find this dock in the dark?'

'I knew where it was so I aimed for it.' A huge breath huffed from Grant's mouth. 'I don't care what you say, whether we find those bastards or not, we're not going back to Luing until daylight at the soonest.'

Fiona held Grant's gaze for a moment. Her night vision was nowhere near good enough to see his expression, but what he'd just said sent chills throughout her veins. Grant had been calm and had exuded confidence in the RIB, but his words told her it had all been a front. He'd been every bit as scared as she was.

Now it was the moment of truth. If Shand and his mates were on Torsa, they'd have to find them. If not, they'd have to stay until Grant judged it safe enough to return to Luing.

SIXTY-ONE

Before she did anything else, Fiona scoured the far part of the jetty where the ground sloped up the hill. There was a set of narrow tracks as if left by an ATV. That made sense to her. Holidaymakers wouldn't want to carry their luggage, food and drink all the way from the jetty to the house.

The grass in the centre of the track and a little to the right side was flattened down. Fiona might have thought it was done by the wind had there not been grass standing to attention to the left of the track. It was what she was looking for. A clear and obvious sign Shand and his mates had dragged their boat up the slope.

After the way Grant had warned her he wouldn't travel in those seas again before daylight, the last thing she wanted was to leave a dangerous escape method the killers could use, if they were unable to stop them.

Fiona went back to the jetty and tapped Grant's shoulder. 'Can you pull some leads from the engine and put them in your pocket?'

While Grant went to work on the RIB's engine, Fiona

removed the key from the ignition of the other boat and pocketed it.

The one pair of handcuffs she'd brought with her were around Betty Jamieson's wrists. There were several sets of Plasticuffs in the boot of the car, but she'd not thought to collect them on her way to Ardinamir Bay. She untied a hank of rope that was hanging over the boat's side and looped it over one shoulder. In the absence of modern police restraints, she'd have to do things the old-fashioned way.

Fiona waited until Grant joined her. Even through the hell that was the boat ride over, she'd been thinking about what to do when they landed.

'Listen up. They've dragged their boat up the hill. If they've dragged it after them, it'll leave us a nice easy trail to follow. We go silent and dark. No speaking and no torches unless we have to. I'd much rather sneak up and take them by surprise than forewarn them of our coming. I know you want revenge for your brother, but don't forget at least one of them carries a knife. We each take one of them down. You'll have to grapple your man, but I'm sure you'll be able to get him in an arm lock. No unnecessary violence, do you understand?'

'Yeah.' Grant held up three fingers. 'What about the third one?'

'I'll take care him.' Fiona's plan was to use proportionate force to incapacitate one with a strike of her baton across the back of his knees. That would leave her free to deal with the third and final attacker.

Grant took a step towards the slope away from the jetty. 'Right.'

A thought came to Fiona. 'Hang on a minute. Do you have a knife on you?'

'Aye.'

'Can I have it?'

Grant fished in his pocket and handed over a short penknife without any drama. Fiona wanted the knife for two reasons. First of all, if it was in her pocket, then it couldn't be used as a weapon. Secondly, if they were unable to capture the killers, there may at least be a chance to sabotage their boat by cutting a fuel line. If she cut the line, it was affirmative police action, but if Grant did it, the action could be classed as wilful criminal damage.

With full night vision to aid her, Fiona found it easy to follow the swathe of flattened grass. Once it had crested the hill, the swathe set a course for the far side of the island.

After travelling a hundred or so yards Fiona spied the unmistakable outline of a roof with chimneys at each gable. If the killers kept a straight course, they'd have missed the house by a good couple of hundred yards.

The swathe travelled in a line that was more or less straight with occasional deviances to round a boulder or collection of gorse bushes. Before long the swathe passed over the centre of Torsa and the going became easier as they were going downhill again.

Inside Fiona's body adrenaline and exhaustion were fighting an endless battle. She felt tired enough to lie down and sleep on the rough grass beneath her feet, but her hands were clenching and unclenching with every step as she also battled with nervous energy. To add to Fiona's discomfort, her bladder was full and she was desperate to relieve it.

The fact they were now descending the island's spine and travelling to the other coast put more energy into Fiona's stride. To have endured the boat ride over to Torsa only to find the killers had already fled the island would be too much. All the same, she didn't dare break into a run.

Ahead of her to the left, Fiona saw movement. It wasn't the billowing of windswept gorse bushes she was used to seeing, this was a different kind of motion. Her first thought was that somehow the killers had become aware they were being pursued and were setting up an ambush.

The collapsible baton was plucked from her utility belt in a flash and snapped to its full extension. A shape broke cover from the long grass and bounded towards them.

But it wasn't one of the killers; the shape coming their way was a dog. When it got within ten feet of them it set itself into a pounce position and started to bark. It was large enough to be a threat on its own, but that wasn't Fiona's greatest worry as there was no way to know whose dog this was. If it belonged to the killers and its barking alerted them to her and Grant's presence, it would scupper her plan of a stealthy and sudden takedown.

SIXTY-TWO

As best Fiona could tell the dog was a pale-coloured Labrador. It now capered around barking as it circled them. She bent to one knee and held out a hand. Heather owned a Labrador and it was a friendly thing that loved to be petted.

The baton was back in her belt as the dog came close enough to sniff her hand. Disgusted at the lack of food it bounded away and then darted back in and jumped at her extended arm.

The Lab's coat was soft as Fiona ruffled the back of its neck with one hand while tickling under its chin with the other. A collar was round its neck and Fiona soon found a tag.

By using the tip of her pinkie, Fiona traced the tag as she continued to make a fuss of the dog. By the time she'd finished she knew the dog's owners weren't the men she was chasing, as the postcode etched into the tag started with NE: Newcastle.

With this information now known, Fiona straightened and pressed on. The dog scampered away out of sight after a few seconds, but reappeared a couple of minutes later.

As they trooped on Fiona saw the grey outline of a dinghy

nestled behind some bushes that were around a hundred yards from the shore. Next to the dinghy were three human shapes.

Fiona couldn't make out their features, but she could tell from their outlines they were watching a point further along the shore. When Fiona cast her eyes that way she saw a light bobbing along the ground. She didn't need to be Einstein to work out the light was a torch held by the dog's owner.

It took Fiona less than a second to realise the killers were hiding out until the person wielding the torch passed. With luck that person would be allowed to pass by unharmed.

Fiona cast a glance over at the mainland and saw the one thing she didn't want to see. Above the Argyll hills, the first light of dawn was clambering over the horizon. There would soon be daylight, and the killers were sure to want to sail across to the mainland under the cloak of darkness, or at least get close enough to the mainland they'd have a chance of disappearing before officers could get to the point where they landed. Even if they couldn't use darkness to hide their movements, they'd still try, as to stay on Luing was to guarantee their capture. All things considered, Fiona knew they'd be desperate to get onto the water as soon as possible, as the cloak of darkness provided them with their best chance of getting to the mainland undetected.

The torch halted its progress even though Fiona willed the person holding it to continue moving. The longer they held up the killers, the more danger they were in. She had to act before the killers decided to take another life.

Rather than have the dog give away their position, Fiona ducked herself down into a depression in the ground and waited for the dog to come back. Grant followed her lead, although he had to be pulled lower so he wasn't visible from the gorse bush. Once the dog had left them again, Fiona planned to close in on the gorse bush and ambush the killers before the dog gave them away.

Fiona crept forward until she could peer between the grasses giving them cover. Instead of coming back to them, the dog had picked up the scent of Shand and his mates and was trotting towards the gorse bush where the killers were hiding.

As the dog was making its way towards the killers, the torch kept coming along the top of the coastline. By the time the dog fell into its pounce position, the torch was no more than twenty yards from the far side of the gorse bushes.

When the torch started rounding the bushes in a way that would lead its user into contact with the killers, Fiona slapped at Grant's arm, rose to her feet and started running towards the killers.

SIXTY-THREE

As Fiona ran down the hill, she retrieved both her torch and the collapsible baton from her belt. Both could be used as clubs or a defensive shield against a slash, and if directed into someone's eyes, the torch had more than enough power to dazzle someone with the severity to leave them temporarily blind.

Grant was ahead of her and sprinting like an Olympian. Fiona was running as fast as she could, but exhaustion and the fact she'd always been a better distance runner than sprinter prevented her from keeping pace with the islander.

By the time they'd got within ten yards the killers were alert to their impending arrival and were turning to meet them.

Grant launched himself into a flying tackle that flattened the nearest one, but while Fiona would have done the same if there were only two people to deal with, the presence of the third prevented her from doing so.

Fiona used her torch to dazzle her opponent, and when his hands went up to shield his eyes from its glare she cracked her baton against the side of his thigh with enough force to deaden the muscle. Her next strike landed on a raised arm, glancing off the elbow with such power that she could hear his yelp even as the wind stole it away.

The man turned so Fiona delivered a swiping, vicious horizontal strike to the back of his knees. The blow landed with sufficient accuracy to draw another howl from him as the attack on his tendons sent him to his knees.

Fiona dug a foot into his side and turned her focus to the third of the killers. He'd backed away from the skirmish and when she picked him out in the lightening gloom, her heart almost stopped.

The killer had a vicious-looking hunting knife in one hand, and the chin of the dog walker in the other. The blade was against the dog walker's throat, and it was clear what would happen if Fiona tried anything. The dog walker was a woman, and from what Fiona could see in the slowly increasing light, she was in her fifties.

Fiona cast a glance to where Grant had launched himself at the nearest of the three killers. He was in full control of the man and had his quarry pinned face down in the grass beside the dinghy, with an arm twisted behind his back.

'Let him go.' The shout from the killer was hard to make out, but Fiona caught enough of it to understand the knifeman's meaning.

Fiona dropped her baton, walked over to Grant and gestured for him to release his prisoner. As Grant did as he was bidden Fiona was reaching into her pocket. What she planned to do was a huge gamble, but she believed the odds were stacked in her favour.

It was a fiddle to unfold Grant's penknife in her pocket without showing what she was doing, but she was trusting the poor light to hide her actions.

Unlike the RIB which Fiona and Grant had travelled to Torsa aboard, the dinghy the killers had stolen was a standard inflatable model. It was no match for the knife in Fiona's hand, much less the power she put into the slashing stab at the rubber side.

The boat hissed out a gush of air that smelled foul then disappeared.

Fiona folded the knife and put it back into her pocket as she walked towards the knifeman. When she was ten feet away she halted.

Due to the increasing light, Fiona could see desperation in his eyes and the terror on the face of the dog walker.

'It's over. You can't get off the island. Your boat's ruined. Let her go. There's no point adding to the charges against you. Frankie Shand, Luke Williamson, Philip Kerr, I'm arresting you for the murders of Charlie Tait and Will Nichol, plus the culpable homicide of a resident of the caravan site.' It galled Fiona that she didn't know Vic's surname, but she ploughed on and read them their rights in full.

The knife trembled against the woman's throat but the man didn't remove it. Instead his face twisted into a snarl.

'You got here. We're taking your boat. If you try anything, she's dead.'

With his terms delivered, the knifeman started moving back the way they'd all come.

SIXTY-FOUR

Fiona eased herself out of his way as he approached. She'd thought that puncturing their dinghy would also puncture their hope, but the knifeman was smart enough to figure she and Grant must have used a small boat to get here.

When the knifeman reached their boat and found it inoperable, she could trade the leads for the woman's life. By then there'd be enough daylight that it'd be so much harder for the killers to land on the mainland unseen. With luck, tipping off Heather as to how she guessed the killers might plan to escape would mean there'd be a reception committee waiting for them when they did make it to the mainland.

All of these thoughts flashed through Fiona's mind in a second, but what she hadn't anticipated was Grant and what he might do.

As the man Grant had pinned down rose to his feet, Grant wound a powerful arm around his neck and planted a hand on the side of his head. 'Let the woman go or I'll snap your mate's neck.'

Whether Grant would carry out his threat was unknown to Fiona, but she didn't like the way this had developed into a

Mexican standoff. She had to intervene before the knifeman called Grant's bluff.

Fiona reached for the pepper spray on her belt, but her hand stopped moving before she'd even located the canister. Grant was upwind of her and although the gale seemed to be easing a little, any spray she discharged would be blown back in her own face rather than covering Grant.

Rescue came from an unlikely source as the Labrador careered out from the gorse bushes and bit the knifeman's calf. The knifeman instinctively slashed downwards with the knife at the dog, but he was too slow to harm the brave animal.

There was a ten-foot gap between Fiona and the knifeman. She crossed it in just over a second. Even so, the knifeman was bringing his weapon back up, and when he saw Fiona's charge he thrust the knife at her chest.

A thudding blow scorched pain across Fiona's chest, but she trusted the stab vest to have done its job. Fiona's momentum carried her into the knifeman and as she collided with him, she was using her arm to push the woman aside.

Fiona and the knifeman went down in a tangle of limbs. Despite her determination not to show any weakness, Fiona couldn't prevent a yelp of pain when she landed on her injured shoulder. As her face was beside his, she could smell garlic on his breath as he cursed in her ear. The reek didn't matter, all that mattered was making sure the knife was kept away from her. She gripped his wrist and tried to twist it so he'd drop the knife, but he was too strong for her to get the purchase she needed. His other hand crashed into the side of her face, numbing her cheek and blurring her vision.

The next punch had Fiona seeing stars, and she knew that if they kept on fighting like this, she'd lose. As the knifeman was beneath her she tried a knee to the groin, but his legs were pressed together. Instead of continuing to punch, the knifeman had changed tactics and was now clawing at Fiona's face, his fingers moving up towards her eyes.

Fiona reared back out of reach, and shot a hard palm strike at the man's jaw. She connected with it and in return received a punch to the mouth that split her lips.

Still her left hand competed with his right for supremacy of the knife. Even without the injury to her shoulder, her left side was the weak side. To now be using her left arm to engage in a desperate wrestling match was akin to riding into battle wearing a blindfold. The knifeman won, and when he twisted his arm so his knife sliced into her forearm, she released his wrist with a scream.

Before the knife could be slashed at her throat, Fiona changed her tactics and jabbed a short punch into the man's Adam's apple. As the man gasped for precious air, Fiona untangled herself from him, levered herself upright, and delivered a forceful stamp onto his groin.

The knifeman folded with a yelp so Fiona wrenched his wrist around until his fingers released the knife.

In an ideal world, Fiona would be wearing gloves and she'd drop the knife into an evidence bag. In the half light of daybreak, things were a long way from ideal, so even as she fished into her pockets in search of at least one glove she risked a look at Grant to see how he was faring.

The second of the three killers lay on the ground unmoving, while the third lay on his back with his hands and forearms covering his head from the series of blows Grant was raining down on him.

The guy's arms drooped down, but that didn't stop Grant from punching away. Fiona had to stop the islander from beating his foe to a pulp, and with the man already unable to defend or protect himself, a couple more of Grant's hammer blows would do just that.

SIXTY-FIVE

As the man at Fiona's feet was starting to recover from the blows she had landed on him, Fiona drew her pepper spray and shot a quick blast into his face. When the irritant hit his eyes he screamed twice as loud as when she'd stamped on his groin.

With an evidence bag in her hand, Fiona grabbed the knife and charged over to Grant.

'That's enough. He's done. Stop.'

Grant looked up at Fiona, his eyes wild and his jaw set hard. He didn't speak, nod or give any sign of having heard what she'd said. His fist when he unclenched it had raw, bloody knuckles. The fist clenched again and powered down.

Fiona had expected Grant to try striking again and she dropped the knife to grab at Grant's arm. She was too late to stop the first blow, but by leaning into him and pumping her legs she managed to topple him from his position on the killer's chest.

Even as she tried to pin Grant down, Fiona recognised the grief-fuelled rage dictating his blood lust. She'd known the anger brought by sudden inexplicable grief, but as much as

Fiona might sympathise with Grant's feelings, she was afraid of what he might do if she couldn't get him to calm down.

'Bitch.' The word was hissed in Fiona's ear as she wrestled with Grant. 'He's one of the bastards who killed my brother.'

'Yes, he is. But you made your parents a promise. Don't break their hearts by getting yourself sent to jail.'

Grant's eyes locked with Fiona's and for a terrifying moment, she thought the islander was going to turn on her so he'd be free to exact a brutal vengeance on the killers. That was not a fight she wanted. Grant would be a far tougher opponent than the knifeman, and there was every chance that in his current mindset, he'd be every bit as deadly.

'I saw one of them try to stab you. He needs to pay.' Grant's mouth twisted in suppressed anger.

'Don't even think about it. Your parents are going to need you to get through the next few days and weeks and months.' Fiona tossed a head nod in the direction of the knifeman. 'Don't worry about him paying. He's going to be looking at some serious jail time. And if you keep on attacking them, so will you.'

Grant slumped back. His body all of a sudden limp as he huffed lungful after lungful of air into his chest.

Fiona climbed off Grant and scooped the knife into another evidence bag, the first having long blown away. Once the knife was inside and the bag sealed, Fiona slid it into a pocket.

Like Fiona, Grant climbed to his feet. Of the three killers, only the knifeman was moving, although he was doing nothing more than thrashing around in the grass and rubbing furiously at his eyes.

Only when she was sure Grant wasn't going to start throwing punches or kicks at the three men did Fiona cast her eyes around to look for the woman. She'd retreated to a point twenty yards away. Far enough that she was a safe distance from the fight, yet not so far away that she couldn't see what happened.

'Do you want to get the rope, Grant?'

Fiona bent to the bloodied man at their feet and patted him over in case he too held a weapon. He didn't, and while his face resembled uncooked mince, he was making feeble movements.

Next Fiona checked the other man Grant had been fighting with. He still wasn't moving, and for a horrible moment she wondered if Grant had carried out his threat and snapped his neck while she charged the knifeman. As she bent to the man, she could see his chest rising and falling. More telling was the movement of his eyes as she knelt by his head and took in the bloody nose and blackening eyes.

Fiona's fear was the man was playing possum and was about to lunge at her with a concealed weapon, but when a fat tear rolled from his eye and his lip wobbled she saw a different reason for him staying put. This guy was the weak link of the group. He'd stayed down because he was afraid of facing Grant's wrath. When it came to the interviews, he'd be the one most likely to turn on the others first. She made a point of memorising this fact.

'Put your hands where I can see them. I'm going to pat you down in case you have a weapon on you. If you have one and you tell me about it, it'll look better for you when this goes to court.'

Two empty hands squirmed out from under his body as he shook his head.

Once she'd patted him down and proven he wasn't lying about a weapon, Fiona took the end of the rope from Grant and bound his wrists and ankles.

Five minutes later all three were tied up and Grant had moved them so they were in a group.

The dog walker stepped forward, the Labrador now obediently at her heel although it was shooting suspicious looks at the knifeman. 'What's going on?' The woman's accent was a Geordie burr that backed up the tag on the Labrador's collar.

'They're killers. I've been after them since yesterday afternoon.'

The woman's face scrunched as she looked at Fiona. 'You've been after them since yesterday? I thought detectives wore plain clothes? They always do on the telly.'

'I'm not a detective.'

'Aren't you? I have to say that was very brave of you charging at him like that. You saved my life.'

'I think more of the credit goes to your dog. If he hadn't bit the guy, I wouldn't have had the opportunity to tackle him.' Fiona pointed to the house. 'I don't suppose there's a phone in there, is there?'

'No, but I've a mobile. It's surprising how much signal I get with it.'

'You get signal here?'

Fiona drew her own mobile from a pocket. No matter how she prodded or swiped at the screen it remained blank. Either it had shorted from a soaking, or its battery had died.

'Do you have it on you?'

'No, it's in the house.' A concerned look swept onto the woman's face. 'I'll have to be getting back. My family will be wondering where I've been. It's time I started their breakfasts. I can get it for you once I've fed them all. They won't be happy with me if they don't get their breakfast on time.'

From the way the woman's eyes flitted across the killers in horror, it was clear to Fiona the woman's family expecting her there to make their breakfast was nothing more than an excuse. The woman just wanted to get away from the horror of the situation. All the same, Fiona needed to contact the mainland as soon as possible.

'It's very important I call this in as soon as possible. My radio and mobile are both knackered.'

'You're welcome to come with me, use it at the house.'

Fiona couldn't leave her prisoners alone, and nor could she trust Grant to stand guard over them. Without her to stop him, who knew what he might do in the time she was away making the call.

'How about my friend Grant here goes with you, and brings the phone here? I promise that once I've made my call, he'll bring the phone back to you?'

The woman nodded and bent to scratch behind the dog's ear. 'Come on, Sandor.'

As they left, Fiona couldn't help but smile at the way the dog had been named after Sandor 'The Hound' Clegane from *Game of Thrones*.

The smile faded as she turned to face the killers. She still didn't know who was who among them, and she planned to have learned as much as she could from them all before any support arrived. She might not be a detective, but that didn't mean she couldn't do as much as possible to ensure that when she handed the three men over, the case against them was already built.

SIXTY-SIX

With dawn illuminating the sky, the wind dropping to a much more tolerable level and the killers apprehended, a sense of achievement was radiating throughout Fiona, although she didn't let any of that distract her. There was still work to be done.

The three killers all lay on the grass in front of Fiona, each of them wearing a different expression. The knifeman looked furious and he was muttering vague threats while wrestling against his bonds. Fiona had no worries that he'd free himself, as she'd made doubly sure they were secure enough to resist any efforts he might make.

The guy who'd taken the hiding from Grant lay on his side and from his body language Fiona could tell he was doing nothing more than feeling sorry for himself. It was the third one Fiona was most interested in. He looked terrified and Fiona sensed playing on that terror would be the best way to get some answers.

'You do know that my colleagues and I have this all worked out, don't you?' Fiona let the question hang over them.

It was the knifeman who bit. 'You don't know nothing. You can't prove nothing.'

The pedant in Fiona wanted to comment on his use of double negatives but she let them slide for now, she had a far better target in her sights than the knifeman's grammar.

'We know more than enough to send you to jail for a long time. We know you went after Charlie Tait on purpose. We know you wore hoodies to hide your faces as you bought tickets for the *Each-Uisge*. That you paid cash for those tickets. The other passengers and the crew that were on the *Each-Uisge* were mostly vague about who was where when the boat ran aground. The key word there is *mostly*. Two of the passengers were convinced you were the last to come out of the cabin. I can easily picture the three of you staying back for an extra ten or fifteen seconds. Tait was in the wheelhouse until the last second desperately trying to restart the engines. Two of you would act as lookouts while the third slid open the door and stabbed him. It wasn't one stab, though. There were a lot of stab wounds on his body. I saw them and I could tell whomever wielded the knife that killed Charlie Tait was also holding on to a lot of anger. The wounds to his groin especially looked like a frenzied attack. That led me to think he was killed because of either a sex crime or an affair with the wrong man's wife.'

'You can't prove nothing of what you're saying.' There was defiance in the knifeman's eyes. 'Yeah, we were on the boat. You rescued us, but there's no way you're pinning no murder on us. As for a sex crime or an affair, I've never heard such bullshit. We never heard of no Charlie Tait.'

'You knew Tait by a different name. The name he was given at birth and that name was Oliver Ewart.' Fiona gave them time to digest what she'd just said. Her last conversation with Heather had furnished her with everything she needed to get to the truth and that's what she was doing now. 'Fourteen years ago you all joined the Sea Cadets on the same day. For two years you were daft on the cadets and then all of a sudden you wanted nothing to do with them.'

'So we outgrew the cadets. So what?' The hate in the knife-man's eyes was as intense as the terror in the eyes of the guy who'd stayed on the ground to save himself further pain. Between them, the bloodied guy was shaking his head at her words.

'You didn't outgrow the cadets. You all ended up working on boats in one way or another.'

'You ever been to Wick? You either work the boats or the fisheries. The boats is where the decent money is. You can't prove nothing.'

'Oliver Ewart was the Commanding Officer for the Wick cadets. My colleagues on the mainland have found blog posts with pictures of you and him together. They've also dug into the fact he left Wick around the same time you left the cadets. Apparently he was beaten up after leaving a pub and he just upped and moved on the next day. Left his job, sold his car and furniture on eBay for a lot less than it was worth. That's a hell of a coincidence. So is him turning up in Oban a week later as Charlie Tait. Do you want to know what I think happened?'

'Who gives a shit what you think happened? You're adding two plus two and getting nine.' The sneer in the knifeman's voice was laced with doubt.

The guy who'd played possum stared at the knifeman. 'She knows, Phil, she knows everything.'

'Shut it, Frankie. She doesn't know nothing and nobody else does. We swore, remember?' As soon as he'd finished speaking Fiona could see in the knifeman's eyes that he knew he'd said too much.

From the exchange between the two friends she now knew the knifeman was Philip Kerr, the possum was Frankie Shand and the bloodied one was Luke Williamson.

Better than that, she'd also heard enough for her to be confident in her theory as to why they'd set out to kill Tait.

'He abused you, didn't he? That's why you left the cadets. That's why you attacked him as he was walking home from the pub. I dare say you laid some kind of threat on him. My guess is you either told him you'd kill him, or you'd tell your parents what he'd done to you if he didn't move away.' None of them spoke, but for Fiona the looks they were sliding each other were all the confirmation she needed. 'It was a brave thing for you to do as boys, and it would have been better for everyone if it had ended there. It didn't end there, though. Instead what he'd done to you festered in your minds. None of you have settled down with a wife or girlfriend. Nor a husband or boyfriend for that matter. At your age, at least one of you should have found love, yet none of you have. Like I say, his actions festered in your minds and you decided to hunt him down, to kill him. I reckon you thought that was the only way to erase his abuse from your minds. Am I right, Frankie?'

Frankie Shand didn't answer, but from the way Kerr sank back against the grass, all the aggression gone from his body, he didn't have to.

'When you were being rescued from the *Each-Uisge*, you must have been terrified to see me, a uniformed police officer, waiting on the shore. You got desperate and didn't dare go back to the caravan on Luing that you'd rented, so you hid out in the eco-pods. It was bad luck that the mechanic, Will, went to the eco-pods. He was actually looking for a missing child. Not you. Unfortunately for Will, you didn't know that, so you killed him and dumped his body in the skip. I was looking for the lost girl too. As I drove around the island, I had my lights and siren on in the hope of attracting her attention. That must have seemed like I was coming for you. That's when you decided to sever the mooring straps on the caravans as a distraction. What you didn't know was that an elderly couple couldn't evacuate their caravan in time. She's got a broken leg and he passed away shortly after we got him out of the caravan. That's two definite murder charges and one culpable homicide against you so far.' Fiona locked eyes with Shand. He was the one who she wanted to frighten into a confession. Whatever he said now wouldn't be usable in court, but once he'd taken the step to making a confession here, he'd be more likely to repeat the confession in an interview suite. 'Add in Kerr's attempted murder of me, assaulting a police officer and a whole load of criminal damages charges for the caravan site, and I'd say every one of you is looking at a significant amount of jail time.'

Shand found his backbone as he glared at Williamson. 'You idiot, Luke. This was all your idea, you were the one who said we should kill Oliver Ewart for what he'd done to us. You were the one who stabbed him, and the one who killed the mechanic. It was your idea to cut the caravans loose. I'm not doing time for murder, Luke. I love you like a brother, man, but you know what'll happen to us in prison. It'll be ten times worse than what he did.' Shand turned to face Fiona, his voice cracking with emotion. 'My name is Frankie Shand, and I want to state for the record that neither I nor Phil Kerr killed anyone. Phil only had the knife because we took it off Luke so he couldn't kill anyone else. That's right, isn't it, Phil?'

'Aye, it's right.'

'Bastards.'

Fiona knew the truth when she saw it. Had Shand and Kerr intended to shift the blame for the murders from themselves to Williamson, he would have used a different insult. He would have called them *lying* bastards. He'd left the accusation of lies out of his response, which told her the others were telling the truth. The accusation may appear at a later time when interviewed with a lawyer at his side, but for now, he wasn't savvy enough to think beyond his sense of betrayal.

As she looked down at the three men, Fiona knew that on a

certain level they were to be pitied. They'd been abused by an adult they felt they could trust. That abuse had turned out to have a long-lasting effect on them, and the desperate measures they'd taken to try and exorcise their demons had backfired on them all. There was little chance of them being able to cut a deal that would see them avoid jail time. Williamson would, of course, face the stiffest sentence if the other two kept to their insistence that he was the one who'd murdered two men and caused the manslaughter of a third.

Fiona cast a glance over her shoulder and saw Grant returning. She'd be able to call this in and if the wind kept dropping, support would reach them in a few hours. Then once the prisoners were handed over maybe she'd have time for a bite to eat. And a pee.

SIXTY-SEVEN

The lessening of the wind brought with it a whole array of changes. From where Fiona and Grant stood guard over the three prisoners they could see life returning to normal. Fishing boats were back on the water, their captains no doubt desperate to get back to work after losing a day's catch.

By the time support came, the sun was high in the sky and Fiona was on the point of disappearing behind a gorse bush to relieve her aching bladder. DI Baird led the support group along with a clutch of uniformed officers and detectives. Heather was beside Baird, matching her stride for stride, although Fiona could see her friend was almost jogging to keep up with the taller inspector.

Baird directed the uniformed officers and as they set about replacing the ropes with handcuffs, she moved away to one side hooking a finger at Fiona as she did so.

'Want to explain why two of them look like they've been run over by a tank?'

'They resisted arrest, ma'am. I had to sanction the use of appropriate force to subdue them.' Fiona pointed at the rent in the front of her stab vest, and the arm Grant had bandaged up with a first aid kit he'd brought from the house. 'One of them tried to stab me. When that didn't work, he slashed at my arm.'

Baird's eyes widened a fraction. 'And the civilian you roped into this caper, am I right to understand he's the brother of one of the victims?'

'You are. Without Grant's help I could never have got to Torsa and thwarted their plan to escape. His presence meant I had a form of backup. I know it's unorthodox, ma'am, but I did what I had to do to make sure the killers didn't escape justice.'

'I see. And just how do you think their lawyers will spin the involvement of a civilian? A grieving relative no less?'

'I don't think it will matter. Grant made a citizen's arrest.' That was the story Fiona had told Grant to stick to. It was flimsy, but it was a way of mitigating any claims of assault that may be made against him. 'I stand by what I said earlier. Without Grant's help I would never have caught them. By now they'd either be on the mainland or lost at sea.' Fiona looked Baird dead in the eye. 'When it comes to the interviews, Frankie Shand is the weak link. Philip Kerr is the brains, and Luke Williamson is the one who killed Charlie Tait slash Oliver Ewart, the mechanic, Will, and cut the mooring straps at the caravan park.'

'And you know this how?'

'Because I talked to them.' Fiona cast her eyes back towards Luing. 'There's a young lad who lived and worked with Tait. Bit of a rascal, but basically okay. His name is Davie, and considering Shand confirmed our theory about Tait having abused the three of them as children, I'd suggest he's been doing the same to Davie.'

'What makes you think that?'

'When I broke the news of Tait's murder, Davie was in pieces as if Tait was a father figure, but the more I think about it, I can't help but wonder if they'd had a sexual relationship, or

Tait had been coercive with his sexual advances and Davie had mistaken Tait's abuse for affection.'

Baird's eyes narrowed as she applied her thought processes to Fiona's theory. 'That stacks up, doesn't it?'

'Sadly it does, ma'am.' Fiona flexed her shoulders and tried not to think of the pressure on her bladder. 'Davie is in a house opposite the shop with Ian Caldwell. Everyone else from the *Each-Uisge*, the holidaymakers from the wrecked caravan site, and Betty Jamieson are in the Kilchattan Church. As for Mrs Jamieson, she's in handcuffs, but I have to say, ma'am, her mind is failing, so when it comes to interviewing her, you're probably going to have to get her checked over by a doctor first.'

'Is there anything else?'

'No, ma'am. That's everything.'

'It's enough, is it not?' Baird reached out her right hand for Fiona to shake. 'You have achieved a great amount in a short time without support. You ought to be proud of yourself, you've solved two cases, caught three murder suspects plus a kidnapper and delivered them more or less oven ready.'

Fiona shook the offered hand. 'Thank you, ma'am.'

'There's one last thing.' Baird leaned in close, her mouth by Fiona's ears. 'The way you're hoatching about tells me you're bursting for a wee. Go on, bugger off and find a discreet bush. I'll not have one of my officers pissing their pants.'

'Your officers, ma'am?'

'You have keen instincts and a good brain. Your methods are unorthodox to say the least, but should you ever make detective, I think I could find a place for you on my team. Something to think about.' Baird turned and walked over to supervise the officers who were already managing fine without supervision.

* * *

Fiona rounded the gorse bush and trotted back to the line of people walking back to the small dock. Heather was at the tail of the line, not her usual position, but Fiona knew her friend well enough to realise Heather had opted to hang back so they could chat.

As was always the case when Fiona walked anywhere with Heather, Fiona had to lengthen her stride to keep up with the taller woman and her boundless energy. Neither of them had enjoyed any sleep in the last thirty-plus hours, but Fiona could only tell Heather hadn't rested because she was a close friend.

There was a smile on Heather's face that puzzled Fiona. All she wanted to do was grab something to eat and then sleep for a decade or two, yet here was someone who was sure to be every bit as tired as she was looking happy. Yes, Cait was back with her parents and they'd apprehended a killer, but a lot had gone wrong, and they were far from being finished for the day.

Heather handed over a package of throat lozenges. 'I got you these. Every time you called you sounded more and more like you'd been on a four-day bender, drinking own-brand vodka and smoking cheap cigars.'

'Thanks, it was all the shouting to make myself heard. What are you so happy about? Don't tell me you're looking forward to dealing with all the questions and paperwork when we get back to the station. You've got to be as knackered as I am.'

'I don't care about the paperwork. That's the last thing I have to worry about. I spent most of last night worrying my mate was going to get herself killed trying to be superwoman. She didn't. Life is good. Paperwork is shit, but life is still good.' Heather stopped talking long enough to flash her best smile Fiona's way. 'Come on then, tell me, just how much of a bollocking did Baird give you?'

'Hardly any. In fact, she more or less offered me a job if I made detective.'

'That's wonderful. You should do it, Fiona. We'd be

working together then.' The excitement in Heather's eyes died when she realised her mistake. 'I'm sorry. I know you've got that whole exam phobia thing going on. And that if you did make detective, it'd be so you could look into your parents' murders, not so you could work with me.'

'Working with you would be a bonus. Anyway, I've been thinking about my parents. What if they were killed because they blew the whistle on an abuser? The only time I ever heard my dad get really mad was when there was a news story about a paedophile or a rapist. He despised them and I know that if he'd ever learned of any, he'd have gone right to the police.'

'It's worth looking into.'

With a possible reason for her parents' murders to look into, the exhaustion fell away from Fiona as she strode back towards Torsa's jetty.

A LETTER FROM G.N. SMITH

Dear reader,

I want to say a huge thank you for choosing to read *The Island*. If you did enjoy it, and want to keep up to date with all my latest releases, just sign up at the following link. Your email address will never be shared and you can unsubscribe at any time.

www.bookouture.com/g-n-smith

The Island holds a special place in my heart for many reasons. As a Boy Scout I camped on the mainland near Luing, yet it was many years later when I visited the island as an adult. That visit was a research trip on a cold December day rather than the summer which is when the novel is set.

No amount of online research can ever substitute for a visit and what a visit I had. Luing is beautiful, barren, wild, ancient and a dozen other contradictory adjectives. I apologise to any of the islanders who may take issue with my descriptions of their nature and their homeland. I tried my best to be true to the reality, but there are some authorial embellishments about the islanders' nature, although it's my understanding they do possess a fierce community spirit.

If you're ever thinking of visiting Luing, do, it's a wonderful experience that starts with a drive over the humpbacked Clachan Bridge onto the island of Seil. Such is the hump of the bridge, drivers have to crawl along in first until they are sure nothing is coming up the other side. Once you've crossed to Luing on the Belnahua ferry, the island is great fun to explore and it left me feeling a deeper connection to nature. It's a beautiful place and one I plan to return to.

Now I've waffled on about the setting, I suppose I ought to say something about the novel itself. As with the other novels featuring Fiona MacLeish – at the time of writing I'm a third of the way through book three, *The Shelter* – I had immense fun weaving a whodunit plot around a specific location that can't easily be exited by any of the characters and nor can other characters enter it. The locked location means Fiona has to battle not only to solve the cases, but stay alive and protect others as the weather is also a dangerous foe. The sprawling but contained landscape of Luing gave me a larger playground than previously, but I feel it really added to the tension and drama. As for Fiona and her quest to conquer her phobia of exam rooms so she can investigate her parents' murders, I've a few ideas up my sleeve and I'd be honoured if my wonderful readers followed Fiona's journey with me.

www.grahamsmithauthor.co.uk

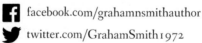

facebook.com/grahamnsmithauthor

twitter.com/GrahamSmith1972

instagram.com/grahamsmithauthor

ACKNOWLEDGEMENTS

As always, my first thanks go to my loved ones as without their support and understanding, I'd never have made it as a writer. They all have to put up with me zoning out when an idea strikes at the weirdest times, blathering on about plot ideas or some strange fact I've learned while researching a point, and me being 'busy writing' when they have other uses for me.

At Bookouture I'd like to thank both my former and current editors for their work on *The Island*. Isobel Akenhead brainstormed the original idea with me, but it was Harriet Wade's keen eye that elevated the manuscript to what it is today. Both ladies deserve huge thanks, and a certain amount of apologies for the comments I send back to them as part of the editorial process. Together with the wonderful work of the publicity and marketing teams they've helped me produce a novel that has found its way into your hands.

Col Bury and Paula Morrow both deserve a mention for helping me with my research and keeping me more or less on the straight and narrow. Any mistakes are mine, not theirs. Although I will probably try and pass blame towards Col as I love watching him squirm.

Finally, I'd like to thank the whole raft of friends, readers, bloggers and fellow writers who've helped me along the way, not just with this novel, but with all the ones that preceded it.

Printed in Great Britain
by Amazon

37210103R00192